THE TENDER TIES HISTORICAL SERIES

Hold Tight the Thread

JANE KIRKPATRICK
AWARD-WINNING AUTHOR *of* *ALL TOGETHER IN ONE PLACE*

WATERBROOK
PRESS

HOLD TIGHT THE THREAD
PUBLISHED BY WATERBROOK PRESS
2375 Telstar Drive, Suite 160
Colorado Springs, Colorado 80920
A division of Random House, Inc.

Scripture quotations are taken from the *King James Version.*

This book is a work of historical fiction based closely on real people and real events. Details that cannot be historically verified are purely products of the author's imagination.

The floral design on the cover is reminiscent of the Iowa Nation beadwork and is used by permission of The Museum at Warm Springs, an entity of the Confederated Tribes of Warm Springs, Warm Springs, Oregon. The design is from a beaded bag in the permanent exhibit gallery.

Grateful acknowledgment is made for use of the poem "The Way It Is," copyright 1998 by the Estate of William Stafford. Reprinted from *The Way It Is: New and Selected Poems* with the permission of Graywolf Press, Saint Paul, Minnesota.

ISBN 1-57856-501-4

Library of Congress Cataloging-in-Publication Data
Kirkpatrick, Jane, 1946–
Hold tight the thread / Jane Kirkpatrick.— 1st ed.
p. cm. — (Tender ties historical series ; bk. 3)
ISBN 1-57856-501-4
1. Dorion, Marie, 1786–1850—Fiction. 2. Women pioneers—Fiction.
3. Oregon—Fiction. I. Title.
PS3561.I712H65 2004
813'.54—dc22

2003024238

Printed in the United States of America
2004—First Edition

10 9 8 7 6 5 4 3 2 1

Praise for
Hold Tight the Thread
by Jane Kirkpatrick

"Jane Kirkpatrick writes from a depth and richness of detailed research and from a genuine affection and respect for her characters. She gives us strong, admirable women with sensitive spirits, courage, and the capacity for unconditional love. *Hold Tight the Thread* is a thoughtful, skillfully prepared feast for those of us always hungry for more quality historical fiction. Like her other novels, this is a story that allows us to experience the struggles and adventures and faith of another time through characters we can learn to know—and love."

—B. J. Hoff, author of the American Anthem series and *An Emerald Ballad*

"*Hold Tight the Thread* is such a satisfying ending to a wonderful trilogy on the life of such a memorable woman: Marie Dorion. I learned so much even as I felt a range of emotions—sad, happy, bittersweet, and triumphant. I love this book!"

—Linda Hall, author of *Steal Away* and *Chat Room*

Praise for Books 1 and 2 in the
Tender Ties Historical Series

"I highly recommend *Every Fixed Star.* Jane Kirkpatrick's storytelling is deft and true; she breathes life into the long-ago Oregon country with warmth, emotion, and a deep understanding of the region's people and past. With depth, creativity, and inspiration, *Every Fixed Star* provides a fresh view of this period in the Pacific Northwest's history, showing the complicated dynamics between settlers, fur traders, missionaries, natives, and visionaries. Jane has vividly captured the history of the fur trade for intelligent women readers."

—Laurie Winn Carlson, author of *Seduced by the West* and *On Sidesaddles to Heaven: The Women of the Rocky Mountain Mission*

"Jane Kirkpatrick has a rare gift, for her novels touch both the emotions and the intellect. She fills her stories with living history, each rich detail carefully researched and woven into a very particular time and place—the Columbia country of the 1820s. And yet, *Every Fixed Star* is far from a dry history; rather, it is the moving, heartfelt story of one woman's journey toward accepting her own failings as a wife and as a mother—a struggle common to every woman in every century. Through Marie's 'heart knowing,' we are forced to examine our own hearts and lives and emerge the better for it. Jane's novels are more than a good read; they are a life-altering experience."

—LIZ CURTIS HIGGS, author of *Thorn in My Heart*

"[An] evocative, imagined retelling of the story of Marie Dorion, the remarkable Iowa Indian woman who crossed the continent with her young sons and her mixed-blood husband in 1811 as part of the first grand expedition after Lewis and Clark.... As always, the historically accurate details are woven in with care, and the characters are fully imagined. At the story's end, the reader absolutely believes 'Marie was an Ioway woman of the Gray Snow people; gray like the stuff that strengthened bones.' A truly fine book."

—*The Denver Post,* in praise of *A Name of Her Own,*
book 1 of the Tender Ties Historical series

Hold Tight the Thread

OTHER BOOKS BY JANE KIRKPATRICK

NOVELS

Tender Ties Historical Series
A Name of Her Own
Every Fixed Star

Kinship and Courage Historical Series
All Together in One Place
No Eye Can See
What Once We Loved

Dreamcatcher Collection
A Sweetness to the Soul
Love to Water My Soul
A Gathering of Finches
Mystic Sweet Communion

NONFICTION

Homestead
A Simple Gift of Comfort (formerly *A Burden Shared*)

This book is dedicated to

the Iowa Tribe of Oklahoma
and
the descendants of Marie Ioway Dorion Venier Toupin.

Cast of Characters

Madame Marie Dorion	an Ioway Indian woman
Jean Louis Toupin	French Canadian; Marie's husband
Marguerite Venier	Marie and Louis Venier's daughter
Jean Baptiste Gobin (JB)	Marguerite's husband
Toussaint; Jean Baptiste II ("Doublé")	JB's sons
François Xavier	firstborn
Angelique	daughter
other children	not named
Marianne Toupin	Marie and Jean's daughter
David Gervais	Marianne's first husband
Joseph, Marie, Marguerite	children
François Toupin	Marie and Jean's son
Angelique Longtain	François' wife
Jean Baptiste Dorion	Marie and Pierre Dorion's son, known as Baptiste, b. 1806
Josette Cayuse	Baptiste's second wife
Denise Marie	daughter
Pierre	son
Genevieve	daughter
Paul Dorion	Marie and Pierre Dorion's son, b. 1809
My Horse Comes Out	Paul's wife
John Dorion	b. 1800
Thérèse Constant	John's wife
**Barbe*	Marie and Jean's godchild
Angele Indian	Marie and Jean's godchild
Baby Marie	Marie and Jean's godchild

(continued)

The French Prairie People

Joseph Gervais	early settler; David and Julie Gervais' father
Angelique Clatsop	Joseph Gervais' second wife
Julie Gervais Laderoute	David Gervais' sister; friend of Marianne Toupin Gervais
Joseph, Isadore, and others unamed	Julie's children
Marie Anne Ouvre	Julie Gervais Laderoute's helper
Louis LaBonte	French Canadian and former Astorian; employee of Hudson's Bay
Kilakotah LaBonte	Louis' Clatsop wife, friend of Marie
Michel LaFramboise	French Canadian and former Astorian, Hudson's Bay
Joseph Klickitat	child rescued and living later with Dorion/Gobin family
Françoise (Frani) Gervais	child of Joseph and Angelique Gervais (and niece of Kilakotah LaBonte)
Daniel Waldo	emigrant of 1843 wagon train

Catholic Missionaries, Priests, and Layworkers

Sisters of Notre Dame de Namur	first sisters on French Prairie
David Mongrain	servant to Father Blanchet, catechist on French Prairie
**Sister Celeste*	a composite of sisters serving St. Mary's on the Willamette
Father Francis N. Blanchet	first priest at St. Paul, first Archbishop of Oregon
Father Pierre Desmet	early priest on French Prairie
Father A.M.A. Blanchet	bishop and brother to Father Francis N. Blanchet
Father Jean Baptiste Brouillet	priest at St. Rose of the Cayuse

Walla Walla and Cayuse Connections

Narcisse Raymond	uncle to Josette; French Canadian
Gray Eagle and Five Crows	Cayuse wanted in Whitman murders

THE MISSIONARIES

Jason Lee	superintendent of the Oregon Mission (Methodist)
Josiah Parrish	Methodist Mission at French Prairie and Clatsop Plains
Elijah White	physician for Methodist Mission and subagent for Indian Affairs
Henry and Eliza Spalding	Presbyterian missionaries to Nez Perce
Marcus and Narcissa Whitman	Presbyterian missionaries at Waiilatpu, Cayuse country
The Wallers	Presbyterian missionaries at The Dalles and Oregon City/Willamette Falls

HUDSON'S BAY COMPANY (FORMERLY NORTH WEST COMPANY)

John McLoughlin	chief factor for Columbia country, Hudson's Bay, stationed at Fort Vancouver
Marguerite	John's wife
Tom McKay	son of former Astorian and stepson of John McLoughlin; also interpreter, guide, horse breeder, and rancher on French Prairie
Peter Skene Ogden	a Snake River brigade leader; negotiator for hostages

SITES

St. Paul	present day St. Paul, Oregon
St. Louis on the Willamette	present day site near Gervais, Oregon
French Prairie	present day south of Champoeg, Oregon
Fort Nez Perce/Fort Walla Walla	on the Walla Walla River, present day Wallula, Washington
Astoria/Fort George	present day Astoria, Oregon
Fort Vancouver	present day Vancouver, Washington
Waiilatpu	present day Whitman National Historic Site
Crossing, Rivière des Chutes	present day Sherar's Falls, Oregon
Oregon City/Willamette Falls	present day Oregon City

* denotes fictional character

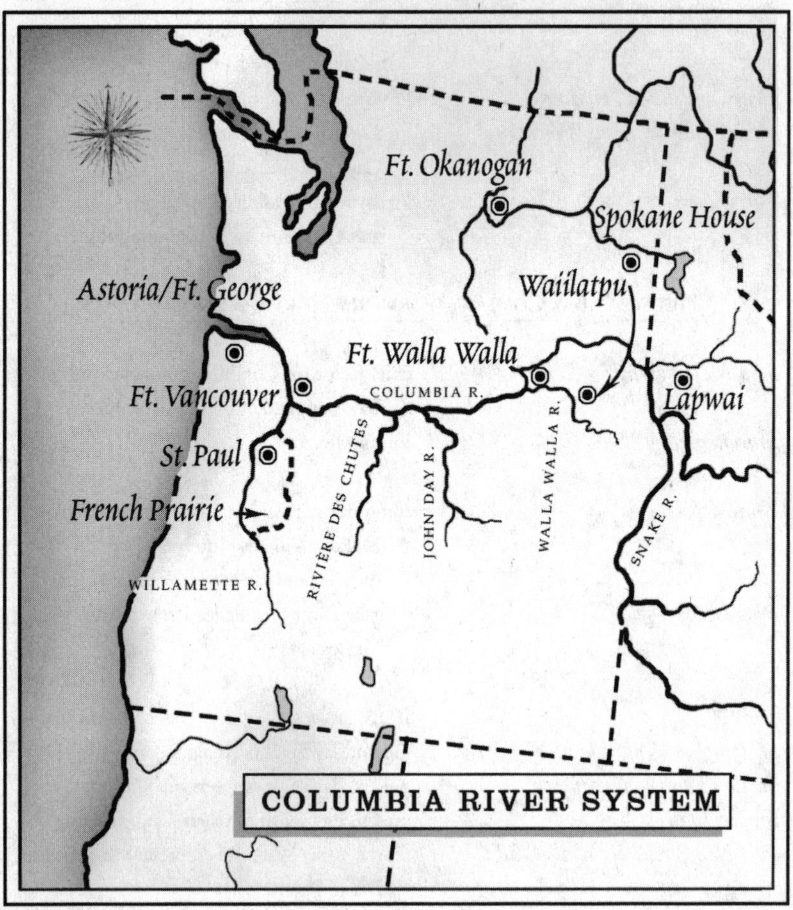

Ft. Okanogan
Spokane House
Astoria/Ft. George
Waiilatpu
Ft. Walla Walla
Ft. Vancouver
COLUMBIA R.
Lapwai
St. Paul
French Prairie
RIVIÈRE DES CHUTES
JOHN DAY R.
WALLA WALLA R.
SNAKE R.
WILLAMETTE R.
COLUMBIA RIVER SYSTEM

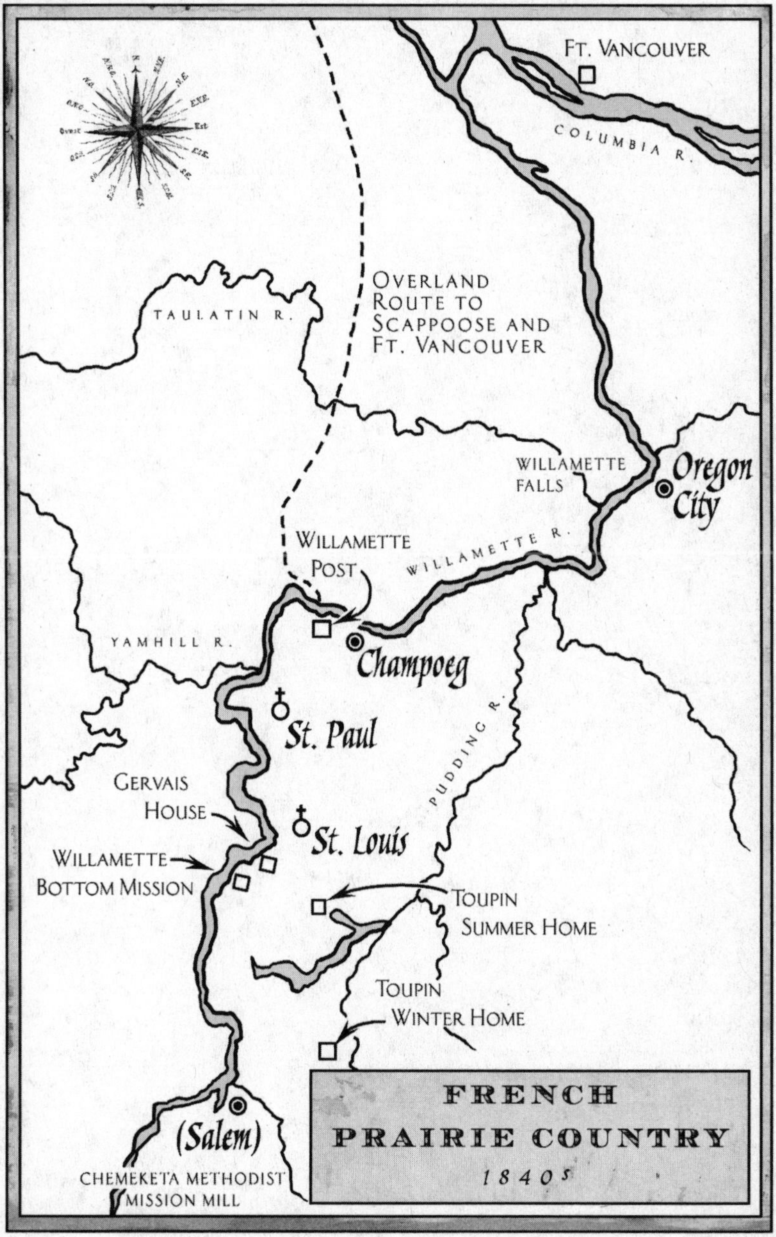
FT. VANCOUVER
COLUMBIA R.
OVERLAND ROUTE TO SCAPPOOSE AND FT. VANCOUVER
TAULATIN R.
WILLAMETTE FALLS
Oregon City
WILLAMETTE POST
WILLAMETTE R.
YAMHILL R.
Champoeg
St. Paul
PUDDING R.
GERVAIS HOUSE
St. Louis
WILLAMETTE BOTTOM MISSION
TOUPIN SUMMER HOME
TOUPIN WINTER HOME
(Salem)
CHEMEKETA METHODIST MISSION MILL
FRENCH PRAIRIE COUNTRY
1840s

Hold Tight the Thread

The Way It Is

There's a thread you follow. It goes among
things that change. But it doesn't change.
People wonder what you are pursuing.
You have to explain about the thread.
But it is hard for others to see.
While you hold it you can't get lost.
Tragedies happen; people get hurt
Or die; and you suffer and grow old.
Nothing you do can stop time's unfolding.
You don't ever let go of the thread.

WILLIAM STAFFORD

Ye shall know the truth,
and the truth shall make you free.

John 8:32

We turn away, we avoid.
Finally, we forget, and forget we have forgotten.

Daniel Goleman, *Vital Lies, Simple Truths*

1

Bright Shining Light

August 1841, French Prairie, Oregon Country

Marie let loose her daughter's hand, then stepped behind her, gently guiding her into the darkness. *"Maintenant,"* she said in French. "We go now." She placed her hands on the young woman's cedar-caped shoulders, inhaled the wood scent of her hair. They were nearly the same height, one of the few things they shared in common—that and a worry over whether they'd be enough.

"We don't have time for this, Mother," Marguerite protested. But she allowed Marie to prod her to an area of prairie grass where Marie motioned her daughter to sit.

"We need to make time for this," Marie said. "Lie down." She patted the grass.

A vast darkness arched over her and her oldest daughter. The women's heads touched, as though they were two logs reaching out from a center post. The air felt moist. The moon would rise late tonight. The dry grasses tickled her ankles. She should have put on leggings before convincing her oldest daughter to walk a distance from their log home to feel the night air breathe in the dark sky. Getting Marguerite to come with her at all had taken convincing. Dozens of tasks waited finishing before the big event tomorrow. "There will never be another night like this one, not ever," Marie told her daughter. Marie meant to savor it. She'd begun to cherish these feathers of peaceful moments floating into her life, even when it took effort. It still took such effort to name the good in her days. Learning new ways, she found, both stimulated and strained her. This was a happy occasion. She refused to let worry scar it, and so she controlled her troublesome thoughts, even now, when they pushed like a bullish child elbowing his way in uninvited.

"Did you see that?" Marie asked. She pointed. "That light? There's a special prize for the one who sees the first star."

Marguerite shook her head, rubbing Marie's hair as she did. "Papa Jean's spectacles must let you see something I can't. It's still just dark sky to me, Mother. Where did you see it?"

"East," Marie said. She adjusted the lenses given her as a gift by her husband just weeks before. "Toward Hood's Mountain. An arc of light. There's another."

"I don't see them. Maybe they're coming to find us with the lanterns." Marguerite said. "Maybe they think I've changed my mind and have run away."

Did her daughter warn her of worries? The man was twenty years her daughter's senior. He had sons already. Maybe Marguerite wished more time before she committed to this man Jean Baptiste Gobin. Does a mother encourage her daughter to walk through the uncertainty of marriage, promising her that peace will come, or does she make a safe place for a daughter to turn around, to reconsider her heart's future?

What was right for a mother to do? was always Marie's question.

Ripe gooseberries scented the August air. An owl hooted in the big cedar tree in the center of the timbered section that marked the border of their land. Prairie wolves howled in the distance, a sound distinct from the larger wolves that roamed in packs. Marie took in a deep breath. There were more blessings here than dangers; that's what she must concentrate on, encourage her daughter to think this too. New ways took time. Her friend Sarah had told her that long years before, and Sarah was seldom wrong. Unlike Marie, who was a mother named by her errors.

She took another deep breath. She would count her blessings like the beads of her rosary, designed, orderly, and obvious, the way the priests said God revealed himself in the created world. Hadn't her husband of many years become her friend, someone with whom she preferred to spend her time? That must have been part of a grand design.

Wasn't this prairie land they'd found to live in ripe with promise, predictable with seasons of planting and harvest? Hadn't she found a quiet way to ease the ache of a lost and troubled son, soothe the disappointment of rarely seeing distant friends, survive the deaths of a child and two husbands? The landscape, her newly forming faith, and her family promised peace. These were the life threads that she wove into a healing robe of comfort.

Memory, too, served her. It brought the conversations she'd had with her friend Sacagawea to mind whenever she wished. Memory reminded her of what she had endured in her fifty summers. Even Kilakotah she called neighbor now, though to touch her fingers to her friend's cheeks meant a three-day ride to the horse ranch of Tom McKay. Still, the two would see each other more now, when they gathered at the parish church on the Willamette River when the priests traveled south for Mass. And in between, she had the memories of those who brushed against her and changed her life forever.

She had troubling memories too, but surely she deserved now a time to set those aside, cut those ties. Her friend Sacagawea would tell her to expect kindness in life. This she would do, especially tonight. After all, she was a mother whose children told her their secrets and honored her with their questions. What mother didn't want to be known for her careful tongue and modest wisdom? Her husband, Jean, tolerated her many wonderings over varying views of faith of native people, of Presbyterians, Catholics, and Methodists who populated this prairie area. Perhaps he understood that her baptism was a beginning of another questioning journey and not one simply ending with acceptance as it had been for him.

Marie questioned. It was part of who she was.

Marie blinked again. She'd seen the pinpricks sometimes even in the daylight, when she stood too quickly or when she first awoke. Their presence interrupted her sleep, too, and she'd awake with a start, a gasp that would wake her husband and stir the household trying to sleep in the upper loft.

Perhaps her eyes were learning new things even while she slept. She had spectacles to wear during the day, to stop the squinting that had been a part of her life for as long as she could remember. Yes, that was probably all it was, her eyes adjusting to the dark and daylight, seeing clearly with spectacles.

This piercing light tonight was likely just the first sign of the stars filling the night sky. Nothing to be alarmed about.

"Will this always be my home?" Marguerite asked then. Her voice had changed to wistfulness.

"You'll always have a place with us, but you'll have your own home after tomorrow." Her daughter took in a sharp breath, and her breathing quickened. Marie heard discomfort in the sound. "This is your choice, *oui?*" Marie asked. "To marry this man?"

"I'm glad we moved here with Papa Jean," Marguerite said.

Hadn't her daughter heard her? Or did she deliberately avoid?

"You might not have met your JB if we hadn't."

"There are more French Canadians here," Marguerite said.

"More people like your papa."

"There's one," Marguerite said, lifting her hand quickly to point. Marie felt rather than saw her daughter's arm reach up. "In the northern sky."

"I see it too. *Bon.* You receive the treasure. You have the first star in your basket," Marie told her.

"What's my prize?"

"It comes to you later."

"You made that up, Mother. There's no 'first prize' for seeing the first star of a night sky."

"You'll see," she said and smiled.

Marie had coaxed her daughter away from the cheek bread pans, those rounded tins that resembled a baby's bottom when the dough rose. She drew her from the chatter of Marguerite's younger brother and sister so she could rest a bit before taking on the role of a bride. A peaceful moment was her daughter's treasure. A new wife had few of them after the wedding, and Marie wanted her daughter to have the memory of a special evening before the days filled up with the work of living.

Marie would have a prize too: a memory of a last quiet time with her oldest daughter alone, a moment of hanging on to a daughter before Marguerite became a wife.

Marie thought to offer sage advice, to say something to sustain her daughter in this time of transformation when a woman became a bride. Words failed her at times, even French words, her first language. Marie thought of her mother. What might her own mother have spoken if she had lived to see Marie's marriage day when, as a young girl, she had committed herself to Pierre Dorion? Would she have been proud that her daughter chose a man affiliated, however briefly, with the Corps of Discovery? Or might she have stepped in to intervene, suggested that she was too young to wed?

No way to know. Her mother had died before Marie spoke marriage vows.

Marie was pleased her daughter had waited until she was twenty-two to marry. And her youngest girl, Marianne, while fifteen, showed little interest in boys. A blessing. Marie touched the beads around her neck, ran her hand over the smooth metal cross that her friend Sarah had given her. Blessings. Count the blessings.

"What are you thinking about, Mother?" Marguerite asked. The girl had a gravelly voice, husky almost, her throat scorched perhaps from leaning over the cook fires. Marie imagined the tiny wrinkles that flowed like rivers toward the pools of her daughter's dark eyes, eyes that tonight looked tired even before the wedding plans consumed her. As a child, Marguerite had been known by the French Canadians for her thick eyebrows lifting in question and by her firm lips reserving expression for rare occasions. Even with impending joy so close, Marguerite's full round face hadn't eased often into a smile. Marie wished something different for Marguerite.

"Remembering," Marie said. "It's what a mother does on a day before her daughter weds. A bride-to-be should have stars in her basket, *n'est-ce pas?*"

Marguerite said, "To light the darkness she finds there?"

"You worry over darkness?" Marie said.

"Just a rule of thumb," Marguerite said.

Marie shivered. Such a phrase. Could this JB Gobin be a man who used the rod against his wife? Had she missed some rumor about him? Why otherwise had her daughter chosen the term *rule of thumb,* the legal size of a rod allowed by a husband to strike his wife?

"Does he hurt you, this Gobin? You do not need to marry him, then." Marie sat up. Her daughter was asking for a way out.

"No. No." Marguerite answered quickly, pulled her mother back. "I only meant I'm just a little worried, a slender worry, the size of a rod. About…"

"Do your thoughts go to someone else? to Richard?"

Marguerite laughed. "That Nez Perce boy? No. He was just a friend." Her voice sounded light, as though she coaxed a child to eat her porridge. "No." Marguerite hesitated now. "I think of Paul," she said.

Marie felt a chill go through her. "The day before your wedding you think of your half-brother?" Marie moved her head, felt the hair at the back of her neck bristle.

"Didn't he run away on the day Baptiste married Older Sister?"

"He did."

"It was the first wedding I remember, and it ended in sadness. Papa never came back. Paul never came back. Even Baptiste left, and before he returned Older Sister died."

"Leave those hard thoughts behind now, Marguerite."

"They never even said good-bye to me. None of them," Marguerite said.

"This is what you think of when you prepare to marry?" Marie said. "*Non.* This is not good. You were little then. You should think of other things. You shouldn't think of a sad time. See, there's another star. This will be a full sky night."

"Don't you wonder where Paul is?"

Another light, as tiny as a pinprick, flashed before her eyes. Marie blinked, and the glimmer broke into flickers and disappeared. She felt no pain, but uneasiness snaked though the tiny hole as though the opening might rip into something larger that could consume her. When had they started, these flickering lights, tearing at the fabric of memory and mind? She lived in safety, surrounded by family and friends. Why did the uneasiness pierce her now?

Marie held her jaws together, made herself breathe in through her nose. "I have put my thoughts of Paul in a past place, to make room for new joys, like my daughter's wedding."

Marie could hear voices in the distance. Marianne's girlish pitches poked into her husband's and her son's low tones. Someone would be calling them back soon.

"What do you think really happened to Paul? And to Papa?" Marguerite asked. She sat up now. "They're linked together for me, their disappearances."

"They happened years apart," Marie said. "Our memories tell tall tales to us sometimes."

"Not for me. I wonder about the stories I should tell my children about their grandfather."

"Papa Jean was more a part of your life. Tell your children of him."

Moments passed, and Marguerite sat so silent that Marie thought she might have fallen asleep. Marie imagined her daughter's long eyelashes closed against her cheeks; she reached to touch the bone beneath her daughter's left eye, a bone left flattened when a horse raised its head to Marguerite's and cracked it long years before. Maybe Marguerite worried about injury or death, this young woman on the eve of new living. Marie was no *femme sensé;* she had no explanations. Her baptism weeks before had answered some questions but added even more.

"I want to tell my children stories of Papa," Marguerite said, her fingers clutching her mother's now. "So they'll know about a good father. He was good, *n'est-ce pas?* He had scars in his fingers. I remember that. And he sang, didn't he?"

"*Oui.* He loved music and he sewed with me. Even with his fingers that would break open in icy water. Tiny stitches we used."

"Sometimes I think that Paul…"

"What? What do you think?"

"Nothing," Marguerite said. She let loose her mother's hand. "It is a never-mind thought."

For Marie, stories of Paul arrived on an arc of pain that hit new marks each time they were spoken as words. She wanted to forget that wound, put it away as she'd put other painful times behind her, times that were better tucked away as forgotten thoughts, not brought into present memory. "Tell your children of the good your stepfather brought to your life. Don't dwell on the death of your father or the disappearance of Paul or the death of your sister-in-law," Marie said. "Baptiste married a woman he loved. Remember that. And he is happy now. He did come back. Not all who leave stay gone. Papa Jean lived away for months trapping, but he always returned."

"Older Sister lost her life…giving birth," Marguerite said. Her voice was so low the words sounded like the hum of bees.

Marie put her arm around her daughter. "You're worried over childbirth?" Why hadn't she thought of that? Of course. What kind of mother was she not to know a daughter would be concerned over such things?

"To have something and then lose it," Marguerite whispered. "It might be better not to have it at all."

"Look around this French Prairie. See how many children run here and there. Babies are a natural thing. You'll see. This is an orderly world created for us. A peaceful world. Baptiste loved again. I loved again, after two husband's deaths. Our hearts are large enough to love more than once, to fill the empty places of those who leave or are even sent away."

"Are they?"

Had Marie gifted her daughter with a mind that always worried rather than one that reveled? Was that the legacy she would leave this child on the eve of her wedding night? Not one of hopeful joy but of the weave of worry?

"This match frightens you because JB was wedded before," Marie said. "I understand this now."

"Non," Marguerite said. Too quickly. "It is not the marriage that frightens." Marie imagined Marguerite's obsidian eyes piercing the darkness, could almost see her daughter smooth her hair back, the lovely widow's peak marking the center of her high forehead. "It's the unanswered questions that trouble me. We need to go inside. We have bread to bake while the night is cool."

This was not the conversation Marie wanted to have with her daughter. She wanted to tell her of the joys of companionship, about light shed upon a marriage journey that moves two people back and forth across the bridge of separate and together. She wanted to tell her not to stay as unbending as her mother had. "I loved your father. The uncertainties of his death still haunt me, but I can find no answers when I search there."

"It is hard to move to a new place in my life while old questions still hold a claim. What about Paul? Is his disappearance related to—"

"Don't wait as long as I did to cherish good gifts, daughter," Marie said. "Desire met is more than longing for past pleasures. Desire attained is as sweet as molasses. Think about such sweetness instead of all that might be unfinished in a life."

Marguerite moved to stand into the darkness.

What could Marie say that would be supportive, encouraging, kind? "You can change your mind," Marie said. As her daughter reached to pull her up, Marie grunted with the effort. She held Marguerite's wide palm, squeezed her long, slender fingers. "Even now. At this moment. Though the banns have been read, you can still decide to wait. JB will wait. The guests will understand. What you wish is what matters most."

Am I saying the right thing? Am I suggesting caution where it needn't be?

"It's just…there, see that one? Oh, it has a tail as it falls through the sky. A falling *etoile.*" Marguerite sighed, and Marie knew that a moment of opportunity had passed, that she hadn't comforted her daughter. She hadn't given her the gift of peace the day before her marriage. They hadn't even had words Marguerite might someday wish to tell her daughter on her marriage day. She couldn't say, "My mother told me this wise thing the day before I married your Papa, and now I tell it to you." Her daughter was apparently as good as her mother at slipping good things into worries and intended affection into distraction. It was not the legacy Marie had hoped to give her daughter.

"Come, Mother." Marguerite squeezed Marie's hand now. "I have a garland still to weave for my hair. We've lain around enough." She slipped her hand from her mother's and walked on ahead, alone.

"Where are they?" Marianne Toupin tapped her bare foot on the puncheon floor. Jean Toupin looked up from the brass music box he polished to glance at his youngest daughter. "Your mother took your sister out to look at the sky. The night's dark as a raven, so the stars will soon look like a flowing river. The sight of *les etoiles* lifts her, your mother. She wants Marguerite to share this night sky. A mother and daughter together, eh?"

"Why didn't she ask me? I'm her daughter too."

"You're not getting married tomorrow. Hush now. No lower lip," Jean said.

"Get me a cup of hot water, *gosse,*" François said. The boy had a sharp tone to his tongue, always, as sharp as his Adam's apple that bobbed in his slender neck. "That'll keep you occupied."

"You can get your own if you call me a *gosse.* I'm no brat," Marianne told him.

"My own what? Water or new little sister?"

François reached out to pull on the apron strings surrounding Marianne's small waist. She squealed, moved out of reach, and stumbled her way toward the door she then pushed against. She draped her arms at the door opening, a look of longing filling her face. Jean wished he could find the chalk to erase his daughter's lonely look.

"Don't bother your mother and sister, now," Jean said instead. "I don't want them coming back in before I finish the polish on this brass."

"I'll just go to catch the night air," Marianne said. "What's in here reeks of...brassiness." She turned and stuck her tongue out at François, who stood and walked for his own cup of water. He jabbed at his sister's arm as he swaggered past her.

"Here now," Jean said. "Respect each other. This is no time for nonsense."

"Where Marianne's concerned, it's all such as that," François said.

"Maybe if I had an older brother who wasn't such an *enfant terrible* I'd—"

"Maintenant!" Jean said. "A man seeks a little silence in his own house."

François straddled a plank bench; his back met his sister's glare. He whittled on a piece of wood now that Jean hoped might be a present for Marguerite's wedding, though if it was, the gift would be delivered late. Jean couldn't even tell yet what it was meant to be.

Had his two children always bickered like this? No. It was worse this past week. Probably all the activities related to Marguerite's impending marriage and their having to face yet another change in their lives. He'd forgotten how change, even good change, could catch a soul off guard, swirl a man around like a *bateau* in a whirlpool just before it spit him into calm water. At least he hoped calm waters would follow the swirl.

"Your mama and sister will come inside soon," Jean said. "Someday you, too, will have a special memory walk with your mama, the night before you wed. But this is years off, *n'est-ce pas?* You do not want to leave your old papa just yet, eh?"

Marianne ignored him, stared out into the darkness.

Marguerite was almost like Jean's own daughter. He'd taken her into his life along with Marie's two sons long before he'd had the joy of holding his own flesh and blood. He wished the girl well and believed he'd helped make a good match for her, as any father would. But he held something special for Marianne. His baby. He imagined a fine marriage match years from now. She was just fifteen and had time enough for love.

"Come, help your papa with this brass box, Marianne. You rub for a while. It will be your part of the marriage gift, eh?"

"They're just standing there, Papa. Can't I go out now?"

Marianne had her father's lean build, while both her mother and Marguerite carried heavier bones that made them able to heft heavy baskets Marianne buckled under. Her mother had told Marianne once that she was still growing into herself. "Like those strange little warts that sometimes grow into the bottom of my feet?" Marianne had asked. "Is growing into myself as painful as that?"

They'd all laughed, though Marianne hadn't. She could be such a child at times, but at others she could startle him with her womanly beauty, which made him wonder how such loveliness could have come through him. As with her mother, Jean wanted to protect Marianne forever from the eyes of prying men. He thought of that now as she stood there, the lamplight flickering off the tendrils that framed her narrow face. Her hair wasn't nearly as thick as Marguerite's or her mother's hair either. It kinked up like his, and she complained about it often, not wanting to be different, Jean supposed. And at the same time, she wanted to be as unique as every star in the sky. Jean shook his head. Women were a strange lot. But he loved them all, the women in his life. He just wanted to keep them safe.

"She's probably telling her the secret of my birth right now," Marianne said. "I was probably one of those changeling orphans left at the doorsteps of the Methodist Mission, and no one has wanted to tell me."

"What? *Blesid Maria,*" Jean said. "Where do you get such ideas? They do not talk of you. Besides, you were born in the Okanogan country. I was there when you arrived. Why do you say such things?"

She faced him. "I'm just so different, Papa." She spoke in a whisper. François didn't turn around. "Marguerite says if I wear my hair rolled into a bun at the back of my neck the way she and Mama do, it won't frizz up so much. She says I shouldn't rub it with alder leaf tea or let the wind pull it loose from the ribbon, but none of that will make me look more like her or Mama. And my eyes, Papa." She wiped at one now. "Where did I get these eyes? They leak, and they're pale as weak tea." She wiped her hand on her apron, then stared at her fingers. "And fat little fingers? Whose are these? Mama and Marguerite have delicate fingers." She'd begun to cry now.

Jean put the music box down, stood. François turned, frowned, then shook his head in disgust as Jean moved toward Marianne. He pulled his daughter into his chest, patted her back.

"I just don't belong, Papa. I'm ugly and strange and will never get married, ever. And Mama prefers Marguerite's company, I know she does. And Marguerite's leaving and—"

"She'll be a little short ride from here," Jean said. He patted the thick hair that cascaded down his daughter's back. "Your sister doesn't go far away. You'll have time to visit. She'll come here often, you'll see." Marianne was sobbing now, shaking. "You will fall in love, little one. Is this what troubles you? You have plenty of time." His words appeared to make her cry harder. He held her shoulders away from him and wiped at the girl's cheek with his thumb. What had he said to make it worse? Her mother could fix this. "*Maintenant,* you go on out then," he said. "They'll welcome you. Keep them there while I finish up with this box, eh?"

She sniffed and lifted her chin. *"Oui,"* she said. "I do it for you, Papa."

Her voice sounded light, no longer dragged down by despair. She put her finger to her lips as though to silence him, cracked a half-smile, and then she crept low into the outside shadow, as though she were a small child, out to play hide-and-seek. How had she gone from weeping to childish as quickly as a star falls from the sky? Youth. It was a gift of youth to shift quickly.

"She tricked you, Papa. She just wanted to go out," his son said.

"Eh? You think this?"

"They use tears, Papa. It is their weapon."

"We men have tears too," Jean said. "They come unbidden at times. It's so for women, too, eh?"

"Maybe," François said. "It's not been my experience. They pour out tears and turn them off as easy as…as easy as that music box."

"Women have more complicated parts than you might think," Jean said as he returned to his polishing, the oil pungent in the room. He'd probably never understand women, even those he loved the most. Jean smiled without letting his son see. François sounded like an old man who'd had his heart broken many times, and Jean knew that wasn't so. His son, though seventeen, had never even asked a girl to dance so far as Jean knew. His son made judgments about women while watching from a distance, which left room for speculation. He had things to learn if he wished to get closer, but time to learn it in, just as Marianne did.

Jean's family was changing, but much of the giving a father had to do still remained undone. It was worthy work that needed doing.

Marguerite stopped, pulled her mother's hand back. "What's that?" she said. "Over there."

Marie turned to the sound of swishing, like wind picking up inside a pine grove except it was low to the ground. Pale light filtering through the cabin's skin windows helped her see a large mole-shaped form shifting back and forth as it moved through the dry grass.

"Porcupine," Marie whispered. "A big one. Quick. Get a blanket and tell your Papa Jean."

Marguerite lifted her skirt and set off running.

"It's no porcupine, it's me," Marianne said, jumping up. "Can't you tell your daughter from a rodent?"

Marguerite gave a whoop of surprise and said something Marie couldn't hear. The swishing sound continued though, off to the side of Marianne, who circled and now came beside her mother.

"Shh," Marie told her. "There is a porcupine. Listen." She pointed.

She heard Marguerite say, "Papa Jean, there's a porcupine out here. Bring a blanket, François."

Marguerite stood in the pale shadow of door light now. Marie hoped Jean had had time to polish the wedding gift and put it away before they returned. Jean soon filled the doorway and joined Marie. François and Marguerite followed.

"Where is it?" Jean asked her. He held a pistol in his hand.

"See there, just this side of the fence," Marianne said.

"We four will take the blanket and as soon as we throw it over him, you—"

"I know how to shoot a porcupine, wife, eh?" Jean said.

Marianne whined. "I can't see very well." Marianne clutched her corner of the Hudson's Bay blanket François handed her. "I don't want to get too close to him. Papa, don't shoot me."

"Such a thing you say, daughter," Jean told her.

"Just stay behind me," François told Marianne. He raised a sperm oil lamp in one hand, the blanket corner in the other.

Marie and Marguerite held the other corners, and the four crept quietly toward the animal, which was humped over like a treeless hill shuffling through the grass in the growing starlight. They worked their way up behind him.

"Now!" Marie shouted, and they ran, two people on either side of the creature. They tossed the blanket down over his back, still holding tight to the corners. The porcupine thrashed and turned. Marianne squealed.

"Hang on!" Marie shouted.

"He's whipping around the other way," François warned. He laughed, and Marianne squealed into the night.

"Step back, step back," Jean said as the animal, blinded by the blanket, turned in a circle, this way, then back, like a disturbed bull.

Marie felt the tug of the quills release. "Lift up your ends. Now!"

The drag against the quills lessened, and they pulled the fibers free.

"Move now, all of us at once. Flip the blanket but hold tight," Marie said. "Move toward the house now."

"Let Papa shoot!" Marguerite said.

Marguerite's words were followed by the flash of light burning from the powder of Jean's pistol.

Birds roosting in the trees beyond scattered in the night sky. "Missed him," Jean said then, but Marie didn't think he sounded disappointed. "He would have made a big stew, Marianne." Her youngest daughter groaned a protest. "You'll wish we had him later." To Marie he said, "You'll have enough quills to decorate a hundred moccasins. Some left over to trade."

Marie had just enough light to see what she needed. "These belong to Marguerite," Marie said. The starlight let them all see the dozens of white quills in the blanket, their dark points disappearing into shadow.

"A gift fit only for a bride to be," Marie said.

"Quills are my special prize, mother?" Marguerite asked. She laughed then, a deep, hearty laugh, and Marie hugged her oldest daughter with one arm.

François picked up the lantern and held it high enough for all to see this gathering of the Toupin family. How Marie wished all her family were here this night—all her sons and the one daughter who had died. Weddings and births should have all the family gathered, leave no one outside that circle. A good mother stitched a family together no matter the rips and tears of past years. *Rips and tears.* Marie frowned. Her mind covered something. "We've things to do yet," Marie said. "To make tomorrow a special day for you, Marguerite." Jean handed François the pistol, and he took the blanket from the women. The men started back for the house while the women followed. Marie put her arm around her oldest daughter's waist, and Marguerite wrapped hers around Marie's. They followed the men inside.

"Mother," Marianne said just as Marie was about to close the door. "I'm not inside yet. You pushed the door in my face."

"Pardon," Marie said.

"You didn't even remember I followed you."

"Your mother didn't mean to forget you," Jean said. "You make too much of a thing, daughter. A mother doesn't forget a child, eh?"

"Well, I hope not," Marianne said. "What kind of mother would do that?"

Another pinprick of light flashed at the side of Marie's eyes. The light unsettled her. Marie sensed it had nothing to do with moonlight or stars.

2

In-Between

"Isn't this a fine time," a woman at the wedding told Marie. She stood close to Marie, as though she knew her. Or perhaps the woman needed to be close to hear above the din of music and glee. Someone had brought spirits to Marguerite and JB's wedding celebration, stored it beneath the firs, cooled it in the river. Men moved in and out of the Gervais barn, took the path to the water, and returned with pinker cheeks than when they'd left.

"My daughter has married well," Marie said. Marguerite wore a white buckskin dress with rows of shells across the bodice that tinkled quietly when she swished through the clusters of French Canadians and former Hudson's Bay men and their Indian wives. She'd blushed when, after the priest finalized their vows, old trapper friends wrapped the blanket around JB and her, a custom of the river Indians to mark the binding of a couple. The white blanket with a black-and-yellow stripe hung folded over her daughter's forearm now, draped nearly to Marguerite's feet. Marie smiled. Marguerite wore hand-cobbled leather shoes instead of moccasins. She always did like her shoes. It was a grand gathering of French Canadians and former Astorians. French and English words filtered through the fiddle sounds.

Marie pawed her memory for the name of the woman. She knew she knew this woman. Why couldn't she bring up her name? "Didn't we always say we hoped it would be so?" the woman said. "I remember when we went with Ross after your marriage to Louis. We talked of children then. That was before Marguerite was even born to this land. A long time ago."

Marie caught her breath. Here stood a woman she'd known during those years. And yet she didn't recognize her enough to say her name?

Lately, the space between seeing and recognizing was deep and clouded as a flooding river. Paul came to mind. If she couldn't remember a close friend seen only now and then, would she recognize a son not seen for years if she were given the gift of stumbling upon him?

"Kilakotah!" Marie said then, tossing the name into the night. How could she forget the face and name of someone she cared for? Her heart pounded.

"You say it as though we've just met," her friend said and laughed.

Marie couldn't say what had just happened. It was as though half her mind wore one of Jean's heavy boots while she walked barefoot with the other half. Maybe it was part of the excitement, all the activity of the days previous.

They talked easily then, of old times, these two women, Marie relaxed with her memories intact. Marie ate and served the guests throughout the night, naming each familiar face. She had a good memory. Her friend Sally Ross commented on that often. She felt the presence of someone behind her as she stood replacing food in the flat woven baskets. An arm reached around her holding a mug before her face. "It smells good, *n'est-ce pas,* this home brew?" he said, and Marie nodded. She recognized Jean's voice. She turned to face him. Maybe he would understand this strangeness. But before she could speak, two knee-hopping mountain men danced by and knocked Jean's mug, spilling the brew onto Marie's dress.

"They will pay penance in the morning, eh?" Jean said as he dabbed at the stain, brushing against her bodice.

Penance. The priest gave her things to do to pay penance, to make amends, for what she confessed. The doing never seemed to relieve her of the weight, though. Saying assigned prayers was never enough to lift her spirits fully. Could this space in remembering her friend be a penance, for some past wrong she had yet to confess?

Marguerite Venier Gobin awoke as a married woman and wondered what she'd done. Her mother hadn't prepared her for this, for what happened after the ceremony when the French Canadians she'd known since birth returned to their homes along the Willamette River and she didn't. Instead, she'd walked down the dusty path with her new husband, neither touching the other, followed by his sons. She'd climbed into the wagon only to be surprised that the two small boys had scurried around the wagon and already sat beside their father.

"I've a soft feather pillow for you, there," her husband said, pointing to the body of the wagon just behind the seat. "More comfort for you than up here."

Neither had her mother told her what it might be like to enter into a house once ruled by another woman and maybe still was, though her husband's first wife had been dead for a year or more. And where was her mother's wisdom, her sage advice everyone spoke about, when it came to the marriage bed? She hadn't heard any sage words related to...well, *that.*

Marguerite turned over in the feather tick, blinked back tears. How had she gotten herself into this? A month after her mother and stepfather had reaffirmed their marriage vows before a priest, making all the births of their children legitimate, Marguerite had taken her own vows. With a man she hardly knew. With a man nearly as old as her stepfather, with a man who already had two sons.

"Femme!" her husband shouted now. Jean Baptiste Gobin, JB as his friends called him, had a booming voice, not unfriendly, but loud. "*Femme!* Come see the morning," he said. "Clear as spring rain. The natives and good French farmers will be starting the fires soon, and the air will never be so clear then. Come now. Rise up." He laughed then, not an unpleasant sound. "You, married woman." He'd moved closer. The coarse linen that divided their bed from the rest of the one-room house flew open. Their house was a story-and-one-half high, but the little boys hadn't slept in the loft.

Marguerite felt August hot and, though fully covered by a night dress, the thought of a stranger seeing her like that forced her to pull up the blanket to her chin.

Behind him, she saw the little boys, their eyes like owls, staring at her from their bench beside the table. Rumpled robes lay in the corner where they must have slept.

JB's eyes softened when he saw her. "*Femme.* There's no need for fear, eh?" He patted her on her head as though she were twelve instead of twenty-two. "Dress quickly then. I will make up the coffee. The boys and me, we are introducing the back of our belly buttons to our stomachs with no food between them. Been some time since a woman's fed our bellies, eh boys?" he turned to his sons.

Both boys sat staring at her.

She'd thought them four or five years old, but now she could see they were older, surely six or seven. Toussaint, the oldest, had thick curly hair, black as new-tilled soil. Jean Baptiste II, Doublé, his father called him, making it rhyme with *away,* moved his thumb slowly to his mouth, then popped it in. Neither boy blinked, not once.

When she'd first met them, somehow she'd thought they were JB's grandsons, who belonged to someone else.

She'd met JB when they'd first come to French Prairie, when her mother had finally agreed to join her older brother Baptiste and his family, already here. She'd known of him a whole year, but her Papa Jean had only recently arranged the marriage to JB, a fur trapper turned farmer. Marguerite didn't really feel her cheeks grow warm in JB's presence until the Feast of the Epiphany in January. The priests had celebrated the first Mass in Columbia country at the little log church named for St. Paul at the north end of the prairie.

JB was one of many French Canadians she'd encountered again in the summer, through all the ceremony and sounds of shuffled moccasins on the puncheon floor as people came forward for the wafer. JB wore a blue-and-red sash around his waist and the tassels flew as he walked, *strutted* might be a better word, down the aisle after the Mass. Dozens of children had scampered around the chapel built by French Canadians three years before, awaiting the arrival of a priest. These little boys must have been there, but she didn't remember them that day.

Later, the fiddles had come out and JB had asked her to dance, his knees high stepping. Toussaint and Doublé must have been taken to a neighbor, but then everyone was a neighbor that night, so many French Canadians and their native wives enjoying the pleasure of one another's company and the arrival of the priests. Carts and horses and mules lined the muddy road leading up to the church, and the air was filled with smells of roasted goats and swans, fried fish and fresh-baked peach pies, the dried fruit coming to life with water. Over six hundred people had journeyed miles to participate in the Mass, her parents among the many well-wishers.

Well, not her parents exactly, nor well-wishers exactly either. Her stepfather had come with a light and willing step; her mother had been more cautious and only after much consideration, from what she could tell, had her mother knelt when Papa Jean did, bowed her head when Papa Jean did, spoke quiet prayers with her lips moving but not loud enough for Marguerite to hear her mother's words. Her mother had smiled as Marguerite remembered, but she stood off to the side, watching more than being a part of things until it was time to serve the food. Her mother was a gifted server.

She wasn't sure what kept her mother from embracing the faith the way Papa Jean did, openly, with words of appreciation for the priests and the candles and the stations of the cross where he said a man "had time to think, to consider. To be present in the light of wisdom and love." Papa Jean used words in romantic ways.

Her mother held the faith at arm's length as if it might bite when she least expected. Papa Jean just received. He confessed to the priest, was given guidance for traveling the trail of forgiveness, and did his best to not make the same mistake again. When he did—because men always do, he'd told her—he could expect greater penance would be required. Such was the way of faith, or so her stepfather told her. Papa Jean visited the little log church even when there was no Mass, which struck her as strange. No priest would be there to hear his confession. Not even a catechist, a teacher, to answer questions. "I go for the stillness away from the swirling places," he'd told her. "I am filled up by the silence of a holy place. It makes me less irritable, eh?"

So perhaps there was something more to his acceptance, something Marguerite just didn't understand. Still, Papa Jean spoke about his thoughts; her mother rarely shared her views about either the cheer or the complications of faith.

She wasn't privy to her mother's knowledge of marital ways either, or she'd have been prepared for these owl-eyed children staring at her the first morning of her wedded state. She'd have understood the hot cheeks she felt now as her husband grinned at her in an intimate way.

"My little *etoile,*" JB said. He ran his fingers at the point of hair that peaked perfectly at her forehead. He brushed his hands over her ears, knotting his fingers gently through her thick, ropy hair. It kinked like the end of an unbraided rope, though not as much as her younger sister's hair did. She usually kept it in a knot at her neck, but the pick had come out in the night. No, he had removed the pick, her husband had. She'd smelled the sweetness of his breath and savored the gentle way he placed his hand at her neck and pulled her close to him. She shivered with the memory.

"You're cold," he said. "Come. Get up now." He stroked the top of her head. "Etoile." He kissed the widow's peak, his lips soft as ripe plums.

"You call me *star?*" Marguerite asked.

He frowned. "This does not please you?"

"We have a cow we call that," she said.

"You would rather I call you Madame Gobin, maybe? Or woman? Something in English? French? *Femme?*"

"My name is Marguerite."

"*Oui,* I know this, my *etoile.* But there are so many Marguerites. I will call you Etoile because you shine, you sparkle. You have brought this into my home, into my life, my bed. Does she not sparkle, my sons?" He didn't wait for them to answer, nor look to see their expressions. "Come now, Etoile. Get up. You waste the day." He kissed the top of her head again and turned his back.

Waste the day?

Both boys' eyes moved as one to their father.

Marguerite sat straight as a headboard. "My name is Marguerite," she said. Her voice was firm. "It may be a long name and there may be many others but there is only one me," she said. "I am distinctive."

Her husband halted midstep. Standing with his back to her JB said, "There is only one star that bears your name. I know you are…unique."

The owl eyes moved back to Marguerite. Would these little boys be ready to witness an argument so early in the morning? Was this issue worth one?

JB turned around, raised his one eyebrow. *A warning? Agreement?* "Etoile…"

"Marguerite."

The owl eyes moved back to their father. She thought she saw Toussaint's little eyebrow twitch or start to rise.

Do I have the right to disagree with my husband, in front of his sons, on our first morning together? She didn't know. If only her mother hadn't kept her so much in the dark about marriage and life. For having had three husbands in her lifetime, her mother surely had more wisdom than what she'd chosen to share with her oldest daughter.

"Get up now," he said. "Or do you need teaching?" He raised an eyebrow, and Marguerite pulled the linen closer to her chin. She could hear her heart pound in her ears.

"Do you teach by…striking?"

"Striking? With a rod?" He sounded wounded. "No, no, no. Why would you think such a thing?" He came back over to her, sat beside her. "I am an old man," he told her. "But I am your companion, too. Would the moon want to strike at the stars? No, no, no. I would never raise a hand to harm you, never." He held her then, kissed the top of her head. "You have been worried over such as this?" He moved so he could see her face. She nodded. She didn't want to describe her real worries; couldn't even name them to herself. "Ah, we have much to learn together, then, my *etoile.* Much to learn."

She let him hold her. She had wanted her mother to offer her confidence about what she was doing, marrying a man mostly unknown to her but recommended by her parents. Her mother hadn't really let her share her fears. Their last time together, watching the stars, her mother had wanted to talk about light things and good things when what Marguerite needed was information about getting through the hard places. Her mother had even said she could change her mind if she wanted. *Does my mother think I've made a mistake?* Her husband stood, then said, "Marguerite. It will be as you wish, Marguerite. It is more important that we eat now and that you prepare this meal for your family."

"Oui," Marguerite said. "As you wish, husband." She pulled on her buckskin dress over her night linen and padded barefoot to the table.

"Bon," he said and slipped past her. "Today it is Marguerite. Tomorrow you are Etoile. We accommodate, tie the sash to fit us both, eh?"

She watched the owl eyes of the boys grow larger and thought better of what she'd planned to say. One could be known by worse names. Her mother had said what one did in life named a woman better than anything else. This morning her name was Wise.

"Be careful now," Marie told Marianne. "Around this bend the current quickens and there's that old tree root that looks like it is mostly above water but the worst of it hides below."

The two women kept the oars in the Willamette River mostly to guide rather than paddle as the river carried them downstream. It was still a startle to Marie that the rivers in this Oregon country ran north. In the country she'd known first, along the Des Moines, the Ouisconsin, the Mississippi, and the Missouri, rivers ran south to the sea. She expected the sun to rise on the other side of her when she first slipped a canoe into the water heading downstream. After all these years, she still expected something different.

Jean kept a small craft at the Gervais place where a wide gravel bar made launching easy. The river narrowed here, and in August, before the rains swelled it, it was a natural crossing place.

Marie's intent was to paddle down as far as the falls where a little settlement grew. The Hudson's Bay chief factor, Tom McKay's father, had claimed land there with some dispute. He called it his own but for the Company, too, and Jean said people grumbled over that. The man wasn't living on the land. He had someone else doing that, and the Company wasn't really allowed to "claim" the way a person was. The Company always acted like a person to her, requiring debt, hiring and firing, setting people out for years at a time.

For Marie, the chief factor's interest in that land meant others took notice too by opening cooperage shops and providing blacksmith work.

It saved time for the French Prairie dwellers, who didn't always have to travel all the way to Fort Vancouver. Choices benefited everyone. She intended to enjoy having such choices.

At her feet, the wrapped canvas sail lay beside a *shaptakai* of leather holding several pair of moccasins she'd beaded. No coinage or currency existed here as it had back in old St. Louis. Everyone just traded and tried for the best value they could. The Americans at the mission and commercial men at the falls liked the soft hide shoes she shaped and adorned. They realized quickly that thin-soled leather shoes were best reserved for weddings and funerals, while feet stayed warmer wrapped in deerskin or elk.

"Look there," Marianne said.

"Where?" Marie turned.

"I think it was a lion," Marianne said. "Maybe she tracks us."

Marie squinted. She hadn't seen the willows move, at least nothing large enough to be a cougar. A blue heron lifted its legs, dragging against the dark fir trees, then rising above into blue sky. "Are you sure it was a cougar? I don't see a thing."

"There." Marianne pointed to the other side of the river, and Marie could tell by the light tone of her voice that her daughter teased her.

"I suppose you see a bear there, now," Marie said.

Marianne laughed. "Didn't you see it? Your eyes are aging, Mama."

Marie grunted.

"I was only fooling you," Marianne said. "It breaks up the journey."

"You need to fool your old mother as a way to entertain yourself? You have too much time on your hands. Watch the river. Learn it, Marianne. Remember its ways. Someday you might need to make this trip alone, and you'll need to know how to avoid the rapids. Coming back, you can take the lead and set the sail."

"Upriver is harder work," Marianne complained.

"You'll need no entertaining then."

Marianne groaned and Marie smiled. She vowed to talk more about what she saw as they moved downriver, to teach her youngest daughter, give her the attention her daughter craved. She would have preferred to use the time in silence, listening to bird calls or smelling the scents of this lush land. But Marianne found ways to pull her mother's thoughts to her.

"We'll take out here for a bit," Marie said. They beached where Champoeg Creek flowed into the Willamette. Tom McKay had a mill on this creek, and sometimes Kilakotah and her husband, Louis LaBonte, were here tending Tom's horse ranch instead of farther north near Scappoose. She hoped her friend was here. She wanted to see if she would recognize her. She searched. A jaw harp twanged in the distance.

Marie yelped with the splash of water. "You were daydreaming, Mama," Marianne told her.

"I was," Marie agreed. She brushed at the river water Marianne had splashed on her bodice.

Marianne said, "You should ask for forgiveness."

"For what?"

"You ignore your baby," Marianne said.

"My baby gets my attention." She wiped at her face with her hands. "You need to confess your abuse of your mother, *n'est-ce pas?*" Marie smiled when she said it.

"Will we stay long at McKay's?"

"Only if Kilakotah is here."

"I suppose you want to apologize to her," Marianne said.

Could the girl know? No. She'd told no one. "I've done nothing to hurt an old friend," Marie said.

"You walked right past her and didn't say anything about the beadwork on her dress. She told me, Mama. She said you were so busy you didn't even seem to recognize her."

Kilakotah had noticed. Marie swallowed. But Marie had been busy that evening; many strains and stresses had kept her preoccupied. So many people in one place always troubled her. A marriage ceremony transported a person back in time, then shot her like an arrow to the present. Marguerite's wedding flooded her with memories of the girl's birth, to the pain of her father's death, to the empty place beside this child where a father should have stood. No grandparents stood behind her, either. Marie had to remember for all who weren't present, for grandparents, for the girl's dead father, and for herself. Grief crept up in a time of joy forcing some memories out. No wonder she hadn't remembered. Today, she'd recognize Kilakotah. Today, all would be well.

"Mama, you're not listening," Marianne complained.

"I'm taking our boat to the landing now. You notice how we do this so you can do it at the falls."

A woman walked toward the gravel bar as they pulled the craft onto the bar. She waved. That wide gait, that short, thick neck, those almond eyes. "Kilakotah!" Marie said as her friend approached, her hand shading her eyes from the sun. "My heart knows you," Marie said, and she began to sing the Ioways' welcoming song. Marie waved back. Kilakotah. *Merci, Dieu.* No lopsidedness in remembering. *Bon.*

Just when Jean Toupin thought he'd brought calm to his world, order skittered away like poorly packed mules.

One, sometimes two, of the hard-earned cows now permitted milking without the usual tail-swatting across his wife's face. They did still have to corral the calves to get the cows to come in. He hated the bellowing of those little babies, but one did what one must and the result was that at last he could drink a tin of warm milk and look out the window of his own house and gaze at a small wheat patch he and his family had tilled and made ready for harvest. The truly rich land had been taken by earlier settlers, but he'd found a way to plant. He'd been a man content in his own country.

Now this. Sometimes he wished it wasn't so easy to see his French Canadian friends so often. He didn't need to know certain kinds of news.

He'd have to tell Marie.

Jean rode his horse toward their square-log home, pulled the bridle from the gelding, and rubbed him down before putting him out on the fenced pasture. Jean was killing time. He knew that. Still, the animal needed tending, and wiping down the big Cayuse mount after a long ride certainly made sense. And Jean did have a bad right shoulder, so it would take him longer to tend the horse than for some men. Marie would understand this, wouldn't she?

Jean looked around for his son, François, almost relieved not to see him. The boy would have offered help so his father could go inside but would've questioned him. At least Jean had had the good sense not to take François with him. The boy could be hot-tempered. He wasn't sure where he got that quality from. Probably Marie's lineage. Jean smiled to himself. Both streams that formed his son had rapids and boils in them. He couldn't blame François' bad behavior on just one.

Dust no longer caked at the horse's chest. He'd brushed out the mix of dirt and sweat beneath the saddle blanket. Jean opened the pasture latch, swatting the animal on the rump. The horse hurtled through the gate, then turned and nickered, lowering his head for a scratch. Jean obliged. More blessed delays.

"I thought I heard you," Marie said. She'd come up so quietly behind him he startled. "What did you find out?"

"Only fifty cents a bushel," he told her, not meeting her gaze.

"Baptiste said the Russians are paying a dollar and a half to the Company."

"The Company's men will have a market. They'll get their money. But if we want credit to trade at Fort Vancouver, that's the amount McLoughlin will give us in trade. Fifty cents a bushel."

She'd been weaving tules and bear grass into a basket, and her small fingers wore dark stains though her fingertips were nearly white. They were always cold. He lifted her palm, kissed it. "At least we'll have grain for flour. Bread will be plentiful this winter. We won't go hungry even if we have to grind it in the coffee grinder."

"But the sperm oil, cloth, stoneware, salt—"

"It's what is, Marie." He sounded harsher than intended.

"Does McLoughlin cheat us?"

"No. He has orders too. He's a good man. The Methodist's mill takes some of the grain we Frenchies raise now, so he needs to make sure he doesn't overpay or he won't have enough to meet the Russian contracts. It is not so simple as it used to be, my Marie."

"*Oui.* It used to be that a free man was owned by the Company through debt and that an employee was owned by the terms of his contract. Now both debt and contract affect us all." She paused to pull a loose thread from his coat. "I wanted new thread," she said. "Your clothes are more patches than cloth, and I lack even thread to sew them back down. Our neighbors will think you acquired a lazy wife."

"It's the same for everyone, Marie. No one notices patches. Especially when we eat well. I will say I have burst my seams with your cooking, eh?" He pulled her to him with his good arm. "There's more news." He cleared his throat. "There is talk of the Americans pushing this prairie for a government assigned to them. Not the British and not independent as Texas is, but to make us come under the American rule."

His wife frowned. "Why would we? When we've needed things done we've formed ways to make it happen our way. The cattle came north without help from the Bostons. The Willamette Cattle Company didn't need an American government to bring success here."

"More Americans come," Jean said. "Two months ago, several families left the Red River to come settle the British side of the Columbia. One hundred and twenty-one people make their way across the mountains of Rupert's Land and come down the way Sarah and Ignace did those years ago. If they're fortunate. Then things will change here, Marie. If the Red River group makes it with wagons and children—there are seventy-seven children coming—then more will follow. The British will want to settle northern land to make their claim on the country, and that will press the Americans to do the same in the South. It will be a…competition, a challenge of two great nations, and we French Canadians will be in the middle here, just as we have always been."

She pulled her hand from his. "These Kalapuya people are in the middle, what's left of them," she said. "And the Cayuse and the Nez Perce. These people are trampled between, more than we."

It had always been so for them, as far as Jean could remember. The trails Indians made were always taken over by carts of the British or the Americans. Something drove them, no matter what the landscape.

"Maybe Father Blanchet will help us keep a still place in the midst of this," Marie suggested.

"The priests want no part of the government, I think," Jean said.

"He led the meeting, with the Methodists," Marie reminded him. "They worked together, you told me." They moved slowly toward the house. "People of faith know how to work together, *oui?*"

"One would hope," Jean said. "The Methodists would like to remain in power, making their own rules against drinking and horse-racing and such."

"I think this is not a bad rule," Marie told him.

"A New Year's grog never hurt a French Canadian," he said.

"Maybe someone else," she cautioned.

He remembered then, her first husband's weakness for gambling and drink. *"Oui,"* he said. "Maybe the Methodists have a good idea about drink. It's better we stay apart from them anyway. We Frenchies have our priests now who know our ways. We stand together, we French Canadians, but alone."

"There is no place alone, I think," Marie said.

"We should count on the priests to guide us," Jean said. "Stay with our own kind. This is what I meant to say." He hoped he didn't upset her with that comment. She didn't see the priests the way he did; and she was often quick to remind him that her people viewed things differently, even when they wore the same kind of spectacles that non-Indians did. His wife had a good grasp of men and change and how they tangled.

"I thought our years here would be easy," Jean said. "Even the soil breaks with little effort and grows wheat overnight. It never grew so easily at Walla Walla. We have friends here. Our children. It's these other people who—"

"It's not your fault, husband," she told him, motioning him inside. "The Company pokes into our lives like a fat awl; government tangles with treaties. Trouble gets stirred up everywhere people gather. Even in families. There is no safe place."

"That awl doesn't have to tear us up, it doesn't have to make holes in the Toupin family, *n'est-ce pas,* my Marie." He nuzzled her neck. She drew away.

"No?" she said.

"*Non.* Our fabric is too strong for that. We don't need new thread for patching."

3

Out of the Ashes

September 1841

Marie lost herself in a world awash with sunflowers and smoke. She worked at the fence line beside her youngest daughter, Marianne, while thick vapors blanketed her September days. Indeed, that seemed to describe her life here these past years. A kind of haze had wrapped her. Seasons had drifted, quickly, and yet it had taken her a lifetime to be here on this western prairie with her family within reach.

Almost all her family, though not all her sons.

She could barely see the house from this fence through the smoke. Licks of low flames danced across the prairie devouring tarweed and the grasses that covered camass fields. Despite the flames, tall firs and oaks kept their branches supporting platforms of dried salmon for which she'd traded her beadwork to Indians at the Willamette Falls. Sunflowers stood like silent sentinels through the dusky veil. The stalks, growing here and there, rarely burned in the set grass fires, and she'd watched the Kalapuya people—the few who survived the fevers and ague—torch individual plants with sperm oil–soaked rags to purposefully set the flower heads on fire. Later, along with the other Indian wives, she'd gather up the seeds for winter storage. The new grass would come up with the fall rains and grow thick to feed the horses and cattle through the winter. They didn't even have to cut the grass for winter hay, though some did. Just in case. Marie liked the sweet smell of cut grass filling mangers.

She could make out the outline of the fence close to the peach tree they'd planted from Fort Vancouver's rootstock. Beside it they'd constructed a square-log home on this north claim and formed their chimney out of thonged sticks plastered with grass and clay. Her husband had said he felt at home the day he participated in the Mass after long years of waiting. For Marie, learning to love the land made her feel at home.

At least this newly scorched earth kept government and Company expeditions and trapping brigades from moving through the blackened region in autumn. The grass stubble discouraged horsemen for a brief time, as they feared cuts to their mounts' feet. She wondered if the Indians knew that and burned the grasses for that reason too, keeping expeditions at Fort Vancouver or headed farther east where the land remained free of planned fires. The few remaining Kalapuya had cunning ways or they wouldn't have survived. They'd been stepped over like old dogs by the British and Americans boots as they tromped through the Kalapuya land. Americans didn't expect any old curs to circle around and bite them. Perhaps that's why Jean said that new Americans would most likely settle here rather than near the Cayuse and the Whitmans. Her oldest son's wife was of that tribe. Her people still rode hard and strong and wouldn't likely be run over as the Kalapuya had been.

It was good that something kept the Americans and British from coming south and the Spanish and Californians from working north. They were in the middle here on this prairie settled by former Astorians and their Indian wives even though the French dominated. Michel LaFramboise lived down the road. Joseph Gervais, who had been a part of Hunt's journey, farmed many acres and wore the robe of respect. George Gay built a brick house across the river. But their wives, they were mere Indians.

Mere Indians made the homes. It had been less than a year since they'd moved first into an old cabin and spent their spring turning black soil beside the finger lake Jean called Labiche. They'd planted a garden fed by the springs of the slowly drying slough. Abundant crops grew. She and her husband bought out the man who'd built the cabin then, a former Hudson's Bay man. The land could not be sold but improvements could, and Jean said they'd keep clearing trees to broaden the meadows and someday, when there was a government, they'd own land too. This place of oaks and tall grasses beside a changing slough promised peace.

This fall, Jean said he wanted to go farther south, too, to seek another claim. The Methodists had moved south to avoid the fevers and ague. But sometimes, Jean said, he just wanted to be with his family off the trails and let others manage the swirls of Britishers and Americans, priests and Methodists and government flags. Perhaps none of it would touch her in her own home.

Not seeing Marguerite did touch her. She'd vowed to give the girl time to settle in as wife and mother, something Marie would have liked when she married her first husband, Pierre. They'd remained in the lodge of Pierre's mother and little changed after Marie's arrival. Her mother-in-law made suggestions for how to tan a hide, how to cook up buffalo tongue. Her first husband had opinions on everything and shared them with Marie, not expecting protest since she was a very young wife. It had taken some time, but he soon got some. Her mother-in-law had added words of wisdom, though, and offered help just when she thought a young wife might need it. That mother didn't have to wait to be asked. One thing had changed: Marie's introduction to the mysteries of the intimate, the feel of skin to skin, and the times of tenderness that earned forgiveness for her husband's often brusque and hurtful ways outside the comfort of the buffalo robe.

It had been nearly a month since Marguerite's vows, and in all that time, her daughter had not come to visit her, had not asked for her advice. She'd done something wrong in raising this child or surely her oldest daughter would have wanted to see her mother's face, wanted to tell her of her days.

"Father Blanchet can relieve a mother's worries," Jean once told her. "You tell him of your worries about your daughter, eh? He makes it better for you."

But whenever Marie confessed her concerns, the priest gave her tasks, duties, and though she performed them, the acts of worship didn't revive her spirit. Perhaps she should confess more than small confessions, of thinking unkind thoughts of her husband's snores or her exasperation with her youngest son's irritable comments made of others. These were never-mind sins, as her daughter might call them. She hadn't even told the priests of her largest faults.

She was probably doing it wrong, the penance, because it didn't prevent her from bringing the same concern up again and again. "Your worries revolve rather than resolve," the priest told her once. "You must allow God's Spirit to move through these dark places. The Comforter leaves us with peace and light," he told her. "You do a disservice when you hang on to past hurts or dwell on future ones that might never come."

A disservice. She continued to struggle and displeased the Lord in the process.

But it was the priest's suggestion—that she could choose her thoughts the way she could choose to say the rosary prayers as many times as needed—that gave her hope. She worked on this, but it was a mountain of learning. She hadn't been able to learn to read words, and she wasn't sure she was capable of putting truly painful memories or deep wounds into a basket from which she never took the lid.

Marianne coughed as she placed pickets tighter around the hen's scratch. "Put another there," Marie directed. "They'll push that aside."

Marie hadn't remembered the smoke as being so dense that season long years before when she'd been here with her first husband. She hadn't remembered that the land burned for so long, covering the whole prairie like a river fog.

Marie adjusted her glasses. She looked around at their square-log house, the ends all whitewashed as chalk. She watched the narrow back of her youngest daughter as she worked. Despite the heaviness of the air, she could breathe here on this prairie.

"I hate them," Marianne said. She jabbed at the earth with her shoulder-blade shovel. The two knelt side by side now, making fence repairs.

"Who?"

"What have we been toiling over for the past hour? Raccoons. You go to a different place in your mind sometimes, Mama."

Marie made herself concentrate. *"Pardon,"* she said. "I will pay more attention to you now."

Marianne didn't respond. The girl craved her mother's attention more than her other children had, obviously more than Marguerite did. Baptiste had been independent at Marianne's age, forming a marriage bond. Marie had objected then, and she certainly didn't want such a thing for Marianne, who was nearly as old as Baptiste had been, taking his first wife. She hoped to see François settled into a family first, long before Marianne left home. The girl was sometimes almost infantlike in her need for Marie to comment on the way she scrubbed a *wappato* they'd cook or how well she sewed a patch. Everything she did was followed by a pause that elicited Marie's comment, as though Marianne's concerns were all Marie had to think about.

"I saw them when you raised the lantern last night," Marianne said, back on the animals. "There were six, weren't there, already inside the fence? Good thing you latched the henhouse. They milled around like old bald trappers at the fur houses waiting for their cigars after supper." Marie smiled at the picture of those raccoons as milling old men. Her daughter had a gift with stories. "At least with skunks we'd have the oil when they were dead. Raccoons are useless." Marianne jabbed at the hole the creatures had made in the picketed fence surrounding the chicken pen, set another branch deep into the ground.

The raccoons had scampered out when Marie lifted the lantern. At least the light had shown them where the fence was weak. Together, Marie hoped they could block the entrance the raccoons used to assault their few chickens. She had plans for those eggs. If the Company paid little for wheat, they might be more interested in eggs.

"We have to be shrewd traders, Marianne," Marie told her daughter. "And trappers, too." She wasn't about to give up such bounty to raccoons.

"They're just so...dirty," Marianne said.

"You've eaten their meat easily enough."

"I've never eaten raccoon." Into the silence Marianne turned, said, "Mother, you haven't served those...filthy things."

Her fifteen-year-old daughter's eyes widened, her mouth dropped open. "How could you?"

"Easy," Marie said. "I had dead raccoons and hungry children."

Marianne dropped her shoulders with an exaggerated sigh. "Oh, Mama." She returned to her work, pulled with her hands at the broken pickets composed of crooked oak branches. "They even left their scat on top of my moccasins," Marianne complained. "Right next to the door. They came that close to our house."

"To remind you to bring your footwear inside at night."

Marianne coughed. "Rest a minute," Marie said. She handed her daughter a twine-wrapped water jar. "I put some vinegar in it, to clear the thickness in your throat."

Marie watched her youngest daughter as she drank, her long neck glistening with sweat, her throat bobbing as she swallowed. She had short stubby fingers, a wide hand like her father's. Marianne's face was long and narrow and surrounded by hair as twisted as tobacco, not straight like Marie's. Marianne's movements were as fluid as the swans that settled on the river. She reminded Marie of her friend Sacagawea. That Shoshone woman swayed too when she walked, with the gentle ease of a breeze.

Marianne wasn't the prettier of her two daughters, but she was singular in her gentleness to children and her ability to draw people to her, to chatter with ease. She had a spirited side, holding her own with her brothers when they tried to boss her about. She was just a child. Marie didn't think Marianne even noticed boys, and this was good.

Was it right for a mother to assess her daughters in that way, to compare them? She loved them both, each welcomed, each unique.

Marianne had been the first of her brothers and sisters to be baptized when the priests arrived from the East. She was only thirteen. Marguerite, her eldest daughter, had made that decision later, just before she'd married.

Marguerite, married. An older husband might want to mold her daughter to be like his first wife. Maybe that was why Marguerite hadn't been to visit her. Perhaps JB restricted her. Marie had never walked that path, following the wife of another. All her husbands had chosen her as their first.

The French Canadians who had known JB longer said he'd been a good husband to his Indian wife, who had died following the seasonal fever and ague.

Had her daughter consented out of desperation, for fear she wouldn't find a husband, perhaps? She hoped Marguerite hadn't married just to please her parents.

No, Marguerite's face had shone during the nuptial Mass. The ring of blue flowers capped around her black hair had reminded Marie of a night sky with flicks of stars for color. Candles had reflected in her daughter's coffee-colored eyes. A shadow formed at that flattened cheekbone. She'd been surrounded by many of the French Canadian and Indian families who had seen the girl grow when they'd stopped by the Okanogan and Walla Walla forts. Their presence confirmed the blessing of this marriage.

Now here they were, all the Toupin family living within riding distance of each other on this French Prairie, all of her children.

Well, almost all of them.

Perhaps Jean was right. She should confess her failings as a mother to the priest. Perhaps the penance prescribed did little because she held back the real faults that plagued her.

Marie wiped at her irritated eyes. "The sunset will be red tonight," she said. "All this smoke. And see how the creek looks like red honey?"

Marianne reached for the water jug and took another swallow. She wiped her mouth with the back of her hand, left dirt streaks on her cheeks. This youngest child of hers looked for just a moment as she had when she was little, chasing puppies around their hut. The girl smiled then, and the gesture lit her face. Marie saw there a young woman with flashing brown eyes that would one day sparkle with invitation to a fortunate young man. Her baby was growing up but not away, not yet.

Marie adjusted her spectacles, stood up, surveyed the landscape. The smoke would lift eventually. Learning to live peacefully within the middle, helping her children live within that space, perhaps this was her *métier,* work to which she was best suited, work that needed doing.

"After we fix the fence, we'll need to set traps," Marie said.

"My eyes itch," Marianne said. "You can't convince me these fires are good for anything."

"Maybe when we catch the raccoons the meat will already be smoked." Marie said.

Marianne squinted at her. "You make fun of me."

"Non," Marie said. She leaned to wipe the smudge of dirt from her daughter's cheek. "I make no fun of you. I just practice finding treasures inside a smoky day."

October 1841

"Josiah Parrish," the man said, introducing himself. "I appreciate your assistance more than you can know. I could have freed the wheel alone, but two is better than one." He smiled. "It would have taken me till morning, I suspect. New York didn't have such mud as this."

"Nor Mackinonge," Jean said.

Parrish squinted. "You're new here." He used an accented French, didn't ask it as a question. Jean Toupin shook the man's hand. He was an American, that was certain, though not one of the Bostons, those merchants arriving by ship. He was one of the Methodists. He hadn't said *reverend* before his name, though. An October rain pelted down, dripping off his wide-brim preacher's hat. Jean had just spent the better part of an hour pushing and pulling to free the man and his wagonload of supplies from the thick mud that masqueraded as a road. It was one of the things he didn't like about their move from the drier Walla Walla country to this side of the mountains. The valley bore green because it was wedded to rain.

Jean usually liked meeting people, talking and listening. It's what he'd done for years as an interpreter, a *voyageur,* a trapper and hunter. But at times, people annoyed him. This was one of those times. He didn't feel like exchanging pleasantries in this rain, and the effort at the wagon had made him irritable. Sometimes, he welcomed the chance to exchange news. Tending cows and planting seeds were solitary tasks. A man came up with many thoughts that might go nowhere unless he spilled them out, heard how they sounded arriving on the minds of others. Just not today.

Jean adjusted his soaked woolen hat close to his head. He needed to get home. Marie would want to know that the Red River group had arrived, or almost all of them. Four had died on the way but of the 121 who set forth, most of the children at least had survived. They'd hit British soil, and already he'd learned that some families talked of coming south of the Columbia River to this place, this prairie, defying the decree from Hudson's Bay. She'd want to know that. She'd want to know that they didn't like not having their own cows the way these French Prairie people could.

His wife had said once that whether people came and stayed in this western country would depend on cattle. He'd laughed, and was glad they'd invested in horses, too. They had nearly forty mounts to call their own and ten cows. But he could see now she was right. People wouldn't remain in this northwest Columbia country unless they could make a gain. Turning over the increase from a cow to the Company each spring meant servitude, not unlike life in France or England where only the wealthy could own. Everyone else just grubbed for the master. Jean had no intention of repeating that kind of life in this new place. Independence was his interest.

Parrish stepped around his wagon, the suck of mud bringing Jean from his reverie. The man checked the harness and then stepped up into the now unstuck cart. Neither of them should be out in such weather, especially that man, alone with such heavy-loaded riggings. It was already dusk. Jean's horse was tired, and his one good arm ached from the effort of pulling and lifting at Parrish's mud-caked wheels. It'd be worse if he had a wagon full of supplies to take home instead of some packs lying across his horse's rump.

Parrish said in a schoolboy's French, "I haven't seen you before."

The man's poor French showed his effort to engage his neighbors, and Jean softened toward him. "We've tilled land north," Jean told him in English. "Me, my wife, and children. On the shores of Lake Labiche. Have my eye on a southern plot, too." Jean remounted his horse, removed his cap, wrung water from it, and replaced it on his head. Parrish lifted part of the canvas covering his supplies to let the water pooling there cascade down. It fell in sheets down his back, pelting the canvas covering the supplies so loudly it sounded like raindrops on a cedar shake roof.

"Rain to make the grass grow," Parrish said, smiling. "Does no good inside my wagon."

Jean was surprised at how easily the man talked with the elements pouring on him. He didn't even hunch his back, something Jean still found himself doing despite the fact that it did nothing to stop the penetrating rain from seeping beneath his wolf-skin jacket. Most people who had been here awhile didn't hunch up in the weather. Perhaps that's why Parrish thought Jean a newcomer.

"Came for the good soil then," Josiah Parrish said.

"That and the dozens of countrymen urging us, eh? We had cattle here, part of the stock Company of a few years back. George Gay"—Jean pointed to an area west of where the men stood on the road south of the St. Paul church—"is a friend as well. LaBonte, Gervais, McKay, LaFramboise, LaChapelle, Lucier, all friends. My wife and I came across with Hunt."

"Ah. You're one of Astor's men. Not McLoughlin's."

Jean hesitated. "Both, of sorts. And neither. I'm my own free man."

"You and your wife, you say? I thought only one woman made that trip with Hunt. All written up in Irving's book. A Madame...Dorion. I must have been mistaken."

"*Non.* She was not my wife then, but she was the only woman on the journey. And she brings two children with her. They all survive. She helps the men survive."

Parrish didn't seem to be in any rush. Jean found himself warming to this stranger who came so easily beside another.

"I've heard of you," Jean said, placing him at last. "From the meeting to handle Ewing Young's affairs. Last February. With Father Blanchet. One of my French friends said you were there."

"I'm sorry that your Father Blanchet didn't ever call another meeting," Parrish said. "It would have been good to have all of us in this valley in agreement. I was pleased he'd been named coleader. Disappointed when nothing came of it."

"He has many duties, Father Blanchet." Jean's horse stomped impatiently, raised his head up and down as though he could read his rider's discomfort.

"Rightly so," Parrish said. "But it's good to discuss these things among friends and neighbors, right? One never knows when such discourse will bend a government one way or another, even way out here, far from Washington City."

"We hear rumors of disputes even among you Methodists—so discussion doesn't always lead to results, eh?"

"A people can't move forward without a little dissent," Parrish said. The light banter had left his voice.

The rain chafed against Jean's neck, but he felt heat there too.

"So tell me, will the French vote with the British or the Americans, do you suppose? Or is there disagreement among you Frenchies as there is with us?"

Was he just making conversation? Why would he care? His stepson, Baptiste, thought that was a reason for the Red River arrivals, to infiltrate and push people in the Columbia country toward the British. Why not American spies trying to find support for *their* cause, trying to get votes drummed up for their way of thinking? The Methodists claimed they expanded their mission sites to serve Indians even while the native population grew smaller from disease. Maybe the expansion wasn't for service or to avoid the vermin and plague at the Mission Bottoms, as their lands were called. Maybe they intended to take more land, to grow richer when the boundary was settled. They were after something, the Methodists. But then, wasn't everyone? The prairie looked so calm and placid, but Jean knew that it was an ember waiting for a small wind to flame it up.

"How far away did you say your claim was? I may be needing your assistance again if this rain keeps up," Parrish asked. "Times like this I know why we're looking to make our move to Chemeketa Plains." Jean hesitated. The river landing purged only the supplies for him and Parrish this day, and Josiah Parrish was stuck before they'd made a mile down the road. His horses would be lucky if they didn't sink in to their briskets before he traveled another mile, and it was more than ten miles to the new mission site on Mill Creek. Jean's Labiche place would be a good resting stop, maybe for the night. It was off the main trail, but offering it would be a neighborly thing to do.

"Just down the road a couple of miles," Jean said. He pointed with his chin.

"Lt. Emmons is leading a group south into California and should be at the mission by now. Going overland all the way. Picked up horses at McKay's farm, near Scappoose. These supplies will be needed by that expedition, as soon as I can get them there." Parrish seemed to be thinking out loud.

"Emmons? This is not a man I know."

"Military. Came by ship. I suspect to discover whether we're ready to become a territory of our own. That'll be a more burning question once Americans arrive overland."

So the Methodists were open about their support of this prairie place becoming an American territory, maybe even a state one day.

"Or even if the British will want such a motley group as we are here in this Columbia country," Parrish continued. "Perhaps the Brits will only want those who settle north of the Columbia River, leave thee and me and any Americans to our own devices, right?"

"The British won't abandon the French Prairie settlers," Jean said. What might that mean for their land claims, for the work his neighbors had put into building their farms and planting their fields? Would the Americans honor their claims or just give them away to "real Americans," people from the states, when they arrived overland in their carts the way the Red River crowd did? Maybe they'd let these missionaries with vast amounts of tilled soil and more than four hundred cows grazing inside fences have the French claims. The French were all British citizens or carried Canadian connections, and if the British abandoned them… Their wives were natives, not Americans either. And what about the women? Except for the missionaries, all the men had married Indian women. What would happen to them? And to his children? How would they be seen by a foreign American invader?

He'd thought that when he left the Company's employ and no longer had to worry over their treatment of their French Canadian or half-breed or *métis* employees, that he had nothing further to be concerned over. He could age in peace among his French friends. Even one day, perhaps, have enough resources to hire help so he could smoke his pipe instead of plowing.

He'd have to ask the opinion of his friends Michel and Tom McKay. They'd have thoughts about this. Even his stepson Baptiste might have some ideas about what the future held for the French Canadians and their Indian families. The British desert them? This was a whole new thought.

Jean had been spending too much time walking behind a horse.

Parrish squinted at Jean. "Are you all right?"

"Oui." Jean told him. He picked up his reins, pressed them against his horse's neck, heard the suck of the animal's feet against the mud.

"Emmons brought a whole tour of botanists and such with him, too." Parrish continued the conversation as he stepped up onto his wagon seat. "McKay and LaFramboise are guiding them. Have a fellow named Brackenridge along who I hear was on that journey west with Astor too. Who knows what news they'll take back with them. Probably that the area's not habitable, if they got stuck in the mud as I have." He laughed.

Talking to himself, Jean thought. He didn't envy the man his journey through the muck and mud. "Gee-up now," Parrish told his team.

Jean heard the slap of leather against the horses' rumps. He scrunched his neck against the rain, realized again it did no good. No man should be out on a night like this, and certainly not alone. What kind of a neighbor was he? He didn't really want to invite Parrish to his home. There must be something amiss with the Methodists or else Father Blanchet would have continued on with those meetings. This Parrish and the missionaries in general might be men meant to avoid.

He heard the clank of strain of the hames and harness. The wagon made five feet before Jean heard a moan of disgust escape the man's mouth. The wagon dragged, then pulled back into the mud.

Marie would understand.

Jean pulled his horse up next to the rain-drenched man. "I've an offer for you," Jean said. "We can take your supplies to my claim for the night, load them on our horses, and pack them leaving the wagon there. Or we can wait until morning when the roads may be more passable. Or I can ride with you now, keep tugging at your wagon that seems attracted to the muck, eh? You'll have to board me for the night once we get there. One thing is sure: You'd best not try to make the rest of this journey alone."

He hoped Parrish would choose to go to Jean's home where Jean's warm wife awaited. Marie would have a good sense of the man within minutes. She had wisdom that way. Still, an evening with an American expedition had its draw, too, like a fox among the chickens. He might gain news from the East and view firsthand how the Columbia country was seen by those sent to assess it.

His curiosity about what the inside of the mission looked like could be quenched too. Michel would be there, he said, and Tom. This rainy afternoon and evening could turn out quite well.

Either way, he'd already made a decision for himself: He needed to hire some help for the field work so he wasn't always behind a horse, tilling. He needed to have time to jabber with men and share ideas. Information was the flame of passion.

"You are most kind. I accept your offer to spend the night at your home," Parrish said. "Two are better than one, or so Ecclesiastes says."

"I did not know that Ecclesiastes lived on our prairie."

"His words do," Parrish told him. "I found them in you."

Marianne had it all planned out. Her mother said she was good at that. She put the soup bowls and ladles and mugs onto the shelf in order each time after she washed them. Marianne liked things tidy. Maybe she preferred it because her hair wasn't. It couldn't ever be with its frizzled and fried strands that danced about her face no matter how hard she pulled it back behind her neck. Her skin clothes, as few as there were, she chalked often and made sure the seams were tied tightly. But she preferred cloth. She handled the washing stick with the hottest water possible even though her older sister had said she shouldn't bother. Marguerite still wore skins, cedar skirts and capes, or the same patched dress.

Marianne even kept the buttons sewed well onto the single good cloth dress she had. It had a lace collar, just like the women at the mission wore. Tiny buttons made of pewter lined the front. Each button held a picture of a bird on it with little lettering around the side. The words were written in another language. Latin, the catechist, David Mongrain, told her. He was Father Blanchet's servant. She wouldn't have dared bother the father with such a question, but Mr. Mongrain had noticed her looking at the buttons while she waited, twisting the little circles to read. He'd told her what the words meant.

Fortunately he hadn't asked her where she'd gotten them. A Catholic child ought not to show such interest in the Methodists, she supposed. But anything forbidden held interest.

" 'I rise from my own ashes,' " he said. "That's what the words say. It's a phoenix bird. A story goes with it," he said.

"About a bird that lived through a fire?" Marianne asked.

"It means never allowing yourself to be defeated. At least that's my vision of it." Mr. Mongrain had pockmarks that pitted his cheek, and Marianne wondered if the disease had been his fire and that he still lived the sign of his phoenix. He'd come from someplace in the Eastern provinces, or so she'd heard. Everyone had a hard story to tell of their arrival in this country or right after. Even her friend Julie Gervais, who was actually Julie Laderoute now though everyone still called her by the more famous name—her father was so well known—had a story. Julie's was a suffering story. It was a birthing one. Marianne only let her tell it once.

Marianne had no suffering story, much less an interesting one, try as she did. Maybe after today things would be different.

"The father will see you shortly," Mr. Mongrain said. "He won't have much time. So many wait for him." His pewter gray eyes looked kindly at her. "So be thinking of what you wish to say."

"Thank you," Marianne said. She hoped Father Blanchet would ask for her quickly, before her parents decided it was time to go home. They'd be eating and chattering with neighbors as they always did after Mass at the St. Paul church. Twice a month they traveled the ten miles or so to this north end of the prairie to worship and to catch up with neighbors.

She fingered the ridge of the bird on the buttons. She'd treasure these buttons even more now that she knew what the words meant. "I rise from my own ashes." She would do this. She wondered if that had anything to do with the "growing into herself" that her mother told her about.

The door to the priest's quarters behind the sacristy opened, and

Marianne lowered her face so whoever just departed wouldn't worry about being seen by her.

"He'll see you now," Mr. Mongrain told her.

Her heart beat a little faster even though she wasn't confessing. The church had no little rooms like her father said lined the side of a large cathedral in Montreal where people stood in lines to confess and receive absolution. She was just having a conversation with the priest, that was all.

A scarf of linen lay over her head, and she'd pulled it down against the frizz of hair. It hung on both sides of her eyes like the blinders on a horse so she wouldn't be recognized either. "Come along then," Mr. Mongrain said. "Speak quickly, now." He swept his arm out to push open the door.

Marianne stood. She swallowed. She'd do it well. She had it planned.

Both she and Mr. Mongrain turned at the sound of the heavy door opening at the far end of the chapel. Marianne gasped. Her mother's form entered the back of the church. No other woman was as tall on this prairie. She recognized the way she walked, small steps on such long legs. *She picks this moment to want her daughter to be closer to her.* Marianne quickly ducked beneath Mr. Mongrain's arm.

❖

Marie stepped into the cool shade of the log church. The priest's quarters consisted of a small room behind the church that held only a bed and crude desk that permitted him a place of rest when he made the journey south from Fort Vancouver. It was said he roamed out from there, north to the British forts where so many French Canadian Catholics lived and worked, as far east as the Shining Mountains. A few more priests had joined the earlier arrivals, and new converts were sought too, but these Masses at St. Paul were for the faithful, as Marie saw it, serving the *engagés* and retired Company men who wanted their children raised in the faith as their fathers had been back in the provinces.

The mothers were mostly converts, brought into the Catholic faith of late, weaving the spiritual traditions of the Chinook and the Clatsop and even the Kalapuya people with the new teachings of the priests. Marie saw the strands of belief as separate and distinct, like tulles and grasses of many thicknesses and colors that were woven into one strong mat.

Lately, a studied man—a catechist, Jean called him—remained behind after the priest left. He offered assistance in between the Masses. He was tall with a wide forehead and dark hair that thinned. His face was pitted. From the pox Marie assumed, though she had not heard the catechist talk of it. What was his name again? Hadn't Jean told her? *Mongrain.* She sighed in relief.

She waited to be sure whoever waited for the priest had gone behind the door. Mongrain motioned with his arm for her to proceed down the aisle.

She hadn't spoken with the catechist much, but she recognized him. He lived on the prairie, was one of them. She reserved any confessions for the priest and still would. That was the rule, Jean told her; confession and absolution arrived through the priest.

"May I help you?" he said. The words were halting, spoken in Chinook, the trade language most Indians knew. He must have forgotten she wasn't a river Indian, but of the Ioway, the Gray Snow people, who spoke French. Or perhaps he'd never known.

"I didn't mean to disturb," she said in French.

"You haven't." His French now sounded Canadian, not Dutch like the priests. His smile looked full and warm. "Ah, you are Madame Dorion, *oui?*"

"Toupin," she said. "My husband is Jean Baptiste Toupin."

"Pardon," he said, corrected. "You wish to see the friar?" he asked.

She shook her head. "*Non.* I think to talk with someone…less of a mountain," she said.

Mongrain laughed. "I'm a little *butte,*" he said. "They are more easily conquered, *oui?*"

"More easily approached," she said. "With a greater hope of success." He would be an easy man to speak with. Perhaps she might one day ask him of her mothering questions; maybe about the strange flickering light, though she supposed a doctor might better answer that concern.

"You have a question," he said. He sat on the plank bench beside her.

She nodded. How to begin?

Mongrain waited.

"My husband wishes for years to have me choose the baptismal water, and so I do this, at the big Mass in the summer. We marry that day." Mongrain nodded. "So I accept that gift, decide I am not without flaws but that it is as expected. I am not dishonest in receiving the gift before I think I'm worthy."

"Oui," Mongrain said. "You understand this well. You're not having second thoughts?"

"*Non.* But it was powerful water, from the Up-In-Being, *n'est-ce pas?* So I wonder if I do it wrong." She hesitated. Forming thoughts about things inside her mind, things without a way to hold or touch still troubled her. "I still make mistakes. I still worry over my children," she said. "Once I accepted this worthy gift, all old fears and thoughts and wonderings should wash away, *n'est-ce pas?* Mine are still with me."

"It takes time," he said.

"For the water to cleanse? How can that be if it is so powerful? Unless I do it wrong. Maybe my heart wasn't ready. Maybe what I try to leave behind is too great a thing to wash away. Maybe I don't do the penance well. I should work harder at it?"

He cleared his throat. "Perhaps this is a question you should explore with the father."

"Am I confessing?" she said. *"Pardon."* She started to rise. She thought it was a question, but perhaps it was admission.

"No, no." he said. "It's an important question, a worthy one." He clasped his hands together and leaned his forearms on his knees. She eased back. "When we first fall in love," he said, "all troubles wash away." He thought for a moment. "We feel fresh as new corduroy, all the ridges firm to the touch. As it is worn it doesn't feel so new. It gets marred and scratched and smoothed. We long for that newness. It doesn't mean we love less or did something wrong. It is part of the faith to have nicks and wearing and to wish for what we once had. It is still the same corduroy. We must come to see it as better, *n'est-ce pas?* More familiar. The ridges are not so distinct, but we are warm and we know it will keep us that way in storms because it already has."

"Other things keep us warm, maybe better. If the peace of the water washes away, then it is no better than not being washed. What has the faith changed?"

He gripped his hands as though in prayer. "I don't want to misspeak. I think you should talk to the father. He'll be free soon."

She'd offended, been pushy with her thoughts. It was her way. More than once she wished she could just accept a thing the way it was given without having to tug at the seams to make it fit her. But the Sarahs—one a Chipewyan woman, the other a missionary from the Sandwich Islands—spoke of a *métier* that had not looked worn, even after years. It guided and strengthened and gave up such light, they had enough light to give away. Marie had not found this with the baptismal water, or at least if she had, she had lost it.

The light through the small windows faded as they waited. She should look for Marianne and Jean and François and start home.

"My husband waits," she said, rising. "I'll come when he has more time." She stood to leave, wishing now she hadn't come at all. She hadn't thought the question through, not really. And the forgetting was her real worry, not remembering the faces of friends. And her missing son haunted her. Something else too pricked at her mind, threatening light but instead slipping through without leaving words. It was just that she wanted the quiet, the calm, that the Sarahs had, wanted it to remain forever, and it had merely visited her. It hadn't made a home in her heart. She couldn't begin to explain that to Mr. Mongrain or the priest. She hadn't even told her husband.

"Let me ask him for you," Mongrain said. "Others must have this question too but not know how to ask as well as you have. It will be a good lesson for me to hear his answer. I can share it with you and others, too."

"You are still a student?" Marie asked.

"Oh yes. I was his servant for many years learning a little English. I know very little Chinookan, as you can tell. And to be in service here when he travels north or east to Cayuse country, I must know the questions that trouble the new converts as well as those long faithful to the church. I'm always learning new things about the faith. I'll ask him."

"I come back to get the lesson," she said.

Mongrain tapped his finger against his closed lips. "We need such a class for converts," he said. "We've been praying for more priests and trying to recruit sisters to teach. Our children here are taught by Methodists." Mongrain wrinkled his nose. "If they were taught the faith as children, perhaps they'd have answers to the questions you now ask. We have a new building set to be a school. But we'll have no schooling in the faith except through faithful servants, faithful mothers. So you have asked a good question, Madame Toupin. I am grateful."

The door opened, and Marie lowered her eyes, to give privacy to whoever visited with the priest. She smelled the faintest scent of familiar soap as the woman swished by.

4

Progress

Baptiste Dorion took the knife to his own hair. Holding dark strands in one hand and the knife in the other, he stood in front of the small piece of mirror. He cut the slender lengths that had hung down his back for the past year. The black hair marked the Bah-Khe-Je blood of his Ioway mother and that portion of his father's blood that was Sioux. His father had been more Indian than French, at least that was how Baptiste saw it. He'd worn his hair short before when he'd interpreted for the Army that time. A few times later too. Each time he let it grow back. Maybe because his wife preferred it that way, worn as an Indian since that was how she saw him. This time he'd keep it short. Like the Americans and the merchants and the Methodists wore theirs.

The long hair made the Americans falter when he rode with them, he could see it in their eyes. Was he trustworthy? Would he turn on them? That's what they were thinking, always wondering just what a half-breed might do. Their worries prevented them from inviting him into their conversations as easily as they did Tom McKay. Tom was a half-breed too, but no one thought of him as such, not with his step-father so influential.

The eyes of the French Canadians sometimes held judgment, too, as though he wasn't one of them, either, though his father had been. His hair wasn't thick and curly like the hair of other middlemen, where a shake of a man's head while paddling a *bateau* could send the buzz of gnats and mosquitoes flying. It was thin and straight. And long.

The knife tore at his hair, leaving a ragged edge. He took a sharp-ening stone out to work the blade. He wasn't even sure why he'd decided to cut it now. Maybe it was Tom's influence.

Tom was like an uncle to him, a good man, who stood separate from Tom's own stepfather, the head of all the Hudson's Bay in the Columbia country. Tom made his own way in the world, didn't rely on the reflected glory of his father, and Baptiste didn't want to do that either. He'd be his own man, do things his way.

He cut his hair because it was time. The arrival of members of the Bidwell-Bartelson party with Father Desmet at Walla Walla told him it was time to choose sides. That little gathering of men rode mules overland with carts. They eventually discarded the wheels and loaded packs on their horses' backs. But for the first time, a group of Americans without the protection of a fur brigade had come overland. They'd made it across the continent on their own and with a set of wheels. Fitzpatrick, an old mountain man, had experience, but not over the trail they'd taken. Yes, they had a priest with them, someone whose prayers might be larger than their own to keep them safe. He wasn't sure about that. But most overlanders headed south into California and didn't even consider reaching the Walla Walla region. A fur trading company had even protected Marcus and Narcissa Whitman those years before. They hadn't arrived on their own. But if a priest and a few farmers could do it, then soon, anyone could.

And they would.

He'd tried to tell his wife, Josette, that. Told Gray Eagle, the Cayuse chief, too. He'd warned them that Whitman's arrival was just the beginning of their trouble, that they'd best find a way to receive payment now for the land he'd taken from them, because without the land the Cayuse were nothing, they would never be anything. Not with the Americans coming. The British and Scots came to trade, to take riverbanks for their forts and storehouses. The Americans came to take whatever hills and plains they could, as much as they could. Whitman was the example for that. He wouldn't settle for a small piece of earth; he'd want more, always tilled more.

At French Prairie, the Methodists had little resistance from the natives. A few Klamath and Molalla understood what was happening, but they stayed farther south. Baptiste thought the Cayuse would see what was happening, but several of them used Whitman's mill for the grain they grew. Some even took Mrs. Whitman's classes and were learning English and accepting the Methodist faith. In time, they'd forget where they came from. They wouldn't recognize themselves.

The Cayuse needed payment for the land Whitman had already put into wheat and covered over with houses, a mill, and barns. He'd fenced in his cows, and he'd fenced out the Cayuse horses that had grazed at Waiilatpu for as long as any could remember. If Whitman refused to compensate them for the rye grass, there'd be nothing anyone could do to help the Cayuse. Or the Whitmans, once the Indians realized what had happened. The Americans looked at everything through the lenses of law and property and rights. They overpowered the land instead of finding the power within it. Family lineage did not matter. The shame of taking away a man's ability to feed his family did not matter. Land and their claim on it mattered to Americans.

Even his mother had succumbed and now had "property" in French Prairie, though his stepfather worried over the lack of a title; a way of saying it was his. As if a title to something meant anything should an American want the same thing for himself.

Baptiste claimed no property. He shared in the ten cows of his mother and stepfather and in the forty horses. But no land. He'd set up their teepee at the far edge of his mother's claim so when he traveled the rivers for the Company, his wife and children would have people close by. Josette was forever longing to be back along the Walla Walla where her people were, but that was a woman's way, to long for where she wasn't.

Gray Eagle, the Cayuse chief, had laughed at him when he warned them of the coming bad times that would follow Bidwell and Bartelson's success.

"There are too many of us to worry over a few stragglers and a man who wears black dresses," Gray Eagle said.

"He's a holy man," Baptiste told him. "He has powers."

"Ours are stronger."

Baptiste had been dismissed as someone who had walked too long on the paths of the Hudson's Bay Company. Josette had dropped her eyes in shame.

Baptiste made another slice at his hair and winced at the pain against his scalp. He thought of his father's death and how painful it must have been dying at the hands of his own people.

Baptiste had warned the Cayuse, he'd told them this was just the beginning. More Americans would come. And he, Baptiste, would join them, though not to take more land from the Cayuse. He had no use for land that way. But he would be on the winning side. That was the only way to protect his family.

And the Americans would win.

As young as he was when they'd left the fort at St. Louis, he never forgot the bustle, the men and horses and *bateaux* that ruled. Creole, Spanish, French, Scots, English, they all had a say in St. Louis. But it was the Americans who persisted, who stood above others, even without a top hat on. Hunt had endured over Manuel Lisa, over Donald Mackenzie. Americans were like geese in flight, always higher than the others, always pursuing and sustaining themselves for the long journey.

It was where he wanted to be. On the American route, not on the dusty trails worn down by Indian ponies' feet, regardless of how handsome the Cayuse mounts were.

Cool air now hit the back of his neck. Short enough, Baptiste decided. He'd get his wife to even it once he arrived back at Waiilatpu where she was now, visiting her mother and uncle and sisters. He'd likely be part of the brigade taking supplies from Fort Vancouver that way before the hard snows. The Company usually tried to give him duty that took him closer to his family. Even though his mother had no time for the Hudson's Bay, he found them usually fair as long as it took nothing from their profits. They, too, would fall by the way of the Americans, he was sure of that. But until then, he'd use them as they used him.

He wondered what his wife would say about his short locks. Probably nothing. Josette accepted whatever he did, rarely made any demands on him these days. That wasn't exactly the Cayuse way. Her sister had been outspoken. So had his first daughter. Both of them were gone now, both taken before their time.

Sometimes Josette acted as though she were still just the little sister of that first wife, just the woman who had outlived her older sister and had eased into his marriage bed because it was what he'd wanted and she hadn't anything better to do. He tried to remember their marriage day. He couldn't recall the details. Instead he remembered his marriage to Older Sister, the woman he'd loved first.

His brother Paul had tarnished that day, disappearing at the end of an angry confrontation with his mother. His brother's timing was perfection, always bringing eyes to himself, making sure no one else got his mother's attention. Paul performed, rode a fast horse standing on the mount's back, kicked up dust at people's eating fires, anything to bring notice.

That day he'd run away, and then later his mother had sent Baptiste to look for him.

Everything had changed after that.

He'd been seeking his brother while his wife lay dying.

In time, the pain of her death had moved to another part of his heart, still there, still holding the emptiness, but it was smaller, less piercing. Then he'd married Josette, sister of his first wife who had cared for his infant child.

With each child of their own—they had two now, Denise and Pierre—Josette moved away from him, spoke less, held her smiles hostage. The only thing she'd stood firm about was making him choose between her and his love for whiskey.

He'd chosen her, but he missed the excitement that whiskey brought.

He'd tried to lose himself instead in horseracing and running river rapids better portaged around. He kept himself clear of the amber. The laws passed against selling it helped. The Methodists at French Prairie had even formed some kind of temperance society when they'd first arrived, though he knew the chief factor, John McLoughlin, brought his own wine when he visited the Methodist Mission. At least Baptiste had been asked to pack bottles in the barrel when the factor headed south. Baptiste was pretty sure the wine wasn't for the reverends there or for cooking.

He shook his head. Josette would have her work cut out for her getting the chop lines on his hair to look even. And she'd want them to line up. It didn't matter to him. They were as different as fire and rain, he and Josette.

The more he was away from Josette, the harder it was to remember why he'd given up what the whiskey brought: warmth, a fog against boredom, the easing of pain.

Lately, the sinew tying the two of them together could be severed with a dull knife. He sometimes wondered if he'd made the right choice when she'd asked him to give up drinking. Maybe the only thing holding them together was his commitment to leave behind what had once kept them apart. He snorted. She would laugh at such a statement as twisted as a juniper tree trunk. She'd laugh at him, something a wife shouldn't do. He deserved solace sometimes, he did.

He realized he'd grown terribly thirsty.

Marianne told her mother, "You ease the idea to Papa, let him think slowly about it." Her father usually needed time to consider an idea not of his creation. Her mother would talk with him, help him see how she was growing up, would soon be ready to leave their home to make her own. Then Marianne would follow up with her news and the rest would slip down his throat easy as cider, all sweetness and none of the bitter.

Her mother said nothing, just stitched on a set of moccasins. Her lips were pursed over the dark ends of the porcupine quills that stuck out like a fan. She pulled them one at a time and twisted the sinew thread around them, tugging them into the tight design. Marianne was sure her mother understood her part.

"You spoke with the friar?" Marie asked finally.

Marianne nodded. "I knew that if I asked you first, you'd never agree to let me even discuss it with Father Blanchet. But now I have. And you see, it's fine with him. Papa will approve too. If you do it as I tell you." Her mother grunted. "You do understand?"

She'd taken the silence as agreement.

In the morning, as her father finished his grain coffee, Marianne tried to get her mother's eye, to see if this might be the time to tell him. But she rubbed at the table with a wet rag. "I'm getting married, Papa," Marianne said finally. Her mother looked at her, furrowed her brows, had a dazed look in her eyes.

Her father laughed. "What is this story you tell?"

"No. I am. It's no story. Didn't Mama tell you?"

"What?" He looked at her mother. She looked away. "Married?" he said to Marianne. "No. No, no, no." He stood, knocking a tin of coffee onto the puncheon floor. Her mother moved to wipe it up while he paced. He'd never paced over anything she'd said before. Sometimes what her mother did could agitate him, but she'd never caused his face to turn so red. Marianne watched him stoop to look at a nail working its way up above the surface of the floor. *Good. He's distracted.* It would give her time to think. Her wide palm felt wet. She brushed her hair back from her cheeks.

She should have checked with her mother first, to see what he'd said when her mother told him. Now her mother wouldn't even look at her.

"Papa?" He'd stepped out onto the porch. She turned to her mother. "Mama, didn't you talk to him? Did you forget to?"

"You said I should talk to him," her mother said. "But you didn't—"

"You talk to me, Daughter," her Papa said. He poked his finger at his chest. "I am your papa, eh?" He'd found his tool pack and returned with a hammer. He lifted the handle, glared at her, then bent to pound the nails. "You speak to me if you're such a grown-up woman. Don't blame your mother." He pounded the floor in front of her, hammering on a nail that didn't really look as though it needed it.

"Well, Papa—"

"Speak up!" he said. "Can't you see I have things to do here?"

Marianne crossed her arms over her chest. She put them at her side. She clasped her hands behind her back. She jumped at the intensity of the sounds of iron against iron, pressing her hand against the tabletop now, drumming her fingers. Stopped. She took a deep breath, swallowed.

"Didn't you remember, Mama? I asked you to talk to Papa about David and me."

Her mother frowned. "I—"

"This is not your mother's duty, to be your voice. You talk when you want to, eh? Apparently to a boy who thinks you are old enough to be a wife."

"I don't see why you're so upset," Marianne said. "I'll marry within the faith. David Gervais is a fine person. I thought you'd be pleased."

"Arranging a marriage is a father's duty, not a child's. How do you know this person long enough and well enough to be talking of marriage?" Her father kept pounding, and he shouted above the sounds. The veins in his neck stood thick as willow shoots. They throbbed.

"He's Kilakotah's nephew," her mother said. "Joseph's son. They're good people, the Gervais family. David works with his father."

"I know who he is," Jean said. "I traveled on Hunt's journey too, remember?"

"We've already spoken to the priest," Marianne said. "Not together," she added quickly.

Her father's eyebrow raised. "The priest did not ask why your parents don't accompany you, a mere child?"

"I told him of my baptism two years ago. I'm a woman in the faith, not just a young girl, Papa." Her father shook his head, stopped the pounding. His shoulders sank. She heard a horse whinny into the silence. "The banns can be read, and we can marry in November." She kept her voice light, as though announcing a party. Her father always liked parties. She'd find out later why her mother didn't talk with him. "It'll be a good time for a celebration. After the harvest..."

Her father stayed bent over so she couldn't see his face, just the place at the back of his head where the hair thinned. He lifted his head. He stared at her mother.

"You knew of this," he said to her mother.

"I know the Gervais boy," she said.

"Well, so do I, woman. But that is not the same as wanting him to know my daughter. You are only fifteen," he told Marianne. Marianne wished he'd stay angry with her mother for not telling him rather than growl at her. He held the hammer like a pointing finger. "And *must* you marry? Is this why the priest approves the banns being read without a parent's request? Is this why you do not tell me, you two women? Because you are afraid of what I'll do to this boy and to you if—"

"Non, non," Marianne said. She reached for his right arm, the one that hung loose by his side. She touched him. "Papa, no. We are in love—"

He pulled away from her. "Love," he said. He'd never brushed her off before.

"But, Papa, it's true. We don't act on—"

"Then wait until you are old enough to know what you want. Love is a flame that can burn as well as warm," he said. "François is older than you, but he hasn't made such a choice. Yet you think you can?"

"We have to find new ways to do things, Papa. We're in a new place now. Americans—"

"This is because you are envious of your sister. That's what this is. She marries, and now you think you must too."

"No!"

Her mother shook her head, motioned with her chin for Marianne to stop now, to not push further. "Go tend to your chickens," she said. "I'll talk with Papa."

"Can I trust you'll remember?" Marianne said as she pushed through the door, tears stinging in her eyes.

November 1841

The full moon cast a light so bright the few remaining wheat sheaves formed wispy shadows across the fields. Deer fed openly and played, darting like comets in the moon's beams. Marie rubbed her temples with her fingertips, sat on the log bench and leaned against the cabin wall. Smoke from the chimney thinned into the night sky, tickling her nose. She pulled the beaded pins that held her hair in a knot at her neck, then felt the weight of it cascade down her back. She began pulling an ivory comb through her long hair.

Maybe it was the full moon making her crazy. Marianne was right to be angry with her, and Jean, too. She could have intervened, gone to the priest herself to protest this child's impulses. She might have told Jean so he could have turned their daughter around before it got this far. She'd failed them both. She hadn't forgotten it, though. It wasn't like not recognizing Kilakotah at Marguerite's wedding; no, she'd chosen to put the thought of Marianne marrying aside, hoping to later find the right words to dissuade her. She done so poorly with Marguerite the day before her marriage, she wasn't sure if she could do what was right for her youngest daughter. Marianne was even more ignorant of the meaning of slipping into the bed of a boy. Maybe it was the *charnel,* the *historique*—the sensual, the sexual—that distressed Marie, made her delay talk of her daughter's choice with Marianne's father.

Yet wasn't this part of a mother's *métier,* to prepare her daughters for the intimacies of marriage along with preparation for the duties of walking beside another, discovering how to carry equal weight? Marie tugged at a snarl in her hair. Her own marriages had consumed years of learning how to walk beside her husband, how to let him lead without making her feel that her only gift was to follow. She hadn't always done well. Now that they lived on this French Prairie, she'd had to find new ways to walk, not just because she tired more easily but because they were staying in one place, all of them. There were few hides to clean and stretch for trade. What she'd known first no longer mattered here. She hadn't seen much of Marguerite except at Mass, and then her daughter talked of simple things, nothing that mattered. She looked tired and weary. The girl was busy, that was all, busy raising her husband's children on her own, without the need of a grandmother's intrusion.

Marianne's going to the priest without his knowledge had shamed her husband, made him nothing more than a gnat on a horse's ear. That's why Jean was so upset. That and being surprised by his daughter's plans. Marie might have protected him from that, prepared him. She wondered what the priest might think of a mother allowing a young girl to approach him for permission so boldly. Marie hadn't been back for confession, and she hadn't stopped to speak with David Mongrain either. He'd know of Marianne's rush to marriage by now. He must think her a careless mother to not contain her daughter's passions.

Marie pulled the comb through the long strands reaching into her lap. Streaks of white lined her dark hair that shone like silver in the moonlight. She was just getting old and somehow hadn't even noticed her youngest child's scampering into the marriage season. When had Marianne met up with David Gervais? At Mass, she supposed. But how many hours had they had together to arrange something so formidable as a wedding and all that went before it? She'd thought Marguerite bold to marry a man twenty years her age with two children already, but Marianne had a streak of independence that put both Marguerite and Marie to shame.

Marie felt the part in her hair. It hadn't widened in all these years of her hair growing long enough to sit on. She supposed this was so because she kept the strands bound up, tied into that knot instead of bearing all the weight of it down her back. She didn't see the silver that way, either. She could trick herself into thinking little had changed. She was still the mother of a growing family. But now...

Maybe she hadn't wanted to believe Marianne would really choose to move away from her. Maybe the thought of losing both daughters within a few months of each other was too much for her mind, and so she put it out as soon as the request came in.

Here she was, a woman forgetting familiar faces and then choosing to forget the longing eyes of another.

"The moon shines bright when it overpowers the rain, *n'est-ce pas?*" Jean said. She smelled the sweet smoke from his pipe as he came to stand beside her, his weak arm barely touching her shoulder as he sat. "We should have had a night like this one to get that Parrish reverend on his way."

"Then he would have had no reason to visit us."

"They're different, the Methodists from the Presbyterians, eh?" Jean said.

"I haven't met this Parrish's woman," Marie said. "It will be harder now, to make a friend of her with the mission moved south to Mill Creek."

"When we grind wheat, we have a choice with the Methodists' mill," Jean said. "And maybe we'll spend more time at our little claim south and they'll become true neighbors. A good comes of their move. They understand that the illnesses come from the river bottom. It shows they can make changes."

"Not like those at Waiilatpu."

"Oh, the Whitmans change, just not as some would like." Jean drew on his pipe, making little slurping sounds not unlike the whistle of bats swooping into the night. "Mrs. Whitman's daughter died, did you know this?" Marie nodded that she did.

"It will make her softer," Marie said.

"Maybe. Sometimes grief does this. Sometimes it makes the mind a brick."

Marie didn't want to talk of Mrs. Whitman. She wanted to tell Jean about the empty spaces in her own thinking, the lopsided thoughts, but words failed her.

"Marianne says they need clothes sewn for the children. They cook two meals a day now, for over sixty people at that mission," Marie said.

"Our Marianne knows this how?"

Marie shrugged.

"The priests will build a school soon," Jean said. "The Methodists will have fewer to feed then."

Jean tapped out ash on the hitching rail, stuck the stone pipe into the sash he wore around his waist. He reached for Marie, put his arms around her, and nuzzled her neck, tugging at her hair. She leaned back into his chest. He smelled of the tobacco and linseed oil he'd been rubbing into harness tack. The warmth of him offered safety and soothed her scattered thinking.

"Don't go thinking of taking babies in," he said. "Helping out the Methodists. They will manage on their own."

"I'm so forgetful of important things, I might forget where I put a baby," she said.

Jean laughed. "Their howls would remind you where you laid them down."

Marie heard an owl hoot in the oak stand. "I didn't mean for Marianne to surprise you," she said then. "I should have prepared a way, given you silence to consider before your daughter came to you with her coyote spirit, everything already settled. It's what a mother does, and I didn't."

He squeezed her more tightly. "She is her mother's daughter, our Marianne. Doing things her way. It's better she went to the priest first, or I would have forbidden it. Maybe you knew this without knowing, so you did not talk of it sooner."

Marie hadn't considered that she might have purposefully forgotten something and then forgotten that she had made that choice.

"I've had time to weather this," Jean said. "Marianne was the first to choose the faith," Jean continued. "And so I trust she's guided by a godly force in this." He kissed the part at the top of Marie's head. "Forget the worries you have tonight about what you failed to do. Mothers are human, Marie. You are a loving mother, a loving wife. Once François finds his way, it will be just you and me. You take care of your old *voyageur,* eh?"

"It is my *métier.*"

Jean nodded. "And it is enough."

Baptiste held his beaver hat firmly with his hand. It had a few rub holes against the felt, but they were under the brim, mostly. The hat must have blown off some British head during a windstorm that rolled up the Columbia or been left behind by an American arriving on ship. No one said they'd lost one.

He'd found the hat thatched among the orchard cuttings pile and reached in to pull it out just before setting the pile aflame. He'd brushed and reshaped the hat as best he could. Then he stuck an eagle feather around the band he'd formed from a rattlesnake he'd skinned back along the Walla Walla River.

He put the hat on. He looked even taller, and he was already well over six feet tall. A legacy from both his bloodlines. The hat would mark him as a confident man who walked in all three worlds, French Indian, English, and American. He looked at himself in the silvered mirror. His shortened hair came just below his ears. It would be good enough to wear at his little sister's wedding. He might even catch the eye of some young woman. He thought of Josette. This was no betrayal, just to entice a look.

He walked outside, tapping the hat tighter on his head. He pulled his wolf-skin jacket, hide-side out, around him, tightened the belt. The rain had stopped, but the gusts of wind still carried moisture. He didn't want to lose his hat to the Vancouver breeze the way the hat's former owner might well have.

He walked head bowed into the wind, taking long strides between the men's lodging and the fort's store. He'd pick up some little trinket for his sister. Both of them now would be married off. The whole family married, except for his half-brother François and maybe Paul. Paul—where might he have disappeared to all those years ago? Could he have lived to marry, or would someone have taken his brother's life in an outrage agitated by Paul's angry ways?

Baptiste bumped into someone, and both men grunted.

"Excuse, *pardon,*" the man said. He was not as tall as Baptiste. He had dark eyes and almond skin, and black, curly hair sprouted out like wings over his ears. Baptiste didn't know him, but they began talking in French mixed in with bits of English. The man said he was with the Red River group. They shook hands in that soft-finger Indian way.

"I know something of that country," Baptiste said. "My father was Sioux and French. My grandmother lives not far from there."

"I didn't realize," the Red River man said. "Who are your people?"

"Dorions. I'm Jean Baptiste Dorion."

He looked thoughtful. "Oh, you say it a little differently. We encountered a man with such a name. In Saskatchewan," he said. "He tells us he has been in this country and that he follows our trail." The man pulled at his chin. "It might have been Dorio. It might have been that name. He said it a little differently than you."

"DeRoin?" Baptiste asked. "Did he say it like that?"

The Red River man thought, nodded agreement. "He says he'll travel with us to the Columbia country, but then he doesn't. He sends word he'll follow. He may have."

Could it be Paul after all these years? It would be just like Paul to arrange his entrance around another wedding and take his mother's attention from her daughter onto her long-wandering son.

Accompanied by a drizzling rain, Marie rode her horse to the crossing place on the Willamette not far from the Gervais place. She uncovered her canoe from the blackberry shrubs and could see by how it lay that someone else had used it and returned it. It was the way here. She pulled the heavy craft to the water and shoved off, drawing her cedar cape tight around her shoulders to ward off the rain. She needed to talk to Kilakotah. The more frequently she saw her friend, the more she remembered the details of that woman's lined and aging face and the less she worried that she wouldn't recognize or remember her. She needed her sage advice.

"You're not losing your daughter, not like you lost Vivacité all those years ago, to the cold and snow and poor choices. Marguerite began a new life," Kilakotah told her. "Marianne wants the same. You still have them; it will just be different. My girl weds. I have her as a friend now. Change. It is just another change."

"I remember when I comforted you," Marie said.

Kilakotah patted Marie's hand. "Maybe you are upset because it was a surprise, something you didn't know about before the priest did. You don't like to be left behind." The two women winnowed grain that Kilakotah and her daughter had harvested earlier. They listened to the rain pelting the shakes over Tom McKay's barn they worked in. "Maybe you're jealous."

"Jealous? *Non.*" Marie lifted the wheat heads to the air, caught them again in her flat basket. "I think she isn't ready to marry. When she is ready, when she is old enough, then—"

"I'm old," Kilakotah told her. "I'm ready to have a house with just me and Louis and my slaves. That's what you need. A house empty of your children with some slaves to do the work for you. Then you won't be wondering how to fill your days. You keep them in line, and then you go visit your children. Your Josette and her brood. Your son. Your daughters. You have earned this place of rest. My Louis can get you some slaves from California at the Dalles—"

"Slaves are not the answer," she said. "Jean says even the law forbids holding sl—"

"They need a roof, food," Kilakotah defended.

"Only because they are orphaned or someone took them from their mothers. *Non.* No slaves."

"They like working the fields and handling horses," Kilakotah said, her jaw jutted out in firmness.

"Have you forgotten what it was like to be married to someone who took your child with him but left you behind?"

"I wasn't his slave."

"You were treated like one," Marie said. "As though you had no wishes of your own, no name of your own."

"You think you're too good," her friend said.

"No, never that," Marie said. She softened her voice. She wanted no argument with her friend. *I can't even explain to my best friend this discomfort.* Her own old bones could only take so many shifts and twists before they'd break. Perhaps her thinking worked in the same way. Perhaps her friend was right and she envied her daughter's beginning something new, moving along while Marie watched her own hair turn to silver and her own bones creak with age. Marie tried to remember what her life was like before she had children in it, before their cries and sighs and smiles marked her days. It had been so long ago. She'd been so young... Small hands always reached for her. She'd been filled with sadness and a longing.

"My firstborn was taken away," she said out loud. *What a strange thought.*

Baptiste was her firstborn, and he was still living close by her, though he traveled. Paul, well he was somewhere, but he hadn't been *taken* from her. He'd chosen to leave. Kilakotah's eyes formed a question. Marie was thinking strange thoughts now and not just forgetting what was worth remembering.

5

Caves of Concealment

November 1841

Marianne enjoyed her moment, the next scene in the continuing drama she'd composed that was part of the prelude to her marriage.

She'd begun the script when she'd been a witness to Isadore's baptism, her friend Julie's baby. Julie was her intended's sister. Marianne smiled at the young man as he stood across from her inside the church at St. Paul. That was the first time she'd let herself imagine that she might someday be David's wife, the mother of his children, and, like her mother, wear the mantle of a respected matron of French Prairie.

While the priest spoke the words and laid white linen on Isadore's wet hair, Marianne's thoughts were on things less spiritual: the thickness of David's arms; his soft, shy smile; the slight color rising at his neck. David hadn't known then of Marianne's preying nature. No, she wasn't a huntress and David wasn't someone she meant to devour. Goodness, no. She was merely protecting David from some virago who might swim in like a hungry fishwife and take him as her husband and then drive him to distraction. David could look forward to a good life with Marianne. And Marianne would at last be on equal footing with her sister and her mother.

Her mother and Jean had renewed their vows the day after Isadore was baptized, and then there'd been all the talk about Marguerite's wedding. Her family hadn't noticed that Marianne was busy with her…rehearsals too.

It had taken little effort to capture David's attention. A kind word after the service, then a question about how he thought the autumn wheat crop might fare, and he soon talked about himself. Men liked to speak of their exploits and share their knowledge, and somehow they believed whoever listened wore a higher intelligence as well. Her mother often stayed silent in the presence of men talking, but she listened. Her mother listened well.

David had sad eyes, still grieving his mother's death and his younger sister's. His hands were callused, marking the pull and grip of the harness as he worked the fields behind the ox. Dark earth lined the creases of his fingers. Hard working, her father would say of him—as long as he didn't see David as a potential suitor. A good prospect for some young woman her father might add, as long as Marianne wasn't written into that scene.

It strengthened Marianne's resolve, believing her father would find value in David should he marry another. She had hope, then, that in time her father would allow those qualities to shine inside the name son-in-law. His son-in-law. David Gervais.

She'd made all the rehearsals, gone backstage to get permission to have the banns read and then on stage, survived her father's outrage, even her mother's betrayal at not doing her part in this drama Marianne had so carefully composed. Now the wedding, and she and David together could simply take bows at the end of the performance before slipping off the stage and out of the performance to real life.

The guests danced, the fiddles and tapping feet of invited friends and neighbors filled up the parish hall built next to the St. Paul church. Even the November rain had chosen to stay away for the day.

"May I swing you about?" David asked.

"Oui," she said, thinking his invitation sweet. Her husband barely lifted her feet from the floor. "I'm not porcelain," she said, gripping the shoulder of his homespun shirt.

"I'd not want to risk injuring such as you," David said.

"Swing her!" one of David's friends shouted from the corner near the ale.

"You're her master now!" yelled another.

David's neck flushed pink, and the little bone in his throat bobbed up and down. He set her feet on the floor, careful not to step on the flounce of her dress. She'd worn a woolen dress, the patches stitched with thread she'd acquired from the Methodists. It was better than those skins her mother wanted her to wear. She wasn't an Indian, despite what some might say.

"I like the wind in my face," she told David. "Swirl me higher." She leaned her head back away from him and closed her eyes.

David whispered to her, gently pulling her up. "They're all watching," he said.

"My point exactly," Marianne said.

Her father invited her to dance then. She curtsied as she released her husband's hand.

"Don't forget to come back," she told him.

David nodded, then slipped away with a look Marianne didn't want to say was grateful, exactly, but his face looked as though balm had been applied to a painful wound.

Marie thought the gathering of French Canadians and their wives, dancing and eating in Joseph Gervais' barn in celebration of the New Year of 1842, would be a happy time. But the closeness of so many people inside that wooden box and the rain dripping down through roof cracks made her pull her cedar cape closer around her shoulders. At least the cedar repelled the rain. New Year's Day always reminded her of the birth of her first daughter, the one she lost and buried seven days later. She tried to distract herself by watching the card games played in the lean-to hay shed. *Vingt et un* the men called it, and wagered sticks to represent wealth, currency being so scarce.

She felt edgy watching the games. *Vingt et un.* Twenty-one in English. Her first husband had played that game, often. He lost large sums at it. His father before him had too, the latter even bringing suit against a man who failed to pay up one of the times her father-in-law had won. The memory of that story made her sad. She coughed and moved nearer the huge barn door, where puddles formed in the mud outside. Pipe smoke swirled out into the night, graying the mist. She could still taste the pork that the Americans Baker and Anderson donated to the gathering. Well salted. Apparently Baker and Anderson had much to trade the Company in order to receive precious salt. Four quarts of salt, four pounds of sugar, four ounces of saltpeter per one hundred pounds, the recipe for preserving beef. She wondered if the proportions would be the same for a hog. Her mind could fill with useless things like this she remembered well.

Sometimes she thought it would be pleasant to write something down as Sally Ross could. Then she could put useless things out of her mind and yet have confidence she'd relearn them when she needed. It might even make room for more thoughts she hadn't even considered.

Marie looked around. So many people she didn't know here. A few Americans attended the New Year event, none of the Methodists from the mission. But merchants from Willamette Falls nodded and leaned into potential customers. They spoke of harness making and mills. Former Hudson's Bay Company men smoked and nodded over news.

She heard a shout of triumph from the card game. Her eyes moved back to one of the Rocky Mountain boys, as the old trappers called themselves. No longer trapping, it was said they took loans from John McLoughlin at Fort Vancouver and tried to pay them back through wagers, though McLoughlin told them just to get work.

Her eye caught the backs of her daughters. Marguerite chased after JB's little boys while Marianne hung over David's shoulder at the card game. Her youngest had said little about her married life that wasn't as chirping as a finch.

François occupied himself with a cluster of young men who raised dark eyebrows at one another when attractive girls walked by. He'd been at the gaming table, but now he stood to the side, his gaze falling on the slender Longtain girl. Her son François would leave soon too. They'd all be gone, her children, and then what? Peace, Jean said. And wasn't that what she'd been longing for all these years? Why didn't the idea, then, fill her up?

"Your eyes are far away," Jean said. He stood beside her.

"Just chasing the chill." She pulled the cape tighter.

Jean draped his arm at her shoulder. "Maybe a dance would warm you. I see Kilakotah over there. And Marguerite. They'd dance with you. Grab your daughters."

Marie squinted, trying to find them. Relaxed when she did.

"Something bothers you, eh? You tell me. I listen."

"I struggle to find words."

"You use words well," he said. "To solve other people's problems."

"I feel bound up," Marie said then, the image coming to her as she clutched at her cape. "As though strings of sinew hold me together, tight, sometimes cutting off my air when I want to breathe deep."

He brushed his bearded face against hers, whispered. "I could cut them one at a time. I would wrap my arms around you, hold you together. They wouldn't cut you then, those sinews."

"No," she said. "Everything inside would spill out. You might not like what you saw."

"*Besid Maria,* woman." Jean made the sign of the cross. "You say things that spin my head. We have no secrets, you and me, eh? I have known you for thirty years now. Thirty. What could there be inside you that I could not accept?"

Jean did know her, better than anyone. Yet he couldn't reach the darkest places, places she'd thought she left behind when she accepted the baptismal waters. She'd confessed all she could remember of wrongdoing. Mr. Mongrain had brought her no greater explanation from the priest about her wonderings. Perhaps they were never-mind questions, puzzles that if pursued only caused greater distress. She couldn't look at corduroy now without noticing the rub marks, the stains, and wondering if her own errors were so obvious to others.

She paid the penance the priests required. Then when she least expected it, when around her people laughed and friends shared stories of ritual and routine, she became aware of caves of concealment she kept distant, even from herself.

"It takes too much to explain," she said.

He pulled her to him with one arm, the smell of sweat and tobacco ripe against her nose as her face brushed the damp wool of his shirt. "I would love anything that spilled out of you. You know this, Marie."

"You say this now—"

"I will say it forever. Come now. We will dance together and set the tongues to wagging that an old man and his wife still like the swirl of the dance, eh? I will cut just the string that binds your legs, so step high, my Marie. Step high."

⯎

"We should have our own house, husband," Marianne pleaded. She held the molasses in the clay pitcher with both hands, offering it up as though it held the Eucharist wafer. "A wife needs time alone with her husband."

He dropped his eyes, sliced through his johnnycake, mumbling.

"What?"

"I said your husband is busy farming and has no time for building. Besides, Mother Gervais needs help with the young ones, and my father needs a good cook for his sons."

"Angelique is a good cook," Marianne said. "And your little sister Frani is already a helper. She skips and sings as she works."

"She's just a child."

"Did you marry me to be a second mother to your younger brothers and sisters?" Marianne said. David frowned. She might have gone too far. "Your sister Julie has her own home," Marianne said then. She rolled her lower lip out into a pout. David loved that look. He'd told her so. "I have your little brothers and sisters in addition to you to look after, and I have to do it in another woman's home. My fingers are callused from the sewing of your leggings and shirts, yours and all the men of this household. I didn't know I married all of you."

David touched her lower lip with his spoon-fork, a gentle prodding away of her irritation. She pulled back from him, set the molasses down, then stood with her hands on her hips. *"Bonbon."* He tried to kiss her, but she backed away. "Don't spoil what little time alone we have." David said.

"It feels as though I am your father's hired maid," she said, making her voice as sweet as his nickname for her. "We've been wed more than two months, and yet it feels as though little has changed. I could have worked less hard in my mother's house."

"You forget the warm nights," David told her. "You couldn't find those in your mother's house, *n'est-ce pas?*"

"I'd hear fewer snores," she said. "And I never know when one of your brothers will appear over the top of the ladder."

"They're only curious."

"They're too old to be so curious," she said. "A wife needs privacy."

Marianne watched her father-in-law and David's younger brothers walk toward the house. Angelique, David's stepmother, had taken her youngest and young Frani and gone to visit her sister, Kilakotah. His father and brothers had at least let him sit down first to this meal, allowing a little alone time with his wife. But it was not enough. A married woman needed the company of others, but only when a wife could ride home to her own place. Dozens of people stopped at the Gervais landing on the river and the guests had to be fed. She'd learned it was a part of her marriage contract to help serve them. She had little time for visiting on her own. Half the time when David's friends stopped by, David would leave with them. Who knew what he was doing then? Playing twenty-one or something else?

She was constantly surrounded by people who might have been part of an audience but who instead took over the stage.

David patted the back of her legs as she stood beside him. "You have my brothers' hands to help bring in water and to churn, and my little sister to serenade you. Be grateful for what you have, Bonbon. Julie has her own house, yes, but she also has three children, one a new baby to look after as well as a husband and field help she cooks for. It is not an easy life as wife and mother. Maybe you should visit her and see how hard it is to be a mother when the baby is little."

She heard voices, stomping of feet. David's eyes darted toward the door, back to her.

"Maybe you will work harder for us to have our own house if I'm not here," Marianne said.

"I work long hours," he defended.

"A woman needs her own place. A mother even more." She brightened, kissed him, barely brushing his lips.

"I need to work a year to earn supplies enough. A child will only delay it," he said.

"I cannot stop what God intones should happen," Marianne said. She wrapped a scarf around her head and pulled leather boots on over her moccasins.

"Your mind challenges even what God plans."

"But didn't you wish to marry such a woman?"

"I didn't want to marry at all." He spoke into his plate, his ears as red as the rooster. "Until you came along and convinced me I should."

"A man's home is invaded by squirrels and sausages. Is nothing sacred?" Jean asked. Marie knew he loved her grandchildren who came to visit, and yet his voice held annoyance. When had they last just lain together in their bed not yet so tired that they fell asleep in midsentence? When work did not consume them, Baptiste's children did. Or as this evening, Baptiste's and Marguerite's children and even Marianne had stopped by and then stayed, halted by a rare and windy snowstorm.

"Squirrels? Where?" Doublé said, his boyish eyes scanning the room.

"You," Jean said. "And your brother and your mother and—"

"I'm not a squirrel," Doublé told him.

"I saw you shake off snow from your behind," Jean said. "You looked like a squirrel brushing his tail. You get wet all over the floor, eh? Your grandmother will slip and hurt herself."

Doublé stood up and mimicked a shaking tail. Children lay everywhere a flat surface allowed. A fire cooked a bubbling pot; sausages sizzled at the iron as Marie returned to her stirring. Despite Jean's annoyance, it was as peaceful a scene as she might ask for, this warmth of hearth and home.

Her large family had eaten and told stories, and François and Jean and Baptiste had played cards while Marguerite tried to quiet the Gobin boys and talk with her mother. At last, Marguerite felt like talking. Marie hoped in the din of family they could cut out a patch of quiet.

Marianne hovered near the men's games, but she failed to take the usual bait her brother Baptiste gave her with a tease. Instead, she'd remained set aside, excluding herself like an unwanted wife, even when Marie smiled at her. Marianne had combed the long hair of Baptiste's Denise until the child's eyes drooped. Denise's little friend Frani Gervais had waited her turn. It was good to see her daughter being tender with the little ones. She'd hoped to share laughter with both her daughters over the cooking pot, but perhaps Marguerite needed a distance from her sister.

"It's worrisome," Marguerite said, bringing Marie back to her eldest daughter's conversation. "JB should be here."

"Perhaps he stayed the night in Oregon City, what with the snow falling," Marie said.

"Papa wouldn't forget us," Doublé said as he came to sniff the stew.

Her daughter stiffened with the child's presence. "No, I'm sure not," Marguerite told him. "He said he'd stop by here to pick us up."

"Then he will," Marie said. "He traps still?"

Marguerite shrugged her shoulders.

"He does," Doublé said. "He works hard to care for us. There is some good reason why he isn't here. I know this."

Her daughter raised her eyes to Marie's, and they held caution in them seasoned with annoyance. "Go make up your bedroll in the loft," Marie told him. "We'll eat and then to bed with you."

"But Papa—"

"The snow delays him, *n'est-ce pas?* Go now. Listen to your grandmother," Marie told him.

"You call him grandchild?" Marguerite asked as he walked away.

"He belongs to you," Marie said.

"No. He belongs to his father. A different thing."

"Papa Jean treated you as his," Marie said.

"Papa Jean would do anything to please you," Marguerite said. "All marriages are not so. I'll shell the peas," she said then. "So we'll have porridge enough for tomorrow."

They'd bedded down for the night; Jean patted the down mattress, then sighed as Marie curled into the crook of his arm. Cooking smells filled the cabin as the porridge bubbled at the andiron. Children made sleeping sounds at last.

"You think of something, eh?" Jean said. He stroked her arm, moved the braid of her thick hair up over the pillow. "Maybe your thoughts wander to me?"

"Marguerite," she said. "The boys trouble her. We should take one of them here. Xavier is old enough, he could help you in the fields. Maybe they need more time to know each other as a husband and wife. Without little ones around."

"We need no new people underfoot," Jean said.

"But we could help her."

"If we offer such a thing, she might accept. How could she know then that she could be the kind of mother who would learn to love her husband's sons? You would deprive her of this? *Non.* You are too good of a mother to take this lesson from your child."

"A good mother would have taught her well, not waited for her daughter to discover such hard things on her own."

Jean kissed her. He whispered in her ear. "You are not only a mother, but a lovely woman. We do not need to add to our family now, eh? The grandchildren go away and leave us in peace but are close enough we can watch them play like squirrels in the snow. It is a good life. You talk of changing it. No. Enough of this mothering talk. I am a husband who has long waited for his wife to come to bed. If you make me wait longer, I myself may need lessons on what to do."

She stroked his beard, and he ran his bare toes up along her leg. She let herself be cherished, if only for the moment. "No man forgets such things," Marie said.

"Oui," Jean said. He pulled her closer. "Especially not a Frenchman."

⌖

"Why didn't you come by for us?" Marguerite asked JB when they arrived safely back at their home. Two days had passed. "Your sons waited for you."

JB shrugged. "I have a large load of supplies, Etoile. I bring them home in a blizzard, risk my life, and you worry that I am here instead of driving back in the night to get you? Ah, women."

Marguerite dropped her eyes. He had come to get them, though a day late.

"You're young. You don't always think of others, you young ones," he said. "I have a family to think of, and I do. You do likewise."

"Yes," she said. Uneasiness settled on her. He'd stacked supply barrels, ready for unpacking. It would have been a difficult trip. "I'm sorry, husband."

"You are forgiven, woman." He rubbed his hands together. "I will help you put these away."

"I would have liked to go with you," Marguerite said. She had her back to him as she pried open the barrel's top. She smelled lard, pounded to release the nearly frozen first layer so she could dig out the pork beneath it.

"When the weather is better," he said. He poked at the flames with the iron.

"But you took the boys with you the time before, when it rained hard."

"I thought you liked the time with your mother, eh? Is this not a gift for you to have me doing the work while you talk-talk with your mother?"

"I watch the boys," she complained. "It leaves little time for conversation. And my sister was there and brother and—"

"Big families are joyful, woman." He wound up the music box that sat on a table all its own. It played the French tune "Alouette." "Our wedding gift sings to us."

Marguerite smiled. She must not worry. It was just a part of learning to be a wife, this adjusting to the unexpected. He had his work, and she had hers. It was how it was. He was right. She was being much too childish. It had been a good family visit. She hadn't been able to say much to her mother, but she'd seen that she looked well, still strong and spirited. Marianne's worry over her mother's forgetfulness was just Marianne's heightened imagination. Her mother was fine.

And JB was fine. He'd been where he said he'd be, here, home, unloading the wagon. He'd had to spend the dark February night alone since the snow had continued to fall.

"A census-taker visits while I'm at my mother's," Marguerite said. "He says you don't answer the questions." Marguerite made conversation as she rolled another barrel toward a storage place. "There is a reason you don't do this?"

"He caught me at a bad time," JB said.

"When you were unloading," she said.

JB stayed silent.

She turned to him. His face had turned the color of fresh beets. "Was this what makes a bad time, that a government man stops you from your work?"

"No." He looked away, pulled his knife from its sheath, picked at the dirt beneath his nails. "He stops by…days ago. When I'm out in the field," JB said.

Marguerite wondered what kind of work he'd be doing in the snow. She opened her mouth to ask but he strode to the door, opened it and called to the boys to come in from outside. "We go now and check the horses." To Marguerite he said, "They want to know what supplies we have in case of a war. Then they'll tax us so we can pay for it. I don't like this."

"Who wants to wage war on us?"

"Maybe the Cayuse or the Molalla or the Klamath. They're still strong enough to see what's happened to the Kalapuya," he said. "Some mistrust Hudson's Bay people, the wives…they wonder where we Frenchies would stand if the Indians attack. Baptiste's family lives in that tipi. He'd be hard-pressed to stand against her people. And your mother is full blood—"

"This war is a real threat?" This was new to her. "So why didn't you answer the questions, then?"

"They don't need to know how much wheat we have. They'll take it for troops if war comes. It's part of the push to make us American. The census is an American thing here, woman. They don't even want to count those with mixed blood or full blood, like your mother. I don't cooperate with men like that."

"But if we need to protect ourselves, then—"

"I told him the number of horses we had," JB said. "I told him that much."

"That's little help," she said with disgust. "Those he could count for himself."

"Dorion! You've been to the Columbia, *oui?* These people, they seek a guide. Are you interested?" The Saskatchewan shopkeeper ran his wide hands through his curly hair. A habit. Dorion noticed habits. "They come from the Red River area and make it this far. A little help from you and they might avoid trouble in the mountains."

"We'll pay," the traveler standing at the counter said.

"And leave my farm? Who would tend my wheat?"

"Thérèse, that pretty wife of yours. She does most of the work anyway, eh?" The shopkeeper chuckled as he spoke.

Dorion hoped the man joked. Others teased him some and he wasn't always sure if they meant to banter or berate. No matter. Dorion and Thérèse knew better. He and his wife were a team. He traveled away often. It was what a father had to do sometimes to keep his family in food and cloth. But his absences from their little flourishing farm on the high prairie in Rupert's Land had merit. He worked no matter where he set his feet. He broke horses, gelded them, bought and sold mounts from one farm to another. He had a way with both horses and matching them to the needs of these Canadian farmers. His Thérèse understood his leaving home to do his work. He always returned. Even from that long journey he'd made to find peace within himself.

He hadn't known Thérèse then, but it didn't matter. Through his stories, she could remember what had never happened and remind him when he felt sorrowful or troubled. Somehow she understood that a man couldn't commit to a loving wife until he found peace with his elders. That had been his journey those years before. He'd made it, and only rarely now returned there in his mind. Now he had no interest in returning to the Columbia country. The shopkeeper knew that of him, but he never failed to offer opportunity.

He'd take it as a compliment that others felt his guiding skills held merit.

"There'll be many more wagons moving through, heading west. Hudson's Bay wants to claim good harbors there," the traveler said. "They've even named a new area already. Puget Sound Agricultural Company, close to the Pacific. We have friends already gone ahead. We had a late start."

"I met some of them. From the Red River, *oui?*"

The traveler nodded.

"You might find good farmland there, Dorion," the shopkeeper said. He pronounced it the French way: DeRoin.

"Here I think you like me as your neighbor," Dorion said. "Now you sound like you would like to be rid of me, my friend."

The shopkeeper smiled. "I only want to assist these good Canadians. If they are successful, we will have new markets, Dorion. More people to buy your wheat. More families heading to settle that country and make it British. It is a patriotic thing we do to help them. We thwart the Americans that way, eh? Besides, you don't leave much currency in my store, Dorion. These travelers do."

"That's Thérèse. She manages our funds well."

"She does," the shopkeeper agreed.

To the traveler Dorion said, "Just head toward the setting sun and listen to where the natives tell you, about where to go, what's edible or not. The trails are well marked, though your carts might not make it. But even as a young man I made my way by listening to the land and the rivers and the people who know them best. Plan to arrive before the snow falls, and you'll be fine. If you have not crossed the mountains by August, don't." He added, "Umatillas are friendly people. Walla Wallas, too, but they're farther down the Snake, closer to the Columbia. Just look as though you are moving through, not planning to stay. And if you trade, don't eat their horses. Dogs are fine if you can't find game. But Dubreuil here has supplies to sell you. Anything you need. Lots of good wheat, I hear." Dorion grinned. "I need to be heading home. I wish you good fortune."

"Merci," the traveler said as he tapped his fingers to his cap.

Dorion watched the man return to his trading then. He pointed to a book of cloth, an oil lamp, other supplies. He didn't envy the man's journey. He'd made it, but now he preferred travel that brought him to familiar landscapes within a month. It was good to have a place to call home. Thérèse always gave him a special gift when he arrived after a long journey, some small item, a clay pipe, a waist tassel with red-and-gold threads. She didn't realize that her being there waiting was her greatest gift. Wherever she was would be home.

"I know why you tell me of these carts heading west, always urging me to lead one or two," Dorion told the shopkeeper.

"Eh? Why is that, my friend?"

"My Thérèse spends more in your store when I'm not here, so we Dorions are loyal Canadians after all."

"Committed to keeping a local man in business," the shopkeeper said as he waived him off.

A loyal Canadian. Dorion was that after all these years of wandering. He indeed was that.

6

Granted Desires

1842

"You stay away from them," Marie said. "It's wise to climb the same tree often, get to know that one trunk well before you decide to scamper up another without study. You risk falling otherwise." She handed back the button Marianne had given her to look at. She was sure she'd seen it before, hadn't she? Both women waited near the fireplace while their husbands stood talking at the far end of the parish hall. The long building had been built to become a school, but so far no priests or sisters had been recruited to this wilderness region for teaching in it. Only Methodists and the occasional tutor employed by Hudson's Bay for those close to the fort weathered the demands of so distant a place for learning. Mr. Mongrain still led the catechism classes, but now that the Methodists had moved their mission and school farther south, no one taught reading and writing, skills Jean said were needed if a child was to survive in this changing place.

Marie's backside chilled while her face felt hot at the fireplace. Nearly everyone else had gone home. She and Jean would leave soon too. They had a grand prairie to cross between this St. Paul parish and the Toupins' southern winter claim. She and Jean and François wouldn't often make the Mass this winter, leaving the roads to the rains and their wagon dry inside the barn. She'd miss the ritual and feast day celebrations. She'd miss seeing her daughters, and today both Marguerite and JB were absent.

Marianne popped the button into her wrist satchel. The girl sighed. "I didn't tell you so you'd get all worried."

"You picked the button up at one of their Masses?"

"They don't have Masses, Mama." Marianne glanced toward the men speaking with the priest. She kept her voice low. "They have a service. It's a funny word, isn't it? David says he has to service the wagons when he greases the wheels, and the Methodists talk of their worship as a service."

"Your father wouldn't want you to spend time with the Methodists," Marie said.

"He does. Besides, Papa can't say now what he wants for me. Only David can."

Marie stared at her daughter, who pulled now on the ribbon of her poke bonnet. "Oh *moi,*" she said, dropping her hands in frustration. "Will you tie this for me, Mama?"

Marie tugged on the fraying bonnet strands. Marianne was still just a child, and yet her chin jutted out like a matron's.

"You let your husband give you advice," Marie said, "but not your mother or your father."

"I'm married now, Mama."

Marie nodded, though it seemed her daughter had entered that joining stream by merely stepping from one *bateau* into a boat poled by another. Perhaps she didn't appreciate all she brought into the journey, nor how much she'd have to travel alone.

"He knows that Parrish, at least," Marianne continued. She stuffed the frizz of her hair at her temples inside the poke.

"Parrish is leaving soon. Maybe for a reason. The Methodists stir for an American government here, and we are fine as we are. We are safer among our own kind. Father Blanchet says this too.

"You didn't stay among your own kind, Mama," Marianne said. Her daughter clutched at her bodice, dropped her hand quickly. Marie noticed her rosary wasn't there. "Besides, they're our neighbors. David's and mine. They're the sturdy Methodists, the ones who'll work the fields and wrestle the building from the bugs." She giggled. "That's what they said. The others have moved to where their mill is," Marianne said. "The sturdy ones want to be a part of us and not just raise bigger herds and be involved in government things. They're not reverends. They're… people."

"People get sick there each summer at the mission site. That's why their leaders moved south," Marie said.

"David says it's because all the good land was taken here so they had to go farther south to have more fields and cattle. I don't know who they're going to service that far away from where people are," Marianne said. "You should get to know them. They had the most beautiful garden with melons and catnip and peaches and even some grapes. They'll probably have gardens at the mill site, too."

"You've been there often."

"I'm just curious, Mama, about what they do there, so I went looking and I...found the button and lost my—"

Marie heard the dog, Knuck, whine then yip, cutting Marianne's words off. He probably lay under the wagon to avoid the January rain pelting down. The new addition to their household had trotted after them this day until Marie had taken pity, not made him run the full eleven miles from home to parish and placed him instead into their wagon making its way to St. Paul.

"You should know what your own beliefs are before you try to learn others," Marie warned. "You don't attend the catechism classes with Mr. Mongrain, so you're missing these lessons."

"You're the only one who comes each time, Mama. No one else comes so far and through the mud with no hope of a priest to pardon you for last week's sins." She sounded annoyed, her daughter did.

"It's how I learn," Marie told her.

"Father Blanchet says it is a woman's curse to be curious, one begun in a garden," Marianne said.

"You're too curious," Marie said.

"You once traveled with a Presbyterian up to Lapwai, didn't you?"

"I was of service to them," Marie replied. "It was before—"

"Papa says you missed my baptism because of it, and you were just interested in something new. I'm just like you, Mama. I am."

Marie blinked at the sharpness of her daughter's tone. "I wanted to help a sickly woman with child be with her husband. It was not a journey just for me."

"Well, I help the Methodists. They grow food they give away to feed the orphans. They take people in. They teach them to sew and cook."

"You go there for the wrong reasons," Marie said. "You are only curious over a forbidden thing, nothing more. This is not a good pool from which others can drink."

"Papa says you just wanted to help take a printing press to the Nez Perce people so you could see your friend Eliza again." Marianne's voice pitched higher, louder. "I can decide my own ways now," she said. She dug at her wrist purse, tightened it, loosened it. She wouldn't look at Marie.

Marie wondered if she should share with her daughter the agonies of questioning if she'd done enough for a child, of her profound guilt when she realized a child had died in her absence. Should Marie share that she had given that grandchild little in the way of faith, and now more than ever she wanted to offer something of substance to her other grandchildren and to her own children as well?

"Little Marie died while I was gone. I hoped…it was your brother Baptiste who taught me about forgiveness, not the journey to Lapwai. I was not just curious about their faith," Marie said. "I wanted to understand it. You go to the Methodists as though you hear a new song on a feast day."

"They're interesting to watch, Mama. They sing and sing, and then one of them rises, and in English mostly, so I don't understand all of it, talks of Jesus as though he was someone standing in the back of the room. They invite him in, and then they wait. Long silences. You'd like that part, Mama. Then someone else tells of their own way of knowing him or how he brought light into their lives. They talk a lot about light, Mama, and how it shines for their work." Marianne pulled at a thread on her dress. "I can hear English spoken there, Mama. I practice my lessons."

Her daughter reminded her of a moth dancing with a hot light at the lamp.

"They talk about sin, just like we do, and I say many Our Fathers and Mary prayers, and I remember that my soul doth magnify the Lord before I leave. Not so they can hear me, of course. They'd answer any questions I had, though. They're very kind, really."

"Mr. Mongrain might answer your questions," Marie said.

"About the Methodists? How would he know?" Marianne said. "I think for myself, Mama. I just want to know what other people are like, for when my children ask me one day."

"Ah. At last you bring news I'm interested in hearing, about grandchildren. You and David will gift us with—"

"No. Not yet." Marianne dabbed at the frizzy halo of hair surrounding her head. "Maybe never." She turned away. The dog barked. "I wish they'd hurry up," Marianne said. "I have things to do."

"What about this place doesn't suit you?" Baptiste said. He sharpened the knife point while his wife, Josette, held the baby on her hip. Wind pressed against the tipi Josette had set up at the far edge of his parent's claim. Denise's eight-year-old eyes stared at him as she huddled beside her brother. Her shoulders shook. Was he being too loud, too frightening?

"I miss my sisters," Josette told him. "And my mother sees little of her grandchildren."

"If I build a frame house, with a fireplace so you stay warm, if I bring help for you—"

"These are not what I miss," Josette told him.

He pushed back against the pile of furs. He heard a pup yelp and then scurry out the flap.

"Things grow dangerous there. I don't want you to go back to Walla Walla." He adjusted his hat, made a sucking sound between his front teeth. "Even here, the mission has changed, which means the Americans are restless. Some go and others come. There is a story that the doctor who was once at the mission was sent back to America and now he brings others back. McKay says Whitman fattens more cows and trades only a few to your Cayuse people. He insults them with poor trades for their handsome horses. Your people don't easily take to such insults. Things rip apart there."

"More reason for me to go, to help my mother and little sisters."

"Dangerous," he told Josette. "For my children. You have no right to bring them into that danger."

"Danger is a knife with many blades," she said. "If what you say about the Americans is true, then this place holds danger too."

"The tribes here are weakened, at least," Baptiste said. "Sick and dying. It's the Cayuse, the Nez Perce, the Walla Walla who are proud and have never faced the Americans. I saw what happened to the Sioux. I know what happened to the Iroquois—"

"I know who's strong," she said. Her voice changed, and he knew she would try a different argument. "These are my children too. My blood flows in their veins too. My people are strong. We don't run away from trouble."

"When have I run?" he said.

She hesitated, and he knew what was coming. "You disappear inside whiskey."

"Not for years, woman! When will you let go of this? Am I not allowed to ride a different horse?"

"You race them," she said. "And it takes you to the same place."

He stood, jammed his fist into the side pole that framed the teepee, and the skins shook like a blast of wind against them. "I do what you ask. I come to you. I bring you here to French Prairie, where we all are now, my family. I take you back when you want, each time. This one time I think we should wait. Am I some stranger to you, you don't know me anymore?"

"But you leave, travel here and there. You refuse to take us with you. And I don't know this place, these people. Maybe, not even you."

"It's not the Company's way now. A *milieu* cannot take his family on the boat. Other cargo, more precious to the Company, must be watched after. The trapping is different now. Harder. I'm sent to meet brigades, not to go with them as my mother did. I'd have no time to protect you even if there was a way to take you."

"I protect myself, as your mother did."

Baptiste grunted.

"If more Americans come here, there'll be trouble in this place too.

The Americans will fill this French Prairie place first so the trouble will be here, not at Waiilatpu."

He stared at his wife, rubbed his sore fist. He'd wanted her to speak up more, to be more certain of things. Just not about this, just not to him.

Denise's eyes stared out like a frightened rabbit's.

Maybe it would be better if she went back to her Cayuse people. Narcisse Raymond, her uncle, still lived there. He'd look after them, maybe even better than Baptiste could here. He'd thought with them close to his mother and Jean they'd feel at home, that this would be family enough.

Josette stood beside him now, her hand on his back. "Let me rub oils on your sore hand," she said.

He nodded, and she led him to the robes where he sat. She lifted the basket and removed the skunk oil. "Two teardrops of oil can soothe," she told him. She rubbed his knuckles. She hummed, then, "Please," she whispered. "I want to go home, to be with people who know me."

"There are no priests there," he said. "When we have more children, they should be born here, baptized here."

"You're not even baptized," she said. "What does it matter where—"

He started to pull away from her, but she shook her head, cupped his hand inside hers. "As you said. It will be as you said. We'll come here if there is need for a baptism."

She continued to rub his knuckles, then his fingers, each one massaged until it was as soft as a rabbit's foot. She smelled of sweet herbs. He could hear her heart beat as she leaned into him. "They won't come to Waiilatpu," she whispered. "The Americans will stay away from the Whitman Mission except to pass through. More Americans will come here than there, and the Whitmans will close their mission as these Methodists did, and move to a different place."

He shook his head, no. "They are a persistent people, these missionaries," Baptiste said. "My mother says they don't see progress as going to another place but changing the place they're in."

"They will want to be around their own people."

"Like you do," Baptiste said.

She nodded agreement. "The Cayuse country will be a safe and quiet place for your children to grow up in." He grunted. She wiped at her eyes. "Thank you," she said. "Thank you for letting me go home."

It was how this conversation nearly always ended, his giving in, his anticipating the loneliness once they'd all gone. He'd feel like a stranger then. Her presence in his life is what made any place he went a home. "We don't go soon," he said. "I have things to do here."

She cried now, soft tears that streaked down her face. "I will be stronger there. Our children will be stronger there."

"The tears of a loved one heal," he said, thumbing her cheeks of their wetness. She looked at him. He shrugged. "It's something my mother once said, told to her by a Russian fur trapper. 'The tears of a loved one heal while the tears of a stranger are just water.' "

❖

By April, winter rains turned into prairie blooms, the dampness disappearing like misty fog. Now only brief showers chased by tufts of white broke the days. The puffy fluffs of clouds reminded Marie of a plant with white blossoms. What was it called again? She stood up, tiny flickers of light dancing before her eyes. It happened when she stood too quickly. That's what it was. She'd find a stick to help pull her up. She closed her eyes and tugged at the word in her mind, hidden as though behind spider webs. She would think of other things, and maybe the plant's name would come to her.

She looked for the child helping her dig in the field, found her near the timber. Marie started toward her, not wanting her to get too far away.

Pearly everlasting. She sighed relief. Her Chipewyan friend Sarah had drawn a picture of those blooms and told Marie it would help a person breathe or could be mashed into a healing wash for open wounds. Today the clouds looked liked pearly everlasting and reminded Marie of that friend. What would Sarah say if she told her it took her this much time to remember even such a simple thing as the picture of a plant?

Marie took another step forward sinking into the soft earth. Spring. She hoped that her foggy mind, "thick" as she called it, could be cut with the crispness of the season. The rains did bother her, made her as sluggish as one of the old sows wallowing in the mud, just turning over now and then or getting up to eat. Weaned of her piglets, the sow simply gained weight. Marie looked down. She could still see her feet.

Today she'd finish filling her waist bag with plants, hang them to dry, then make the journey to St. Paul. She looked forward to that time with Mongrain, even with a few more students now as the settlement of St. Paul grew. Red River people made their way south to the prairie, a few attended the class, and Marie had spoken to some of the younger wives about going. Marguerite had even agreed, though Marie worried her attendance was more for time away from JB's sons than for answering spiritual questions. Still, it was while they waited for Mr. Mongrain to begin one day that Marguerite had told her mother of her pregnancy.

"I should have noticed," Marie said.

"You've had other things on your mind."

"My daughter will have a daughter, maybe. This is good."

Marguerite had smiled. Marie's time with her daughter was an unexpected gift resulting from the lessons. She'd gotten more for her trade with Mongrain. She was learning more about this Catholic faith while sharing with him what she knew of herbs and plants and even the language in this Columbia country. Marie was quick with languages. They came easily to her ear. Knowing she'd be telling Mr. Mongrain about the plants helped keep their uses clear in her mind.

Marie looked for the girl and caught a glimpse of her squatting at the ground near the trees, digging. Good. Marie bent and spread the grasses with her hands. Too early for pearly everlasting. And this wasn't the right place for it to grow, anyway. Hadn't Sarah said it sought the mountains? But it also grew where the land had been burned, as this land had. It might come up through ashes.

Closer to the timbered edge, white tufts of valerian pushed through the dirt and needle-matted soil. Marie approached. Valerian carried with it a scent of earth Marie inhaled. This one she knew. Good. It was just that she had many things on her mind so she couldn't always remember. Her routines had been pushed around like the last of the year's potatoes rolling in the bottom of the basket. No wonder she forgot little things.

She picked a plant that could be cooked, but its leaves, when dried and steeped as a tea, offered help for those troubled by long nights, whose minds raced without ever finding a finish line to rest at. She wished she'd had that when Paul was young. She'd have taken it herself for the wakeful nights and given him some to slow him. Marie stripped the leaves, placed them into a flat wallet at her waist. She saw signs of milk thistle pushing up through the cultivated areas. Marie noted where the plants grew so when they were ready for plucking she could return. They'd stimulate milk production should Marguerite's body need such help once her baby arrived. Marie smiled to herself. This same plant could help prevent another baby from forming. Sometimes milk thistle produced more life-giving milk; sometimes it told the body not to prepare for a baby at all. These were amazing things, these gifts of the earth.

David Mongrain said all things were created for good by one Creator. He said mothers and fathers were creators too, bringing children into being. How people chose to use God's creations—plants, words, farms, friends, even their thoughts—that was what resulted in contentment. People could either leave the path of their *métier* and find themselves separated and lost, or they could reflect and contribute to God's creations in their lives.

Pearly everlasting might be called something different back in Sarah's land, but it performed the same. "As long as you don't mistake it for something else," Sarah once told her. "Many plants look alike but are very different. You must remember which is which. But that's easy for you. You have a good memory," she told Marie.

Milkweed is different from milk thistle.

Yes, she knew that. She'd always known that. Why did she even have to think about it? Milkweed helped her eyes too. They still hurt despite her wearing her spectacles all the time now. Kilakotah told her milkweed was good for aching eyes. Milkweed was different from milk thistle. She must make herself distinguish the two.

Marie would peel the leaves and stems of the valerian and cook them, bitter though they were, and offer some to the remaining mission farm workers, too, for those who came there with the coughs. She smelled the leaves. The scents helped her remember that plant.

Her granddaughter, Denise, approached now from the edge of the meadow where the timber vaulted toward the sky. Marie was aware of a faint breeze cooling the sweat above her lip. She'd miss that child when they headed back to Cayuse country. She hoped Baptiste had chosen wisely for his family. Wouldn't they all be safer here on this prairie, all of them together? She had a vague memory of people gathering in a time of war, when her mother and father still lived. Other mothers, her mother's sisters and their families joined them too, and they settled into their rounded huts, sharing space with cousins who were like brothers and sisters while they waited for news of the battle. It should be like that for her own family, all of them snuggled into one lodge.

But Baptiste said Josette wanted to go back home to her people, and who could know for sure what was best with such uncertain times? At least they'd be with family, surrounded by family. Once again Paul came to mind, and she wondered if he lived, if he had a family to surround him. Always with thoughts of Paul, something more pressed into her thoughts, pushed like a wind against a door. She imagined opening the door, to see what lay behind… She couldn't.

"Grandmother," Denise called. The girl had plucked a thick green plant from the shadow of an oak, and she walked with her arm outstretched to show Marie. "What should I do with these?"

Marie frowned. She'd seen something like those leaves in the mountains and in rocky areas on the upper Okanogan River. Her Okanogan friend there had said they were good for sore throats and could be found even in the winter when the dry reddish stalks pushed up through the snow. But she couldn't be sure these were the same plants. There wasn't any snow here, not even in the shadow side of the trees as there would have been in the mountains. She needed to see where the leaf came from, its source and its surroundings, to be sure. Once she could've been certain, but now…

"Leave them," she told Denise. "Don't pick any more. We need to go to meet Mr. Mongrain soon, remember?"

Denise sighed.

"These are good lessons," she told her granddaughter. Was she the only one of her family who appreciated Mr. Mongrain's stories? "Someday you'll be pleased you had this time with him. The stories will strengthen you in hard places."

"I only go to be with you," Denise said. She had her mother's deep voice, even for one so young. She sounded almost like a boy child, though she had the slender limbs of Josette's family. "Here with you is better," Denise said. "You teach me lessons about leaves and the birds and...what's that one called?" Denise pointed to a bloom of vibrant red. Blood red. "It's the color of your hair ribbon, that one you always wear."

Marie touched her hand to the knot of hair at her neck, an old piece of tattered cloth woven in. The cloth and a set of ivory-handled sewing scissors were all that remained of Marguerite's father, that and the memory of his disappearing. "I know that bloom," she said. *What is it?* Then with a sigh she said, "But I can't remember its name, Denise. I just can't remember a thing."

Marie watched as Marguerite dismounted. She hadn't seen her daughter in some weeks. Marguerite pushed past the blackberry bushes clustered at the edge of the fence, didn't even stop to check the growth of the peach trees she'd help plant last fall. She held her stomach protectively with her hands now, the small rounded form pressed against the leather. She scattered geese as she approached the split rails, her bare feet slapping against the path. Even when she waved to her mother in the doorway, Marguerite didn't smile. A chicken squawked, then lifted, settling on the fence, feathers ruffled as Marguerite sped past.

Was someone hurt? No. Her daughter would have signaled her to come or shouted for help. But something was amiss.

A warm June breeze lifted a whirlwind of dried ash leaves, spinning then settling down. As the slough drained back revealing springs and rich ground, they'd planted melons and corn and tried to keep the cows out. Marguerite's arrival took Marie's eyes from the garden. Marie wondered if her daughter would jump the low rails or take time to unlatch the gate, she was moving with such speed.

Marie stepped out onto the stoop, shaded the sun with her eyes. "What is it?"

Her daughter hiked up her skirt, put one hand on the rails, and propelled herself over them. The fringe of her dress flew against her knees. Yet she approached her mother barely winded.

In that moment, Marie felt the ache of her aging. She was over fifty, she was quite sure, and once she could have jumped that fence too without a thought. Marguerite had done it with a six- or seven-month-old child in her womb. This daughter of hers, not yet married a year, could run and jump, then stand erect, not even gasp to catch her breath. How long had it been since she could say the same?

It was so good to see Marguerite. She wanted to tell her this. Instead she said, "The gate's there for a purpose, daughter," then, "I know it isn't the baby's time that brings you here. *C'est juste?*"

"Too early. Yes." Marguerite brushed at an imaginary bug before her face, dismissing it. "You need to use English, Mother."

Marie started to agree in French again, stopped. "So tell me, what makes you jump like a doe over our fence after so long a time?"

"I came to see how you are."

"I'm fine."

What has she heard?

In the distance, Baptiste's helper, Archange, worked with Jean and François turning over braids of black soil. They were nearly finished and then would start felling timber to widen another cropped land. Today the men rotated with one man managing the plow, another dropping seeds, and the third pulling any tougher, tall weeds. Jean would replace Archange from behind the ox soon, giving the man a chance to rest. Black-and-white birds gathered behind him, tugging at the worms pulled loose by the plow he'd borrowed from the mission.

Now Marie motioned Marguerite, and the two women walked around the cabin so they could sit on the shade side where they overlooked a narrow finger of Lake Labiche. Marie lowered herself to the wood porch. Jean had begun the building of a wider porch with plans to cover the doorway to offer shade from the hot Willamette Valley sun in the summer and the endless rain in the winter. He'd left that task unfinished to begin work in the field. There were always new beginnings here while unfinished efforts yawned for attention.

Marie's knees creaked as she sat on a stump then fanned herself with her hand. She looked up at her daughter. This was no visit to see how she was. Marguerite would begin when she was ready.

"Archange works hard," Marguerite said. She nodded toward the fields.

"Baptiste had him help build their house too, even though they'll go to Waiilatpu as soon as Josette gives birth. I'll miss Denise and the little ones. Josette, too—"

"It's those...boys, Mama. Those...demons," Marguerite said, the words blurting out.

"Your brothers?"

"Must you always think of your sons first?"

Marie felt a worm shimmer in her stomach. She motioned for Marguerite to sit beside her.

"Come. Put your head on my shoulder and let me hold you like I once did," Marie told her. "Tell me what troubles you."

Marguerite sighed as she sat next to her mother on the grass, legs crossed in front of her, her fingers picking at her nails as they lay on her belly that rested like a basket before her. "It's JB's sons," she said. "They're like squirrels, scurrying through my things."

"They bury nuts in your *par flèche?*"

"I don't use Indian *par flèches,* Mother. JB built me a dresser. I have drawers now, with pull handles he traded for at Vancouver."

"I haven't seen this dresser," Marie said. "I like *shaptakai,*" she added. "And baskets." She waited for her daughter to continue. When she didn't, Marie said, "So, they bury treasures in your dresser drawers, your husband's sons."

"No. They take things. They...use my hair picks and brushes. Today I looked everywhere for the tallow candles JB gave me. They're rare, you know they are. I'm making up a drawer for the baby's things, so I'll be ready. The candles belonged there. Those little demons took them. I can't find them anywhere." She shook her head, and the dark hair that was pulled back into a knot at her neck threatened to work free.

"Come." Marie motioned for her daughter to turn so she could adjust her hair. Marie ran her fingers through the ropy thickness, unknotted the long strands.

Marguerite jabbed at the hair pick as she talked now. "They don't mind me. They just do as they please." Marie brushed tendrils behind her daughter's ears, motioned for the hair pick, and finished twisting thickness into a roll at her daughter's neck.

"However did you do it, Mother? How did you manage to bring three families together from three fathers?"

"I didn't." Marie said. "Not well."

"You did well."

"You forget Paul."

"Maybe Paul shouldn't count," Marguerite said.

Marie caught her breath. "He counts."

"But no one could understand him and his…strange ways."

"You don't even remember him, do you? You're just repeating stories."

"Baptiste was like a true brother. And François and Marianne. I would never have done things to them or to Papa Jean's children to upset him or make them jealous the way JB's sons do."

"Is that what you think? The boys are jealous?"

Marguerite's shoulders dropped. "They're so little. I don't see how they could be, but what else explains it? We barely have time alone, JB and me."

"Some time, though," Marie said, and she leaned to pat her daughter's stomach. Marguerite blushed.

"They lost their mother." A meadowlark chirped its song into the silence. "They might be afraid to fall in love with you, for fear that you'll die too."

"I think they wish for that."

"Oh no, Marguerite. Little boys seek out things," Marie told her. "They like to see what you have, not to be mean, but to satisfy a curiosity. They don't think as we do."

"They satisfy themselves, stealing my candles." Marguerite said. She turned to Marie. "What if they start a fire with them? I haven't found them anywhere."

"Thoughts of fires worry you?" Marie said.

Tears pooled in her daughter's eyes. "They don't respect me, Mama," she said. "And JB, he just laughs when I tell him. 'Children,' he says. 'I have a house full of children.' He puts me into the same voice with them, his little four- and six-year-old wolves."

"Your husband shows you respect. You have a good home, he doesn't discipline you with a rod, does he?" Marguerite shook her head. "He has a path to walk with his sons, too. They were there before you came. Think what they must wonder over. They watch JB smile at you and run his hand over your belly and talk of his son. Maybe they wonder if they'll be set aside when your baby comes."

"I didn't worry about François and Marianne joining our family."

"You had a mother who carried you, the same mother. Toussaint and Doublé, they lack that."

"They have their father. I didn't have a father for very long at all."

"It is a loss, but not the same. The hole left when a mother leaves is much wider and deeper for a young child, even with the kindest of fathers to comfort. What you do now for them will make them better husbands when they're older. Better fathers, too. You must put them first for a time. Or beside your own baby."

"How will I be able to keep the baby safe if those boys won't listen to me?" Marguerite whispered.

"You will be enough," Marie said. Her words were echoes of her friend Sacagawea singing in her ear. *It must be a woman's repeated nightmare that she isn't good enough for her child,* Marie thought. "Let them help you plan for this little one. Maybe they can bring gifts for him so they don't need to look for the ones you've hidden aside."

"I wasn't meaning to hide the things I make for the baby."

"Little squirrels see with different eyes."

Marguerite loosened the leather tie, expanding the seam of her dress. She inhaled deeply. She retied the thongs, then said, "Did Paul see with different eyes?"

Marie felt that coldness in her stomach. "He must have."

Jean shouted from the field, and the men changed positions, stopping to drink cold water from the twined jug.

"Don't you wonder what happened to him? Where he went?"

"I think of your lost brothers every day of my life."

"Brother. It's one word in English, Mother. Brother. *Brothers* means more than one."

"Did I say 'brothers'?"

"His brothers are Baptiste and François, and you see them most every day."

"I said 'brothers'?"

"It's just a mistake, Mother. In the English." Marguerite squinted at her. "Are you all right?"

Marguerite curled herself into her mother's side. "I mother you, too, *oui?* A daughter can mother, too. You make a little mistake in English. It means nothing. One brother we know nothing about now. One brother."

This was turned around; she should be comforting her child.

Marguerite sighed. "I miss not living under your roof, with you and Papa Jean and François and even Marianne."

"Marianne has her own home now."

Marguerite nodded. "I hear she visits the mission. She took her crucifix there and tried to introduce it to the reverends."

Marie smiled. "I should have warned the Methodists."

Marguerite laughed. "She'd better convert them now, because when the baby comes she'll be busy."

"I'll help you," Marie said. "Marianne doesn't need to leave her family to help with your baby."

"Her baby, Mother. She says she'll have a baby maybe before I do. Didn't she tell you?" Marguerite's eyes widened. "Don't tell her I told."

Had Marianne told her? Had she forgotten something as important as that?

Marguerite said nothing for a time, then, "I'd better get home, *n'est-ce pas?* And I'll use the gate, Mother. Remember, act surprised when Marianne tells you about her baby."

"That will be easy," Marie told her.

Marguerite stood, turned to her mother. "How did you know I wasn't running to you because of a problem with the baby?"

"Pardon?"

"You said when I jumped the fence that you knew it was nothing with the baby that brought me. But how did you know?"

Marie nodded with her chin to Marguerite's bare feet. "As much as you love your shoes, I know you'd have put them on for something as important as the arrival of a child."

Marguerite stood. "I just don't want JB's sons ending up like…well, like Paul."

"There must have been a reason why he left," Marie said. "I didn't love what your brother did, leaving us like that with no word from him. But I never stopped loving him." She stroked her daughter's hair. "Give them time, JB's sons. You must be a wise woman to figure out what these boys want." Just as she tried to understand what her daughters wanted from her. "Respect them, too, daughter. They'll respect you back."

"Paul showed no respect, Mother."

"Perhaps I held him too tightly. Maybe I didn't know how to let him go, so he had to tear loose on his own."

7

The Light of a Child

1842, French Prairie

It was sparsely furnished, but it was hers. Well, theirs, hers, and David's. A house-raising yielded this story and one-half log house with a cat-and-clay chimney that crawled up the end wall. Two rooms and a loft. Actually one room, but Marianne knew of a way to divide it. Two windows with real glass brought in light. David's father had been very generous with the windows. With other things, too, allowing them four plates and cups and the rounded scoop forks that served both to slurp the soup broth and poke the meat settled in the bottom of the bowl.

Her family, too, had been generous, offering bed linens and even the goose-down mattress she and David laid on the crisscross of rope anchored at the corner. A table and a bench came from the Gobins, and even her older brother, François, carved a stump he said might one day hold a music box. Sparsely furnished it was, but it was hers. Theirs.

A fire crackled at the hearth. She'd found the making of the chimney as interesting as watching the whole house go up. A double crib, one inside the other, tied with sinew to keep them even, was set at the end of the house and then filled with mud and straw. Across the river the Gays were building a house made of brick they formed themselves. Marianne had suggested something similar, and David had laughed. "Too expensive, Bonbon," he said. "And takes much time. We'd have to have a kiln and take days to form enough blocks for a house. The mortar has to come from coral out of the Sandwich Islands. It might take my entire share of wheat to purchase such lime. If you want to wait a few years—"

"No, I want our baby to be born inside his own house," she'd told David and hadn't mentioned bricks again.

She was good at accepting what was and then creatively adapting. The cat-and-clay formation of the hearth meant the fire would heat and harden the mud mixture. Eventually the wooden cribs would burn out and leave behind the mud as hard as brick might ever be. It was the strength of what was inside that mattered, how hot a fire one lived through that strengthened, not how something looked on the outside.

She'd watched the house go up and worked to feed the men who built it. Her mother brought baskets of berries and dried salmon, and her father baked cheek bread he set down on the table before donning a scarf tied behind his head to daub the sweat. All the French Canadians had bright-colored scarves. Her brother Baptiste wore his feather-decorated hat as he hammered.

Children ran about chasing the dog, and even the slave—no, the helper Archange, his long black hair swinging free of a braid—had been invited and did his share of work as though he were family. Only Marguerite and her brood had been absent.

"She's not feeling well," her mother told her. "The baby swirls her stomach. This happens sometimes with a baby. You'll know one day before long."

Marianne almost told her mother right then that she, too, carried an infant in her womb, but her mother would think she was taking attention from her sister. And she wanted her mother to know that she had done this all on her own. Well, not on her own. David, too. Besides, she wanted her mother to believe that her husband had planned this house on his own accord and not because he'd been shamed into it.

Having a child would change David, she knew. He'd be stronger, a little more willing to think of new things and not just see himself as a farmer for all of his days. It was a challenge being married to him. He could be hard as brick and, other times, easily molded. She hated that she could play him, think how he'd want something said, and then say it just right so he'd give in to her whims. At the same time, she did so like receiving what she set her heart on.

Once the baby came, David would be more interested in spending time with her and his son—if it was a son—instead of playing cards with his friends or bantering with his father and brother. Julie said her brothers were all like that, fun-loving and gentle. "They're hard-working," her sister-in-law told her as they set food out on a sawhorse table draped in the shade of oak trees. "Men deserve their rest."

"We work hard too," Marianne said. She reached to set a jar down, straightened quickly. She didn't want anyone to notice the bulge at her waist.

And no one had.

Now, two months later, she moved around the almost empty house, swirling in her bare feet. She was at peace. Her own home. Her own husband. Her own baby soon to arrive. She was a matron as sure as her mother or sister. She did wonder how her sister might be. She didn't want her to be seriously ill, but at the same time, it was nice not having every chatter with her mother be Marguerite this and Marguerite that. Marianne hadn't had one day of stomach sickness. This having babies might be as easy as...baking a pie, not that she took time for that.

She looked out the window toward the river now. The water barrel that collected rainwater at the roof eave stood half full. She could go ahead and use it to water the garden troughs. It would be much easier than bringing the bucket up from the well. The house had been built on the Gervais claim, at the far south end, a short distance from the Willamette River, and the ground was slightly higher here than at the old Mission Bottom site, as they called it. She hoped this new Gervais house wouldn't see the fever and ague the way the mission lowland did.

The air felt hot and sultry. She'd wait until David came home and get him to help her with the water buckets. It was a problem, this waiting. David had to leave earlier in the morning to meet his father and brothers for working in the field now. Marianne rose earlier to feed him without complaint. She didn't have to be under Angelique's thumb or feed the rest of the Gervais men, and that was a relief. Instead, she could begin her own chores: milking the one cow they had, feeding calves and chickens, gathering eggs, shooing the crows away from the garden plot. They had a loan of a sheep from the Methodists, paying with the offspring. Julie had agreed to show her how to clean and spin the wool so she could weave real clothes instead of merely handling skins or brushing and rebrushing the threadbare linen dress that hung on the peg.

There was one other problem to which she would need to adjust. She was sure that once the baby came, that too would change. It was David's habit of staying late at his father's house. Even after they left the fields or had milked the cows, David remained, often arriving home carrying a lantern. After eating what Marianne prepared for him, he'd fall into bed and be asleep in minutes.

"Where were you?" she asked him the first time it happened. "I worried."

David dropped his eyes. "Helping Papa," he said. "One of Calvin Coates's horses got down. He only has three, so we worked to get him up. Other horses needed shoeing. Farm work," David said. "It's what I do."

"For now," she said, patting his hand. "For now." She made her voice light. "I've porridge, and it thickened while I waited for you, but it should be tasty."

Once the baby came, he'd want to be around them more. She'd been raised with her brothers and sisters and parents always together, traveling and trapping, but sharing the same tent, the same closeness. Her father had carried her on his shoulders after the evening meal while there was still light enough in the sky to see the distant hills and, sometimes, count the elk nibbling at the meadow's edge. David would want that for his children, she was sure of that. He liked to be around people. So did she. She just liked to choose which ones and when.

She felt the baby stir. "Oh, David," she said holding her stomach. This had happened more often now, and David had yet to be there to feel this flutter of life. This one felt like a kick. She lifted her eyes to the window. If they'd been still living with Joseph Gervais and Angelique, she could have called to David in the field and he'd have come inside if only for a moment.

But she had her house, and wasn't that just as she'd planned?

❖

The woman-child with the round face and narrow eyes stared up at Marie. They said something, those eyes, but Marie couldn't put the words to them, only that the narrow slits reminded her of Paul. The girl had a wide mouth like Paul's too. She'd carried finished moccasins to the mission mill with hopes to trade for sweet molasses and what few other staples the Methodists might spare. Then out of curiosity—a word that made her think of Marianne—she'd walked into the long building housing the school.

Curiosity led her the first time. Marie wasn't sure what kept her coming back.

The sewing teacher, a white woman, nodded to Marie kindly but never spoke directly to her, either. Marie supposed the teacher thought Marie knew neither English nor any of the Chinook language. She might know some French, but Marie motioned with her hands rather than spoke French as she knew few of the Methodists spoke that language. The woman nodded for her to sit next to the child at the sewing table. This was her third visit. The woman-child who looked like Paul had been there each time.

The male teacher working with the Indian boys at the far end of the building never even noticed Marie. It was the way with Indian women and these American men, and Marie accepted, grateful he didn't ask her to leave. Marie scanned the room. She was the oldest woman sitting here on the wood bench taking lessons at the Methodist school.

But it was the woman-child she came for, not even sure why. Marie sat across from the girl now, watching as her thick fingers worked an awl at the leather. A few other Indian women stitched cloth that the Americans had shipped in to trade at their mission store. She'd heard that the women earned credit from the items they sewed to put against accounts. Fort Vancouver's store had a little competition that way, and Marie hoped to have opportunity to buy gifts for her children and grandchildren, come home with things to give away. But it was the girl with hungry eyes that drew her.

"Deese," the girl said. "Deese." It took Marie a moment to realize she was saying an English word...to Marie.

"Dress?" Marie said. "Or is that your name? Deese?"

The girl shook her head. "Deese." She pushed the scissors toward Marie. "Deese." Her voice grew strident. "Deese, deese, deese." Paul could get irritable that way, so quickly, when someone didn't understand what he meant.

"She offers you a gift," the teacher said in English. "She wants you to take them…these scissors. Deese."

"These. *Oui,*" Marie said and accepted them. She had nothing in front of her to cut, but the girl attended to that, too, by shoving cloth toward Marie. It slipped onto the floor. The girl let out a shout as she bent, dropping the scissors. She was clumsy. She needed extra help to do things; even Marie could see that. The girl glanced at the teacher, then at Marie, holding her mouth open, making her eyes narrow to the shape of watermelon seeds. Marie blinked back tears.

The girl cocked her head to the side. "Sad?" she asked Marie.

"*Non.* It's the new dye. In the cloth," Marie said. She lifted the cloth back toward the girl, the movement causing Marie's eyes to water again.

The child reached then and patted Marie's hand. "Kasa not cry," she said.

"No. Grandmothers shouldn't cry," Marie said.

The girl nodded and returned to her sewing. Marie couldn't stop staring, though she knew it wasn't polite or respectful. But the girl—no, the young woman—sounded like Paul had as a boy. How could that be?

It was the hottest day of the year so far. Nineteen, July. JB should be home before long. He made frequent trips into Oregon City or Willamette Falls or Willamette City, whatever they called it. Marguerite didn't know why he frequented a town with so few structures. Chief Factor McLoughlin's man claimed the land beside the falls, and a few other houses had popped up, houses built by former Astorians and retired French Canadians. He said he was helping with the gristmill in return for unused lumber, but he could have gotten the lumber from one of the Canadians, closer. The few things to be traded for there at the new tinsmith's shop weren't critical. Especially if she couldn't find the tallow candles for the tin holder they fit into.

This time JB had taken both boys with him and said it would be best if she didn't come along. "The ruts in the road could well bring on the delivery, Etoile," he told her. "How would that be, then, bringing a babe into the world in a wagon with little eyes awatching, eh?"

"Maybe Doublé should stay so you can send him for help if the infant is so close." JB rolled his hands on her stomach. She pulled back, not sure why.

"Take me to my mother's," she said. Her mother thought she was as strong as a north wind that could push anything over in its way. She wasn't. And she was certainly a far cry from having the spine of her mother, straight and bone tough. She wasn't half the mother hers was. And she had yet to tell her of her worst fear. She hadn't told anyone.

"Your mother would stay home," JB told her. "She's a good woman, your mother. I'll stop by and tell her you think the time might be near. She can come this way without you having to be discomforted by a ride in the wagon."

"You'd do that?" Marguerite asked.

"You've lots of time yet, Etoile," JB said. "I know about these things." He'd left then, and in the silence of the house she realized she was probably being silly. Here at last was a day to herself. She'd make the best of it.

She gathered up the eggs, spoke with the sheep that gazed at her beyond the fence. She pulled peas from the garden and imagined herself popping them into the bucket. A day alone would nourish her and keep her baby happy where he was.

Marguerite noted the shadow of the sun on the garden plot. It was still early. She had plenty of time. Maybe she'd pack food and take it to her mother's. They summered where the lake beds fed Papa Jean's large gardens. The walk would be good for her. She wouldn't be able to do such things once the baby came. She'd surprise her mother.

She scurried, humming as she gathered bread and butter, slices of pork pulled from the lard. She picked up a bucket of peas on the way back to the house to get the food pack and felt an odd pressure against her belly, then the wetness on her legs. She dropped the bucket, and peas dribbled around her like dropped beads.

She had heard the story of her own birth, born in June beneath the sunshine on the side of an Okanogan hill. Her mother, alone. Her father had been traveling south to Fort Walla Walla. Her half-brothers worked or played nearby, two little boys. Surely her mother hadn't permitted the children to be present. No, that had never been a part of the story. Her mother had done it alone, cut the cord herself, said a prayer, and sung the welcoming song, all alone.

A pain seared into her side. She panted, setting a goal of making it to the cabin. She stumbled over the bucket of eggs she'd set there earlier. A pain flashed across her back as though she'd been hit with a hot poker. She nearly dropped to her knees, knocking over the basket of eggs. *I have to clean it up. I have to clean up!*

She looked around, found a rag, then knelt. She wiped the floor, picking through the eggshells and broken yolks. The slime ran everywhere over her fingers. Her legs were wet. Her back hurt, seared like fire into her legs, her abdomen. *Mother!* She felt hot tears form. She wasn't sure where the baby's father was. How long had he been gone? Had he sounded urgent when he spoke to her mother, or had he merely suggested she might come by, that her daughter would welcome a lazy visit?

Marguerite screamed with an arc of pain. She was no saint. She wasn't sure she was even strong enough to make it to her bed.

The wave of agony moved up and over her as though tearing her from the inside out. Could anyone survive such torture? She screamed again, her voice an echo in the Gobin cabin.

She was alone, all alone here. She had to think. What had her mother done? What would her mother do?

She lay back on the bed, raised her knees. She sat up, pushed the feather pillow into a ball behind her. She looked across at the mats where the boys usually slept. The pain rose and fell again. *Do I push? Hold back? Let go?* She couldn't remember what her mother had said.

The chief factor thumped against the grain bucket with his cane. A double hit and the wheat settled more. Jean hated when the factor did that. A bushel was a bushel was a bushel, except when the chief factor pressed even more grain into the measuring bucket. It made the factor look bad. McLoughlin was known for stretching whatever currency he could to benefit the Company. He'd even claimed land at Willamette Falls. If the residents of this Oregon country chose their own government, he'd have a claim within that land too. He'd even called his claim Oregon City, as though he had a right to name it. It riled some.

McLoughlin had riled people more since he'd learned of his one son's death at a northern fort. The young man had supposedly died while in a drunken rage, and one of his own men had killed him, reportedly in self-defense. The chief factor simply couldn't accept it, and since he'd learned of it, word was, he brooded and harangued even his friends, wanting them to find evidence to vindicate his son's reputation. From what Jean had heard, the chief factor was probably right, but Jean saw little gain in trying to convince any of them about it. It was over and done with. A man's reputation once tarnished was hard to bring back to a fine shine. Jean learned that when he'd challenged Peter Skene Ogden those years before.

At the mill, McLoughlin didn't talk to his countrymen of his outrage. They learned of it by rumor, the way the French Canadians got most of their news. If more of them could read and write, they might be privy to the goings-on at Fort Vancouver, maybe even set something forth as good as an American could. But McLoughlin's tapping of the wheat to get more into a bucket than might otherwise be stuffed was a way McLoughlin hoped to gain something, control something, make something happen. Jean could understand a man's desire for that.

A man needed to achieve, hold some power, even accomplish a less important feat but one that gave a level of satisfaction. Grief demanded power.

He'd never grieved a son's loss. The closest he'd come was Little Marie's death. And learning of Marie's son, Paul, disappearing. She spoke little of it, but he guessed she thought the boy dead. At least she hadn't mentioned his name at the legitimizing when the priest had asked if there were other children. Who was he to mention the boy's name? His wife's hesitation had surprised him, but he'd decided she was nervous after all these years of deciding whether to speak her marriage vows before a priest.

He stared at McLoughlin. He couldn't imagine what it would be like to learn of a son's death. Would there be some sort of knowing ahead of it? Were the souls of a man and his kin so tenderly tied that death would send its echo across the seas, the mountains, the rivers, to arrive in a father's heart so that when the word did come it would be a confirmation and not a surprise? And if it didn't happen that way, did it mean the distance between them on this earth was too great to make love's claim?

He looked at his own son taking a rest beside the wagon, drinking from the water jar. He felt his heart ache with the mere thought of François gone from his life, let alone learning of such news months after it happened and then hearing that somehow the son was being held responsible for his own murder by his foolishness or poor choices. Losing a child. Not being able to bring him back even if one could clear his reputation. Could there be a worse fate for a father? At least he had the hope of seeing his son again beyond this life. He didn't know if McLoughlin had that.

François had removed his shirt, his suspenders strapped over his sweaty back. The boy lifted another basket onto the mill's floor while particles of dust rose up in the shafts of sunlight streaming through the tiny windows. François wiped his forehead of the August heat.

"Our wheat is plumper than what comes to you from your north country," Fran told McLoughlin. "Maybe you should rework the measure."

"François. Perhaps you should wait outside, eh? I will finish up here."

"Someone has to say it, Papa.

McLoughlin rose, his bushy white eyebrows turning to François as though he were a gnat that fluttered at his ear. The big man leaned against his cane.

"You should rework the size of the bushel to better fit what we bring you from French Prairie," François said.

Jean felt his ears grow hot. "My son," he said, clapping François on the back. McLoughlin had a temper. Jean squeezed his son's shoulder to silence him. He'd been more outspoken since he'd been courting the Longtain girl. Come to think of it, he hadn't seen the two talking after Mass. The girl had been off with someone else.

"It makes him look cheap when he strikes the bushel," François said, brushing his father's hand from his shoulder. "Hasn't the Company taken enough money from us, his own kind?"

The millwright and those handling the account books to record the weights and amounts looked up from their work; their hands stiffened. A horse snorted and stomped.

"He speaks his mind, sometimes a little quickly, *n'est-ce pas?*" Jean said. "A son can be brash in his youth, eh?"

"Everyone's treated fairly here," McLoughlin said. "I even carry your father on the Company books so he doesn't need to return to Mackinonge to be released from his duty. It would be a big expense for your family for such a thing to happen."

"You violate a Company rule when it suits you, then," François said.

Jean stepped in front of his son, pushing him toward the outside.

"You need us here, to meet those butter contracts with your Russians," François shouted over his father's shoulder. "Our cows produce better. You know this. Because our grain is better."

The account keeper stepped back, scuffing up more dust that Jean could taste even in his dry mouth.

"McLoughlin is a fair man, François. A big man here, one deserving of respect."

"Things change, and a man must change too. The wheat is heavier on French Prairie. You know this, Papa." Then to McLoughlin he said, "You treat us as though we're Americans you're trying to discourage instead of who we are."

"François, *non,*" Jean said.

"Maybe when the Americans come and he needs his countrymen, we won't be there for him, Papa. Then what will he do?"

McLoughlin slammed his cane with a backhand against the wagon, and the horses lurched forward. Jean pushed his son out of the way before he fell against the wagon. The wooden wheel rolled over his foot. He groaned.

"Papa," François said. "See what you've done!" he shouted at McLoughlin.

The account keeper snatched at the horse's bridle, steadying the animals and leading them away from Jean. McLoughlin blew exasperated breath out his nose and leaned down and put Jean's arm over his shoulder. "Come to the hospital," McLoughlin said. "I'll bind your wounds. It's the least I can do for my foolish burst of disposition."

"I'll get my father help," François said. He brushed off McLoughlin's arm.

"We accept," Jean told him.

"Papa—"

"We accept the help," Jean said. "More than one foolish outburst brought on this wound. Maybe it takes more than one good hand to bind it."

Marguerite held the infant in her arms. "See, Mother?" she said. "He looks like you."

Marie smiled as her eyes pooled. Her daughter's son, a scrunched-face, dark-haired, long-fingered boy, pursed his lips at her. He looked wrinkled as an old potato and yet as lovely as a gourd. Marie sang her welcoming song, and the child moved his head as though brushed by a breeze, opening his eyes to hers.

Marie made her smile wide, adjusted the spectacles that sometimes slid down on her nose. "A fine son you have. A fine, fine son." She looked behind Marguerite, expecting to see JB and the boys. She hadn't heard the wagon, but assumed Marguerite had been set off first to be followed by the other men in her life, a proud papa included.

"We'll name him François Xavier," Marguerite said rocking him as she did.

"For your brother? It will please him."

"And Xavier is of JB's family. I think we'll call him Xavier to avoid confusion," she said.

"Or let him name himself," Marie told her. "Where is JB? And the boys? Are they coming inside?"

Marguerite pushed the soft cloth away from her baby's face, tucked it beneath his chin.

"Maybe I call him Prompt," she said. "He comes on the day planned for and he takes little time."

"Is this why you didn't send for me? I would have come."

Marguerite looked pained. "JB said he would stop by to tell you when he went to Oregon City yesterday."

"Yesterday?" Marie tried to remember what she'd done the day before. She'd spent most of the day near the river gathering berries, hadn't she? Or maybe he came by later while she tilled ash in an area near the house. Failing to find them, JB must have simply gone on his way. Had he found Jean working in the field and Jean had forgotten to tell her? Was her husband forgetful now too?

"I'm sorry to miss him. You should have sent one of the boys. Doublé is old enough to ride this far on his own."

"JB has the boys."

"I'll give your husband a grandmother's thinking when he gets in here. He should know better than to take away a plan for you to ask for help." Marie clucked her tongue.

Marguerite turned away from her, burying her face in Xavier's soft hide wrap. "He isn't coming in here," she whispered. "At least not now. I..." She swallowed and caught her breath. "He talks of government things. He forgets the time."

"You brought this one into the world alone?" Marie asked. "And saddled your horse and came here? You had your first night with your son all by yourself?" Marguerite nodded. Marie put her arms around her daughter, holding Marguerite and her grandson, too. She felt Marguerite sink into her. "Sweet, sweet child," she said. "You are sweet and strong, and I am honored that the first eyes besides his mother's he should rest on are mine."

"I want to have him baptized," Marguerite said. "Right away."

"At the Mass, on Sunday. A father should be present, yes?"

"No. We go now. To the mission at St. Paul."

"There might be no priests there. Not until Saturday. Only David Mongrain—"

"I thought I saw your horse here, daughter," Jean said. He limped through the door, followed by François. "Glad to…ah, daughter." Jean's eyes pooled at the sight of the infant. "You have a blessing to share, eh?" Jean motioned to hold the baby, and Marguerite gave him up to her stepfather, watching as the infant's tiny fist opened for a moment to flutter against Jean's fingers.

"We name him after you, François," Marguerite said.

"Me?" Her half-brother said.

"And you will be his godfather, *oui?*"

"Be proud to," François said.

"And the godmother, that will be your mother, *n'est-ce pas?*" Jean said.

"Oh. I…thought…Pelagie Lucier could be the godmother."

"Etienne's little girl," Jean said. "A good choice." He stole a glance at Marie.

"She's sixteen," François said, his face turning red.

"We have found a new love, have we little brother?" Marguerite teased.

"No. I…just know she's young."

Marie was glad for the banter; pleased she could hide her mixed thinking in the family words. Not being asked had stung. Jean must have known by the way he looked at her. Yet a part of her hoped her daughter *wouldn't* ask her to be the godmother. Marie didn't know how to raise a child into the faith, how to translate, guide, interpret, how to teach a child to lean and let go. She had been unsuccessful with this effort with at least one child of her womb, and those that had chosen the faith, Jean had guided, not her. She still had so many questions of her own about what to hold on to and when to let go that being responsible for a child's journey of the spirit forced a tightness in her chest, made light scatter at the sides of her eyes.

"Mother, you're crying. I didn't—"

"I'm happy to have the son of my daughter healthy and well. We Ioways cry at happy times too. You should know this by now."

Marguerite hesitated, then turned to her brother. "Can you come with me now? We'll stop on the way for Pelagie. And the rest of you, come too," she said.

"It would be better to wait for the father," Jean said.

"No. This baby arrives on time, and we have no right to make him wait. We are all ready for him even if his father isn't. And he is small."

"He looks big to me," François said. He ran his finger over the infant's chin. "Might even need a shave."

The infant moved from a slow sound of discomfort to a wail in seconds, his hiccup-interrupted squeal enough to make François place his hands over both ears. "He's a fireball," François said and laughed.

"Like his grandmother," Jean said. "He already knows the Ioways' greeting song before he was even taught it.

Marie felt comforted by thinking of the child's lusty wailing as his first Ioway greeting song. "He remembers what he's never known," Marie said. "It is the gift of family."

"Will you do this?" Marguerite said.

Marianne ran her hand over her full belly. "If I'm not having my own baptized by then. Why not ask mother?"

Marguerite wasn't ready to tell her mother. In part it was why she'd ridden to Marianne's home, something she'd rarely done in the months since her sister's house-raising. She wasn't sure why. But for now, they needed a witness. Two. "JB asked Joseph Gervais. And the priest, of course. It'll be Tuesday next, the tenth of August."

"Oh. It's a baptism? I thought you'd—"

"*Oui.* It's a baptism. Of JB's…son." She croaked out the last word.

"But you already—"

"Not *our* son," Marguerite said. "*His* son. Doublé."

"But that's wonderful that an older child has come to want the living water," Marianne said. She threaded a needle, then continued sewing a patch onto a pair of David's corduroy pants. "Why not tell Mama?"

"Why didn't you tell her you're pregnant, before she could see for herself?"

Marianne shrugged.

"Well, I don't want Mama to know that JB cares more for his first sons than for mine. My heart has a poker in it," she said. "JB wasn't there for the baptism of our son, our child together, but when Doublé says he's ready to take the vows, then JB makes arrangements. He even asks Joseph Gervais to be godfather."

"Everyone wants Joseph. He's so well loved," Marianne said. "But Mama would understand that."

"I can't explain it. Only I don't think it's good to harbor such anger toward someone, a father or a small boy, especially not while standing at the baptismal font. Mother would never do such a thing. If she did have such feelings, she just wouldn't attend. But she wouldn't have them at all. She loves everyone, forgives everyone. She'd see the outrage in my eyes and..." Marguerite felt tears form. Xavier fussed, and she wiped at her eyes. Her mother was a saint.

"You'll have to tell her sometime, why you didn't want her there."

"Just promise me you'll keep it a secret until I'm ready to say."

Marianne nodded, and Marguerite realized she'd been gripping her hands into fists. Xavier cried from his board, and she went to pick him up, board and all.

It would be easier raising her own son, she was sure. Her own mother had struggled with having her sons raised by men other than their fathers. And maybe Paul's strange ways grew from that very fact.

If she were truly a loving woman, she'd forgive JB for not being there when Xavier was born; for not fetching her mother; for not attending the baptism; for those unexplained perfumes and unwarranted delays, the unanswered distance that had grown between the two of them. Marguerite shivered, her stomach churning with her thoughts.

"Are you cold?" Marianne asked.

"No. Just thinking of what you said."

"Oh, don't pay attention to me," Marianne said. "Mother says I make no sense most times."

"She does not."

"It's what she thinks, though. Was it painful?" Marianne asked then as Marguerite nursed her son.

"That's what I've been trying to tell you about," Marguerite said. "I felt so ashamed that he—"

"No, I mean having the baby. Mother says women don't remember the pain of childbirth, only the joy."

"Ha," Marguerite said. "I should be so fortunate." She sighed. "It isn't that you don't remember the pain; it's that I suppose women choose to do it again, despite it, because what follows is so wonderful." She gazed at the tiny form she held in her arms. "You'll find out about that soon enough."

"If the delivery is anything like carrying this one, I won't have anything to forget," Marianne said. "But I can't imagine doing it all alone like you did. You know, Marguerite, you truly are a saint."

Marguerite snorted.

"But you've been a good mother to Doublé and Toussaint."

"We do have mother as an example to live up to."

"Don't let that set you off," Marianne said. She smiled at her sister, and Marguerite smiled back.

It was one of the first times they'd just talked together as married women, almost as friends, setting aside the petty competitions. "I guess you're right," Marguerite said. "Neither of us will ever be on the highest rung of a ladder with mother."

Marianne leaned in to her sister. "She'd notice you first, though, if we both started to climb."

◆

She felt clingy as a blackberry vine. "Do you have to go to work so early?" Marianne sniffed, almost cried. "Just stay a little while longer."

"Come with me then," he said. "Help Angelique."

She even preferred helping her mother-in-law to staying at home, alone. David helped her up into the wagon, and she sat as close to him as she could on the board seat. She couldn't get too close today.

"It's just the baby," her mother-in-law said when they reached the Gervais home. Angelique, David's stepmother, didn't speak much French, and Marianne knew only a few words of the Chinook jargon used by so many of the tribes. Marianne's mother could speak it, but not her. Angelique's sister, Kilakotah, spoke some English and French, more than Angelique, and she was even older than her sister, so Angelique could learn it if she wanted.

Marianne tried to put on a cheerful face, but Angelique frowned. "What now?" Marianne snapped. A dull ache in her legs slowed Marianne down, but she moved toward the table that held dirty dishes and began picking them up and putting the tin plates into a basket for washing. The smell of gravy and eggs churned her stomach. "I'll get the water bucket," Marianne said.

When she came back in, Angelique frowned, then pointed. Marianne had left a trail of water on the puncheon floor.

"I'll wipe it," Marianne sighed. But Angelique put her hand on her arm and shook her head. She pointed behind Marianne, then leaned and pulled Marianne's skirt up. "What are you doing?" Marianne struggled with her, trying to push her dress back down. Angelique pointed again, shook her head. While Marianne bent to wipe the floor, wondering about the insanity of her mother-in-law, she heard David being called in from the field.

"It isn't that bad, Angelique. He doesn't—"

"Still," Angelique told her. David's younger brothers and sisters sat and stared.

David burst through the door, eyes wildly scanning. He took one look at Marianne and said, "I'm going to get your mother."

Her mother would come? Was this it? Then the pains began.

David rode hard through the split-rail gate, his horse scruffing up dust while he brought the reins up short and shouted. Jean ran up the steep bank of the dry lake bed, reaching David nearly as soon as Marie, who came from the side of the house. She set the egg basket down and wiped her hands.

"Calm down, calm down," Jean said. "What is it?"

"The baby… It doesn't… You have to come," David said.

"How much time has she struggled?" Marie asked.

"She was fine this morning. Angelique's been tending her."

"Has she asked for me?"

"I have," David said.

Marie hesitated. "I can ride to the Methodist mill," Jean said. "See if their doctor can come."

"Let me gather up my things," she said.

She filled her flat bag with herbs and dried leaves while David helped Jean catch up horses. She scurried, scanning the room to be sure of what she might need. Marie hadn't known when Marianne's time would come. She hadn't wanted to push into a place where her daughter had deliberately kept her from entering. But this was a different time. A child might not know when she needed her mother until the mother arrived. She pulled the latch behind her, took the reins Jean handed her, then threw her leg across the horse's back and signaled the mare to follow David's horse.

How did a mother know if she intruded or tended?

It was a question that for now required no answer.

Her mother stayed with her the whole time, held her hand, urged her when to push and when not to, prepared healing teas. She'd had no trouble at all carrying this child. Surely a short little delivery time would pass without peril.

But she'd sweated like a spent horse, riding the pain, resting with sips of water after each run up and over the ridge of it.

After the sun came up on the second day with no baby in hand, her mother had bent with quiet words to David and his family, and then she'd given her a concoction of herbs that made her head swoon as though it had fallen off and now rolled between her knees. Angelique and her mother muttered things then, and she felt certain that someone said a prayer.

Her friend Julie drifted into her memory holding a rosary and speaking words over and over as a chant. She thought Marguerite might have been there too, and then a doctor. He said his name, but she didn't know if he came from the fort or the Methodists. Even her father had leaned down, the scent of tobacco strong on his breath as he kissed her fevered forehead. Mr. Mongrain came, she thought. Someone whispered the words *last rites,* and Marianne feared her baby must have died.

Once she heard David pleading with her to not give up, and she wondered what he could mean. Didn't he want her to give up this baby into the world? Weren't they all waiting for this child to arrive? Then the inside of her twisted like a tree root clinging to the side of a watery bank. The pain seared its way into every crevice and cave of her, then carried her away toward a warm and pleading light.

She felt a glow so peaceful it was as though she prayed without using words. No pain here, just a sphere the color of the Eucharist wafer. She could have stayed inside that glow forever, without the pain, without the wonderings, but the cries of her son brought her back.

"David?" she said.

He stared at her, his face breaking into a tear-stained grin when she opened her eyes.

"It's a boy," he whispered, "You gave up a boy."

"Let me see him."

They laid the small form onto her stomach, and she'd had just enough strength to brush his dark hair with her fingertips. "My son," she said. Then she fell back into blackness.

Marguerite kept her nephew alive with her own milk. "Just until she's well enough," Marguerite told David. The poor girl barely stayed awake for longer than a minute, so Marguerite wasn't even sure Marianne knew who kept her baby from starving. Marguerite hoped she'd have enough for her own child and Marianne's, but there wasn't any choice in the matter. It was the way it was.

For six days, Marianne wavered in awakeness, and then, finally, her own restored strength produced milk to feed her son.

"What could bring sisters closer?" her mother said.

Marianne's fever lessened with her mother's herbs, and she had healed well enough to ride in the Gervais wagon on the day of announcement to the world that Marianne was a mother. She had given birth, and her in-laws would act as godparents at the tiny infant's baptism.

David doted on his wife and newborn son. Marguerite could see that firsthand while she stayed at the Gervais house. He'd be there for the baptism of *his* son.

JB stood beside her now as Marguerite watched the Gervais wagon roll up to the St. Paul church. She watched David run around to help Marianne out. Marguerite's husband never did such tender things. He just waited for her to follow on behind him as he did now that the Gervais group had moved toward them and into the chapel. The church felt cool despite the heat of the August afternoon. The scent of candle wax filled the air. The priest hadn't entered yet, and they stood near the door, their eyes adjusting to the dim light.

Xavier started to fuss, and it reminded Marguerite of a question. She whispered, "Mother, what did you use to balm our bottoms with when those little bumps got all red from the moss?"

"Henbit," Marie said. "Make a poultice of the fuzzy leaves and red flowers. It should—"

"Where would I find it?" Marguerite broke in. "Oh, I know. There's some at the edge of the field, where the ground's been disturbed. Good."

"If I interrupted you like that, Mother, you'd say I was being rude," Marianne said. She held her son in her arms.

"Would I? I don't think that's so," her mother said. "You girls. You see me differently than I am. Your children will see you, too, in ways that will surprise you one day." Her mother looked as though she'd cry. "You are woven together, my girls, through your son, Marianne. Life-giving milk from one daughter shared to give life to the other."

"The milk saved the baby," Marguerite corrected, "not Marianne."

"When a baby lives, a mother lives too." Marie smiled as she pulled the lace scarf down over Marianne's wildly frizzy hair. "You give to your sister as well as to her son. Marguerite is an 'other mother,' Marianne, as your Ioway ancestors would say. You are honored too for allowing your sister to keep life in your son."

Marguerite felt her face flush with such praise. Marianne's cheeks were pink too around her smile.

"I don't know how soon I want to try this birthing thing again, though," Marianne said. "I might need a little more time to forget."

A door from the priest's quarters opened, and Father Blanchet came in, his heavy cross and beads swinging across his wide chest. He motioned them forward, and though Marguerite's child was not being baptized that day, she could hear the words spoken and she knew the meaning of them shared in the rhythmic Latin. She took the moment to renew the importance of her own commitment to raise her child in the faith.

She cast a glance toward JB. Her husband did stand beside her today. She was a mother. She'd brought into the world a being that she would always love, and she'd kept another infant alive.

They all bowed their heads then, and the swish of their hands making the sign of the cross before the priest began the liturgy sounded like music Marguerite would never forget.

8

Season of Giving

1842, Saskatchewan Province

Dorion pushed the horses into the high pasture where the grass, though brown, reached to their briskets. If he could get another month of grazing here, he'd have enough hay made up to make the winter no matter how high the snow piled, even if it snowed in late October, which it sometimes did. Thérèse would tell him not to tempt fate like that, not to propose he could predict what the seasons held, but it was his way and always had been, to push and challenge, even the elements, even the seasons.

Such a push had defined his stay in the Columbia country; his love of rivers and beaver, foxes and trapping, and seeking the unknown, discovering what he hadn't known was there. Perhaps he should return. Who knows how it had changed since he'd been there?

But no. Trouble lived there, too, and a bad mix of feelings that he'd managed to contain. Thérèse helped him to control things. If they had wanted to see him again they could have sent word, and they hadn't. He'd come from a long line of interpreters and guides who knew how to track, how to find a soul they longed for. For him now, the solidness of land was his guide. The soil claimed him, not the rivers that flowed to the sea, not the challenge of what lay "out there." He stayed challenged by a family, by providing for his daughter and sons, hoping to keep them safe until the day he died.

When had that changed? When he realized that all things that lived eventually died and returned to nurture the sea or the soil. All things died, even hopes and memories. Not only those of good but of past wrongs. Perhaps that was how his own mother put him to rest, decided not to seek him after all.

He watched the horses rip at the grass then headed back toward his cabin. In the distance, he watched tiny figures move across the prairie. Wagons, heading west, shadowed the sheaves of wheat his family had cut and tied.

He had suggested to that one Red River man that he might go west again...but then had changed his mind. Even when the shopkeeper asked him to consider, he hadn't, not really. But seeing the wagons, the children walking, reminded him. Maybe there was something there that he might yet find, some answer to a troubled question of who he really was.

He reined his horse back toward the lower fields. Thérèse waited for him there, she and the children. That's who he was now. A father, a husband. It didn't matter what had gone on before. Thérèse had come into his life and given him direction. She served as the point of his compass. What happened west just didn't matter. He couldn't let it matter, not ever again. Those wagons carried no answers for him.

French Prairie

In October, more than the leaves marked change. Rains swelled small streams, and larger rivers like the Pudding transformed the familiar. Water dirtied by the mud-soaked banks pushed the Willamette to the top of its bed, forcing mothers to watch their toddlers closely. For weeks after she learned of it, Marie thought of Narcissa Whitman's young child, whom the Cayuse called Temi. The child had died while having a "tea party," as Marianne described it, beside the Walla Walla River. There'd been no high water, no flooding on that summer afternoon. But the child had slipped beneath the silvery blue and later was found clutched by willow roots, already taken by the deep.

Dangers lurked. Children died, even ones hovered over. "At least they found her body," Marguerite told her mother when she learned of the child's death.

"They might have thought the Cayuse were at fault otherwise," Marianne added.

Marguerite churned butter, lifting and plunging the paddle. "I can't imagine anything worse than not really knowing what happened, can you, Mother?"

Marie nodded agreement. There was nothing worse, she was sure of that.

Wet wool and linens scented the hearths of the houses on the French Prairie this season. Families lingered over meals. For Marie, the fall and winter were soothing robes worn while her husband slept late and her son whittled beside the fire, serenaded by the dog's snore in his sleep. The family ate but two meals a day during this season. And if she wished to visit her daughters, she could still ride in the rain with little worry over the cold. The daylight packed itself away earlier, so a trip to a neighboring farm might result in the visiting family just spending the night. They'd play cards, listen to a music box, sing songs, and tell stories. After the little ones were bedded down, the talk would turn to hopeful things: the next year's harvest, what the ships might bring in, which child might find happiness in marriage. This season when leaves fell matted their lives with hope. Geese honked, a stutter to the steady rain falling through the firs and pattering on the cedar shake roof. Her husband woke slowly, stirring Baptiste as well. François was already up and tending to the stock in the misty morning light. Her husband shook Baptiste's shoulder to wake him, and the two stepped outside to wash their faces at the bucket.

"Did you tell Mother?" Baptiste asked as they stepped back inside. He and Jean had ridden back from Fort Vancouver in the rain the day before, and Baptiste had spent the night.

"Tell me what?" Marie asked as she stepped out onto the porch to hand Jean a quarter of blanket used now to towel his face dry.

"They want us to take some of them in," Jean said. "Over 125 are here already. They left their cattle at Fort Hall or Walla Walla and their wagons, too, arriving on horseback and on foot."

"This is the second group, from the Red River?" Marie asked.

"No. These are different," Baptiste said. "They come as Bidwell and those new priests did. I told you."

"Did you?"

They came back into the main room. Baptiste straddled the bench and sat at the table, emphasizing his words with his chunk of bread stabbed into the air. His hair stood up on end, shaped by the line of his hat and Marie's feather pillows. "I knew they'd come, more and more of them. There'll be trouble."

"McLoughlin will provide grain for them, food for the winter. But they've no shelters," Jean said. "They need homes. McLoughlin and the Methodists, too, ask that we open our doors to them."

Marie looked up.

"We have little to spare," Jean said. "We live simple. Wouldn't it just cap the climax to show generosity to travelers and have them sniff their noses at our ways here?"

"You could watch a family with children squat in this rain without food?" Marie asked.

"McLoughlin can't," Baptiste said. "He's softer than he would have us believe."

"Ever since his son died," Marie said. She paused. "Before then, too. He makes loans, remember?"

"Maybe he's too generous, and now these Americans expect things," Jean said.

"I've signed on to ride with their guide, that Dr. White. He goes to Cayuse country," Baptiste said. "And to the Nez Perce at Spalding's spot. There's trouble there. I guess White learned of it when they stopped at the Whitmans' coming through."

"Mrs. Whitman fed all of those people?" Marie asked.

"White says Whitman charged them good for what they got," Baptiste said. "Dr. White led the party out here from Missouri and places farther east. Those on the trail paid him to do it."

"Not even a trapper by experience," Jean said. "I'm surprised they didn't get lost. Almost wish they had," he said, glancing at Marie. "But now they arrive with no currency, nothing to trade to feed themselves through the winter. So McLoughlin says he'll even put their needs on credit."

Marie said, "If there's trouble at Lapwai, it would be safer for Josette and the children if she stayed closer to us."

Baptiste bit off a piece of jerky, chewed while he shook his head, no. "The baby arrives, so now she pushes to go home."

"Genevieve," Marie said stating the infant's name. "This is not a name I know of. It is not a family name."

"Josette does things her own way," he said, looking away. "She doesn't always listen to her husband."

"Sometimes this is wise," Marie said.

"Not often," Jean said. "See how long it took you to listen to me to come here."

"Does this Dr. White come to replace Whitman at Waiilatpu?" Marie asked. "He's a medical man, like Whitman, *oui?*" Did she remember him correctly? "He was with the Methodist Mission here, *n'est-ce pas?*" She ground cornmeal into a fine powder at the plank table. She lifted the grain and rubbed it between her fingers. Still too coarse.

Baptiste shook his head. "It's worse than that." He glanced at his stepfather.

"He's the one sent away because he charms Indian women," Jean said. "Jason Lee banished him." Marie frowned, trying to remember if she'd known any of this before.

"Who knows what kind of Americans such a man brings with him. No. We have no need of tending to such people through the winter," Jean said.

"The Americans make White an Indian agent, a representative of the government of America. He's in charge of all Indian people in the Columbia country," Baptiste said. "Even though the British still claim joint ownership of the land."

"Americans just assume things," Jean said.

"That's the real reason America says we need an Indian agent here when we are not even under that country's control. These new Americans, even before they arrive, want to change rules. It's why the Cayuse must get an understanding with Whitman before he gives away more of their land." Baptiste's voice rose as he spoke; his eyes stared as though he saw something none of them could see. "It's what I tell you. These people—"

"This White. He says he's in charge of Indians. Even the women now?" Jean said.

Baptiste finished chewing. "He comes too close. He holds their hands too long when he's told their names. He looks into their eyes."

"Perhaps he intends nothing by it. Maybe he needs to be told that unwanted touching dishonors, that staring into another's eyes without knowing a person can steal a part of them," Marie said.

"You always seek the good in someone, *Mère.* Sometimes there is no good way to explain a thing. Lee dismissed this White. There's tension there for a reason."

"Do any on our prairie take these Americans in?" Marie asked.

"Lucier," Baptiste said. "And David and Marianne since they have a big house and only David and Marianne and little Joseph fill it."

"Already the new arrivals complain that the good land is taken by us," Jean said. "Their settling in will pinch like big feet squeezed into a pair of cobbled shoes. He's a clever man, this White. He makes money bringing people here who double the size of this prairie and then leaves it to us to find a way to keep them alive through the winter."

"He's paid twice, too," Baptiste said. "The American government pays him as an Indian agent, and the settlers pay him to guide them here."

"The American way, eh?"

Marie ground harder on the corn. These visitors riled her son, yet he would travel with the Indian agent and take his wife back into Cayuse trouble just because she wished it. Her husband, always a generous man, now closed his doors to those in need. She hung on to everyday routines by a slender thread and yet considered unraveling her household by upsetting her husband and inviting strangers in.

Marie said, "Archange will stay with us after Baptiste goes anyway, so our family expands whether we wish it or not. We'll learn new things if we take some of these Americans in. Winter is a good time for this. You can help with cooking. It was once your *métier,* remember?" She smiled at her husband.

"François shifts mood like wind on a blustery autumn day. He won't like making room. And these newcomers probably wouldn't even speak the language. No. I say *non.* Wife?" Jean asked. "Did you hear me?"

"We should share what we have," Marie said. "Generosity is for the old, *n'est-ce pas?* If we old ones do not give what we have, who will? Who will show the younger ones the way things need to be?"

"I thought you worried about forgetting," Jean said.

He spoke the truth, but his words struck her in an open place. Marie added an egg to the cornmeal. Even the talk of strangers sitting at a hearth brought both worry and warmth.

Marguerite felt like a cow, heavy and lumbering and tugged on. The calves outside bawled for their mothers. It was an odious task, keeping the calves separated so they would cry for their mothers, bringing the bovines in from the fields, their long horns spraying raindrops like sparks from a flint. But it was how it was done here on French Prairie. She wondered if there weren't places in the world where cows munched easily on grass while they were milked, where their babies knew there'd be enough milk for them, too, so this fretful bawling didn't have to echo beneath cedar and oak trees twice daily.

Her own baby slept, and JB's older sons now helped by holding the bawling calves in front of the stanchions JB had built. JB walked behind the animals, pushing them forward, a long stick swirled above his head to show his intention if they balked or turned back.

She supposed she should be grateful JB was there walking with a stick raised high and calling to the animals if they moved too far right or left. She'd be the one milking them, though, and sometimes when he shouted at them as they hungered for their bawling calves, they took longer to let their milk down. So she sat squatted beneath them, her head buried into the flap of skin at a cow's thigh, conscious of a quick back leg that could rip her without warning. Marguerite already limped from where a cow had stomped its foot onto her, smashing the big toe.

It hurt worse than childbirth and certainly took ten times the number of days to heal.

"Etoile, be careful now," JB told her as he struck the back of the cow, startling her forward into the stanchion. Toussaint quickly slammed the brace down to hold the animal that quieted a bit as she licked at her calf. "That toe slows you down. You don't want to have this one step on another foot, eh?

"Tell me news I don't already know," Marguerite said.

"You'd be bedridden."

This time she held her tongue. Having a reason to lie back and merely feed and tend her baby would be a gift. Maybe she should prod the cow to crush her other foot.

"I'll get some grain for her," Doublé said, and Marguerite nodded. At least JB's sons had taken an interest in helping her—when JB was around to see them—and that made this milking time go faster.

When she'd milked what she thought she should, she had Doublé release the calf that butted her mother's bag as she filled herself up. Marguerite scratched the animal's back as its tail twitched and it repositioned itself to get a better grip at its mother's bag. The calf was tamer than its mother. When the time came for the calf to be a mother, it would be easier to manage. Starting young mattered. Maybe that was why she struggled so with her husband's sons. She'd been deprived of the chance to start young with them.

Marguerite moved over to the second stanchion where another cow and calf awaited. Behind her, the first cow was turned out while JB prodded another through the corral toward its milking site. It was their routine through the five cows. JB never milked a one. "It's beneath a fur trapper," he'd told her.

"It's beneath a mother, too, but we do what we have to," she'd snapped.

He'd patted her behind.

When finished, she'd haul the buckets to the bench beside the house. There Marguerite would skim the cream, putting it into the churn. While she nursed Xavier, she'd raise and lower the plunger to make butter. She needed to begin a stew to simmer for the evening meal. Perhaps she could do that between feedings. At least the rain had let up. And at least the cows could graze on the ever-growing grass and she didn't need to worry about getting them food. Not as she worried about feeding the children.

The children. She still couldn't really say "her" children. It bothered her that she distinguished her son from JB's sons with other women. A good person would do no such thing, she was sure. A good woman would take them all in, make them all a family without the walls of their wombs to define them. Papa Jean had never treated her as though she didn't belong.

She wondered again how her father had been with Baptiste and Paul. Maybe he hadn't lived long enough to warm to her mother's first sons. She'd had a year already with Doublé and Toussaint, and they still hadn't warmed to her.

"Watch out!" she told Doublé. "She'll kick you. Don't stand there so close."

"I'll hold the tail, so it doesn't swat you in the face, Auntie," he said.

Auntie. "Well, be careful. You could get hurt. Stand to the side then, so she can't kick out."

He hummed while he held the tail, and she squeezed the milk into a froth in the bucket. When the teats felt flat as a soaked porcupine quill, she stood, pressed her hands against her back. She wished she weren't so tall.

"I'll carry the bucket in," JB said.

"Merci," she told him, her eyebrows raised in surprise. "Thank you."

"I don't want you to stumble," he mumbled.

She nodded and followed him into the house where Xavier slept. Good. Maybe she'd have time to sew a patch onto JB's leggings before her son woke. Xavier required all her attention when she nursed him, as his suckling struggled. His frustrated cries often woke JB and his sons, who would then choose to make a demand on her, that they were cold and could she get them another blanket, or hungry and could she get them a slice of melon. She couldn't imagine how her mother had raised them all, five children, though they weren't all under one roof at the same time, not the way these children were.

For a few days, she'd fed Marianne's boy, too. Those five days she'd felt as depleted as an old elk-bladder canteen drained dry of its contents.

Keeping her secret from her mother, not telling her that she'd raised an unworthy daughter, required enormous strength. She wanted to tell her mother, but just couldn't. Her mother was wise and loving and would see in Marguerite's face the hatefulness chiseled there.

Then she had, spilling her story out to her mother as though she were but a child. Her mother had listened and just the telling had made it harder for Marguerite to stuff the rage she felt for her husband into a space as narrow as a sausage.

She had every right to be outraged, even if JB hadn't struck her with a fist. But the rule of thumb he'd used to strike her had left wounds deeper than any rod slammed against her shoulders might have.

She wouldn't confront him. The shame would sap whatever strength she had left. But she'd have to forgive him. Wasn't that what a faithful, loving woman did? Wasn't that what her mother had done with her first husband?

Josette had been the one to tell her of those frightful times before Marguerite's birth. It was when they'd stopped there after Doublé's christening. Marguerite had carried Xavier in a sack on her back rather than in a cradle board, and she'd stubbed that bad toe over a pup, nearly falling with her son.

"Baptiste says we shouldn't have dogs inside," Josette said. "But Denise and Pierre like to snuggle with them as though they were of one litter." Marguerite reached around her back to lift Xavier from where he slept between her shoulder blades. He'd awoken with her lurching stumble, and he fussed now.

"So sad," Marguerite told him. "You have a poor, clumsy mother."

"Let your son hear good things about his mother," Josette said. "He'll know enough troubled things from others."

"I just tell him the truth," Marguerite said, then dropped her shoulders. "You're right. I shouldn't give him *mal* thoughts. See? I expose him to a father who makes bad choices. I am bad at this wife business, at this mothering, too. My mother would cluck her tongue at the poor ways her grandchild learns."

"She had her own struggles years ago, Baptiste tells me."

"Paul, *oui,* when he ran away."

"No. Before that one left."

"You know something," Marguerite said. "Tell me." She wondered why she didn't know this and Josette did.

"When Baptiste was little. He remembers that his father uses his fists on his mother," Josette said. "Baptiste says it happens when he drinks, but once or twice when his eyes were clear, too. He and his brother huddled out of the way."

"She kept her children safe, then, my mother."

"Maybe. They never knew when he might strike at them. Once, when Baptiste was at Astoria, when he was our boys' age, he remembers being in a dark place and sounds of hitting and this time his father pleading with his mother. His father makes promises."

"Does he keep them?"

"Baptiste thinks so."

"So she forgives him, then, Baptiste's father?"

"She goes with him when he leaves Astoria. She's there to rescue Baptiste and Paul when their father's killed. Not long after, she meets your father."

"She forgave him, then." Marguerite held her head in her hands. "I should forgive JB too."

"Who knows how long she held on to the stick she beat at herself with. Don't you do this, Marguerite. Marriage is a business of putting what matters into a basket and making sure it balances. Things are always taken in and taken out. Each decides what goes in or out. It's the way of people. All deserve to be treated with respect, but we must require it for ourselves as well as give it away to our husbands."

"I honor myself," Marguerite told her.

"We women have a way of protecting others we care for and yet let the same pain pierce our backs without even admitting who holds the rod."

Did Josette speak to her or encourage herself?

She remembered that conversation as she watched JB lean the cattle rod up against the wall of the house. He even poured tin pans full of milk, the first step in the skimming. JB sought to make amends. He commented on her safety at the milking and now offered to carry the milk inside. She had to build on that, push aside the pain of his betrayal, one he hadn't admitted to, at least not yet. She might have to change her own ways first in order to get him to change.

"What does your mother say of us?" JB asked her when he finished with the skim pans. He had his back to her as she lifted her son.

"She says the shame isn't mine," Marguerite lied. Xavier smacked his lips and made the sounds that would soon be a wail unless she lifted him for feeding. Why had she told him that her mother judged when she hadn't?

"So you tell her why I wasn't there at the baptism of our son?"

JB motioned his older boys toward the mats where they slept, and they protested. "Go," he told them. "Etoile and I need to talk."

She was too tired to talk now. She'd pressed the pain into a reasonable place where she didn't have to bring it up to be able to make it through her days.

"This is all she knows? She says it's my shame? Do you tell her everything, then?"

"I tell her enough," Marguerite said.

"The truth," he said. "You tell that part too. Your part."

"I have no part in your betrayal," she hissed. It was like him to hold her accountable for his spending time away...with other women. She was sure that's what consumed him.

"The baby needs to eat," she said. "It's not good to talk of hard things when he's eating." She patted Xavier's bottom as she paced the floor. The child squealed as he lost her breast. She slowed, pulled back the cloth that covered them in this private place, and helped him. She caressed his tight, frizzed curls now beaded with sweat. He quieted, his small hand resting against her.

JB watched but didn't add words to his looks of accusation. Then he moved closer to her. "When you have fed him," he said, "we talk."

The mountain they called St. Helen's exploded, pushing ash high into the November sky. Marie had thought a thunderstorm rolled across the valley and then that they were having an early snow as the white ash drifted down. She hadn't heard many thunderstorms in this valley and told Jean she'd welcomed the rumble, not knowing what it was, and people had talked of little else at the mill or after the Mass. A mountain exploding. Was it just the beginning of bad things to come?

Jean stood in front of Marie while he helped Denise onto her horse. The mid-November rain had been scattered by low clouds that threatened drizzle but so far hadn't delivered much. Closer to the barn, the horse kicked up little pockets of the fine white ash deposited when the mountain had exploded. Josiah Parrish said it would make the soil even richer, so Marie had shoveled the white ash around her apple and peach trees. They kept finding it still in places where the rain couldn't reach, a constant reminder of the mountain's power. Jean hoped to take a trip to see how the lava had flowed. Maybe in the spring, if they survived this influx of people seeking shelter on the prairie and the separating of his family.

Denise's face was flushed a rosy pink inside a hood surrounded with the fur of gray squirrels. Jean couldn't even see her braids. She sat straight and didn't move her hands or give false messages to the horse.

"My horse carries two or three," she said. "You come too."

"You go with your mother and father. Tell your other grandmother hello from us," he said. The child nodded.

She looked so young to be handling a big animal, but Marie had insisted they give one of their finest horses to Denise for her own. Baptiste had approved with a grunt, said something under his breath to his mother about an old bride's price.

"This child is too young for thinking of marriage," Jean said.

Marie had touched his good arm and shook her head so he knew that something had transpired between the woman and her son that didn't include him, some piece of an old story written before he came into their lives. It didn't happen often, but when it did he felt a twinge of regret. At least he thought that's what the feeling was. It differed from the loss he felt when he missed a good shot at a deer that might have meant several meals for his family. So maybe it wasn't regret. He wasn't sure what it was.

"Did you teach him, Papa Jean?"

Jean nodded. The horse would respond to the slight touch of a child and stand still the minute a rein was dropped. A rider could recover it more easily from a horse who knew to stop.

"I named him for an old horse of your grandfather's," Marie said.

"*Lumière.* Grandmother says that's what you called your horse, Gampa."

"*Oui.* For the light," Jean said. He turned to Marie, "You remembered."

"Some things," she said.

Beyond them Josette helped load the packs of their things while Baptiste and François tossed the ropes over the pack animals to hold the loads tight. Jean heard François say, "You let me know if these hitches I take hold better than yours." His son was forever tying knots and trying new ways to secure loads on pack animals, saying a man's very life might depend on learning new ways in order to survive.

Baptiste said he would, and Jean watched his family gathering up to leave. They headed to Walla Walla again, and who knew for sure when they'd be back. Marie would mourn the loss of the little ones running about their house or her walks to Josette's tipi to hold Genevieve while Josette finished forming wheat into fry bread dough. Nothing pleased either of them more than this intertwining of family, and now the strands separated. Again.

He pushed aside the emptiness he knew would move into the space when they were gone. It was difficult to believe that Baptiste and François were not true brothers or that both boys were not his very own flesh and blood. He was a fortunate man to have kept his family so often close to him.

Knuck barked, and the puppies joined in, sending squirrels up the nearest tree. Denise turned, and then they'd all looked toward the gate to note the arrival of several men whom Jean didn't recognize. But apparently Baptiste did as he removed his hat, held it to his chest briefly, and nodded once before returning his hat to his head in a sign of respect.

"This is my stepfather, Jean Toupin," he said then, nodding toward Jean. "This is Dr. Elijah White."

So this was the man, the new Indian subagent of the American government. He sat the horse well, tall and stately, his back as straight as an old cedar, a colorful scarf tucked in at his neck.

"And who is this lovely lady?" Dr. White asked. Jean looked to see how Baptiste would handle this comment about Josette. They'd be traveling together for several days, and the man did come with a reputation.

"My mother," Baptiste said as Jean realized Dr. White rudely pointed with his gloved hand toward Marie.

"Ah, yes, the famous Madame Dorion," White said.

Marie's eyes were lowered, but she said loud enough for Jean to hear, "Madame Toupin."

"She understands some English," White said, delighted. "But of course that would be so with you knowing it well enough, Dorion," he said. "I expected her to be much older." White dismounted and walked past Jean, barely acknowledging him. He stood in front of Marie and examined her as though she were a horse he considered purchasing. "Washington Irving suggested she was well into her years by the time of your father's death, but he must have been mistaken. She's quite...handsome."

"I listen as well as speak," Marie said.

"Oh, spirited," White said. "*Pardon.* You'd have to be to survive that Hunt journey. Having just made an overland trek, my admiration increases, Madame Dorion. Increases indeed."

"Toupin," Jean said, offering his hand. "I'm Jean Toupin, and this is my wife."

"Yes, yes."

"I have a gift," Marie said then. "For the man my son rides with."

"How pleasant," White said. "A going-away gift."

She handed White a pair of moccasins ornamented with porcupine quills of three different colors woven into an intricate design. She'd worked days on those moccasins, dying them red and green, soaking the quills, holding them in her teeth to flatten the ends so she could lay them against the leather, weaving them like a mat. Jean had thought they might have been for him or for Baptiste, perhaps, to mark her son's going away.

"You were raised well, Dorion," White said. "Generosity is the trait of a wise and peaceful soul." After examining her work, he nodded in approval, then folded the gift through the opening of his wolf-skin jacket, patting his chest when he'd tucked them inside. White reached then and lifted Marie's fingers into his palm, his other gloved hand devouring hers into a cup, his eyes searching Marie's face. "Thank you, Madame Dorion. They make a truly fine gift."

A searing pain went through Jean. Who was this man to come here and lift his wife's hand? Who was he to put his face in a place where his eyes could catch his wife's without the protection of a downcast gaze? Someone needed to tell this man how to behave since he had apparently learned nothing from being banished from the mission. Maybe Josette shouldn't travel with this expedition. Baptiste champed at the bit to be a part of White's journey into the Walla Walla and the Nez Perce country, but maybe his stepson missed seeing how this man might treat Josette. Someone needed to let White know that all doors would not open to him just because he carried the title of Indian subagent.

"Monsieur White," Jean said. "It is not good—"

Denise took that moment to ride her horse toward her grandmother and White, sending the doctor scuttling backward and breaking his handhold with Marie.

"Here, here, child," White said, catching himself. "Is the horse out of control?"

"My Gampa trains him," Denise said.

"Denise," Baptiste said. "Go help your mother."

"*Oui,* Papa," she said. She turned the horse with a press of the reins against the mount's neck and grinned at Jean as she did. Then she kicked her little legs against the big horse's side. The horse appeared to move exactly where she told it, exactly as he'd been trained.

David Mongrain, acting as the catechist, held the cloth up. Marie adjusted her spectacles. She identified a church building, many black bars, crosses, scratchings. Marie knew marked words she couldn't read, and the picture of an open book. This was the part of the study she liked best, the Saghalie Stick, the Stick from Heaven, a Catholic Ladder, David Mongrain called it though he said Protestant missionaries used the Ladder too. It was where the stories were told. He pointed to three bars nearly at the bottom. "Mary, Joseph, and Jesus," he said, then, pointing to more black bars, "These explain the prophets."

"We had such men among the Ioway," Marie said.

"From here we can tell the story of Joseph," he continued, "a man mistreated by his brothers, who was sold into slavery and was later used by God to save those very same brothers, his father as well. He became a respected member of a king's household."

"Where was his mother?" Marie asked. She squinted.

"Rachel? She had died. But his other mother, Leah, would have been distraught I'm sure."

Marie frowned. "Distraught?"

"Troubled. *Mal.* Ill. Needing some of your herbs. Joseph was her firstborn, and he came after much...dissension between her and her sister, but this is not the important part of the story."

"Did she go to look for him?"

"His brothers lied to her, so she never knew he still lived. Until he rescued them all. The story tells us we can never see how the struggles at one time may bring great hope into another time, if we're ready and willing to trust in God's guidance."

"The brothers lied," Marie said. "So Joseph was alive, but his other mother never knew."

Barbe, the intriguing woman-child, stood closely to a second set of drawings that filled the cloth nearly as large as the window. Joseph's story was close to the top, and sheaves of wheat were in it along with drawings of men bowing down.

"Bark like dogs," one of the other women said, using Chinook. She pointed to the figures of the bowing men.

"No, no. Those are men. Being respectful, accepting forgiveness from the brother they'd mistreated."

"He forgave them?" Marie asked. "These brothers. And the father, he forgave his sons, too?"

"Oh yes. Underserved forgiveness," he said. "It's an example of grace. The father had received it from Joseph, for not protecting his son and keeping him safe. And the brothers for their cowardly acts. Joseph could have had them killed, he'd become so powerful, but he didn't. He fed them during a great famine, during a time of great hunger. He did the unexpected."

Marie shook her head. "I know no one who could be so generous."

"That's right," David Mongrain said. He smiled. "Alone, no human could be so loving. True generosity requires that we lean on someone greater, someone stronger, who gives us what's needed to be truly large-hearted."

"The way a child leans on its mother," Marie said.

"Even being a mother is nearly impossible without that greater love sent through hands of others. Wouldn't you agree? The noblest work of all, the greatest *métier* still relies on someone else."

"They make their mistakes alone, *oui?* They live alone with those mistakes."

"No tragedy, no act of terribleness, is too great to be forgiven. The story of Joseph shows us that as it demonstrates charity and giving."

A third student pointed to another picture, and David Mongrain told another story, though Marie did not remember it. Her mind was lost to thoughts of Joseph and her own sons.

She worried about Baptiste being with Dr. White. She'd given the man the pair of moccasins as a gift to remind him to look after her son and his family, to be a reminder that a mother worried over this son and his kin even though he had sons of his own. She hadn't told Jean of her plan to do it. His face had tightened with the offering, but he didn't understand what it meant. Maybe she should have told him the gift's purpose. Jean often gave gifts to show his affection to her and to those he loved. He might not understand that her people sometimes gave gifts as a way of shielding. It was why warriors gave up their lives as gifts of defense.

She liked to light the candles Father Blanchet set out at the church. She'd think of them as memory candles now. At the First Communion of John McLoughlin and his wife just the week before, there had been dozens of little lights flickering like starlight when the big man

McLoughlin bowed in prayer. Two choirs, one of men and one of the high voices of Indian women, echoed back and forth across the church, sometimes singing in French, sometimes in the Clatsop and Chinook language of so many of the women. A few were sung in English, the strains of voices filling Marie even when she didn't understand the words. The music wove its way into her heart without ever entering her ears. The lights flickered, and each represented a prayer sent, a hope lifted up for healing, the making of a good memory.

The sounds healed, too, so she'd been able to think not of McLoughlin's son who had been killed, not of her own sons who had gone away, but of the grieving father and his mother and the bond she shared with them in loss. This westering place they'd all come to was engraved with loss.

When McLoughlin stood up, the candlelight lit the wetness on the old man's tired cheeks, and Marie blinked as her own eyes spilled with the tears of regret, holding back the sobs of longing known only by a parent who has outlived a child.

Jean had put his arm around her and whispered that the candles would remind them all of those they loved who had already died. He could know her thoughts that way sometimes, as though words formed on her soul. "We light candles later as prayers sent out for those still living, eh?" She'd nodded and leaned into him, inhaling the scent of leather worn on his chest.

Her gift of moccasins to Dr. White had been like a candle lit for Josette and Baptiste and Denise and all the rest, nothing more. She'd tell Jean that when she returned home, so her giving of that gift wouldn't trouble him.

"Have you heard from your son?" David Mongrain asked as Marie pulled on a wolf-skin jacket. She fluffed up the fur at her cheeks.

"No. Baptiste sends no letters to Jean Toupin."

"The grist mill at the Whitman Mission burned," David Mongrain said. "We had word from an Indian runner. I thought you might know something of it if Baptiste sent word. It was purposefully set. They'll have trouble grinding wheat now, for the natives. A hard winter threatens there too."

"This is not good," Marie said. "The Cayuse—"

David Mongrain lowered his voice. "Your son…his name was linked with it," David Mongrain added. His eyes were gentle, carried no judgment.

"My son? Baptiste?"

"A Dorion," he said. "Spoken in the French way, though I assumed it was Baptiste they spoke of."

"Who sends this news?"

"A priest, at Walla Walla now."

"They say this Dorion started the fire?"

David nodded, yes.

"My son wouldn't do such a thing," she said.

"Maybe he just knows something of it." David Mongrain turned his back and took down the Holy Ladder parchment, then the second set of drawings. "Next time, we look at the Holy Ladder that tells the stories of the whole church and of the priests coming here." He looked puzzled. "I knew a Dorion, pronounced in the French way. In Saskatchewan. He worked for Hudson's Bay then, and so did I. Before I came to Columbia country."

"His other name, this Dorion?"

"I don't remember," Mongrain said. "It might have been…Joseph or James." He busied himself rolling up the cloth stories.

"Not Paul?"

"Do you know a Dorion in the provinces?"

Marie kept her head still, didn't speak a word. How could she still hope this much after all this time? Was there a God so generous as to answer a mother's unworthy longing?

"Paul?" she said.

David Mongrain looked thoughtful, then shook his head. "People just called him Dorion, but I don't think I ever heard his first name as Paul."

9

Harmony's Horse

Smoke billowed out around the palisades. The flames licked into Mackenzie's fort, devouring sawn timber thirty inches wide and six inches thick, rising over the pillars and reaching twenty feet high. Both of the 150-gallon water tanks that once throned over opposite corners of the fort had been emptied against the inferno without success. Flames swallowed their contents, too.

Baptiste stood watching. Mackenzie had built the Walla Walla fort to keep Indians out and protect the Company and the worthy people the Company permitted inside. He'd built it, too, so all would see, Americans and Indians alike, that the British would prevail. One hundred feet square. A double row of palisades. An iron door at the gate. None had prevented this fire.

So much for Mackenzie's plan.

Now even one of the inner structures, a barracks, blazed into the sky while men like ants carried water from the Walla Walla River hoping to douse it. At the main structure, where former factors like Ross and Pambrun and brigade leaders like John Work and Peter Skene Ogden had once held court, where the Whitmans and Spaldings had spent days in respite while their mission was being built by borrowed hands onto borrowed land, the flames dipped and danced with swirls of wind that carried ash high into the cold November sky.

Baptiste felt himself drawn into the haunting movements of the air currents. He watched the way the wind chased the flames down then up, driving smoke from one side to the other, flames from the roof meeting up with the blaze from the walls as though seeking each other's arms. He thought there was a kind of beauty to it.

At the same time he hoped such horror might put a stop to the presence of the Company here, allow the Cayuse to go back to the way their lives had been before the British came and before the American mountain men brought in their trading ways. His own father had been a part of that intrusion, and his father had paid for it with his life.

Maybe conflict could be avoided if they replaced the past. Maybe burning the fort down would be a beginning to the end of the ways that had changed Josette's people for the worst.

"Help them!" Josette shoved at him. "Help them put out the fire!"

Baptiste moved forward with the bucket to stand in the brigade formed from the river to the walls. His face felt hot, and he coughed with the intense smoke. Men, women, even children threw water at the fire, as many Indians as Hudson's Bay Company employees. Dogs barked and horses whinnied their frantic cries as men yanked at their ropes, attempting to lead them beyond the flames into outer corrals.

The Indians, like the horses, sought rescue in strange ways, Baptiste thought. The horses had to be led away from the danger. Josette's people needed to be led away too, but instead, they helped preserve this symbol of their downfall. Why didn't they just let it burn?

Maybe they'd found some good in the forts. Maybe the copper pots and flannel cloth many wore instead of skins made up for land they'd lost for grazing their horses and for feeding the growing herds of cattle they nurtured. Or maybe they didn't know how to do anything different when a disaster struck. They just did what they'd always done—helped when called—without thinking of the consequences.

Water splashed against him as he swung the bucket to the next man. The river water singed against the timbers, the sound a kind of music to the blazing dance. He was in the line trying to save it too, so who was he to wonder over futile actions of others? But he was there because Josette asked to be.

With his in-laws and Company men, French *engagés* and visiting Indians, Baptiste spent the better part of the day with buckets, and in the end they saved only small portions of two of the inner log buildings and the single stone house where Chief Factor McKinley and his family resided. Everything else was gone and would have to be rebuilt before hard winter set in.

Maybe they wouldn't rebuild, Baptiste thought. Maybe they'll close this fort and just move on, letting the wind and the snows and next summer's sun return this place to the sagebrush and dirt. Black soot drifted and settled on the river. He was thinking wishful thoughts, making up a story to tell himself.

No one knew how the fire started. Baptiste supposed at the blacksmith building where sparks easily kissed old dried timbers. But the rumors rolling like thunder whispered, "Cayuse," and there was no reason not to believe the truth of that, either. Even Josette's uncle, Narcisse Raymond who'd lived near the fort since it was built nearly thirty years before, said the Cayuse might have done it. "Things haven't been good here," Narcisse told him. Still, most Cayuse had helped put out the flames.

Maybe someone had just tried to speed things up by burning out Whitman's closest protection, hoping that without a fort for rescue, Whitman would move out too.

"This is why the grist mill was burned," Narcisse said later when he sat at the family fire with Baptiste and Josette and the children. "You stopped by there?"

Baptiste nodded. He'd been at Whitman's to have wheat ground. He'd seen no sign of anything unusual that day, and yet it was said his was the last wheat ground on November 15.

"This is not good," Narcisse said. "Over time, a people should come to know and respect each other living so close together, like a husband and wife, *n'est-ce pas?* Instead, we grow farther apart, we who come here after the first people. We pay little attention to each other. Forget that all alliances require constant altering to make them fit. We learn nothing." He shook his head.

Josette served her uncle and Baptiste as they leaned back against the furs lining the inside of her tipi. She was as happy as Baptiste had seen her, his wife. Surrounded by children and dogs and his long-ailing mother-in-law, she was at home here in this place. He didn't really have a place he felt at home in anymore.

A small flame with a thin line of smoke billowed up through the smoke hole. Baptiste watched it, imagined the vapor disappearing up into the night sky no longer recognizable, the form just a wispy scent, a mere reminder that the smoke had once been flame easily seen and respected for its heat and ability to warm. Now it was nothing.

Josette's people were at risk of becoming the same. Nothing. He could do little to prevent it. More Americans would come, more men like Whitman, like White, even those like his stepfather. Not bad men, just men following their hearts to a new place. Yet wherever they stepped, they changed the rivers and the roads, the meadows and the game that fed there or were taken in traps. Then soon they changed the people there before them, carved by those mountains and forests and fields. And then the intruders were changed themselves.

Life here was a never-ending dance between landscape and man. Perhaps that's why he'd never found a recognizable place to call home.

What did a man hold on to that was strong enough to never change while he did, while all around him life and land built palisades of transformation?

He didn't know. He only knew it was a man's job to find a safe place for his wife and children. Josette felt secure here near her traditional lands, but he wasn't sure where safe was, after this fire. Could he take them back to where his father had come from, back to the Sioux land where his grandmother Holy Rainbow might still live? No, there were intruders there, too, men who built forts, men who made fur deserts of the streams just as the Company hoped to do here in this Columbia country.

There was no safe place to retreat to. A man had to make safe the place where he was.

⌖

"She reminds me of Paul," Marie said. "And she is too old for the Mission School." Marie smiled at Barbe, who sat like a boy might, her knees out. Her thin dress caved in between her chubby legs catching seeds from the melon she relished.

"Where's she been living? Can't she stay there, go to work?"

Marie shook her head. "She…comes too close. She doesn't learn. It takes her time to—"

"You have too much already that takes you from your duties.

François and me, we need you to pay attention here. Archange is already another mouth to feed. You go off to your lessons with Mongrain, and we fend for ourselves. Now you want to bring another mouth, a hungry one from the look of her."

"I honored your wishes, husband," Marie said. "No Americans stay with us."

"They found other places, so our generosity wasn't required," Jean said. "Don't use that one, woman."

"Marie," she said. "My name is—"

"I know, I know." He sighed.

"We do her a favor," Marie said. "She will keep me company while I dig for roots or gather cedar for capes. You can go visiting as a prosperous husband."

Jean grunted. "We fill our cabin already. We even have a dog, too, who robs me of peace."

"It's why we named him Knuck," Marie said. "A thief." She wouldn't let him divert her argument. "She is in need," Marie said. "Maybe she was a slave set free. Perhaps someone sent her away, gave her away." She held her cedar wrap tight around her against the sudden chill she felt. "And when Denise left, I lost not only the laughter of a granddaughter but of little Frani Gervais, who came to play with her. She wouldn't visit an old woman unless that old woman has someone younger to play with."

"What is this 'old woman' talk?" Jean said. "I thought the flickering lights had lessened? If you're so old, maybe you need less to do, not more people to help you do it. Why do you always want more in your house, my Marie? And this girl," he lowered his voice. "She does not look like one who will help you so much as you will need to help her, *n'est-ce pas?*"

The girl had kept her eyes focused on her melon, but Marie suspected she knew they spoke of her.

"When I go to hunt, what then? Will you bring her along?" he shook his head.

"This girl must be doubly lost, with neither a mother or a father, no one to tell her the stories of where she came from," Marie said.

"And so you'll tell her yours," Jean said. Marie nodded.

"Did you ask Marguerite? Maybe she could use some help?" Jean said.

"She has her troubles," Marie said. "You wanted many children at your feet," Marie reminded him. "Do you remember saying that?"

He nodded agreement. "But now I'm old and it's grandchildren," he said. "Why do you do this, Marie? You can't wait until—"

"When I see her I see a child that needs a mother," Marie said. "Who is there for me to mother? Even François allows little from his mother. It is what I do. She is a child."

"Looks older than a...child," Jean said. He sighed. "She comes free, not as a slave. She does the work needed," Jean said, caution rising in his voice. "We feed her, give her a fire to warm herself. If she doesn't work out—"

"Non," Marie said. "She comes as family. We don't send family away. She can leave if she wishes, but she won't be sent away, not ever." Marie rubbed at her cold fingers. She felt uneasy. "We will ask her. Her name is Barbe. Maybe she doesn't wish to live with us."

Jean scowled but took steps forward as Marie did. She said a few words to the girl in the mix of English and French and then said, "What do you want?"

Jean said, "How do any of us answer such a question, what do we want?"

"Mama?" Barbe said.

"And don't we all want our mothers," Jean said. He scoffed, pressed the air away with his hands.

But the girl reached beyond desire to action. She placed her arms around Marie.

The weave of cedar Marie clutched to her shoulders as a cloak dropped to the floor with the girl's motion. "Mama," Barbe said. "Deese my mama."

"You think so?" Josette asked her husband. She touched his hand then, pulling Baptiste from his thoughts of uncertainties that formed around them all like ever-tightening arms.

"I didn't listen," he told her.

"He goes back to get more," Narcisse said. "This is what they say. Do you think this is so? You know him a little."

"Who?"

"Whitman. He left already to go back to Missouri Territory."

Baptiste frowned. "This late in the year? He can't cross the mountains."

"He left days ago. He's desperate to bring more Americans back. They say he'll make money bringing a wagon train this way in the spring as White did. The more people who come, the more he makes with his supplies he sells them."

"But the gristmill isn't rebuilt. And who tends his cattle?" This made no sense to Baptiste. "Does he leave his wife there?"

Josette nodded. "She's alone. Only one helper stays on to milk the cows. Some of the Cayuse who accept the Whitmans' faith camp near by."

"She'd better hope they've accepted the faith," Narcisse cautioned. "Especially if it is true that the mill and now this fort were torched by disgruntled Cayuse.

"This man is mad," Baptiste said. "He misunderstands the meaning of sheltering those he loves."

Baptiste raised these concerns with Elijah White when the doctor sent for him the next morning. White intended to leave in a few days himself, heading east along the Clear Water to check on reports of tensions between the Nez Perce and the Presbyterians there. As White and Baptiste talked, they pressed dough around a stick, then held it over the low fire to bake. Strips of bacon sizzled in the iron pan. "If ever the Cayuse could take back their land, it would be now, while the woman is alone there," Baptiste said. "Narcissa Whitman isn't safe. And if she's injured, your position as one sent to represent these people will be challenged."

"Thank you, my good man, for your interest. But the truth is, I'm sent to keep the peace. I intend to bring her here. She'll stay on with the Lees at the Methodist Mission. There'll be no worries over her safety. Of course, I'm required to work with those already here serving the natives. I plan to visit Lapwai soon."

"My mother makes friends of those Presbyterians," Baptiste said. "It was where she visited when my firstborn died."

"I didn't know," White told him. "Well, they're to move to the area around Spokane where the work of the Eells family has been successful. That will free up the Waiilatpu area and the Lapwai lands…for other uses."

"To be returned to the Cayuse and the Nez Perce?"

"Perhaps."

"And the Whitman Mission—"

"Whitman appears to aggravate people, but he hopes to negotiate with his mission board about getting more funds for his work." White looked thoughtful. "Are you sure Whitman's already left? They were going to send letters with him, the missionaries. I, as well, to let my government know of the impact the Indian agent has already had here."

Baptiste didn't correct the man with his less than accurate title. He was an Indian subagent. Instead Baptiste said, "My family came west during this same season, and the snows and cold could not be negotiated with. Many of Hunt's party died."

"Oh no, goodness. Whitman intends to head south through California and east to Sante Fe and then north up the Mississippi. I certainly think he might have waited for my letters and dispatches, though," White said. "It's the least he could do since I'm the one who conveyed the news that will make the mission even more critical in years to come."

"It's to be closed you said."

"Well, it can be converted into what we Americans will need in the future, which is a storehouse of goods as people cross the mountains with their wagons instead of coming down the rivers. They'll arrive at Whitman's place first after they cross those wicked Blue Mountains and need refreshment and revitalization before heading toward the prairie and the valley along the Willamette. Especially if Hudson's Bay doesn't rebuild the fort, Whitman's resources will be critical for the American emigration. And serve the inner tribes as well."

Baptiste felt his once clear thinking grow foggy in the smoke of White's words. *Americans.*

White sighed. "An Indian agent like myself may well be propelled into the governorship of an expanding territory. Not just for a fort and the little space that might take up, as the British used, but acres and acres.

For farming. There'll be hundreds and hundreds coming then, linked together by little homesteads. They'll want a governor, someone who will carry on my work settling Indian disputes and all, though I truly hope to establish the way to manage the land issues while I'm here now."

"It won't matter that the British and Americans still hold the land jointly?"

"Oh, it'll all go American, I've no doubt of that," White said. "Americans are much more persistent once we set our minds to a thing and quite creative with how we deal with others when necessity demands it. Even the natives will be treated...as is appropriate. Consider the Iroquois and those farther east. They've come to understand the best way for them to survive in the face of an American directive is to become a part of it. I'll look out for the Indians' land. My, my, did you hear my stomach growl?" He clutched at his vested belly. "Oh my," White said then, holding an empty stick up from the cooking fire. "Mine baked through and dropped." He bent to poke at the now-blackening dough that lay like a black rock in the fire. He wore the moccasins Baptiste's mother had made for him, the toes not too close to the flames. "And I was so hungry too." White looked up and smiled a sheepish smile.

"Here," Baptiste said. "Take mine." He pointed the dough ball toward White.

"You shouldn't have," White said and popped it into his mouth.

"Don't forget now," Marianne said.

"Maybe you'd better go out with her," Marie said. "It might be hard for her to reach the latch."

"I can do it," Frani Gervais told her. "I'm Papa's biggest little girl."

Marie smiled at the child. Since Barbe had joined them, Frani found her way to the Toupins with more frequency. She'd seen maybe ten summers and Barbe must be twice that age, but their minds ran in the same riverbed.

"I go her," Barbe said.

Marianne's little one began to whimper from the fur he lay on near the hearth. His cries began like a coyote's, low, then rising to a hiccup of yips unless Marianne responded quickly. Instead, Marianne stood squinting into a sliver of mirror, touching a dark place below her eyes. "Do you think I'm looking old?" she asked.

"You're like a young colt," Marie told her.

"I am?"

"You wear yourself out bolting at dry leaves while a more dangerous snake lies coiled beside the road."

Marianne looked away from the mirror. "Mama, your word knots get more twisting every day. What's that supposed to mean?"

"You have years before you look old, and yet your son—"

Marianne turned to look at Baby Joseph, then back to her mirror. "He's impatient," she said. "Angelique says I should let him cry a little before picking him up. It will make his lungs grow big. And he learns patience."

"I go her," Barbe said, her voice rising above the baby's wail. The girl grabbed at Frani's wrist now.

"Can't I go out alone?" Frani asked. "Please, please, please."

"She'll pick at you until you let her," Marianne said.

"Barbe knows what to do with the chickens," Marie said. She nodded to the young woman who smiled her lopsided smile, then picked up Frani's hand in hers.

Frani jerked her hand free. "I can do it by myself," she said. "Papa lets me do it at home by myself."

"I go you. I help you do right. Deese way," Barbe told her, reaching again for the girl's hand.

"No!"

"Let her go alone, Barbe. She's old enough," Marie said, though she would have liked to be sure Frani could latch that chicken door. But if children weren't given the chance to risk mistakes on their own, how would they ever learn? She could secure the door later, after Frani went to bed. Jean and their son would be coming in from the field soon and she had a meal to prepare before darkness set in.

The baby gulped large mouths of air in between his ever-increasing shrieks. His frizzy hair, so like Marianne's, curled at his sweaty temples.

Marie hated to contradict something Angelique said, but teaching patience in that way didn't seem right. The Ioways taught differently. A crying child marked a sign of poor mothering. The baby was just as likely to learn to scream louder learning that until he did no one would come to hold him.

"Our fence repair worked," Marianne said, laying the mirror down. "No trouble with raccoons?"

"Marianne..."

"David says the wolves are getting braver, though. He hopes they take on some of their Spanish cows because those old nasties defend with their horns. He says they're as good as an arrow poked into a wolf's side."

Barbe turned back toward the raging infant. Marie walked over to the baby and picked him up before Barbe did. Marianne didn't like the girl to fuss with her son, but at the moment Barbe acted more aware of the baby's needs than his mother. When Marie lifted him, Barbe crossed her arms over her chest. She stomped toward her favorite stump stool and plopped down on it, turning her back to Marie and the baby as she did.

"Barbe," Marie pleaded. She swayed with the baby in her arms aware now that in his distress he hadn't noticed that someone heard his cries. "Shh, now."

Barbe stood up and lumbered to the door. "I go outside."

"Let Frani be now," Marie said. "I gave permission. She can do it alone."

"I let her," Barbe said as she lumbered out.

"They got seven or eight of the mission's sheep," Marianne said. "Ran them into each other like they were herded by dogs. Wolves circle, then go in for the kill."

Marianne had to talk louder over her son's wails. Marie cuddled the infant to her, singing softly to quiet him. He was a sensitive child, and the tension of the room clung to him like cottonwood fluff.

"Angelique says firstborn children are strong. They're made that way by learning they can survive the failures of their mothers to meet all their needs. A young mother just can't do it all at once, she says."

Marie felt suddenly uneasy, lightheaded.

"They made a dreadful mess, those wolves," Marianne continued. "I didn't see it, thank goodness. Who needs to see such ravage?" She shivered.

Marie handed Joseph to Marianne. "I've melons in the barn. I need to get one."

"Send Barbe."

"No. Tend your son, now." She sounded sharper than she'd intended.

The girl took him. She pressed her thumb gently on his cheeks to dry his tears. "Mama's here. Mama's here." He hiccupped into harmony.

Marie felt that lopsidedness pressure at her head. Her daughter's easy way of allowing the child to cry? No, something about Angelique's observations about firstborn sons and a mother's failures made her thinking foggy.

She needed to get the melons. To check on Barbe and Frani. That's what she needed to do.

She stepped out into the misty afternoon, her eyes cast toward the barn. Despite a slow drizzle, she could see the closed latch on the chicken house door, no chickens in sight. Good. She noted heavy tracks made by Barbe in the mud heading toward the chicken house. She scanned the yard looking for Frani. The girl was a favorite of Joseph Gervais, his youngest daughter now. Another daughter had died the year before, not quite three years old. The scent of burning branches and tree roots drifted from the fields where the men worked to open up ever more soil.

"Frani," she called. "Come help Grandmother carry melons to the house."

She heard a shout from the field and adjusted her spectacles. Jean waved toward her. Even after all these years, her heart still took a little jump when her husband singled her out, wanting her attention, giving her his. She waved back and smiled.

He didn't smile.

Instead, Jean started to run, their son behind him, yelling.

What are they shouting about?

At an oak tree, Jean lifted his rifle leaned there. Marie heard the thundering sound, felt the earth move.

The horses charged forward then, racing behind the barn. Marie lost sight of them, and she moved her eyes to where she expected to see them appear between herself and Jean. She glanced back to see what she knew chased them. She felt her skin bristle at the back of her neck. She started to run. She hoped she wouldn't be too late.

❖

"I think they'll mostly settle at Oregon City from what Papa Jean says. A few head south toward Chemeketa Creek and the mission mill. They find the winter here is not so cold as the places they come from. They can live in lean-to shelters," Marguerite said. She held a flensing knife made of deer's leg bone and scraped at the hide held at the post. Geese heading south overhead marked the season. "We lived that way with John Work when we trapped."

"But even in French camp where everyone says it is warm in winter months, in old California, a child can still be cold," JB said.

"So you have just invited people to stay here? I'll cook and clean for strangers?"

"It is a man's right," he said.

"To create more work for a woman. Yes. It is a man's right to do whatever he wishes while I'm left to carry out what you propose."

"I thought you might like the company," he said.

"The company of my husband is preferable, but he's too busy, he has other—"

"Etoile. Must we go through this every time? I have asked forgiveness."

"But how am I to trust you?" She jabbed at the hide with the sharp knife.

"No man would go back on his word while a woman wields such a weapon," he said. "Let me have it. The handle needs to be rewrapped or you'll cut yourself."

She let him take the knife, wiped her hands at her apron, and walked past him inside. She had a meal to fix. She washed her hands, and when he came inside with the knife rewrapped with a buckskin twine, she turned her back on him. She busied herself with unbolted flour. She wished again that she had a sifter. If JB did convince her to take people in through the winter, they'd know the flour wasn't bolted from the husks that stuck in their teeth when they chewed her coarse bread. They certainly wouldn't have brought sieves with them across the mountains, and the sieves at the Fort Vancouver store cost more than she wanted to spend. She'd have to hope they understood, these newcomers. A small thing, one she shouldn't worry over with so many other things troubling her. Or maybe as her mother once told her, she was one of those women who worried over little things so she could avoid facing the larger problems.

"It will be more work for you, Etoile," JB said. He used his soft fur voice. "I know this."

"Would you make your sons help?" she said.

"They help now," he defended.

How could she tell her husband that she really wouldn't mind more people underfoot? She wasn't ready to give him what he wanted even when it was something she wanted too. He'd hurt her deeply with his admission. He'd said he'd make a change, but she was wary. He needed to pay penance. She doubted if he'd confessed his sins, and if he had, well, the priest was another man who might just offer forgiveness with a little too much ease.

"I expect some of the settlers will live with your mother so you and your mother will have stories to compare, about how to sleep so many in such a small space and how many dried peas to grind up for coffee. It will tie you to your mother even more."

"Barbe helps my mother," Marguerite snapped. "I don't think she'll go against Papa Jean and take people in."

"You wish to take a slave?" JB said. "You should say so. We could buy from the Klamath who bring them north. This would work good." He rubbed his hands together. "A slave would help if we took in Americans."

"I don't want a slave. I just want…"

"Father says we must offer compassion—"

"He doesn't say to open our homes to Americans. I don't hear him say this."

"Yes. He does. If they're the ones who need it. 'Even a bad man prays for his friends,' eh? The mark of a faithful person is one who prays for his enemies, one who offers help to those who may least deserve it. This is what brings a man peace."

"I don't get the same lessons from Father as you get," Marguerite said. "But I don't have to confess the same things."

She could imagine him now casting a glance at his two sons as though the three of them had to indulge this mere woman. She wore a scarf tied behind her neck, and she straightened it now, wiping perspiration from her forehead with the back of her hand. She brushed at her cheeks, feeling the flattened place where a horse's head had knocked her down, cracking that bone.

"If you don't want to feed bread to strangers, we will understand," JB told her. "Joseph Gervais takes in a Methodist this winter. It is what a good man in a community does. But I do as you wish. We'll do what you want." He nodded toward her hands. "The dough is ready."

"I know how to make bread," she said.

"I'll put the dough into the pans," he said. JB had built an oven for her, trading wheat for the bricks, the same bricks made for the Gay house across the Willamette. She glanced at her son to see if he still slept.

"I'll watch Xavier, Etoile," JB told her.

He wanted to invite the Americans but said it was her choice. She wanted to make the invitation, but she resisted doing what he wished. This was about justice. He hadn't paid enough.

"I've never seen you do such a thing with dough," Marguerite said.

"I built the oven. You think I would know how to build such a beautiful oven if I didn't know how to bake in it?"

"It didn't cross my mind," she said. "I only noticed it's a big oven, enough for me to feed many people from. I suppose you had this in mind for some time."

"I had in mind many children," he said. "I am not too old a man for many children. Look at Joseph Gervais, eh? He has many sons and daughters and enough godchildren to form his own army." JB turned her around, forced her to look at him while he stuck his chest out and sucked in his stomach, puffing his cheeks out at the same time. She laughed. It was the first time she'd really laughed in weeks.

"You look like a bullfrog," she said.

"See, I make you smile. This is all I want. To make you happy." He took her face in his two hands and he kissed her, then rubbed her nose with his. "Flour on your face, Etoile. Like magic dust." Her hands were occupied with pans, and he held her cheeks gently with his bearlike paws. "I make a mistake in not stopping to tell your mother it might be your day to bring our son into the world. I make a mistake. I make a mistake thinking I can be with another woman without you knowing, without hurting you or my sons. It is what old men did when they trapped, eh? I'm an old man who needs much forgiveness. But I can still learn with a patient teacher. You will take pity on me, eh?"

"I have bread to bake," she said.

He didn't release her. "We bake it together. I will tell the Americans we have no room, eh? To make you happy."

"Maybe there are children with no mother," she said. "I'll decide, *oui?* When we meet these Americans."

He kissed her then released her. "Whatever you say, Etoile. I'll do whatever you say."

⯐

Jean held his wife's hand, cold as a rock frozen in ice. Not a good way to end the year, all this coldness. He squeezed Marie's fingers, hoping his would be warm enough to penetrate. He knew his son François huddled somewhere in the gathering at the graveside; he just couldn't see him right then among so many people on the prairie offering support. These prairie people, they were a family. When he died, it wouldn't matter where in the cemetery they put him as long as he stayed here on this prairie at rest with so many other good people, his family, people he'd served and been in service to.

His friend Joseph Gervais cried openly, tears pouring down the deep wrinkles of his face. He wiped at his jaw, his cheeks. No one ever expects to outlive their children, and now Joseph Gervais had outlived two.

The girl had survived only a few days after the accident. Jean was glad for that. A lingering death would have been even more difficult for them all. Why, he'd even prayed the girl would go quickly, but not until her closed eyes and labored breathing said clearly she was already gone, just her body there, the mark of horses' hooves at the side of her head. He supposed he'd have to mention that prayer in confession, though he thought it a merciful prayer, not one spoken out of malice or ill will.

They'd sent François for the Gervais family and meanwhile carried the child into the house. Marie had washed the little one's face, and his own Marianne had rushed away to comfort the Gervais family, she'd said. Barbe surprised him as she sang sweet songs while she knelt beside Frani on the floor.

He'd been glad he'd seen it all, or at least most of it. He still wasn't sure why the child stood there in the first place. He guessed just playing as little girls do, exploring the mouseholes near the barn, ignoring the rain, forgetting the fading hour. She hadn't heard the thundering herd, hadn't been aware of the wolves that chased.

His greatest regret? Not a one of the wolves had been shot, not one. Like gray shadowed arrows, they'd paralleled the horses, almost as though pacing them, placed in such a way that to shoot one of them risked shooting a horse as well. He'd been able to disperse them at least with the gun blast, but not before the horses had stampeded right toward the child who stood as though frozen in their path.

If only Barbe had been able to move more quickly, Frani might have been saved. But Barbe was a lumbering woman-child, heavy and slow to think of what she might do. She had made an effort, ambling forward, yelling, "Barbe help, Barbe help." And she had, her presence startling the horses off course. Her act pushed the wolves closer to Jean. But the last two horses didn't make the turn. They'd raced at the child as startled by seeing her, he imagined, as she was to be there in front of them.

The first knocked her down; the second trampled her, and even the soft, moist earth was not enough to save her. Barbe's efforts had fallen short. Jean's had too.

He squeezed Marie's hand, hoping the pressure of his skin to hers would keep her here a little while longer. He knew she'd disappear from him as she always did with a tragedy. She'd shed tears, many, many tears.

She'd comfort the grieving families, pat the backs of those she held. Even Joseph Gervais would let himself be comforted by Marie's arms, soon widening to take in Angelique, too. The three of them might stand in the rain while the heavens wept.

Then they'd go home where her hands would cook his meals, her body lie stiff beside him. Her lips would smile at his feeble efforts to make her laugh. But her eyes and her spirit would stay far away. It was her pattern, one in all the years with her he had not broken.

He'd been introduced to it when he first met her after years of separation. He'd won her over with the help of friends and time, but he never forgot how distant this woman could be even when he tasted berries on her lips or smelled sweet herbs from her hair spread on the goose-down pillow beside him. He hated those times, and a part of him feared that one day she might never come back. That she would go to a cave of concealment and just stay there, leaving him alone with the bones of her body. She hung on to something in the past and it wouldn't let her go—or she couldn't release it.

They rode home in silence, Barbe buried beneath a pile of furs, asleep in the back of the wagon, Knuck tucked into the folds. François had remained behind to talk with friends, or so he said. Jean couldn't tell which of the many friends he had might appeal to his son's interests that afternoon. It was good that someone could focus on love in the midst of grief.

Jean had rigged a kind of canopy top over the wagon seat. Ironwork held it up. He'd asked the Methodist Josiah Parrish to make it for him, the man being skilled as a blacksmith as well as a preacher. A forklike structure fit into holes at the end of the board seat, then rose up to hold bars shaped like an X that stretched over them. Around that X he'd tied the tanned hide. It didn't keep their knees from being wet, but at least rain didn't pour down onto their heads and their hats. They needed the canopy that night with the drizzling rain. He could remember times in December in Spokane country when no burial could occur because ten feet of snow covered the ground or the earth lay frozen too deep to dig. Here, on this prairie, burials were timely. Little Frani was dead only two days before being placed in the soggy ground. Nothing stopped for the rain.

He pushed up against the hide, forcing water to slide off and away from them. "Works pretty good, *n'est-ce pas?*" She looked at him, confusion in her eyes. "The canopy. It works. We can talk without the rain coming down into our throats." She nodded, patted his thigh with her hand, then turned back to stare out into that place she disappeared to that Jean couldn't visit.

He shook the ironwork. It felt firm. "Parrish is a good man," Jean said. "I guess he and Lee have...disagreements." Jean couldn't tell if she listened or not.

"People of faith shouldn't argue," Marie said.

"Maybe it's like a good marriage where even those who love the same thing disagree about how to show it. As we do sometimes, eh?" Silence. "The priests, they don't marry at all, but they argue, too, with the Methodists and each other."

Marie stared straight ahead, then said, "Do these men of faith listen only to each other or to the one they say they follow?"

She never failed to surprise him with the way she saw the world.

"Maybe Parrish wasn't meant to be a preacher. Only to work with iron. They go to the Clatsop country soon. Did you know this?" She looked at him now. "No? It's true. I tell him about Young's Bay, where you lived, and about Young's River. He already knows. They have a mission there." Jean looked at her, wondering if his idle chatter bothered her as much as the rain might. "I think he gets sent there, he and his sickly wife and three children."

"He has three children?" Marie turned to him.

"*Oui.* And they expect another. I don't think he would leave here. But he signs a petition that complains about Lee, and that one is recalled, back to the states now. And everything is closing down here now. Except for the school at Chemeketa. The Oregon Institute, he calls it."

"Frani might have gone there," Marie said.

"Joseph will send her to St. Joseph's." Then, realizing what he'd said, he added, "It's not your fault, my Marie." She patted his hand again, and he leaned into her, not wanting to let loose the reins. "Much of living is grieving, *n'est-ce pas?* If we are not faithful, we might wonder if God truly cares for us, *n'est-ce pas?*" Should he go further? "But he does."

Silence filled the wagon box. "I wish the blows did not sweep you away," he said. "The tragedies of others always haunt you, maybe more than your own."

"I'm here."

"This moment, *oui.* But you drift away like some wispy smoke up through the cook hole."

"I look for silence," she said.

"Bring it to me," he said. "What hurts you."

"My pain could burn you like a hungry fire," Marie said.

"It's that great?"

"A child lost is always a consuming flame."

Paul again. They rode without speaking for a time, the sounds of the horses' hooves in the mud breaking the evening still. He wondered if he should name the missing son as the fire she feared would consume them all.

"You have a stronger faith than mine," she said then. "It gets you through on steadier wings."

"I would lift you up beside me. You don't let me."

She looked up at him, her eyes like empty baskets. "You're beside me now," she said.

10

Protective Ash

1843

"Mrs. Whitman! You've forgotten your package." The man, a Methodist, Marie supposed, stepped out of the Institute door and gave a string-wrapped item to a woman as thin as a bonnet ribbon. Without her name being called, Marie would never have recognized her. She wouldn't have known her anyway, Marie suspected, with her memory playing hide-and-seek with her mind as it did, but there was little to remember in the face of this woman. Her husband had left her behind while she still grieved the loss of their daughter.

Her long pale neck had lines of age despite the white collar wrapped against it. The flair and flirt that Marie remembered no longer marked her carriage. Her eyes were chunks of coal inside a face as cold as gray snow.

Marie had heard that Narcissa Whitman awaited the return of her husband as a guest of Mrs. Lee while their husbands rode back East to save their missions and their good names. Then this past March, Lucy Lee, Jason Lee's second wife, had died. There'd been no word of the fate of the men.

Maybe Mrs. Whitman was teaching at the Oregon Institute to fill her time while waiting. There'd be more education for all the prairie's children now with the two new priests working at St. Joseph's College at St. Paul. Some of the French Canadian students attending the Oregon Institute could live closer to their homes—and their faith.

Mrs. Whitman accepted the package, then nodded to the man. She pulled her coat more tightly around her. She didn't smile. A cold wind fanned the wolf skin surrounding her face, and as she looked at Marie, her blue-gray eyes gazed right through her as though she weren't there.

Marie started to speak, but Mrs. Whitman brushed past her. Perhaps her memory, too, was confused so she didn't recognize a woman she'd once spent time with. Marie watched her walk toward the Lee House where the Methodists resided. Maybe Marie should follow her, ask what she knew about the Whitmans' gristmill fire that David Mongrain said her son was linked to. Maybe she should offer to sit with her as another mother who grieved a lost child; as a woman whom death seemed to follow. But nothing in the woman's manner and nothing in her face invited that. Marie understood that face.

"So will they come to French Prairie?" Marianne asked.

"A few might," David said. "But most are looking near Tuality Plains, on the west side of the Willamette River. Some Red River people ended up there. Good meadows and forests, too."

"They've had a hard time of it, the women especially, from what I hear," François said.

"Women always do," Marianne said. She set thick slices of pork on the plates before her husband and her brother. "And we're supposed to keep our mouths closed about it and suffer in silence. That's a truth."

"Not something I can imagine you ever doing," her brother said.

She looked at her husband, wondered if he'd defend her, but he had busied himself with the tub of butter.

She set the mugs and the pink-flowered plates on the plank table David had built. She remembered once seeing a table at Fort Walla Walla arranged for some dignitary, the dishes composed of all the same pattern. Variety was much more extolling.

"I've never trusted the Company the way Papa did," François continued, "so I could have told you there'd be trouble. It wasn't farming country, and they wouldn't let them take the increase from their cattle. They were never going to get ahead there, so close to the cold ocean winds in that Nisqually country. Of course they'd have to leave."

"The Company treated us well," David said. "And my father."

He defends McLoughlin but not me.

"The Company supported them as they could too," David continued. "The Red River people signed agreements, not like the Americans who just came on their own."

"Such independent people won't likely form together in a government then," Marianne said.

"Bad agreements should be broken," François said. He stepped right over his sister's words. "They even charged them for the oxen that died while they tried to plow that rocky soil so they could attempt to plant wheat. The Company almost starved them while the fort's stores were full." Her brother could sound so angry over things that didn't really matter.

"Oh well, it isn't happening to us," Marianne said. She heard her son whimper, and she moved to the back of house. Everything men talked about led to disagreements. Her brother could be as grumpy as her father, sometimes.

Always tension. First the Americans arriving in a loose kind of wagon train last fall had everyone stirred. Their presence caused people to rally and find supplies for them, though most had decided to settle together near the falls at Oregon City. Here they were, Americans, and they built on land claimed by a Britisher beside water Indians had fished in for years. Now this British group, part of the Red River train that had come earlier and gone north to Puget Sound, moved south. The French Canadians were troubled by whether they'd come to their prairie and whether they'd be loyal to the British or to the Americans, and where would they worship, at St. Paul's or at the Methodists? David said men like his father had petitioned the priests to come, and even John McLoughlin of the Company had approved that and provided escorts, though many of his officers were Episcopalians.

She couldn't keep it straight. All this splintering over property and religion and the ownership of cows and plows. Conversations swirled like muddy water, and she didn't believe men could leave such issues alone. She had no hope there'd ever be a time when they'd all see things as clear as David's tears.

She leaned over her sleeping child. In the middle of these arguments and interests lived the children. And the women. And the Indians.

Maybe even those of mixed blood lived in the middle. She hadn't thought of that. Maybe all of this was happening to her and not just to people "out there" somewhere.

She and David were both mixed blood, and their children...what would their children be with all these degrees of blood swirling in their veins? Even more important, what could she do to prepare them for all this confusion and uncertainty? Those Red River mothers hadn't expected their children might starve. Didn't mothers always hope to do the right thing?

It was a mother's job after all, to prepare her children for life's unknowns.

"Sweet Baby, I've just had a thought that sounds like something my mother would think," Marianne whispered. "I'll have to remember it so I can tell her. A mother's job is to prepare her children for life's unknowns. A mother's job is to prepare her children for life's unknowns." The baby smiled up at her and kicked his feet. "Of course, I don't know how to do that," she told him. "I'll ask Mama." Marianne smiled at her son. "She'll like my asking. She'll see it's a sign that I take you seriously, if nothing else."

She propped Joseph then, so he could sit up surrounded by rolls of warm furs for balance, and she repeated the phrase to herself.

"We could make mortar," David said. They were on to some other project.

"Only if the Company lowers the price of coral coming in from the Sandwich Islands," François said. "And you can doubt they'll ever do that."

They still argue?

"Finish eating," Marianne said.

Her voice must have startled the baby, who cried out, a sound that brought David immediately to his side. He picked his six-month-old son up and folded one arm over the baby's chest while he turned him as he sat, the baby's legs straddling his father's knee. David slurped his soup while Joseph clapped his hands together and rocked forward, nearly bumping his head but stopping just before he did.

"See that? *L'enfant* is brilliant, *n'est-ce pas?* He applauds his mother's soup."

"A diplomat in the making," François said. "He knows the ladies need to be noticed."

Marianne frowned at her brother. Joseph had begun to fuss. He really did seem to be aware of the pulse of the people around him, his own irritation going up with the rise of a voice, the quick look of judgment sent from one person to another. When her mother had told her that once, she'd laughed. A baby couldn't be so wise as that.

But maybe her baby could be. Would she be wise enough to teach him?

"Have you seen any more wolves?" she asked François. When she saw David wince, she wished she hadn't brought the subject up. Of course, she shouldn't have, not with the wolves being the cause of his little sister's death. Maybe François would know enough to skip over it or ignore her as he often did.

"Dozens." François finished chewing the corn bread stuffed into the side of his cheek then answered. "We're keeping the horses up because they run 'em otherwise, and Papa and Archange and me are rotating guard at night."

"My father says we need a bounty on them," David said quietly. "Maybe that way we'll rid ourselves of the damage they do."

"That's a ruse for forming a government," François said. "Next thing they'll want to tax us so we can pay the bounty. Then there'll be collectors for the tax and then enforcement for those who don't pay. It's all a plan. We don't need a government. We're doing all right with just ourselves here. We'll take the wolves out, one at a time."

"There'll be a meeting next week to talk of it."

"Who calls it?" Marianne asked.

"One of the Methodists. They meet at the old Mission Bottom so there'll be enough room for everyone."

"It's a ploy," François said.

"But they have large herds of sheep. I'm sure they've lost any number to wolves," Marianne said. "They must be wanting a way to control them."

"Father Blanchet resigned and never called another government meeting because he knew what this was, about taking away how we work together as a community, we French Canadians. We former Astorians—"

"You were never an Astorian," Marianne said.

"Papa and Mama were both Astorians; they both tell the stories about doing better when they did it on their own, without interference."

Joseph's fussiness rose like hot air, and Marianne lifted him from David's arms. She held him close, facing away from her, patting the top of his thighs in a gentle rhythm. It sometimes calmed him. A change didn't always distress; it sometimes brought ease.

"Will Papa attend, even if Father Blanchet doesn't?"

"I know my father will," David said. "It's about wolves. Some things really are just what they seem, François."

"Nothing is what it seems," François said. "I'm learning that."

⌖

"Did you remember?" Marie asked the catechist.

David Mongrain shook his head. "No," he said. "My poor brain. I wasn't sure the name was even Dorion, if you recall. I thought it might be DeRoin, and it could have been something totally different. Names get changed here in this country." He tapped his finger at his temple. "Brains get changed too. Too many things stuffed into them sometimes. Little things just squeeze their way out. Sometimes we push them out." He smiled at her. "I'm sorry that what I said led to your thinking of it for so long."

Marie nodded. "It's my choice to let the words spill over my rocky brain without finding an outlet."

David Mongrain smiled at her. "I do like the way you put things, Madame Dorion…Toupin," he corrected when she lifted an eyebrow. "See, I forget still such things as you've told me. You are learning more words, Chinook words; you will share with me, yes? And you've brought more plants?"

"I hope to learn more English words, too. Our French makes it hard for newcomers to understand us," she said. "Words bring people together and they separate them. My husband says this."

"*Oui,* this is an interpreter's learning," Mongrain said. "Words help us know things we didn't realize we knew, and they can keep some things separated and forgotten in our minds."

Marie furrowed her brow. It felt good not to have Barbe along with her every time she studied with Mongrain. These required concentration, less worry over what Barbe might do or say. She'd brought the girl the first few visits, but Barbe had rocked back and forth and turned her head this way, left the bench, walked around until Marie found she couldn't concentrate at all on what Mongrain told her. Barbe learned by doing, not by listening. David Mongrain taught with words.

With Barbe at home, she and David Mongrain could speak together like old friends, then, the way she once spoke with her Sarahs, Eliza Spalding, even with Sacagawea. What David Mongrain said during these lessons made her reach further. "I do not understand this," she said then. "How can we know something but yet not know it?"

"Something learned as a child, perhaps. A lesson taught us by a parent that we've forgotten. Maybe the lesson caused such pain for us, we don't want to remember the day we were forced to learn it."

"Then it is not learned."

"I think it is. It affects us still. We simply stuff it like a sausage, then forget what spices we put in it that still upset our stomachs."

She tried to remember something she wanted to forget. *The times Pierre struck me.* She had wanted to forget that, and yet she hadn't. She remembered it well, the shame of it, the outrage, and her not being powerful enough to stop him until that one time...and then not because she thought she should for herself, but because she knew she must, for the sake of her sons. She couldn't tell David Mongrain about that, though. It was a woman's churning, something only a woman would understand.

"We forget so the pain stays away, the way you said to scrub house ashes into my cracked hands." He turned his hands over to show her the smoothness. "As long as I use the ash, my hands have no cracks."

"Marguerite's father had deep cuts he would sew up in the winter. I learned later that the ash would help, better than the skunk oil," she said.

"But if I stop using it, then they return. The ash is like memory, protecting."

She felt her heart throbbing at the side of her head, tempered by flickers of light. She didn't hear what he said next.

"Are you all right, Madame Toupin?" He leaned close but didn't touch her. "Perhaps we should begin the Ladder stories."

A story called to her, her story. And yet she'd put that story to rest, learned the lesson from it. A woman's story not easily shared with a man. Maybe with this man she could…

"Let me tell you first," Marie said. "A long time ago, my mother told me to stay, to take care of my sister. I didn't want her to leave us, but she'd run for help. She burned with sickness, both of them. I should have gone instead of my mother. I should have listened to my sister, who wanted to follow her. I didn't do either one."

"What happened?"

"My mother died. So did my sister."

"Tragic," David Mongrain said. "The pox?" Marie nodded. David touched his fingers to his own pocked face. Marie dropped her eyes. "So many died of it. And other diseases. Even here on this lovely prairie, I would imagine. Your Barbe is an orphan, yes?" He remained silent, and she was aware that he probably stared at her, but she kept her eyes lowered, out of respect, out of fear that he might see into the emptiness of her shameful soul.

"How old were you?" he said.

"Maybe seven winters, maybe older. Old enough to know I didn't want to stay."

"But you obeyed."

"I obeyed, yet they both died."

She wasn't aware of how long she sat remembering what she'd forgotten, and yet she had remembered this too, had told Jean the story, and Sarah. David Mongrain said, "Frani Gervais, your granddaughter's friend. She was about your age when this happened?"

"Such a tragic thing, a child dying."

"Yet she disobeyed, wandered away from where she was supposed to be, yes?

"I should have gone out to the chicken house with her," Marie said. "I should have protected her."

"Do you think she behaved badly, this child?"

"No, no. She was a good girl, exploring, seeking her own way."

"And you, you were also this kind of child. One wanting to do things her way, the way you thought best. You didn't disappoint your mother, I'm sure of this. That your mother died and your sister, too, doesn't mean you failed them, Madame Toupin, or that you were the cause of their dying." She stared at him.

Mongrain's face had a dark shadow of beard that made him look tired, but his voice was firm and strong. "A child blazes a trail she changes along the way. She learns, crawls over obstacles, jumps across streams, begins again, but she is never at the same place along the path. A young child doesn't wear dishonor for having chosen to obey. You need not carry the weight of their dying. It was not Frani's fault she stood where the horses ran from the wolves."

"If I had done what I wanted, maybe my sister—"

"It would be good to remember this in a new way." He tapped his finger on his lip as he thought. "Let the words change your memory. You can find honor in the little girl who wanted to save her mother and her sister. You can forgive the child who went seeking and faced obstacles."

"Father Blanchet said my wrongs were all forgiven."

"He's wise, you know this. There would have been obstacles no matter what route you chose. You learned to be strong, yes? Your ability to survive Hunt's journey when many died, keeping your sons alive after your husband was killed, this strength came out of that same little girl. You can remember her now. Put your arms around the child who was too young to have caused the death the pox must take credit for. Remember new things."

"My heart knowing, my memory is fluid as a river," Marie said. "It seeks its own level through a people and a place."

"And a time. It brings things to the surface when it's ready," Mongrain told her.

"Often when something floods it over."

"Then, too," David Mongrain told her.

"Why not us?" Marianne said. "Why aren't we allowed?"

"We're married women," Julie Gervais said. "Our place is with our families."

"Washing clothes," Marianne said.

"Washing clothes," Julie answered.

Both women stood beside the black pot, their sticks still steaming from the boiling water where they'd placed their clothes. David had shook his head as though she was a wobbly woman when she told him she would lug the baby and their clothes to his sister's home where the two would wash clothes together.

It made the drudgery a joy. Well, not a joy exactly, but at least inventive. She liked seeing that Julie patched poorly too, and that some of the pants of her husband had been worn enough times before washing they could stand by themselves and salute. She could see that Isadore, Julie's son, still didn't have all his teeth, though she knew most children almost two usually did.

"But isn't that the whole point? How will we raise our babies to be good men if they have mothers who are kept in the dark?" Marianne said.

"I thought you could read a little."

"A little French. Very little. And I write even less. I can't even make up the supply list for David without drawing little pictures of things to tell him what we need."

"I do that too," Julie said, and the women laughed.

They lifted the steaming clothes from one pot, then doused them into another. They'd bring more water up from the well, boil it, then rinse the clothes again until the wash water ran clear. When they finished, they'd lay the clothes over the ropes strung from an oak tree to a peg Julie's husband had pounded into the side of their house. They had several loads to do before reaching that finishing place.

Marianne scanned the grassy area where they'd set their boys, Isadore tied with a long rope around his middle and the other end to a tree to keep him from stepping underfoot near the hot washtubs. Joseph would be up and running before long. He approached his first birthday.

Julie's voice took on a serious tone while she swirled the cloth, the rhythm of her words like music to Marianne's ears. "As long as a mother knows where to get answers, she doesn't need to know all things herself."

"But think of how wise our sons would be if we could read what the provincial government papers really say," Marianne said. "We always have to accept what the men tell us. David says it's all in English, that a man named LeBreton is the clerk who took it all down, but he's an American. And they selected an American for governor. A Methodist. Don't you think it's in our interest to know what these foreigners are thinking?"

"Papa says they explicitly spoke of fair treatment for the Indians," Julie said.

"We're not Indians," Marianne said.

"Some say so," Julie said.

"That's my point. How do we know what people say, or anything else? Unless we can read it, we have to take a man's word for it."

"Or a woman who can read."

"I don't know any. Do you?" Marianne asked.

"Not personally," Julie said.

"The Methodist women can. They teach at their school, and girls can go there."

"Young girls. But none our age. And they teach them sewing more than English. We'd be college age, but we can't even go to St. Joseph's College. Just boys can." Marianne smacked her lips. "Divine madness, giving only half of the set of future parents the tools to teach children."

"Our mothers did well without knowing how to read or write. And they lived in troubled times. Your mother still lives, and she's highly regarded. My father says that of her often. 'Inherently intelligent.'"

Marianne frowned. "What's in my mother's hair that makes her intelligent?"

Julie laughed. "You're mixing English and French," she said. "*Inhérent* is something she is born with."

"But our mothers weren't wondering what would happen when their children knew more than they did. And that's what will happen, Julie. Our sons will know more than we do because they'll go to school and we'll be…set aside. They'll look down on us as less worthy than their fathers."

"Your older brother, Baptiste, he can read."

"And he and my mother, they…argued. For a long time, we didn't see him. Maybe he looked down on her. He learned to read when they lived in Okanogan, and his brother Paul, too. He disappeared. See, how children and parents disagree? My mother had a friend, the wife of a factor, who gave lessons. Marguerite showed me a few words she learned, but I have to find them written somewhere and recognize them. I can't produce them myself."

"It's the way it is," Julie said. "We just have to accept it."

"*Non.* Your father didn't accept that he would live where there were no priests, so he petitioned to get them to come here. Twice. And the Americans didn't accept that this was a grand *French* Prairie. They came to make it a prairie with different names, their own. Then they didn't accept that we'd done fine living here without a government from America, so now we have a provisional government, Julie. Our children will not grow up in the same world we did."

"The Champoeg vote came close, fifty against and fifty-two in favor. I don't know if this push for an American territory is strong enough. Things could change again."

"They will. Which is why we should be ready. We need to arm ourselves and our sons. With words."

"No. We need to get fresh water to rinse with."

They leaned their sticks against the house, noticed that Joseph had pulled himself up against the tree where Isadore stood. Both poked little fingers into the bark as they gripped, their bottoms naked in the hot July shade.

"Should we wait until they nap? I wouldn't want Joseph to crawl over this way and try to pull up on the wash pots," Julie said.

Marianne paused. "I don't think they could push it or pull it over. Besides, Joseph falls flat on his nose every time he tries to kneel into a crawl." Julie laughed. "I think they'll be all right. If we hurry."

"Stay there," Julie told the boys as both girls lifted their dresses so they could move more quickly to the stream. "We're taking a young girl in," Julie said as they fast-walked. "She'll help me out with the children. She has maybe thirteen summers and wants to be baptized. Will you be her godmother? She has your same name, Marie Anne."

They lugged the bucket full of water up onto the sloping bank then, on either side. "That's not how I say it," Marianne said. "But it would sound more like my mother's name, wouldn't it?" She lifted the handle with Julie, and they started back toward the washtubs and the boys. "Next time, let's build the fires closer to the stream, so we don't have to drag it so far.

"But I like working in the shade—oh, look!" Julie pointed. "He isn't walking or crawling toward the tubs. Your Joseph is rolling."

They set the bucket down, and Marianne ran forward, swooping her rolling son up into her arms. "No you don't," she said. "I'm going to watch you like an owl." She buried her face in his sweaty body as he giggled.

She set him back by the tree, then ran to help Julie. By the time they had the new bucket of water poured into the pot, Joseph had rolled to within feet of her again.

"You won't have a moment of peace now," Julie said. "He'll be following you wherever you go unless you rope him up. You'll need a Marie Anne to help you, too."

They gave the boys balls of tied leather to play with while they finished their laundering work. The line of clothes dipped low with the weight of two families' clean linens and shirts.

"Joseph's given me an idea," Marianne said as she stood, her hands on her hips. "He skipped crawling and is rolling instead. He'll learn to walk in some different way. I can do that too."

"Marianne, what are you thinking of?"

"Just you wait. More than one Gervais can be involved in a campaign of change."

They came like leaves that fall, drifting down the trail overland from Oregon City, past La Butte, and south onto the prairie. All shapes and ages and sizes they came, with sounds to their words that reminded Jean of John Day, the Virginian. All Americans. All from back East. Nine hundred men and women and dozens of children, in wagons this time, not just carts loaded with the lightest tools their mules or oxen could haul along with the few family treasures the women cried hardest to keep. Jean told Marie of their coming, and that this was too many and too late, it already being December, for them to winter in Oregon City. They'd be offering refuge, he told her, and he made it sound as though it had always been his intent.

Marie perked up when asked to help others. She'd been missing that cause of late. Barbe worked a piece of leather, punching designs into pieces of hide she'd give to François for his saddle. She helped with the food and laundry and didn't take nearly so much time to remember things he asked her to do. "Stay home," she'd told Marie once as his wife prepared to go to David Mongrain's class. He guessed the subjects were getting too hard for Barbe to follow.

She was good help, Barbe was, and would be for people arriving right here. It would be pleasing to his wife and to himself, too, to talk and hear the news from others' points of view. Now that they had a government, there was always something a man should be made aware of. François certainly had his opinions, but Jean thought they lacked perspective; the boy staring so long into his own pond he couldn't tell it was still pretty shallow.

In addition, Josiah Parrish's move or exile to the Clatsop Plains had meant he had little opportunity to use his English. He didn't want to lose his skill, especially not now, with so many Americans arriving. And without Baptiste around, Jean found he heard little gossip from the Cayuse world, either. Maybe that was good. He didn't understand the turmoil that painted every tipi he'd ever entered. Some people thrived on stories of trouble. Josette stayed calmer than most Cayuse he'd met, but even his Marie carried a certain level of discordant swirl to her life that she rarely let settle. A man needed to keep aware of his neighbor's troubles, but so he could be prepared for how they might turn into his own. He guessed maybe that worry fired up the Indian talk.

Things going so smoothly on his own farm might make a man defend his ease, forget how his peace still depended upon strong threads spun among his neighbors, threads he didn't even make but were given him as gifts.

On a late December morning, with low hanging clouds coloring the day pewter, Marie and Jean fed a family named Waldo a breakfast. Barbe and François headed out to milk cows.

Mrs. Waldo's eyes teared when Marie handed her an egg. She started to refuse it. "I can't pay," she said.

"Not necessary," Jean answered, speaking the English words distinctly so Marie might understand them too. "Just pass the kindness on to someone else," Jean said, repeating it in French for Marie. "You're welcome to stay a day or two," he told them. "While you find what you're looking for."

Marie nodded her approval, and Jean winked at her. He loved to see her eyes twinkle.

"How come you settled so far south of the others of your kind?" Daniel Waldo asked. "You're closer to the Methodists from what I can tell than you are to the church at St. Paul. You're Catholic, right?"

"This is our wintering place," Jean said. He liked being able to claim two pieces of land. "We've another place on a little lake, a slough really, closer to the Willamette River. And to kin. Hunting's better here. My wife had spent a little time with the Astorian group, and we've friends closer to the Willamette. Spend summers that way. I'm of that Astor myself, but never made it up these streams. And the people here, the Indian people, the Molalla, they're friendly, or have been to us."

"Well, that's good to know," Waldo said.

"They're cousins to the Cayuse. My wife's grandchildren are Cayuse."

Waldo wrinkled his nose, and Jean felt his face grow warm. The man took food from Jean's wife, his Indian wife, but when he realized she had Indian blood, he wrinkles up his nose?

"Those are the ones protesting Whitman's place," Waldo said.

"Can't say as I blame them over that. That Whitman traveled with us coming back on our train. Expected special treatment. Only had a ham to eat from, and after it was gone, we all rotated feeding him. He lied to me too. Said I should leave my cows at Waiilatpu because there wasn't any grass beyond his place, but we found some of the best grass I've ever seen just a few days west. And these cows are worth twice what he said they'd be worth. Now I see your cows, no offense, but mine will give three times the milk your Spanish ones will. And they're not so wild. My wealth went up in a bovine minute."

"We worked hard for our cows," Jean defended.

"We got to meet his wife," Mrs. Waldo said. "Mrs. Whitman has a lovely voice. She met her husband at Fort Walla Walla, all nicely rebuilt after the fire. She didn't look well, almost as thin as some of us and hadn't even crossed the mountains."

Waldo ate a hard-boiled egg now, too, while he stood at the door looking out across Jean's fields. Low clouds danced with the mist from the creek. "Good land," he said. He turned back, then, "You say your wife came here with Astor?"

"That she did. Well, with Hunt's party, as I did, eh?"

"Only one woman came across with Hunt," Mrs. Waldo said. "We read Irving's book, before we started out. Scared me half to death, all the tragedy they faced. She lost a baby." She turned to look at Marie. Jean translated what Mrs. Waldo just said.

"Traveling out here was my best time, Whitman not withstanding," Waldo said. "I was sickly in Missouri, living my life like a scoured calf. Isn't that right, Mother?" Mrs. Waldo nodded, returned her gaze to Marie. "Look at me now." He pounded his chest. "Trail over the mountains made me whole."

"Then, is that, I mean, are you, that woman?" Mrs. Waldo asked. "Madame Dorion?"

But Waldo said, "Whitman acquired a pair of spectacles for her. Like yours, Mrs. Dorion.

"Toupin," Jean corrected.

"He said her eyes were going bad."

"I thought that sweet of him," Mrs. Waldo said.

"Then he left them on a rock and remembered days later and actually tried to get the wagon master, Peter Burnet, to send someone back. Whitman doesn't think well, you ask me," Waldo said. "Got all fussed that some Indians met us with grain before we got to his place, said they were competing with him. A scrappy fellow Whitman called...Dorion pushed his woman at us with her load of wheat. Kind of an odd-looking fellow. Short with long hair. His wife had a whole passel of kids with her. Same name as the Hunt interpreter."

"My wife's son and his family are there. He travels with White. I don't think they raise wheat," Jean said.

"Pretty sure that was the name used. Dorion. Like in the Irving book."

Jean translated for Marie, and her eyes took on an icy glaze.

"Made me wonder what Whitman was doing the most of, tilling for souls like he was supposed to be or farming for riches like he seems to be."

After the Waldos moved on down the trail, Jean walked to the well he and François had dug their first summer at this more southern site. The cabin needed work, but the privacy made up for it. Barbe, François, and Archange stood by the shed, getting ready to grain the horses. Jean lowered himself down the ladder into the level cooling space where they kept meat and milk. A bucket could extend down into the pool of water, but this level worked as a cave pantry almost. Jean imagined it to be like the inside of a beaver lodge, water around, but a high dry place inside.

He picked up a ham, checked its weight. He remembered the day they'd butchered the hogs. All the family helped. They'd eaten well in the evening. Good food would settle his stomach and his thinking.

As he climbed back out, Marie met him. He knew she'd be there.

"Maybe Paul has come back," Marie said. "These Waldos, they mention a Dorion. They don't describe Baptiste. Someone else."

"Josette's family might be raising wheat to sell to overlanders," Jean said. "Pretty enterprising, that Josette."

"*Non.* These people remember the name. They read it in a book they say. They remember. It does not sound like Baptiste's family. We should go."

"Why do you want to go and scuttle up that old ash, after all these years?"

"A mother's love for her son never burns out. We should go to Waiilatpu."

"Not a good time of year for traveling there. Snow could come early," Jean said, though he knew weather would never set his wife off.

11

The Anxious Chair

1844

Barbe's skin lesions kept them wintering inside the small cabin at the southern end of the prairie with no chance to follow Waldo's story, which Marie felt sure included Paul. Marie wasn't sure what caused the sores, and the girl couldn't point out any plant she might have eaten or touched that brought them. Smaller wounds became infected, and Barbe found comfort under a thin blanket while she lay close to the fire. Barbe didn't complain, though she scratched at the sores even with the salves Marie made up to relieve the girl's discomfort. Marie thought the mixtures should work better than they did, and she wondered more than once if she might have forgotten some portion of the concoction. She went over the ingredients in her mind, first trying an elderberry wash followed by alumroot she'd pulled from a rocky place and dried when they were at Walla Walla. Even the slender sage leaves didn't do much to relieve the blotches. Perhaps she had forgotten, not needing to use the information for so long. Another thing to add to her list of lost thoughts.

They had plenty of game to meet the needs of the three of them, the only ones to winter south. François chose the Labiche site closer to the Frenchies. Together, he and Archange tended the larger herd of horses and their cows. "I will do this as a husband one day," he told them. "I can begin to do this now." Marie suspected he didn't like being cooped up with Barbe, who wanted endless stories told to her, stood too close, and still talked with food in her mouth despite Marie's efforts to teach her otherwise. François tired of Barbe's interruptions and clapped hands of joy.

Marie watched her son ride off. Wasn't it a goal to raise a child to independence, to want him to leave his parents and do things on his own? She'd sent Baptiste off earlier than she thought wise, but he had found his way. And her girls, they'd propelled themselves like maple seeds weighted to her and yet winged toward families of their own. They'd launched all her children one way or another. Still, Marie found herself wondering every morning over one whose face no longer appeared for her to touch in love, a face she wasn't sure she remembered.

Jean hunted and "looked after his women," as he called it. As Barbe slowly healed, Marie wove strands of cedar into capes and baskets in between lifting Barbe's head to drink the sage tea she brewed. Barbe needed her. Barbe might be a child who would never leave, who would never need to be launched.

The occasional encounters with Molalla or Klamath Indians proved peaceful enough once they made the family connection of Josette's Cayuse tribe. The braves traveling through shared little news that might distress nor bring comfort, either. They squatted around a firepit and smoked with Jean, motioning with their hands of where deer and elk could be most easily found. Jean said it was a perfect time, a perfect peace, his only regret being they did not make the trek to St. Paul for Mass for most of the rainy winter months.

"No place, even so remote as this, offers isolation," Marie told Jean when he boasted that no more bad news would reach them this winter, no more stories of new American settlers disturbing the prairie's peace. "My peace has already been torn," she told him.

Jean nodded. *"Oui."*

"If Barbe had not taken ill—"

"You would have insisted we go to Waiilatpu, I know this," Jean said.

"I accept what is," Marie said. "If Paul was there, he will still be there in the spring. He would not be foolish like Whitman and set out in the winter months to go back East."

"It is only a story, Marie. From an overlander, someone we don't even know, who doesn't even have a good ear for the language, eh? Who knows what he heard as 'Dorion'? Someone might have been speaking of the stars, of Orion, eh?" He smiled at her and pulled her against him with his good arm.

"All stories have some kernel of truth to them, even those spoken by Americans," she said.

❖

"Does mother know you're here?" Marguerite said when she opened the door to her half-brother.

The spring air held the scent of a well-kept root cellar, a moist earthiness wed to decay.

"I come here first," Baptiste said.

"*Oui.* JB will be pleased when he returns. He traps. My husband keeps busy," she said, aware that she chattered, filling in spaces. She had soap to make, mending to tend to. She didn't want her brother judging her a lazy mother with so many unfinished things so obviously lying about. "JB is gone long days, but he would want you to stay here. Where's Josette?" She looked behind her brother. "You came alone?"

From the side of the barn then she saw Josette with their brood of children she pushed before her, one on her back, another she carried in her arms. His children carried bulging *shaptakai.* Denise and Pierre strained with the weight.

Baptiste might have assisted, Marguerite thought, reaching out to help lift their leather satchels and invite them into the house.

Inside, cousins eyed each other. Denise stood most bravely in front of her mother while nine-year-old Pierre peeked out from behind his father and cast shy glances toward JB's two sons. Josette eased the toddler, Genevieve, off her back and set her on the floor. She pulled herself up onto her mother's skirts, a fistful of hemline fringe now stuck into her mouth. The room took on the scent of smoked leather from their clothing and painted satchels plopped on the floor like stuffed, oversized letters.

Baptiste's children, tall and with skin the color of acorns, were handsome but appeared...*obtus* was the word that came to Marguerite's mind. *What is the English word?* When anxious or excited, her words formed more easily in French, her first language, her father's language.

Obtus. Dull, without the sparkle of a child whose body and soul were well fed. Dark circles surrounded Josette's eyes too.

Marguerite scurried her stepson off his chair so Josette could sit down, ignoring the boy's scowl. The boy thought himself the man of the house when JB left, and men weren't told by a woman, any woman, what to do. "My husband's sons don't always think of what others need," Marguerite said. "I apologize for them. *Pardon*." With a section of tanned hide, she brushed the plank chair of a thin layer of spring dust.

"I can ask to sit," Josette said. "I don't expect a boy to know my thoughts."

"You expect men to know them," Baptiste said.

"Boys," Marguerite said, "go out and tend to their horses. Brush them down good and bring in potatoes from the well pantry when you're finished."

Her boys hesitated. "Come," Baptiste told JB's sons. "You, too, Pierre. We men will go together to get peace."

Marguerite watched them through the window. Her half-brother was a handsome man. He held his tall hat against the March winds lifting oak leaves into a swirl. He towered over JB's sons while he gave orders and then boxed their ears with a gentle touch when they ran back toward him, letting the wind spin them around. The boys laughed loud enough she could hear them inside.

"They enjoy themselves," Marguerite said.

"They get to know their cousins. *That* will be good," Josette said.

Marguerite thought to pursue her sister-in-law's mood but said instead, "It'll be good to have you close again. You plan to stay, *oui?*"

Josette nodded. "JB's boys are willing helpers," she said.

"For some," Marguerite said. "I'm surprised you came here instead of going to Mother's. Not that I don't want you here, I do. I'm just...curious." Marguerite unwrapped the scarf draped around Denise's head as she talked and moved to heat up water for tea.

"They have Barbe staying there, and we would add too many." Something in her voice made Marguerite turn to look. There were never too many people at her mother's house, never too many at Josette's either.

"Mother loves the gathering of the clan, as she calls it," Marguerite said. "I'm sure she'd—"

"Baptiste can tell you," Josette said. "When he chooses."

"We'll have a feast here, then," Marguerite said, making her voice light. "And sing welcoming songs here, yes girls? But you should sit, Josette," she said. "You look so tired."

Her sister-in-law sank onto the plank chair then, holding her youngest, David, in her arms. She wore her hair in two braids that rested on her breast. She'd chalked the part into a perfect white line in that tidy way she had. But her eyes drooped and lacked their familiar light. The boy was but a month old, from the size of him; but his eyes followed Marguerite as she moved in the room, making her think he was older.

She's having too many children too quickly.

"We came for the baptism," Josette said. She smiled then for the first time since she'd arrived. Her baby looked up at her with wide eyes and yawned. "We'll ask Marianne to be his godmother."

Marguerite felt a pain beneath her heart. She had no time to consider its source, as Xavier, her son, who'd been hiding under the table with the arrival of the Dorion family, crawled out now, scampered across the room. "He hides when he gets…*angoisse.* Nervous. Anxious," Marguerite said in English.

Josette held her hand out to set his distance from the baby. A tall child at two, Xavier stared at Josette's baby, then touched the tiny shells that hung from the board's brace over the child's head. They made a tinkling sound, and he turned to his mother and laughed. "Yes," Marguerite said. "Music. To entertain the baby while he's in his board." Xavier cast his eyes toward the music box perched on its own table. *"Oui,"* Marguerite said. "That's music too."

She hoped she didn't look prideful, but it was good to see that her child made connections with the words. He understood so much. To Josette she said, "I've missed you. Now I'll have a wise mother under my own roof to ask questions of."

"The invaders don't stay with you?"

"Invaders? Oh, the emigrants you mean. Only for a short time," Marguerite said. "Some went back already to get their wagons they left at Dalles City and even farther, at Walla Walla. A few actually brought wagons over the mountains. Imagine. Floated others down the Columbia, too."

"More will come," Josette said.

"Yes, and they bring their own ways, make all kinds of changes. There's even a passenger boat now between Champoeg and a landing south. It takes people up and back to Vancouver, just anyone who wants to go. For the price of salt or tea."

"Your child does well," Josette said, nodding toward Xavier, who continued to respect a safe distance from the infant.

Marguerite felt her face grow warm. Father Blanchet said that pride went before a fall, but this was just an acknowledgment of a son's uniqueness, wasn't it?

"He's a handsome boy, isn't he?" Marguerite said. "*Ingénieux*, too. Already he knows English words as well as French."

"He's clever," Josette said. "Needed to survive these changes."

Baptiste walked in then, carrying dried wood for the fireplace. "The wind brings up a chill," he said.

"Sit, Mother," Doublé said. "You look tired." JB's youngest son pushed a stool toward Marguerite.

"I didn't see you come in." *He is so secretive.* "You were told to tend the horses with your brother."

"I brought potatoes in," Doublé said. He needed a haircut. His dark curls hung loose nearly over his eyes so she could barely see them. He hid from her, that's what he did. The curls bounced as he nodded toward the basket now full beside the door.

"Cut them up, then," Marguerite said. She turned back to Josette. "He doesn't—"

"Sister," Baptiste interrupted. "That's women's work." He nodded to Denise. "Help your other mother," he told her as Denise slipped between Josette and Marguerite and began scrubbing the potatoes.

Doublé stepped away from her. He looked at Marguerite, then back to Baptiste.

"I'll help," he said and reached for his waist knife just as Denise reached for hers.

Xavier took that moment to notice Josette's toddler, who had ventured at last away from her mother's skirts. Xavier strode across the floor, his small chest thrust outward. Marguerite beamed with the child's confident walk.

With both hands to little Genevieve's shoulder, he pushed her to the floor.

The child plopped, her eyes surprised, and for a moment all in the room stared at her. Josette said, "Being clever is good. But *ingénieux* without kindness is dangerous."

"A terrible cough," Baptiste said when Marguerite asked later why they'd left Waiilatpu. The boys were in their loft beds, Pierre and Denise and even Genevieve were rolled onto a fur mat beside them. Marguerite could hear chattering, but she said nothing. They'd quiet down soon enough. Xavier stayed awake, bringing objects to her she gave the names of in between her conversations with Baptiste and Josette. Baby David slept propped in his board beside the hearth. A log snapped, and he startled but returned to sleep.

"The cough kills quickly, though not every one. Mostly old people or the very young. Babies. They're not sure how it spreads. They bark like Sitka seals," Baptiste said, "and think their insides will come out. We wanted to be free of it." Marguerite looked at the baby breathing easily, then at her own young son standing sturdy and tall.

"We have no cough. We should be all right," Josette said. "There are other reasons we returned."

"Bowl," Marguerite told Xavier in English when he shoved the latest object under her nose. "You know that one." He turned to get something else.

"Josette doesn't like her baby to be around Barbe, either," Baptiste said.

"She's been good," Marguerite told them. "I wish I had such help."

"She's good if she's watched," Josette said. "She doesn't know when she startles a baby. She flaps her hands by her face if the baby cries too hard. Genevieve would cry when she came near. Barbe wanted to hold her, then pushed her away if she didn't quiet. Would you leave her alone with your child?"

Marguerite thought for a moment. *"Non."*

"We'll see Mother," Baptiste said. "I want her views on some things."

Marguerite smiled. "Mother tells me when I ask her opinion that the giving of advice is like an unveiling for the person asked. She doesn't reveal much."

"She did to me," Baptiste said.

"Orders. She gave you orders," Josette said.

"That I didn't disobey." He blinked quickly, and Marguerite wondered what he might have done. She knew he'd stayed away from their home for a long time when she was little, and only in the years since they'd moved to this French Prairie area had the separation between mother and son been bridged.

"Advice is different," Josette said. "You know now you can agree or not with your mother and she'll still respect you. She doesn't have to live with your decision the way a wife and children do."

Baptiste shrugged his shoulders.

"Tell her," Josette said. "Tell her why we came back."

"You say it if it means so much to you, *femme,*" Baptiste said. He pulled out his waist knife and cleaned his fingernails with it, the slow scraping breaking the silence.

Marguerite could feel the tightness in the room. If tensions were high at Waiilatpu, wouldn't Josette have wanted to be with her family? The baby could have been baptized in Walla Walla. She was sure there was a priest there now.

"He wants to fight," Josette said at last. "To join the militia."

"To protect you," Baptiste said.

Josette scoffed.

"This White, the Indian subagent, I traveled with"—Baptiste talked to Marguerite now—"at times I think him a *bouffoon* who paints himself up as a chief. But in Lapwai, he spoke with heart. He convinced Five Crows and Ellis, a chief there, and even old war chiefs to come to Waiilatpu to treat. Nearly five hundred came. He even got Whitman to kill some oxen for meat."

"He thought it was the first time women had attended such a feast," Josette said. "He knows so little of us."

"Who came to the gathering, then?" Marguerite asked.

"Walla Wallas, Cayuse, Nez Perce. I never saw your Richard," he said.

"He wasn't my Richard," Marguerite said. She felt her face grow hot.

"They voted," Josette said. David fussed, and Josette picked him up and removed him from the board, placed him at her breast. "White thinks they've chosen one chief over them all."

"Like the governor, Abernethy, appointed at the Champoeg meeting," Marguerite said. "They chose Ioway rules, from a state named for our mother's tribe. Did you know this?"

Baptiste shook his head, no. "Neither this Ioway government on the prairie nor the treaty will hold unless they get blankets and food to the people east where they've suffered a hard winter," Baptiste said. "The cough and the drought all add to the tightness there. There will be trouble and they will call up a militia to settle unrest, to protect the streams of people coming this way."

"They need to mark the places where new wagons can move through. Not to stay," Josette said.

"I've even seen the letters White writes back to the states saying we need things here to be safe, to keep our families safe," Baptiste told her. "He gets no answers, so he makes his own rules. White's in the thick of the government. Has an office at the falls now, but he plans to go back East to carry his messages. He says we'll need an army that's not connected to the British."

"He thinks he goes as a...representative of us," Josette said, disgust in her voice.

"He wants to keep you Indians safe," Baptiste said.

"You are Indian too," she said. "We need to defend against hunger and no place to set our tipis and finding a home, where no one invades. Whitman builds fences to keep the Cayuse cows out," she said to Marguerite. "He takes on these...emigrants' cows and feeds them through the winter and they use our forage. Then he shouts because our people meet them and sell grain to them first. And your brother wants to join up with rifles. Rifles won't stop what's coming or what will happen after. I just want him to tend his family. If we are here, then he should be here too."

They'd had this argument a dozen times. Marguerite could hear it in their voices. She was a new audience, and the words gnawed at her stomach because JB left her alone often too. But there was something more in their arguments, something not rising to the surface.

"What else might stop what's coming?" Marguerite asked. "What else could we do?"

"I ask my mother's advice," Baptiste said.

"The only woman you listen to," Josette told him. "Will you tell her of your brother, ask her advice about seeing him too?"

Baptiste's dark eyes narrowed, and he stopped the cleaning of his nails with his knife, holding it quiet in midair. "You go too far, woman," he told her.

"Paul? You've seen Paul?"

David, the baby, cried openly now, no longer interested in the nipple.

"Your milk sours him," Baptiste said. He replaced his knife in its sheath. "A mother needs to take care what she does to her son. You make him *angoisse.*"

Baptiste had his suspicions. He'd never shared them with a soul, not even with Josette. He had often wondered if his mother held those same thoughts about Paul and if he and his mother had healed their differences enough that now he could share this news with her without it separating the two of them again.

He'd made a wise decision coming back to the prairie with Josette and the children. If Jean were home today, that, too, would be good. Jean could help with the aftermath, the sorting through of a painful thing. Jean had no part in any of it, so he could look with fresh eyes. This would be good.

He rode up to his mother's home on the edge of Lake Labiche.

Chickens scattered as he did. Two hogs lay on their sides asleep in the March sun. Their pen had recently been moved, and Baptiste could see the square where they'd marked their eating and sleeping. The former mud patch stood out against the lush grass like a dark square on a quilt.

He found his mother stirring ash in a pit, readying soap. Barbe stood with her. Baptiste could send Barbe off to do something else, although he doubted the girl would remember anything he and his mother might say to each other. He didn't see Jean or François, but maybe they were both in the barn. He hoped he wouldn't have to do this without Jean. He swallowed, his stomach churning more than he wished.

"Mère," he called out, and she turned to look at him, quickly raising her stirring stick up to wave a welcome.

She looked older, her shoulders more bent than he remembered. Even from a distance he could see the rain of wrinkles that engraved her cheeks.

"Baa-tease, Baa-tease," Barbe said waddling toward him. "O-o-oh, Baa-tease," she sang in a flat tone of joy. The woman-child had gained weight, and her stomach rolled as she lumbered.

He stepped down from his horse, and Barbe engulfed him. She smelled of smoke from the fire, and while her dark hair was clean it carried tiny particles of ash. He peeled her hands from him. "Good to see you, Barbe," he said, enunciating the words. He couldn't remember how much English or French or Chinookan she knew.

"The face of my son is fresh air to these eyes," his mother said as she approached.

Baptiste smiled. His mother's eyes looked large behind the spectacles, a sight that still surprised him when he saw the tiny circles perched there on her nose bridge. She wore her hair pulled back into a bun, and the sunlight made the strands of gray look like gold.

"It's good to know a mother remembers her son," he said.

"A mother always remembers her son," she said, touching the sides of his face with both hands. She had tears in her eyes. "You surprise us. When did you get back? Where is your family?"

"They stay at Marguerite's."

"Then they come tonight. It will be good to see them all. Barbe, go tell Papa Jean his boy is here."

"François with him. François his boy," Barbe said.

"*Oui.* Do as I say, now," his mother said, shaking her head at Baptiste as the girl set off toward the barn. "She doesn't understand everything," his mother apologized.

"None of us do," he said.

"You came back with White?" Baptiste nodded. "Will you stay then? You must tell me of the news at Waiilatpu."

"People agitate there," he said as he started toward the house with her. "White receives a letter from one of Whitman's helpers saying the Indians are anxious over their hogs and cattle."

"So much uncertainty over food? What does he recommend, this White?"

"He petitions the American government for help. We can talk of this later, *Mère.* Jean will want to hear too."

"I forget my manners," she said, patting his chest with her small hands. Her fingers were white. They must be cold. He covered them with his hand.

"Come. We go inside. Marianne's there. She'll make us tea."

He hesitated. "Marianne's here?"

"Something is wrong?"

"No." Baptiste started again to walk. "I can ask her if she'll be David's godmother. It will save me the ride to her home," he said.

"Your sister will be pleased to see you."

He nodded agreement, aware that he felt relieved. The swirl in his stomach lessoned. With Marianne there, he wouldn't be able to talk of Paul with his mother. Even if he asked her to step away so he could, it would create a pressure on his mother he didn't want to hand her. He'd already decided that the younger ones, Marianne and François, needn't know what he knew unless his mother chose to tell them. It wouldn't be him cutting a wound into unsuspecting skin. He could at least defend his family against that pain.

The afternoon ended too quickly. Marie followed her son to his horse. He'd been edgy, that's how she'd describe it, as though he stood on a summit ready to go over or back down. When she told him Marianne waited inside, his shoulders sighed and his words came out with greater ease. She heard more conversation than she ever remembered the two of them sharing. Pleasant to watch, but lopsided. He fast-walked to his horse, anxious to mount and ride out. He didn't linger, commenting on changes in the landscape the way he often did. He didn't acknowledge the peach tree's growth, the increase in chickens and pigs.

"You'll bring Josette over later, then. You'll stay here," she said as he lifted the stirrup over the saddle to check the cinch.

"We're settled at Marguerite's," he said.

"Oui," she said. "She'll like that." Marie didn't want to sound disappointed. Sometimes, when she did, it made Baptiste irritable. Jean, too. "You are healthy," she said. She patted his shoulder. "She feeds you well, your wife."

He lowered the stirrup, reached for the reins. "We're fine, Mother," he said.

"I know this." She couldn't seem to say the right things. She cleared her throat. "You see many wagons in Cayuse country, *n'est-ce pas?*" Baptiste nodded. He kept his back to her, but he didn't mount up. With his gloved hand, he brushed at the horse's rump. "We hear the winter is harsh, grain difficult to get. Josette's family had enough?" He nodded. "We hear…a story is told that some Cayuse, some Indians, sell grain to the overlanders. From Whitman's own storehouse, maybe. Do you hear this?"

"I hear it. The mill burned the day I was there, the last to get wheat ground was a Dorion. Me."

"You. *Oui.* There was no other Dorion around, *n'est-ce pas?*" She could feel her heart pound at her temples, her cheeks warm. She blinked back little flickers of light. "No other Dorion."

"Why do you ask this, Mother?" He still hadn't turned back to face her.

"We hear stories. Someone says a Dorion sells wheat to them but who the man describes doesn't sound like you."

"No?"

"*Non.* You will think your mother old and foolish. Jean does, but I wonder if it could be Paul, your brother, Paul."

"I know who Paul is, Mother," Baptiste said.

"I think Paul might be there, and I plan to go, to see for myself."

"Forget him, Mother." Baptiste mounted up, setting himself down with such force the horse grunted.

"You think I waste my time if I go there."

"Hasn't he brought enough pain to this family?"

"Paul wasn't there then."

"Haven't you—"

"Your forgot your *chapeau,* brother!" Marianne shouted as she ran toward them from the house. She carried Baptiste's tall beaver hat. Barbe followed and arrived behind a breathless Marianne. "Here," Marianne said. "Don't say I never gave you anything, brother."

"Never," he said as he took the hat and placed it on his head with a tap. "Now I can go," he said, and he pressed the reins against his horse's neck. He ran his fingers across the brim and nodded at his sister, Barbe, and took a last look at his mother.

Marie thought he looked much too grateful to have only received a forgotten *chapeau.*

⌖

"We shouldn't be here," Julie Gervais Laderoute said.

"Why not?" Marianne said. "It isn't as though we're doing anything wrong."

"These are sacred places. Private. We wouldn't want someone coming to Mass just to gawk at us."

"I'm practicing English," Marianne said. "And I'm learning. If I'm not allowed to learn English in schools, then I'll learn outside of them."

The Methodists had set up a tent in a pasture on a wide prairie outside of their church building in Oregon City, and the women and their young sons had traveled on horseback, leaving early in the morning with plans to spend the night along with dozens of others. The June evening might cool, but Marianne and Julie had plenty of blankets to wrap themselves and their sons into. Blue lupine speared the hillsides, and wild strawberries promised a treat, if not that day, then soon. The girls laid their blanket near a sapling. "Mrs. Waller, the minister's wife, planted that apple tree," Marianne said. "It grew from her garbage." They laid out the blanket. "Besides, this event is for people of all faiths. They want us to come and hear them. They know the Indians like celebrations."

Julie looked around. "But we're the only Frenchies here."

"You can't tell by looking," Marianne said. "I like to listen to people talk. That's how you find out where they're from. Besides, you don't know everyone here anymore. There are close to four thousand people in this country now, David says. You couldn't possibly know them all. That many people means we probably won't see a single soul we know."

She noticed where a canvas awning had been set up against the sun for the speakers and musicians. "That's the *angoisse* chair," Marianne whispered. "Near the front."

"Why do they call it that, an anxious chair?"

"They're anxious for their souls. It's what the tent meeting is for, to bring those anxious about what will happen to them after they die to a place of peace. That's what my papa says. The Congregationalists across the river have the same chairs at their meetings. When the time comes, people are said to jump up and give their souls away, and then others pray with them and they're happy and go home."

"It can't be that easy," Julie said. "What about the hours of catechism, the study toward First Communion, and the holy sacraments?"

"They do the study later, Papa says. He also says they preach to each other now that more Easterners have come and there are so few Indians left to convert. And we have our priests, so there's no sense in trying to reach our anxious souls. The priests know how to do that." She smiled. "Papa says the Protestants had to branch out." She looked around, took in the purple wildflowers that dotted the shady areas beneath the white oaks. Seagulls dove at the thundering falls, and downstream Marianne could see platforms jutting out into the water where Molalla and Clackamas and other tribes fished. She looked back toward the awning. "I've heard one talk once. He's sitting over there on that chair."

"When did you do this before?" Julie said.

"There's more than one way to advance a girl's education," Marianne said. "Shh, Joseph. Quiet now. You'll wake your cousin. See how well he sleeps?" Julie's son lay curled on the blanket making soft sleeping sounds. Dogs barked and played hide-and-seek among the rows of people seated on the grass. Joseph waddled unevenly across the green, then ran back toward his mother, hugging her from behind. Marianne patted his arms laced around her neck.

"They must not be expecting many people since they only have four anxious chairs out there," Julie said.

"If they're really just supporting the faithful, they won't need many more than that. Though I suppose some of the people arriving from the East are Methodists or Congregationalists or without any faith at all. Imagine that. They might have a few sins they want to confess."

"So they do that, too, in front of everyone?"

Marianne shrugged. "Papa says so. Not out loud, though. He used to talk a lot with that blacksmith Methodist, Parrish. The one they sent away to the ocean after he signed a petition against his boss. At least that's what François told me, and he knows a lot about political things."

Julie's two older children walked near the water's edge, hand in hand. Marianne handed her son a wooden top his father had made for him, the toy bringing David to her mind. "Did your husband try to keep you from coming?"

Julie shook her head. "I didn't actually say where we were going other than we'd be with you."

"Your Laderoute is trusting," Marianne said, and she laughed.

"He knows I wouldn't do anything that might endanger any of our children," Julie said and patted her tummy gently. "He'll eat at Father's, and our hired girl will carry what's left over from supper for him to have tomorrow, so he'll be content."

Marianne wondered if David would do the same. She hadn't really thought much about what he might do for supper. David did well fending for himself.

"Will your mother come, do you think?" Julie asked.

"I don't think she even knows about this sort of thing. She's studying her catechism with the friars and David Mongrain. She knew I went to the mission on my own, of course. Oh, not about the night meeting. And no one ever found the crucifix I dropped. I might go back and try to find it. She's very devout, at least that's what Father Blanchet says about her. Very devout." She made her face long and her voice deep to mimic the priest.

Julie laughed. "It'll be a stormy day in Eden before you'd ever be described that way," she said.

Her words pierced Marianne, surprised her. She wouldn't mind being known as devout. She was the first to be baptized in her family. That should count for something. But listening to David Mongrain drone on about the Ladder stories bored her. She had them memorized by now, the Joseph story fit higher up on the picture Ladder than the Moses story and so on. Every week the same. She loved the Mass and the candles and the singing, but the listening... This camp meeting had excitement to it. The speakers waved their arms and even shouted sometimes. And who was to say that the Lord might not make an appearance in the midst of that kind of frenzy as anywhere else. Father said he loved everyone the same.

"I still miss that crucifix," Marianne said. She reached for her neck, patting the place where the cross used to hang, the one her father had given her on her baptism. It had been the central point to the rosary beads she wore.

"You'd better be careful you don't lose something here," Julie said. "I'd hate to try to find it around all these people."

"Oh, and there's that Dr. White, whom Baptiste traveled with." She looked around. "My mother would not approve of my being here, I'm sure of that."

"She might think you were anxious for your soul," Julie laughed.

"I was the first to be baptized in our family. I'm not anxious for my soul at all."

"Then you should be at peace," Julie said. *"N'est-ce pas?"*

Marianne frowned. She was at peace. She just needed…excitement. "I'm all right," Marianne said. "I'm a good mother. I'm—"

"Silence!" A woman wearing a wide bonnet turned around and put her finger against her lips. She must have been from Oregon City since Marianne didn't remember seeing her before. Or maybe she was one of the ones arriving with those last Eastern newcomers. She'd met a few when they stayed at Marguerite's. She couldn't believe her sister opened her home to total strangers. Marianne never would. Her mother always said it was total strangers who had helped them survive along the trail when she and her first husband had come from St. Louis. "Even my closest friend was once a stranger," her mother told her more than once.

"My mother wouldn't approve our being here, probably," Marianne said. "She'd think I wasn't being respectful." She thought more. "No. She probably wouldn't even notice. It's Marguerite she hovers over. And François and Barbe. Even Baptiste and his children. You should have seen her the day Baptiste came by to ask me to be David's godmother. She left her soap-making aside and spent the rest of the day just talking with him. Of course, I was there too. But after he arrived, she took no notice."

"If this is for people of all faith, shouldn't Father Blanchet and Father Langlois be here?" Julie asked. She looked around.

"They aren't anxious for their souls," Marianne said.

"Well, neither are we."

Julie could take a thing apart until all the fun had spilled out. Everyone was just out for the good air or maybe, like those who gossiped for their entertainment, to see who found their way to that chair.

Marianne heard the commotion and turned to see several stately looking Klamath men ride in on tall horses. The men were dressed in leggings, painted chests, their arms banded with beaded leather bracelets. They had bows and arrows in fringed *par flèches,* and they stuck their chests out. Black hair hung loose down to their waists. They held the reins tight on their mounts so that the animals arched their necks and danced around, and several people once settled now picked up their food baskets and moved away, scowling and pointing. One of the tent speakers came toward them chewing his lip, and as he approached the Indians kicked their horses and sped past him on either side, laughing and whooping as they did. "That makes a few people anxious," Marianne said.

"Oh look, there's someone taking that chair," Julie said, pointing. "Maybe they will fill them all up before the program even starts."

"I like the singing. They do that first," Marianne said. She stood to get a better look. She sat back down. "It's Barbe," she said, loud enough the woman in front turned and scowled again. "And Archange, Baptiste's old worker, is right beside her." Marianne looked up, then ducked her head again. "I bet they were just looking for a place to sit down. Barbe's become so heavy it's hard for her get up off the ground."

A woman said, "Isn't that your baby scampering up there, toward the front?"

"Oh no," Marianne said, recognizing her mother's voice. She didn't even turn to look at her. She just headed forward, toward that anxious chair.

12

Coming Slowly to a Place

1844

Marie preferred riding a horse, but Jean loaded the wagon with garden harvest, filling baskets of potatoes and melons he wanted Marianne to have, so they harnessed horses. Joseph Gervais grew a garden the whole community raved about, so Marie knew David, if not Marianne, would have more than enough potatoes and kale of their own. But Jean liked to give gifts. And these were treasures he'd grown himself.

"I'll surprise her," Jean told Marie, as she became his right arm so he could lift the items into the wagon box. "You may not like the unexpected, but Marianne does."

"I just don't like to be ambushed," Marie told him.

He'd smiled and told her then to be ready for something that would move her *bateau* but that wouldn't set her adrift. "I told them it had better be a joyous surprise," he said, "or I wouldn't help deceive you."

"So you don't really know what this is about?"

"Trust your children, Marie."

Her children weren't very good at surprises, Marie decided. Jean could still startle her with a gift, a phrase, an observation that made her smile or think a little differently. But he knew her well enough to know she didn't like to be caught off guard or to be rushed into some kind of quick decision. He never presented anything really important to her as a surprise. She came slowly to a new place; this man who loved her best knew it.

She settled next to him on the seat. François rode his good Cayuse horse beside them. Barbe begged to "be home now." She flapped her hands and lost some of her good behavior when challenged by many voices, many people giving orders. "Odors," Barbe called them in English. Maybe they were to her.

So Marie had consented. Jean nodded approval. "You can't protect her from life," he said. "She has to learn about the unexpected too."

Marie didn't give her children much practice, she supposed, planning surprises. But trusting them challenged, too. Baptiste talked more of wars and retaliation with an intensity that alarmed. Josette had actually disagreed with him in front of Marie. She had never witnessed that before. It was over something meaningless, she'd thought, about how Barbe played with the younger children, sitting on the floor and rolling a leather ball. Even the dog had barked his delight, and yet Josette had snatched up the toy that Baptiste said Pierre could play with.

Maybe it wasn't about that toy at all.

Marie found it difficult to engage in what she called infantile things, but she'd seen no harm in Barbe's play.

Marie remembered promising Denise she'd somersault more and whip cream even without a special occasion, but Denise was just a child and it was good to play with children. Now that Baptiste was back, she did find herself taking a little more time for such pleasures with his children. They weren't staying with her and Jean, but she still saw them often.

Yes, Marianne liked to play, but it was time she grew up, too. Her youngest child had turned eighteen this past summer, with a child of her own. Yet she acted sometimes as though she were still just fifteen. Maybe it was just her getting old, and not Marianne's problem at all. Maybe Barbe did tire her more than she admitted. Maybe the trips she made to St. Paul for study and for Mass wearied, though once she arrived she was always invigorated. The idea of going there tired her out; being there did not.

Surprises usually brought joys in the end, at least that was what Jean tried to tell her. Mr. Mongrain did too. "Seek to think on things worthy of cherishing and remembering." He said a man named Paul had said those words. Surely her children wouldn't surprise her with anything that alarmed.

"Peace and joy don't need sunshine or good days," Jean told her. He patted her knee. "It's the words. What is said from within your heart that'll make this surprise something happy or not."

She nodded. Getting through depended on her secret words, the blessings of Scripture and spirit, and not on the actions of others. It was that part of her life that still needed teaching.

A family gathering at David and Marianne's for a Marianne surprise. That was all Jean had told her, claiming he knew little of the purpose himself except that Baptiste would be there with his family and Marguerite with hers.

She hadn't been surprised at all to see Marianne at the tent gathering because that girl was always coming up with something to get herself noticed. Marianne embarrassed herself more than anyone else with her antics. Besides, there was a good chance she'd mentioned going to the tent meeting in Oregon City and Marie had forgotten. Marie had been passing through, having gone to the tinsmith there to make trades, then stepping aside for those Klamath Indians who'd made themselves noticed.

She did remember learning of Julie Gervais' pregnancy, that the baby was due sometime in November. A cold month, though less so on this prairie than along the Wisconsin River where Marie had grown up. Babies born in cold months had to be stronger if they hoped to see the spring. She knew that from firsthand experience. It was something she remembered.

She wished she'd had a mother to watch grow older, to see how it was done, to know whether this was what could be expected or not. But she didn't. It didn't really matter, she'd decided, these occasional lapses she had.

As she grew older and inhaled more ideas from the catechist's lessons, more thoughts vied for space inside her head, so something would have to move out. That's how she explained those forgetful moments, a spilling over to make more room for what mattered.

So far, nothing major had slipped past her. *But then, how would I know if I'd forgotten it already?*

"What are you smiling about?" Jean asked her.

"Just thinking of our children," she said. "And their forgetful mother."

"You're not distressed they didn't gather at our home? Marianne has the most room for our big family, eh?"

"*Non.* I will have nothing to clean afterward this way," she said. "I bring along good bread. My part in the gathering. When the children make too much noise for my old ears, I'll stay peaceful as a leaf on the water, knowing I can drift away home and leave the whirlpools and rapids for their mothers." She folded her hands in her lap.

"These are words I never thought I'd hear you say, my Marie," Jean said. "That you would leave a child behind without trouble." He lifted his elbow to poke at her side, and she leaned her head against his shoulder.

"I'm old," she said. "But even the old change."

The wagon lumbered into the lane that marked David and Marianne's home. The *sappolil,* the tarweed, looked ready for harvesting, and soon fires would be set, a ritual of fall Marie always enjoyed. Barbe had shown her how to gather the near-bursting pods and how to fix the seeds into cakes. The Molalla people, too, harvested them, though this year, with more emigrants wedged into distant places, there might be confusion about the purpose of those fires. Complaints were likely from people who didn't understand the native ways. Deer nibbled in a grassy patch of meadow along Marianne's lane.

"There are horses I don't recognize," Jean said.

Marie squinted. "Maybe David's parents join us. They're family." She felt a little disappointment though, wanting this to be just her family, her own people. She took in a deep breath. She could adjust.

"David maybe has new horses," François said.

"Tied at the hitching rail?" Jean said.

Jean was right. They'd be corralled or in the field, not tied.

Denise saw her grandparents first and came running out of the house followed by Marguerite's stepsons. Doublé carried Marianne's only child on his shoulders, high enough that David could put his hand near his son in case he lost his balance. François leapt from the box and searched the group as though looking for someone. Maybe the horses belonged to his someone special, though Marie didn't know who that might be. Her son was a secretive one. Maybe an announcement about that, her last child going off, was Marianne's surprise.

The adults moved out slowly, helping tend the team. Marguerite carried Xavier on her hip, his legs dangling down. He was getting big to be carried. The thought startled her. Marie lowered her eyes. It was what Pierre used to say to her about how long she carried Paul around. That son had been a late walker, which was why she carried him. Or had she just liked the warmth of him close, his small body a protective barrier between her and her husband?

Such a cluster of people, Marie thought, good people. Her family, descending from her line, her mother's and as far back as Marie could remember. What a joy this family was, and there would be more, someday. She still hadn't seen whom François looked for, but he'd marry one day, she was sure. It was enough, this moment. Marianne had given her a surprise she could cherish, the surrounding of family. She would have to tell her how much the child pleased her.

The gathering parted then, and strangers walked out.

They were all women, dressed in long robes not like the dusters worn by emigrant women coming on the wagons but as though they were priests, wearing necklaces of beads, rosaries that disappeared in and out of the folds of their gowns. They held their hands wrapped inside their sleeves, and black and white hoods framed their faces.

Were there women priests then? Was this Marianne's surprise?

"These are four of the Sisters of Notre Dame de Namur," Marianne said. "Six came West. This is my mother. My famous mother, Madame Dorion," Marianne added. "They wanted to meet you. I invited them, to surprise you."

The women nodded their hoods in acknowledgment.

What had that child told them about her? What Marie had done those years before was no more than what any mother would do to keep her sons alive. Why did people keep talking of it as though it were something uncommon?

The women varied in age from Marianne's to one who looked as old as Marie. She suspected the years of leaning over hot fires most of her life had baked her skin into wrinkles. Perhaps this Sister cooked too.

"Father Desmet brought them with him, and they began a school last month, Mother," Marguerite said. "And many more priests are here. Father Louis Vercruyses finds a place closer to where you and Papa Jean summer at Labiche. And Father Delorme serves there too."

"A school," Marie said. Why hadn't she heard about it? "Did you come over the mountains?" she asked.

"On board the ship *Indefatigable,*" one of the Sisters said. "Around the horn." She spoke in accented French, but Marie could understand her easily.

"We'll teach both English and French," another Sister said.

"Girls," Marianne added. "They're calling the school St. Mary's on the Willamette."

David added, "We already cleared ground for a two-story house near the church at St. Paul. It'll be the center of the Catholic Church in all the Columbia country. Even for the Fort Vancouver area east, to Walla Walla and Fort Hall. We've started the barns," he said. "Lay workers came on the ship too. Baptiste and François helped, and so did Archange. And my father."

"And JB," Marguerite said. Her husband stood beside her today. This was good, though Marie noticed Marguerite shifted Xavier to the hip between her and her husband as they talked.

"Let's go inside," Marianne said. She stepped aside for Marie to enter first.

"Did you help?" Marie asked Jean.

"No, not yet. There's more to do," Jean said.

"I would have helped," Marie said. "If I had known."

"The school isn't finished yet, Mother. We meet outside and pay with flour and eggs and candles," Marianne said.

"And tea," Marguerite said.

"You go too?"

Marguerite shook her head. "But if I help, then my godchildren will have a school and my sons."

"I go," Marianne said. "Julie may come too, after she has her baby."

Baptiste said to his mother, "Our children will attend. Josette insists."

"You can come too, Grandmother," Denise said.

"Oh, I'm too old to learn anything new."

The long-faced Sister wiped crumbs from her chin. "Your daughter is a fine baker," she said as she sat next to Marie. Marie nodded. "I'm Sister Celeste," she said. "And there is no upper age to the school. Someone who has lived as many years as you may still attend." She crossed her hands in her lap. Such calm hands. Such a peaceful voice. "I confess," she said. Marie looked up at the word. "Oh no, not like that." Sister Celeste smiled. "I confess to being a little nervous about meeting you. I so want to hear your version of the Hunt journey. I have read some portions, including what the American named Irving wrote of it. But to hear your words…to have you write them down for others, this would be a true gift to leave behind."

"This Irving wasn't there," Marie said. "How could he write of it?"

"*Oui.* He reads things written by Hunt and Franchere, a Company clerk who published his report in France years before. Irving reads Mackenzie and Alexander Ross's journals, too. He reads his own ideas, from a distance of people and years, but writers still find truths there. And readers, too, when we are given the story later. It is a fine gift to read of someone we know. Finer still to meet you."

"Those men all wrote about mother?" Baptiste asked. He stood beside his mother now, one of Marianne's cups dwarfed in his wide hand.

"You are in the story too," Sister Celeste said. "Two boys came with Hunt, Irving says. You're one of those, *oui?*"

"It speaks well that a mother is still tended by her sons as she grows older," a wrinkled-face Sister said. She pulled a stool closer to where Marie sat. "Does your other son live near too?"

A simple question she couldn't answer. Marie stared at the dust at the bottom of the Sister's hems. They were all dusty. Long dresses of cloth gathered up dust in this country.

"Baptiste's boys will go to the school too, Mother," Marianne said then, reaching to touch her mother's arm. Marianne spoke fast, and her cheeks had red spots on them, Marie noticed when she looked up.

"You come, Kasa. You come," Denise said.

"I gather a crowd," Marie said.

"It's always been so," Jean told her, and he laughed. "They want to hear what you have to say."

A *femme.* Who would want to hear a woman's story, even if she could write it down?

"It's so far," Marie said. "A long ride from home." She looked at Jean.

"You'll be the same age next year at this time whether you go to school or not," he said. "Why not live doing something you told your granddaughter you would do one day, eh? Learn to read."

"I read," she said. "I read the seasons and the Lake and—"

"In English and French," Marianne said. "There are tests, lessons to memorize, and—"

"Keep talking, and she'll be too frightened to go to school," François said. "I'm getting that way."

Marie's head felt light, and she took in a deep breath, glad she wore leather that let her breathe deeply. "Did you think it would take all of you to convince me of this schooling?"

"Your mother needs time to consider."

"It was Marianne's idea to surprise you," Marguerite said.

"Barbe comes too," Marie said, not asking.

"If you insist, Mother," Marianne said. She sighed.

"We also prepare them for First Communion," the older looking Sister said. "Your diligence will be an inspiration to the others, should you choose to join us. A good model as a mother."

"We could try it," Marie said. "Only until the snow flies. Or if I don't forget."

"Well, the surprise is finished, eh?" Jean said.

"Not quite, Papa," Marianne said. She inhaled a deep breath. "I'm changing my name." Marie frowned. "Marianne is such a child's name, Mama. You always said we were named by how we behaved. Well, I choose from now on to be called by a different name. So you'll think of me not as the child I was but as the woman I am."

"Marianne…" François groaned.

"It's my surprise," she told him. "I can do what I want, and David said it was fine with him." She turned to her mother. "From now on, I want to be called Marie. Marie Anne. In honor of my famous mother."

The fire raged through the timbered high country east of the prairies, the smoke burning the sun orange and scouring the sky to pewter. High winds flamed the seasonally set fires and tossed fiery embers like comets into the treetops. Each tree leaned and handed them off, flaming wands in a relay race. The newcomers complained. More people meant challenge to old traditions. Fires out of control added to the American demands to place blame.

At night, Marie and Jean watched a faint glow in the distance, but nothing man could do would stop it. The rains would come and put it out in time. Defending cabins and homes of their neighbors, should the wind shift, meant the need to stay close to the lake cabin's hearth. It was where Jean liked to be anyway, as he was now, his back against the house as he minded the distant glow.

He had two hearths. This one, in a neighborhood of sorts not far from a chapel, with family close and old Astor men and their wives within a day's ride. The second, warmer hearth was wherever Marie was. When they left this house on the prairie and moved south to the timbered country to hunt and trap and winter, as long as she went with him, it was home. His wife enjoyed herself washing her hair in the stream there in the morning, taking a swim in the moonlight along the Pudding River. If she'd trust leaving Barbe behind, she might even enjoy it more. But for now, the girl almost always went with them, even when they headed east, toward the mountains, to camp and hunt *le biche,* deer, they then smoked and made into jerky, readying for winter. Acorns littered the ground like brown hail, and Marie gathered them for later roasting. She didn't want a harsh winter surprising them. A holdover, he supposed, from that winter long ago that did.

He really hoped that the influx of Americans would stop, not that they weren't most of them a jolly lot. And he supposed it was wishful thinking that they'd settle east instead of on this prairie ground. Men like Jesse Applegate had brought their whole families West, even brothers and their children. Once Joel Palmer took wagons right over the mountains, lowering them by ropes like men climbing down a mountain; Jean knew nothing would stop them. Persistent as beavers, gnawing down everything in their path, that's what Americans were.

So they'd probably keep coming, and then there'd be enough shanties and cabins wedged into the timbers or pushing the prairie's edges that newcomers could stay with Americans instead of with Frenchies.

Through the smoky haze he watched a rider approach on a big horse. He didn't recognize him until he could see the tall hat.

"I came to see if you needed help," Baptiste said.

"I'm beyond help," Jean said. He smiled up from the stump he sat on, sharpening his knife with his left hand, using his right as the holder. "Haven't seen much of you of late," Jean said.

"I've been occupied."

"I'm sure your mother will be pleased to see you."

"Maybe," he said. "Is François here?"

"He's courting the Longtain girl these days," Jean said. "Better he's visiting with her and her family than standing around all cow-eyed doing nothing here but show his ornery side. Reminds me too much of myself at his age."

Baptiste stepped off his horse, a tall Cayuse mount, tied the reins to the hitching rail and removed his hat. He turned the rim gently in his hands, kept looking down. "I smell like smoke riding through that."

"Go on in. I'll be there in *une moment.*"

Baptiste took a step, then stopped again. "I'll wait for you," he said.

Jean stood and put his hand on Baptiste's shoulder. "I'm right behind you."

Marie lifted her eyes from the acorns she cleaned from the shells. Her fingers were black with soot, and she had a smudge on her cheek where she'd been sampling.

"Making sure they're roasted through?" Jean teased.

"A mother does what she must," she said and wiped at her mouth, smiling.

"To keep her family safe, eh?"

Marie put the basket from her lap down onto the floor, stood up, and walked to her son. "You're tired," she said. "Come. I'll feed you."

"He comes to see if we need help," Jean said.

"Where's Barbe?" Baptiste asked.

"She's..." Marie looked around. "Oh. She was going to milk Etoile. That one's tame enough. I thought she could manage. Can you see the dog out there? He usually goes with her."

Jean nodded as he looked out the window. Baptiste still hadn't sat down, so Jean pulled out a plank chair. "Made it myself," Jean said. "Stained it with a little red dye and a little milk I talked your mother out of. Looks almost like red maple, from my province."

"I've never been to Canada," Baptiste said.

"So what news do you bring your old parents, eh?" Jean asked. He'd missed having Baptiste keep him abreast of doings at the fort.

"A British ship sits in the harbor at Vancouver. Some go to plays and musicals there. Party."

"How do you know of such things?" Marie asked.

"The ships stay to remind us that the British will fight for that River boundary and everything south," Baptiste said.

Jean scoffed. "Both countries want a harbor at the sea, and Astor's harbor is fickle as a young girl, sometimes smooth and calm. Sometimes not. The Spanish have Yerba Bueno, so what does that leave? Eh? You know the answer?" Baptiste shook his head. "Puget Sound. The British will settle for what is north of the Columbia so they can have that deep-water port. Who cares that it can't be farmed anywhere close, that the timbers march down steep slopes to sea. It is the rivers and the ocean-going vessels that will make their nation in this country. And they only go where the water is deep."

"François says the Company never intended farming to be successful there. Too timbered. Too wet. They just lured the Red River people out to use them to hold the land around the harbor."

Jean brushed away his words. "The Americans want Puget Sound, too, this is true. It is a harbor worthy of a war. So this boundary thing is not settled yet."

"Husband. My son looks hungry, and I wonder if he came to talk of boundaries." Marie said.

"No," Baptiste said. He sat and inhaled deeply. "I came to tell a story."

Baptiste never let go of his hat. How much should he tell her? This thing with Josette, did his mother need to know that, to explain why he hadn't told his mother sooner? Should he start there and come back to Paul, or begin with Paul and then tell of Josette at the end? Both would injure her. Maybe he didn't need to tell her at all.

"Where did you say Barbe was?" he asked.

"Outside," Jean said.

"The story," his mother said. "You wish to tell a story. Were you there for this story or is it like that Irving, where you tell someone else's?"

Baptiste put his hat on the floor beneath the chair. "First, I tell you of a mistake I made," he said. "It was my mistake. I made it. Josette says I should tell Father De Vos and make it part of my confession. But I was not baptized. I don't follow her faith."

"So you confess to your mother instead?"

"I should go find Barbe," Jean said. "See if she has trouble with—"

"No! You stay," Baptiste said. Jean sat back down. *What must he think of me?* "So you will grant me forgiveness," Baptiste continued. He gave his mother a half-smile. There was a time when it would bring her joy, that smile. "If I'm worthy of it."

"I give to you what's given to me," she said.

He nodded. Her eyes watered behind the spectacles. She removed them and thumbed at her eyes, then replaced her spectacles. He looked away, sending his words to the side of her face so he didn't have to see how she'd respond.

"Your granddaughter, Genevieve, is my daughter," he said. His mother furrowed her brows.

"I know this."

"But she is not Josette's."

The dog barked in the distance. Barbe would be coming back in. Maybe he wouldn't have to tell her everything.

"Your wife raises another woman's child as her own?" his mother asked. "How does this happen?"

"I met her, this Nez Perce woman, when I was at Walla Walla. She follows me here—"

"So this is her fault?"

"No," Baptiste said. He lowered his head. "Mine. My choice. Josette ...we...this is why I was not at the baptism of Genevieve," he said.

"But where is the mother?"

"She brings the baby to Josette and tells her and then she leaves. I don't know where the mother is now."

"And Josette raises her as her own child."

He leaned forward, resting his forearms on his thighs, reached under the chair for his hat. He held it before him, still bent over, twirling the rim.

"This is not all," he said. "When all this happens, when Dr. White comes and I leave with him, I take Josette and my family back because she wants to go. I don't want this, as there's danger there near Waiilatpu, but who am I to shut her off from her family after what I do to her?" He took in a deep breath. "We argue and—"

"You hit her," his mother said, her jaw set.

He sat up and looked at his mother, surprise in his eyes. "I never struck her. Never. Even when she says words that are a fire in my stomach, I leave, walk hard, brush my horse until all his hair would fall off if I didn't stop. But *non,* I never hit her. I watched my father hit you, and I chose something different."

His mother's eyes watered again, and Jean moved over to stand behind her, his hand on her shoulder.

"I am ashamed for you, Baptiste. That you hurt your wife in this way, betraying her trust in you."

"She's forgiven me," he said.

Marie dropped her eyes and nodded. "She is a good woman."

"But I don't tell you of something else, because so much happens with Josette and me, then. My mind got stuck in trying to make a better way with her, to please her. So I don't take the time to tell you this." He inhaled. "A Red River man told me he heard of a Dorion, someone who was going to come with them but fell behind. He spoke the word as DeRoin, the way I hear it when I visit Grandmother, in '25. I mean to tell you because I think it could be Paul."

"It could be a cousin," Marie said. She said it warily, as though she held no hope for such a thing. "Your father had many brothers."

Baptiste nodded. "It could have been a cousin. That one. I didn't tell you because I wasn't sure. And because I forgot. I wanted to forget."

"If this not telling has been a worry for you, then you are forgiven," Marie said. "I forget important things too."

Now would come the hard part. "He was at Waiilatpu," Baptiste said. "Last year."

"This DeRoin you heard of?"

"No. Paul."

"You saw your brother? You talked with him?"

Baptiste nodded. "He followed some emigrants west," Baptiste said. "He'd been at Fort Laramie, a fort Indian, he called himself. Said he sometimes hunted for the Company. He'd been back to grandmother's, came back west. He says he goes back and forth."

"How did he look?" She whispered as though in prayer.

"Like he always did. Scruffy as a mongrel. Only now his ears seem to better fit his head; they don't stick out quite so much. Most of his teeth are gone, so when he smiled that big smile, it looked like an empty cave inside. He had a woman with him."

"What was he doing in Waiilatpu?" Jean asked. "Or don't you know?"

"Stealing wheat is my guess," Baptiste said. "He had some he sold to people coming from the East. Whitman was riled about the Cayuse selling wheat to those emigrants before they reached his place. He'd have been real disturbed if he'd known some of it wasn't what the Cayuse had grown themselves, but his own, taken right from his storehouse."

"He was there when the mill burned down," his mother said. She was looking past him, as though she could see him in the back of the room.

"I don't know," Baptiste told her. "I don't know."

She turned on him then. "Why didn't you tell me? Or send word?"

Marie said. "We could have gone there to see him. When you came back, last summer, I asked you if—"

"No. You didn't ask."

"You knew what I meant. You chose to hold the truth, not share it."

"I...couldn't tell you, not then."

"Why do you tell me now? Is this a story I can believe, now?"

How could he tell her that Paul didn't want to know how she was or what had happened through the years? What could he say to make this brother of his look like a responsible man, a loving son? He never asked one question about his mother or any of the French Canadians or Astor's men they'd traveled with. He'd made only two references to his former life. One, he said he'd seen Tom McKay around and that he noticed the big man still limped. "Found himself a skunk pit, remember?" And the other words were of Louis and a beaver lodge he said the two encountered on the day that Louis died. That's when he had smiled that cavernous smile. Paul still saw his own reflection as though it were a king's.

Baptiste hadn't wanted to hurt his mother. He would have sent word, but he didn't know how long Paul would stay and he hadn't asked for her; he had talked instead of his exploits. It wasn't that he wanted to put old things to rest; it was as if Paul didn't care one way or the other.

"Why do you tell us now?" Jean asked.

Baptiste dropped his shoulders, still didn't look up. "Josette says I should confess, empty all the stories from my burden basket that weigh me down like stone. She says I do things to hurt myself because I carry a too full load. So I empty the basket and tell you of Paul."

"We could have seen him, my poor Paul." She cried now. "After all these years." She wrapped her arms around herself and began rocking. "We could have welcomed him back."

A hot poker of fury shot up into Baptiste's back, and he stood up. "There's nothing poor about him. It was his choice to leave, Mother. His choice to hurt you as he did those years before. He kills your husband, leaves us for years with no word, I search for him and come home to pain, and you say 'Poor Paul'? I should have kept this secret. I should have. You think only of your Paul."

His mother's face looked white as bone. Her fingers held against her lips trembled. "You don't know that he killed Marguerite's father," Marie whispered.

Baptiste shook his head. "I'm sorry. One other time I say this and you strike me. I don't know why I said that. No. No one knows." This was what he'd feared. He'd stirred up old ashes that could still burn.

"Poor—"

"He didn't tell me a thing I didn't already know." If she said "Poor Paul" again, he'd leave. Baptiste ground his teeth together. "It's what I believe to be so, Mother. We all do. Your French Canadian family, too, Tom McKay and Michel and Louis LaBonte. Even Joseph Gervais. They all think the same, those who love you. We think he killed him and took his body into that beaver lodge, that's what we all think. You devote too many years to a son who betrayed you, who failed us all."

His mother rocked herself. "Marguerite? Does she think this?" She turned to Jean. "Do you?"

"We're careful never to speak such thoughts in front of you or Marguerite, my Marie. Or the younger children. They have no need to know this, to speak of it."

"Now I have," Baptiste said. His eyes burned from the smoke or perhaps the pain he wanted to bury deep. He thumbed his eyes, held his head back as though to keep the tears from spilling out.

"I give what I get," his mother said, and she put her arms around her son.

His sob wrenched the silence of her embrace. He'd been ambushed by his brother's betrayal, his mother's unfailing love.

"I knock and the door opens," Father Bartholomew Delorme said. He smiled at Jean and Marie standing behind. "I knock on every door on this grand prairie."

"And I know why," Jean said as he invited him in.

"So you approve?"

Jean nodded.

"*Bon!* I give the land from my own allotment," Father Delorme said, the dimple of his clean-shaved face as impish as a child's.

"Land that once belonged to the Kalapuya," Marie said.

The priest lifted his palms to the air as if to say his hands were clean, and they were, Marie supposed. Sailors and trappers and trail-makers like Astor and Hunt and even her family had more blood on their hands than this priest or even the Methodists. Who would protest a priest naming a piece of land as his own? No one had protested the Toupins' choice oak stand or the meadows or their log house nor the cabin they raised farther south on timbered land. They were as guilty as the priests or as innocent. They invaded as well as everyone else.

"What we need now," Father Delorme said, "is the bounty counting." He cupped his palms and bounced imaginary coins in them. His eyes twinkled.

"A tax," Marie said.

"An opportunity to avoid a debt," the priest said. He had a wide face with a high forehead toppled by kinky curls. Young. The man was young to have come so far. "An opportunity to be in service, to extend the faith to families who otherwise cannot make the trek to Mass at the St. Paul Parish. It will be a stone's throw from here."

"You'll build a church that close," Jean said.

The priest nodded. "There is even an American who says he can help us form it up, a Mr. Rees. But we need to pay him for his services. So I knock on doors."

"I can give logs," Jean said. He turned to Marie. "Can't we?"

"You'll teach classes there?" Marie asked.

"Not as the Sisters do, no," the priest said. "But catechism, yes. And baptisms and marriages and burials. The sacraments. Feast days will be filled with laughter and celebration, making joyful noises as we're commanded. Think of it. The Lord's house within an hour's ride. It will fill a great need, a human need we all have. And we will name it for the king of France, to honor this French community. St. Louis." His eyes had stars in them, the way her Sarahs' eyes sparkled with light when the women talked of their faith.

"A building is necessary for this?" Marie asked, more interested in how he'd respond than in being resistant. "The stars, the fields, the rivers, they are not enough to fill this human need?"

"Ah, you've encountered St. Anthony of the Desert," the priest said, surprise in his voice.

"I don't know this man, no." Marie said.

"Nor I," the priest laughed. "He died three hundred years ago. But his idea was that when he wanted to read the Word of God he could merely read the rocks and trees and hillsides, watch the rivers and birds, all creation, to know of God's character and mind. He needed no books in his life, he said, though he missed hearing the words of Scripture. I suspected he memorized much."

"He's a man of my liking," Marie said.

"It's true, Madame Dorion. We need no buildings to know God fully. We need no buildings to fill the human spirit with God's love nor to perform our duties or receive the gifts of grace. But when a building is built and maintained with loving hands, as an act of worship, to glorify God's name, then more than a building is raised. All are touched. Not just those who raise the logs with their hands, but those who help with their prayers and their gifts." He pretended to toss coins into the air and catch them in his palm. "Everyone gains, and God receives the glory. It's an opportunity."

"A town will form," Jean said.

"There'll be surprises," Marie said.

"Such as we can never guess."

13

A Mother's Song

1845

"Vocare," Sister Celeste said. "It's a Latin word that means 'a calling.' In English, the word is *vocation.* Something we are compelled to do with our lives."

"The French is *métier,*" Marie said. "It means the same thing."

"That's right." The Sister beamed.

"Then I have no need to learn the Latin or the English," Marie said. "I already have this word here," she touched her heart.

"Yes, but to be able to write it down someday, to use it as a way to share something that matters, that's why you're learning to read."

"The word is too big," Marie said. "I will never use it."

She knew she was being stubborn, a difficult student, but the work of learning the letters, of trying to remember their sounds, and putting the swirls and circles in the correct places burdened her as though she carried a too full basket on her back.

"Madame Dorion," Sister Celeste said. "Toupin. Madame Toupin. You needn't learn that word then. It was the sound of the *v* that I wanted you to know first. *Vocare.* To call. An English word with that sound…is *voice.* Or *venture.* Or *vice.* I just like the sound of *vocare,*" she said. "And the word holds such meaning. Surely you have a calling."

"To be a mother," Marie said. "But I no longer think I need to read to do that well. You have…a calling to teach," Marie said. "But young minds, not this old one that gets things as mixed up as the dog's food."

She and Sister Celeste were the only ones still in the classroom at St. Mary's on the Willamette. Rain pelted the cedar shingles, and a dark mist surrounded them, so typical of a late January afternoon.

"You're not quitting," Sister Celeste said. "I'd have to admit that I'd failed in my *vocare* if you quit." She smiled. She looked so young to have chosen this *métier,* to live her life in service, bound to her faith. "And Mother Superior will not look kindly on me if I lose a student."

"Tell her I am a poor student. I am," Marie said, holding her hand up to stop Sister Celeste's protests. "It is not your teaching that fails. I simply cannot remember the things needed to put the letters together. The sounds, the shapes are twisted as a rope in my mind. Even if I tell myself stories about them, that your letter…I can't recall it's name, but it is like two Okanogan hills, all bent over and bare."

"M."

"Yes, the letter *m,*" Marie said. "Even when I tell that story, I cannot remember its sound or when to use it. Some words, my name, I can remember when I see it. But not to put them together. And I think I do not need to know this in my life now. Not now."

Sister Celeste sighed. "I have to honor your wishes," she said. "But the children will be so disappointed. They love helping you. They love having you there, sitting among them. Your girls, too."

"It is not my *métier* to learn to read," Marie said, "not a part of my name."

She hated disappointing the Sister who had been both kind and generous. "Maybe I could just sit in the class until the end of the term, until the roads get too muddy. The Mother Superior would understand that and not feel you'd failed."

"It's not her I worry about failing," Sister Celeste said. She had the bluest eyes of anyone Marie had ever met. The wimple, the stiff white cloth surrounding her face, made them appear all the more intense. "It's all those people whom I want to know your story. All the future generations who won't hear what you have to say in your own words. So few women put things into writing, Madame Toupin. So few. We never know what their lives were like."

"A mother's life is not so complicated it needs repeating," she said.

"But each of our lives needs honoring. Each is unique, as distinctive as…every star is distinctive. And each of them is named. We would revel in their stories if they could speak," she said. Marie smiled at the idea of all the stars in the sky having their say about things they'd heard and seen.

"My story means this much to you?"

"Not only because I have never crossed the mountains of this country as you did; not only because I will never be a mother; not only for those reasons. But because you have seen so much, so many changes, Madame Toupin. And you watch carefully, I've seen you, so I know you would discover things in the writing that might even bring you joy. I just wish I could teach you how to write it down for yourself. Please say you'll keep trying. Give me another chance, please."

"For you then. For you."

Marie heard the whimpering sound, assumed that the dog chased squirrels in his sleep.

Marie hadn't slept well herself that night, nor the last several, tossing and turning. Not since Baptiste had visited and told her about Paul. Paul was alive. Imagine. Somewhere along the way, she'd come to accept that her son was dead, that something had happened to prevent him from returning or he surely would have. She'd even stopped her prayers for him. She shivered. *Only a poor mother would stop praying for an absent son.* But with Baptiste seeing him, talking with him, it was clear: Paul had chosen to stay separate from his family when he might have been warmed at their hearth.

Maybe Paul knew not everyone would welcome him back. If everyone thought he had…been involved with the death of Marguerite's father, he might have been set aside. She wouldn't have done so. She could welcome him home, as a mother should. Couldn't she? Love the child; let past actions rise up with the smoke of a longing flame finally put out.

She had longed to know what happened to Louis and yet set that aside as well. Some answers eluded. Baptiste's claim that Paul was at fault, had she known this but put it aside? Perhaps she pushed away pain by pretending. Everyone else seemed so sure. No, there was evidence that the story Paul told had been the truth. Her husband had been ambushed and killed bringing horses back from Spokane. She'd seen the blood. She still had a strip of cloth he'd worn as decoration on his wrists. He'd been at that site beside a beaver dam, been killed, and taken away. Paul had only mentioned it to Baptiste in reference.

It was years before, so long ago now. There'd be no way to be sure. There hadn't been then. How the others had come to their conclusion didn't matter to her. She was Paul's mother, and a mother could believe what she should.

What she must. Did it matter now whether she told herself the truth?

It would do no good to ask others what they recalled of that time. Memory faded as well as transformed.

But if Baptiste had seen him last winter, then it was possible Paul remained in the Walla Walla area still. Maybe David Mongrain did know of Paul, though he didn't think the Dorion he'd met had that first name. Paul might have used an alias, tried to become another person. People did that who came west escaping their eastern pasts, that's what Jean said. But Paul had no past to escape, not really, unless...no, he'd been a boy angered by what he thought was a brother's wound. He'd taken offense where none was intended. David Mongrain told such a story of brothers. She tried to recall the names...Esau and Jacob. Did their story describe her sons? Paul had made his own life separate from all of them. Baptiste said he had a woman with him. Maybe there were grandchildren she knew nothing of.

She turned onto her side. The moon cast a bright shadow into the cabin. Baptiste had lived in a shadow of his brother's leaving. For years he must have felt that she'd chosen Paul over him by asking him to look for the boy, by requesting that he change his life since Paul had chosen to change his.

She'd added to Baptiste's grief, though he'd taken a risk to tell her he'd seen Paul. Especially when Baptiste had enough trouble making amends with Josette.

And wasn't Josette a fine woman to receive the child of her husband's betrayal and raise her as though Genevieve was her own. She had so many children to tend to, and now had a new one of her own. Baptiste's confession explained Josette's irritation with Baptiste at times, her short words, all these babies, and then her husband's disappearing into a breach of faith. She would honor her the next time she saw her, make it a point to praise Josette's efforts as a mother and a wife.

Am I supposed to know that Genevieve is not Josette's? Will I offend if I mention it? Is it another secret? Marie wondered about the mother of that child. Was it an act of courage to hand over her child to another person to raise? What kind of a woman could raise another's daughter, another's son and love them as her own? Family, perhaps, could be woven easily into the mat of their days, but a stranger's child, the child of a betrayal, could that be managed under a shelter of love?

Something agitated, pushed at the back flap of her mind. Marie sat up. She felt that pressure in her head again, the increase in her breathing, and that flicker of light. When she stood up, she felt lopsided. She sat back down.

She thought of Marguerite. Her daughter raised another woman's sons. She'd chosen a hard task. Marie hadn't been all that understanding of the challenges Marguerite described to her. Instead she'd reminded Marguerite that Doublé and Toussaint grieved and to give them time since losing a mother is a loss worthy of long mourning. Marie had raised only her own children. That was quite a different task than nurturing to fruit the seeds someone else had planted in neighboring soil.

That whimpering again. Maybe the wind rose and pushed against the windows and sighed through the cracks at the door. Knuck barked into the night, now. He'd perhaps cornered a raccoon and yapped for an audience.

Marie yanked on the covers, holding her hands over her ears. She just wanted to stop thinking so she could sleep. She listened for Barbe. She couldn't hear the girl's heavy breathing, but she, too, might be awake, tossing and turning. All day yesterday she'd been busy in the barn, doing what Marie didn't know, but each time she called to her, Barbe stuck her head out and waved. "Busy be," she said, and would step back into the barn.

Yes, Barbe was busy just being.

Paul, too. Would she ever have a wakeful night and not have Paul at its center? He'd been so close! Just a few days ride to Walla Walla. He might still be there. Maybe they should go there. She and Jean and Barbe could all go now. Some of the Molalla said there was a trail over the eastern mountains that would take them eventually north to the place where Jean had been fired by Peter Skene Ogden, at the *Rivière des Chutes.* It was a shorter route to Walla Walla, though perhaps not now, not in January when the snows drifted like high ocean sands in the Cascade Mountains. They could go by boat, but it would be a hard journey in January.

Perhaps Paul came back to find them and when he couldn't, he'd stayed, hoping to gain word of his family.

No. She wasn't telling herself the truth. If Paul had wanted to see them, he would know now they'd moved to this French Prairie. She may as well stay where she was and be grateful that a mother's son had been brought back to life even if he chose not to be a part of her life at all.

Knuck barked with insistence. He wouldn't be ignored now. She elbowed Jean, but he merely groaned and rolled over. It was probably nothing. She rose and found the river rock Jean had given her, the one with the stripe of color separating—or binding—the two halves of rock. It fit firm in her hand, and she kept it close beside her bedstead. She patted for her knife in its sheath, held it in her other hand. Every time she picked up a knife she thought of the one Sacagawea had given her and she had passed on to Louis, Marguerite's father. It did not speak well of her that she could remember to recall Sacagawea each time she saw a knife, and yet she'd failed to keep praying daily for her son. Who knew what else of import she'd already forgotten?

Knuck barked short, sharp yaps. Jean said, "What is it? What's the dog shouting about?"

"There's something outside," Marie said. "It woke the dog, me before that."

She heard Jean reach for his pistol, and she heard his feet patter toward the door. "I'm standing off to your—"

"I can hear you," he said. "I'm going to open the door. Step aside."

"It sounds like it's close."

"Probably just raccoons."

Marie heard the leather latch creak, and when Jean pulled the door back they saw nothing, then heard noises. Marie looked down. A small form lay huddled in the shadows, Knuck barking at it just beyond.

Marie Anne. No one called her by that name, not even Julie, her best friend. She tried not to be snippy and correct them when they called her Marianne. She'd asked politely and then made note of it when she sat in the classes at the school, so any people she hadn't met before would think of her as Marie Anne, but even that eroded if people who knew her best wouldn't use the name. Even her mother had said, "You'll always be Marianne to me. We could have a naming ceremony as my first husband's family did."

"Didn't the Ioways have naming ceremonies?"

Her mother looked sad. "I don't remember," she said.

"If it's being treated like a grown woman you want, Bonbon," David told her. "You'll have to act like one."

"What's that supposed to mean?"

"Nothing. I was just pointing out a thing. You can't push people to change old habits just because you say to."

"I won't answer to anything but Marie Anne," she told him. "If people want to talk with me they need to do it right or I'll not speak at all."

"That would kill you," David said. "You have to talk. It's in your nature."

"So is my new name," she said.

"You'll be right, then. But you won't be happy."

She pursed her lips at him, but since his head was lowered, he didn't notice. "How's little FX doing?" she asked.

"That isn't my nephew's name," David said. He oiled a bridle, and the sweet smell of beeswax filled the room.

"There are too many François Xaviers to keep track of," she said. "Of course, I'd never tell Julie that, and I'll be sure to use his whole name in front of her, but that's my brother's name and Marguerite's baby's name, and it was even your little sister's name."

"I think she might have chosen the name because of that," David said without raising his eyes. "To remember a life that isn't anymore."

Why am I always bringing up sensitive things?

She lifted Joseph and placed him on a stool next to the table. He'd be three this fall and could well carry himself around, but she liked swinging him even if her back did ache from his weight. "Did you see that Marie Anne Ouvre at the baptism? She was carrying one of Julie's children as though she were another mother."

"She's just being helpful. The way Barbe is for your mother."

"Well, she stood closer to your brother-in-law than she should have."

David lifted his eyes. "Did she?"

"And Barbe is not all that helpful to my mother. She's a constant watch. I don't think mother got many letters learned at all at the school because Barbe kept punching her arm and pointing at this and that. Almost the way Marguerite's little one does, bringing things under your face to be named. I hope he outgrows that. I was beginning to dislike spending time with my sister watching the way she indulged that son of hers."

"Good thing then she didn't ask you to be his godmother."

His mention of that omission wounded, not that he knew. She'd never told him how left out she'd felt when her only sister chose someone else to be a godmother for her firstborn son. And after she'd been the first in the family to be baptized too. Didn't Marguerite know she would have raised that child as her own if anything happened to her? It might be that she and David would only have one child and she could take on another, if she had to. She would have made a good godmother.

"I wonder why Julie chose Kilakotah's daughter to be FX's godmother?" Marianne said out loud.

"She's a cousin," David said.

She was family to Julie, yes. But so was Marianne. *Marie Anne.* "I'd raise that baby like my own."

"They go back to early years on the prairie," David said. "Besides, a godmother isn't asked to raise a child like their own. You want to pick someone you've known for a long time so they'll understand what kind of person you are and what matters to you. A godparent raises the child as the parents would want, not how the godparent might like. Godparent's have to think through themselves and into the mind of the child's mother."

She felt as though she'd been slapped. "Did she say that about me? That I couldn't do that?"

David shook his head. "Everything isn't about you, Marianne."

Soft patter of rain tapped against Josette's tipi. Baptiste thought it formed a rhythm, and he found himself putting words into a song. He'd long ago given up the jaw harp, but music still tumbled through his head. He was never more at peace with himself than when the drummers at a feast day pounded out a beat for the dancers. He could compose a comfort song. It was how he felt. He'd had his talk with his mother. Josette acted satisfied. His children, chanting songs they'd learned from Josette's mother, he imagined, played at stick games near the fire. The old woman had been frail for years, but at Walla Walla, she wore her basket hat and sat with other wrinkled women chanting high-pitched songs and winning bones enough to trade for salt and cloth at the newly built fort. He actually missed seeing the old woman, listening to her crooning. Perhaps they should go there and bring her to this prairie.

He wished his father had taught him Sioux songs. His grandmother had sung some when he visited her on the Missouri, gave him a traveling song, she said, because she knew that he'd go far and do amazing things. He'd told her all grandmothers think this of their grandchildren and she'd smiled, but she sang the song just the same.

He tried to remember the words now. But they'd disappeared, moved out of his head as his mother might say, to make room for new thoughts, new songs.

"You were there all that time but told your mother nothing of your worry over war?" Josette asked him.

"Other things came up."

Josette bent to her weaving. The long fibers had been readied in the spring and fall, and now, in winter, the work of her hands turned to creation rather than to harvest. "How did she take your delay in telling her of Paul?" Josette asked.

Baptiste shrugged his shoulders. "It brought back old things for her. 'Poor Paul,' she said." He snorted. "Poor Paul."

"You could have saved yourself the sting of it if you had told her early, when we first came back. Or sent a letter."

He pressed saliva through the space of his front teeth, thinking. "I might have written, yes. But Paul might have written too. Paul took lessons with Sally Ross, though I don't know what he learned at her hand. If I had written Mother, she would have come to Waiilatpu, and for what? To see Paul walk away from her again? No. It's better this way. I protect her. She doesn't have to face my brother's wind-shift ways. She can blame me for the separation rather than him. I give her this gift. She doesn't have to wonder now if he lives or not."

Josette kept her head bowed while Baptiste lounged beside his wife. She knelt, a position of work she preferred. He tossed a pebble toward the dog, close enough to see if the sound might wake him. Genevieve patted at the dog's tail while he slept. Dogs in the house. He gave in to this woman over many things. He didn't want to lose her, and yet he did things that pushed at her. Stupid things like letting the sweetness of another woman's scent numb his thinking. Stupid things like telling his mother of his misstep.

Josette never brought it up to him, but he couldn't look at Genevieve without seeing pain. This happened to him before, when his daughter had lived while his first wife died. She'd been a good, sweet child, and he'd spent as little time near her as he could, her face, her eyes always taunting him, turning him toward the blame of his brother and his mother. Now here again was a child's face to taunt him about his own errors.

He didn't want to keep doing these stupid things that drove wedges between the loves of his life. He wasn't sure if his telling his mother about Genevieve would offend Josette. Or perhaps she'd feel better knowing his mother knew, at least. She wouldn't have to keep secret that pain. She'd have someone to talk with, and his mother was as good a listener as any. Unlike most men he knew, women needed listeners to get them through their days.

"I told her of Genevieve," he said.

Josette raised her eyes to his. "It's what you went to do, to confess." She snipped the last word as though it were a loose thread. He saw color deepen the chocolate of her cheeks. "I thought you would confess to one who could forgive you," she said.

"She forgives me."

"I do too. Every time."

Such a bold woman, she was, never moving her eyes from his. He'd picked a strong woman, as his father had.

"I want to do it differently this time," he said.

She looked past him in that way Indian women had of shifting pain from eyes to the sky. "There have been others." She was angry now; he could hear it in her voice.

"No, no. No other women. But I go away in other ways, you tell me this. Fast horses. Whiskey. Work."

"Maybe even this push for the militia."

"Maybe. No. That's needed, to protect you."

She opened her mouth to speak. She hesitated, then said, " 'There shall no evil befall thee, neither shall any plague come nigh thy dwelling.' Father says it is a psalm of protection. We have no need of arms."

"You forget," Baptiste said. "My first child died of a plague. My mother's husbands die violent deaths. Evil does befall us."

"I don't forget," Josette whispered. "But all you do does not prevent this. There is nothing to do to keep the sun from rising and setting on both good days and bad. We're promised a sheltering place, even when evil visits. It's how your mother puts one foot in front of the other each day, knowing she has someone who walks beside her."

Did his mother know this? Was that why she could forgive his brother and even Baptiste? "I walk there too," Baptiste said.

"I don't see it," she said. "And I have good eyes."

He tossed another pebble. He disagreed with his wife, but he didn't have the words to say so. He didn't want to push her further from him, nor say something that would send him from this warming hearth. "Paul has missed his life with his family." Maybe he would miss his too, unless he made a change. "Maybe I'm no different. Someday when I come to ask you to take me back after a foolish way, you might not be there. You might say no. Maybe this is why Paul stays away. He doesn't think we'll invite him back."

"It can't be done alone," she said. "You can't change alone."

"You would help me?"

"You see the results of my efforts. Maybe others…"

Maybe Jean. He was a good man, had treated him fairly, as a son. Jean was good to his mother. Jean was a man he could follow after.

Josette probably meant the priests were who could change him. He should have known she would have turned this around to religion. He didn't think his father had been a man of faith, though his grandmother was. His father had no room for religion, not even for spirit quests. At least he'd never told Baptiste of such a journey. He remembered some story being told that his mother was once known as "Her to Be Baptized." Perhaps his father had once been known himself that way.

No. His father gambled, drank, and abused his wife.

Gambled. Drank. Abused his wife.

Baptiste looked up at Josette, his heart pounding. He was living his father's life. He wanted to live his own.

"It's a child," Marie said. "Look there. She's shivering with wet and cold." Marie laid her rock and knife down and bent to help the child stand up, soaked through to the skin. The girl's teeth chattered, and she whimpered.

She should have gotten up when she first heard the noise instead of ruminating on old worries like a cow on her cud. She so easily discounted a thing and she'd done that, thinking the whimpering nothing more than the dog.

Marie felt a draft and the door from the outside opened again, and

Barbe came in. She stood staring at the girl, her tongue protruding out one side. *What was she doing outside? Had she heard the whimpering too?* "Get a dry blanket, Barbe," Marie told her. "Hurry now."

"Follow odors, follow odors," Barbe said as she waddled and grabbed a blanket. She squinted at the child, turned her head this way and that, as though to make sense of something plucked out of the rain. She went back outside and returned in a short time with fresh milk.

"Merci," Marie told Barbe, then turned to tend the child.

Jean poked at the hearth fire and swung the andiron holding the cast-iron pot over the flames. Soft light flooded the room. "We'll have tea," he said. "That'll warm her up."

"Question. You called?" Marie signed, asking the girl's name. She looked up, confusion washed over her face. "Name?" Marie said in English, and the girl answered.

"Angele," she said. "Sister Celeste calls me Angele."

"And so you are an angel," Marie told her, squinting. "I've seen you in the classes. But how did you find us?"

"Follow you."

"All that way? But our cabin, in the night…"

"The dog. I know the dog."

"Angele," Barbe said then. "Angele. Ha-ha."

"I know her from the school too," Angele said.

She looked about the same age as Denise, maybe younger. She was thin as a wrist bone and had pockmarks on her face, most likely from the measles that had raged through the prairie the year before. Marie hadn't recognized her under the blanket, but now that the hearth fire flashed a glow into the room, Marie saw her clearly.

Angele was one of the bright, attentive children whom Marie believed must be living with a French family, since she'd made her way to the school and brought an egg or a pinch of salt each day for payment. The Methodists still ran the Indian school much farther south, and Angele might have gone there instead, so she must have someone she lived with near the St. Paul parish.

Or someone had abandoned this child. Perhaps her parents were dead, taken by the measles.

"Where do you stay?" Marie asked.

"Where my feet find a place."

"She doesn't live anywhere?" Jean said. "How do you eat? Don't suppose she came in with one of those wagons and someone's looking for her? They'll think we took her."

"You're Indian."

The girl nodded.

"She's been at the school since I've been there. Someone provides the payment."

"She can't be eating much," said Jean.

They were talking about her as though she wasn't there.

"Someone gave her a push for learning," he continued.

The Sisters schooled her in her letters and the faith. They would surely have taken her in if they had known she had no one looking after her. It still didn't explain why she was here now.

"You came all this way because you knew of the dog and Barbe," Marie said.

"I will be baptized," Angele said. "Have my First Communion. The sisters say I need a godmother."

"Your mother has a friend who can do this?"

The girl nodded. "I have my own friend. I find Madame Dorion," Angele said. "Sister Celeste says she looks out for children."

Marguerite was pregnant again. She knew as soon as the strangeness hit her. Cravings for sweetness woke her in the night. Pinches off JB's tobacco twists sprinkled on eggs in the morning tasted tart instead of bitter. The smells in the cow pens curdled her stomach. She hadn't told JB yet.

She must not count on her husband to be there through this pregnancy either. He had failed her last time, and she mistrusted his new words of commitment. Sometimes during Mass, Marguerite looked at the children sprinkled throughout the sanctuary, seeking a resemblance with her own. Though he said he found her desirable, she doubted him.

She represented convenience, someone there to warm his bed with little effort from him.

JB was a vigorous man. He often boasted of it, how many children he wanted still. She was not a vigorous woman, she decided. Instead, she was a tired one, looking after JB's sons, tending the cows, gathering sheaves of grain, mending and cooking and polishing pots. Being an obedient wife.

She was being obedient this morning, taking care of the chores before they left for the St. Paul Parish. She'd be pleased when Father Delorme's church he called St. Louis for the French monarch was completed. They'd have less far to travel then. She could savor a few more minutes of sleep before readying her household for Mass.

The two older boys had already eaten and slicked their hair with bear grease. They helped their father now harness the team. It still galled her that for *this* baptism, JB had found a way to be present. He would attend the baptism of her mother's newest changeling, another lost one her mother had taken in. What kind of father would miss his own son's christening but show up for another's? She took a deep breath. She had to let this old anger that tied her in a knot come loose. Her stomach could ill afford such tightness, especially today.

Her mother would be the godmother for the child. What about those of her own? What about their needs and time with her? She had never wanted to be a godmother for one of them.

Had she been asked? Marguerite felt her face grow hot. She was a terrible daughter, thinking her mother stepped away when it was Marguerite who kept the distance.

She dressed Xavier in his wolf-skin jacket. JB had taken that animal, received the bounty payment promised by showing the tail, and as with all the settlers, been allowed to keep the hide for clothing. JB used poison so the hide was perfect. She'd tanned the hide herself and ran her hand now over the smooth fur. The animals were a trouble to their stock, their food supply; but they were also quite beautiful.

"Very soft, *n'est-ce pas?*" she said to Xavier. Her son nodded his approval.

"You are ready, Etoile?" JB asked.

Xavier let her tie the rawhide around the shank buttons JB had brought back from the Vancouver store.

"What does it say?" Xavier asked as he looked at the tiny lettering on the brass button.

"Gilt Rich Orange Color" she said in English. "I don't know what it means. Someday you'll go to school with your brothers and you'll tell me."

"Papa?" Xavier asked.

"It's just the name," JB told him. "I don't think it has any other meaning. Ewing Young carried them at his store years ago," JB said. "I asked him that once."

"It describes the *couleur,* that's all it does?" Marguerite said. She looked at the hue, the shine of a vibrant sunset. *"Orange,"* she said, giving it the French inflection.

"The color of a beaver's tooth after he gnaws on cottonwood," JB said. He put his front teeth on his lower lip and chomped. Xavier laughed. "A kind of fruit it is too, orange. We have not seen such fruit in this place."

"Orange color," Xavier said. "I speak English. Papa teaches me English. Papa's *ingénieux, n'est-ce pas, Mère?*"

"Yes, your father's very clever. The button maker isn't, though. To take such space simply to describe what is."

"Said often enough it becomes the button," JB said. "It comes to mean the same thing."

She pulled Xavier's coat closed and pressed against her knees to stand up. JB had already pulled her own fur coat from the peg on the wall. He held it for her now, then turned her so he could button up the front.

As though I am a child.

"It pulls tight across your chest, Etoile." JB tugged on it. "You gain weight at last." He smiled at her.

She supposed today she would tell JB. He would like knowing today so he could boast about it to their friends and family, so he could say his *femme* would soon give another baby to "this old man." He would smoke a pipe in celebration, and the smell would sicken her. Everyone would clap his back, and men like Joseph Gervais who'd had three wives already and nearly a dozen children would sing his praises as though the man performed these feats of fatherhood all by himself.

So maybe he wouldn't be indifferent to the baby. His passion for his part in a child just excluded her.

She would tell her mother first. Let JB be last to know.

"It's good you fill out, Etoile." He patted her shoulder like a pup. "Your coat is buttoned tight now with your 'gilt rich orange *couleur.*' You stay too thin; people believe I work you too hard or that I don't take care of my family well. Your body tells secrets better left unsaid, eh?"

"It says what is," she told him. "Like the button does."

Jean stood with his hands folded in front of him while the child, Angele, walked down the aisle to be baptized. Marie would be named godmother. It was the first time she had been named this way. His Marie had resisted such a role fearing it meant she must be as good a parent as God.

"No one can be," he'd told her. "It is useless to strive that way. It will tire you. The job of the godmother is to raise the child as God would, be the one who engraves her name in her heart as God engraves the child's name in his palm. Your work is to allow God to guide, not get in God's way."

When they'd arrived early for the Mass, it was the older sister who told Marie that Angele appeared to have no family and that they discovered she'd been staying in the barns, moving when the laborers came to milk. The eggs and salt she brought for payment belonged to the parish itself. "She went off, and we didn't know where."

Angele was smart, ready to answer her catechism questions, and obviously a survivor who knew what she wanted, even for one so young. Her dress looked like a Methodist Mission cloth dress, simple with a tie belt at her middle. She had no head lice that Jean could see, which was a sign that she bathed often or knew that cedar chips repelled them. Barbe, too, had taken to her, rubbing the girl's head with a blanket to dry up her strands of wet hair, chattering with her and even sharing a piece of the bread they had broken their evening fast with. She'd run out to the barn and brought in eggs for breakfast, then run back without being told to milk the cow, bringing fresh milk in, the foam still warm.

François had been less enthusiastic. "Another one, Mother? Will you always be taking people in?"

"When needed," she said. "It's what I do."

"Women everywhere in the house," he mumbled.

"Not all of the household," Jean told him. He punched his son's shoulder gently with his fist. "They have more need of us now, eh?" His son didn't understand his mother, her need to give what she could. Sometimes, though, Jean wondered if something besides compassion called to her.

"You'll live with us then," Marie told Angele after the Sister's explanation. "And there will be rules to follow. No stealing from the henhouse ever again."

Angele lowered her eyes. "No, *Mère*." So that day in early February, they prepared for the baptism of Angele. All were there at the St. Paul church, his daughter and his son, his stepdaughter Marguerite and her children and husband, too. Even Baptiste's family huddled in the log church. Only Barbe stayed away, and Marie had allowed it.

He watched while Angele came forward, her head bowed.

Then Baptiste stepped forward.

"You will be a godfather?" Marie asked, surprise in her voice.

"Non," he said. "I'm here to be baptized."

Marie's mouth dropped wide then closed. He knelt for baptism, and then Josette stepped forward for the same. Jean looked over at Marie and could see tears pooling in her eyes. She would sing a special song when they left here. A mother's song of celebration.

"Angele Indian," the priest intoned the child's name, and the girl leaned over. Marie stood behind her at the baptismal font. Jean could smell the wax candles burning in their sconces. The shuffle of feet on the wooden floor sounded like music to his ears. He'd been a part of this day of dedication, a day of bringing protection to those he loved through the all-encompassing hand of God. It was as a father should be, at the head of his clan.

He'd thought all was finished when Baptiste stepped forward again. With Josette this time. The priest announced the reading of the banns of marriage between them, "the dispensation of the second and third having been granted," so the ceremony could commence.

His stepson baptized and legitimately married. His wife a godmother. This was a good day, a white light day, nothing dark in it at all. He thought his heart would burst with the joy of it.

"My *mère,*" Angele said and grinned at Marie.

Mère, Jean thought. The same French word used to describe the scum of fermentation that resulted in *de vinaigre.* The words were pronounced in exactly the same way but meant something so different. They were connected at that, he decided. The discard, the *mere* from apples helped form vinegar, a liquid of life. Vinegar, what they'd longed for on that journey across country, longed for still if supplies ran low. It was the discard for a healing balm one swallowed that kept bones from crumbling. They were things that went together, *mere* and *vinaigre, mère* and mothers.

He'd already begun to return to the wooden bench when Sister Celeste handed a bundle to Marie.

"Two need godmothers today," she said. "This one is but a day old and hungers for a mother's song. She calls your name, Madame Dorion. Your *vocare,* your *métier,* is for this infant, *n'est-ce pas?* Yours as well." She nodded to Jean.

Marie looked startled. She stared at the infant, then at him, a question in her eyes.

"Another?" Jean said. "Oh, I don't know..." But he could never deny this woman, not ever.

Marie nodded to the Sister, accepted the child.

This was his family, then, led by one woman who kept them all from crumbling, all as strong as bone.

14

Shifting Shades

"Is it a sister to Angele or…" Marie asked the nun as the infant made a mewing sound.

"Unknown parentage. She was found yesterday in the barns."

"An abandoned child? Angele, did you know of this?" The girl shook her head, hid behind Marie. "But who…one so tiny, so young? Who could do this?"

"Someone very troubled, perhaps unable to care for the child themselves. Perhaps the mother died and the father, knowing it would be well tended, brought the child to us," Sister Celeste said.

Marie took a deep breath to open the blanket for all to see. A bronze-colored face surrounded by a halo of dark hair lay before her. Lips the thickness of melon seeds pursed, and the infant's eyes squinted against the light, wrinkling an upturned nose. She fit easily into Marie's small hands and weighed no more than a sturdy knife.

"There is no board for her? No sleeping place?" Marie asked.

The infant opened her eyes then closed them, the gesture as fleeting as a hummingbird's brush against a flower. The act sliced at Marie, pierced a longing place beneath her heart.

She felt a familiar lightness of head, her own heart pounding at her temples, her breath coming short. "No one made a place for her to sleep?"

"Are you all right?" Jean asked her as though from far away.

"What? *Oui.* Just…surprised."

"So many of the younger women have children of their own to care for. We thought of you," the long-faced Sister said. "Your compassion is legend. We didn't realize Angele had chosen you to live with or that you'd accepted her. Of course, if this wee one is too much…it could be too much."

Marie's mind buzzed like a rattlesnake's warning.

"Are you certain you're not ill, Madame Dorion? You look feverish," the priest said.

"*Non. Oui.* I'm well," Marie said. "We'll take the infant." She raised her eyes to Jean's. A flash of light behind Jean's head now took his face into shadow.

"We've called her Baby Marie," the Sister said.

"Oui," Marie said. Jean lifted the bundle from her arms. Her head felt like a seedpod ready to burst.

"Mama?" someone said. Marie felt a hand at her elbow.

"Marianne? Just help me sit. I...didn't sleep well. *Pardon, pardon,*" Marie said to the priest, to the Sisters, to her family. *What have I done? "Pardon."* She spoke the last word as prayer.

⌖

Jean watched as JB helped Marguerite into the wagon. She sat beside him now, the boys in the back, though Xavier still wiggled between them. Marianne. No, Marie Anne, as she wished to be called, walked beside Marie, past David and Julie and her husband. The girl helped her mother up into the wagon, reassured by Marie's words that she wasn't ill. Marianne's hands lifted and dipped as she spoke. He heard laughter from the girl's friends, Marianne at the center.

François, too, was in a better mood with the Longtain girl attending Mass that morning. He'd already said he'd stay behind for a time. This was good. Jean wanted time alone with Marie, with just the two adults around. With an infant in her arms and Angele nestled into the furs in the box, they weren't really going to be alone. He was just grateful they didn't have Barbe along today. He had no patience for answering that one's chattering questions, not when he could tell that something was terribly amiss with Marie.

Jean didn't know what he could do about it until he knew what it was. She might never choose to tell him.

"You are now godmother twice," he said as the wheels broke through thin layers of ice on the road. The seat they sat on creaked and groaned and the harness jingled. Between Marie's feet, she steadied a water jar filled with goat's milk the Sisters had sent home with them. Dusk blanketed, promising darkness. Angele fell immediately asleep curled up in the robes. The infant slept too, in Marie's arms.

"Father Delorme named her Marie," Marie said.

"Another mother name. Marie Anne. Marianne. You. How will I keep you all straight?"

"This is Baby," Marie said. "Until she chooses a name of her own."

"The Sisters know nothing about where she comes from?" Jean asked. "They said nothing more?"

"She's very, very young, born just yesterday they think. See the down on her skin. Like a gosling." Marie ran her finger over the child's brow, the brown fuzz flowing back into her hair.

"She looked at you. She might be older."

"So small. Her mother abandons her sometime in the night. Leaves her behind." Her words caught in her throat.

"You didn't do that, my Marie." His wife perched now on the edge of the seat as though she might take flight, so he spoke the words as soft and as soothing as he could. "Your infant Vivacité passed into the next world with you beside her, hoping to keep her alive, *n'est-ce pas?* You didn't leave her behind."

"We should get a goat," Marie said, firm. "The cow's milk might be too hard for her. But Julie tells me today she has milk for more than one if we need it."

"Good then. This infant will live, Marie. She's small but sturdy, eh?" Marie said nothing. "I hope Barbe's ready for another change." As they passed construction of the St. Louis church, Jean commented that they'd not have so far to travel to Mass in the future. Marie remained silent, her shoulders bouncing to the rutted road. Meaningless talk. Chattering as Barbe did. What else could he do? How could he break through this fence Marie put up? *"Femme,"* he said then, to get her attention. When she turned to him, her eyes held the look of a frightened rabbit cornered by a dog. "It is all right, my Marie. What troubles you, eh? You can say to me. I can fix it, *oui?*"

"Barbe must be asleep," Marie said, pointing toward the house. "No smoke. She let the fire go out."

He nodded. That wasn't what troubled her. She avoided. She wouldn't tell him now. Maybe later, when Angele was asleep, Barbe, too, tucked in for the night. "You'll be all right, while I put the animals up?" He stepped out and took the infant, helped Marie down. He woke Angele, gently, carried her into the house.

"I don't see Barbe," Marie said.

"Probably fell asleep in the barn. I didn't see Knuck either. You tend these little ones, Marie. I'll check the cows."

"Oui," Marie said.

Jean unharnessed the team, led the horses one at a time toward the gate after brushing them dry. With a swat on their rumps, he sent them into the meadow. Stars salted the night, and he let their message of endurance wash over him. "If it is true that we are, every one, as unique as each of these stars," he prayed aloud, "then you must know my thoughts. Tell me what I can do to bring comfort to Marie. Show me," Jean said. "Show me."

Knuck leaned up against his leg then, and he bent to scratch the dog. "So where is your friend?" Jean said. "Barbe. Wake up in there. Time to come inside to sleep." He lifted the wooden milk bucket and, followed by the dog, walked into the barn. He'd begun the day the father of two, stepfather to three, an adopted father to Barbe, and now he'd added two more to his life, one so tiny he could hold her in the palm of his good hand. He wondered if Marie's first daughter had been that small.

This infant must remind Marie of Vivacité. That was what troubled her, of course! He should have known this even though he wasn't there when the child died. Pierre Dorion and his family had stayed behind for the birth of that infant on Hunt's journey to Astoria. But he'd heard the story whispered from *engagés* who knew Dorion better than he did. He'd heard the rumor that her husband might have wanted the child to die, it came so soon, so tiny, with the mother nearly starving already and no food to keep the babe alive and barely the older two. Supposedly that was why the Dorions had stayed back, so Pierre could do what he must to keep the rest of his family alive.

But she had dissuaded him and kept the child living. For one week.

This small Baby must bring all that back. He would find a way to comfort her, if she'd let him. Give her what she needed to endure.

This day he'd colored in white, Jean thought, as a good day with family and friends. But now, he wasn't so sure. Perhaps no day was all black or all white, but rather a rainbow of color known by its shifting shades and pale hues. The colors changed. It was what living looked like.

He pushed a forkful of grass hay into the manger. He stepped out to prod the first cow to the inside stanchion. Etoile ambled in, stuck her head between the two rough boards to reach the hay. Tiny strings of her hide stuck to the rough edges of the stanchion. Her neck moving in and out would smooth those edges down in time.

"You're a fine old cow, Etoile," Jean said. He scratched at the rounded brow. He bent to lift his bucket and begin the milking when he looked down at the hay. Several strands stuck together into a mat. How had manure gotten there? He touched it. His fingernail flaked some off. It didn't smell like manure. He put his tongue to the flecks. He tasted the salt of blood.

❖

"She never should have done that," Marguerite said. She and JB lay next to each other in the feather bed, her arms crossed over her chest. It had been a long day with the events at the church. Marguerite sat up, punched the pillow to get it just right, then lay back down. She held her arms tight to her side as though they were the stanchions in the barn and her body held rigid in one place. "What's the point?"

"What now, Etoile? What is it your mother fails you in now?"

"What makes you think this is about my mother?" Marguerite asked him.

"It's…her," JB said so softly she didn't hear it all.

"What? You mumble," Marguerite said.

JB rolled over onto his side, his arm up over his head. "So tell me. What has your mother done?"

"She isn't failing me. This has nothing to do with her," she said. JB grunted and circled his finger on the arm of her nightdress, his rough hands catching on the cloth. She sighed. "She's too old to be trying to raise two children, one so young, too, while Barbe hovers around her."

"Barbe helps her, eh? Good, big girl like that can do work for her."

Marguerite hesitated, decided there was nothing unusual in JB's voice.

"She should be resting or spending time with her grandchildren." Marguerite said.

"Maybe she likes the sound of little feet on her floor."

"You men don't understand," Marguerite told him.

"This is true," JB said. "The most true of all you've said."

The boys fidgeted in the loft. Marguerite heard their voices rise then fall, arguing going on. They'd keep it up all night if she didn't yell for them to stop. They'd wake Xavier, and then he'd be up demanding something to eat, and then JB would decide he was hungry and there'd be no rest for her. None. All because JB refused to discipline his sons. Well, she wouldn't do it. She'd wait to see if he was aware of what his sons did to distract.

"Maybe you are envious, Etoile," JB said then, cooing like a dove.

"Of the work she takes on for herself? No. I just worry about her. A daughter is to honor her mother and father and give them due respect. I can't do that when my mother acts more like my sister, taking on the tasks of a young woman. She has more children at home now than Marianne, as many children as I have. All girls for her. All boys for me." She sighed.

"It's good you count my sons as part of yours now."

Did I?

"She has no time to give to Xavier, her grandson. No time to tell him of her ways when she was young and of my father's, what she knows of them. What she can remember. She tells things to Sister Celeste, things we've probably never known about."

"I can tell of French Canadian ways," JB said.

"We know so little of my mother's family. How can Xavier know who he is without the stories of his past?"

"Maybe they come through the blood, Etoile. Maybe they don't have to be heard or said; they are felt and lived the way a *voyageur* who has river water running through his veins passes on to his sons how to read the streams."

How foolish men could be. She was surrounded by such foolish men, JB, his sons, and maybe her own unless she could raise Xavier well.

"You two! *Faites attention,* or I will come up there to put you to sleep and you will not have good dreams."

The boys settled down.

Notice what you want more of, her mother had once said.

"Thank you, for quieting them," Marguerite said.

"It is a father's duty."

"One you often neglect," she said.

JB stopped the circling of his finger at her arm. He lay heavy as heartbreak.

"Every good thread you sew, you too quickly tear apart," JB said.

He was right. *"Pardon,"* she whispered.

"You're tired," he said. He patted her shoulder. "She will have time for you, Etoile. She makes time for her oldest daughter if you ask."

"I shouldn't have to ask," Marguerite said.

"All that *should* happen in a life is that the sun should come up and night should follow day. A *should* that is not the brother of something natural has judgment written on it. It would be nice if everything went as we wished, but this desire that all things should go the way we want is wasted. *Shoulds* weigh heavy on a head."

"But if I've asked your sons to do something, and they know how to do it and it's a reasonable request and they don't, shouldn't they do it? Shouldn't you make them do it? Shouldn't a son honor his mother?"

JB thought. "This *should* word is a hammer," he said, "meant to pound you down. It keeps you from finding out what else you could do if you weren't *should*ing someone else, wanting them to change. Your mother should do what she thinks she is called to do, whether it pleases you or not."

JB could be so exasperating.

He turned over, tugged on the blanket. "I have no daughters," he said. "Maybe if I do I can help." He yawned. "We should get some sleep now, Etoile. So we do not wake our sons and they give us bad dreams."

"We should," she said. "But it's not the natural order of things, so it's wasted."

JB lay quiet for a time but she knew he didn't sleep. She had such a cutting tongue. She should apologize. She should stop complaining. She should at least tell him of his expanding family.

"In August," Marguerite said. "Maybe you'll know then what it is to raise a daughter."

JB turned back over. "This is true? It should happen in the summer?"

"Oui," Marguerite said. "And this thread of a good thing I will not tear out."

"We *should* celebrate," JB said, and they both laughed.

Could it be that the lopsidedness revealed itself at last? Flickering lights to keep her from remembering, her heart pounding to make her listen to what stood before her instead of what had been? The forgetfulness, the confusing of faces were so much easier to think about than this. Marie pressed the cloth from the baby's chin so she could see more clearly. Hers had been a boy. A firstborn son. She had failed to find a way to keep him. Had she been given another chance, or was this just punishment, cleverly conveyed? Her *métier,* Sister Celeste said. Her *vocare.* Marie shivered with the contradiction. A double-edged knife: her love of children, her inability to keep them safe, a knife that cut both ways.

"Is Barbe here?" Jean said. Marie wiped her eyes of tears, and the infant startled with his words. Jean lifted the bucket onto the plank table. "Etoile gave little milk tonight. She'd been milked already."

"Something's happened to her," he continued.

"Why do you say this?" It was what she thought too now, with the house all empty and cold, but she had no forewarning, nothing that suggested she should worry. Her thoughts had been far from Barbe. She might have taken a horse out and been injured. She might have wandered over to Josette and Baptiste's, where Archange stayed. Perhaps she'd fallen asleep there. Had she decided to follow them after all? No, they would have encountered her somewhere along the trail coming back.

Jean handed her a swatch of grass hay matted together.

"What's this?"

"Blood," he said. "It's someone's blood. And," he cleared his throat. "I find this too."

Marie took the slender thread of flesh, dried now like the curl of a vine on a ripe melon. "The life cord," she said. She stepped to the wooden box she'd had salt in but which now housed tiny Baby Marie close to the warming fire. "Her cord," Marie said.

"I didn't think that," Jean said.

"The baby was born in our barn," Marie said, "Barbe was well this morning. Remember? And she skips in and out yesterday, is gone a long time and I even wondered if she had been up in the night as well. The whimpering. It might not have been Angele at all. Maybe Barbe's earlier. Maybe I did doze."

"She'd need a father for this, Marie. It may be she's fallen, cut herself—"

"Archange," Marie said, her mind racing backward. "They were together at the camp meeting. I thought he looked after her. I should have watched better so—"

"Don't, Marie. Don't begin with blame for what you did or didn't do. You gave her a good place to live. She is a young girl. She doesn't know. It may not have been Archange, either. It may not be Barbe's. She maybe helped someone else, is helpful like you are, eh? We mustn't judge too quickly."

"Maybe she wants to be with someone who doesn't always give her orders. She wants to be noticed and cared about and left alone without blame. That's why she wouldn't she tell us. The baby could have died in the night."

"This baby has a will to live," Jean said. "I'll ride to Baptiste's to see if Archange has seen her. Remember, this may not even be her *enfant.* She may have her child beside her—if that is a baby's cord. Hers could be suckling even now."

"It's hers. The cord… How could I leave the child behind?"

"You didn't, Marie," Jean corrected.

"What kind of mother would give up her child like that? For another to raise?" She wrapped her arms around herself.

"Maybe this mother understands that two parents would be better than one parent. If it is Barbe's, the child won't have to beg for the occasional attention from her mother. She'll have a family, complete and whole," Jean said. "It is a gift to give up an infant for this reason. A mother's greatest gift, perhaps, next to giving life."

Marie felt the pressure against her eyes, a piercing light flashed then faded.

"I did this," she whispered.

"No. You were good to Barbe. You do nothing to harm her. You taught her well not to hold close to strangers. You—"

"I did this. I left a child behind."

"This is not so of Vivacité. You know this. And if it's Paul you think of, we came here from Walla Walla only after Paul had many years to return. Now we know he is alive. You did not leave him. He left you. He was ungrateful...or young, and then didn't know how to come back to you. He misses out on growing up by not facing you after that much pain. You've left no one, my Marie. You're a good woman. A good mother."

"Another son," Marie whispered. "I left behind another son. His name was John."

The rainy winter separated the prairie families, keeping them close to their hearths. The rivers ran full and fast, and roads sucked horses' hooves into mud so deep it had taken ropes and many men drenched to the skin to pull them out. Better to stay home.

In June, when the rains ceased, Baptiste took his beaver pelts, wolf hides, a cougar hide, and a lynx and loaded them on his packhorse. Along with his oldest son, Pierre, he headed north, the summer sun already warm and the earth rich with the scent of rebirth. They'd left Josette busy tanning two deer hides. The one would have brought a good price. It still would when she finished. The other was from Pierre's first kill. The meat had already been given away, as was the custom of Josette's family. His too, he thought. Hadn't his father told him of that practice?

When Josette finished the tanning, she'd make a dress for Pierre's grandmother and a *par flèche* for Jean, his only grandfather still alive. He guessed she'd save something back for Josette's mother too, but all would eventually be given away to an elder, to honor the bounty of his son's first hunting success. When she finished.

Josette tired easily, and it took her longer to do things. Before he left for the fort, he'd tied the ends of her flensing tool, from Pierre's deer's leg bone, and he'd filed little teeth into the edge. Then he'd wrapped the bone tool with rawhide so she wouldn't cut her hands as she stabbed at the fur, scraping it off. He'd set up the plank against the barn so she could gouge the flesh stuck on the hide. Denise was a good helper, looking after the children. He and Pierre would be back in four or five days. He had business to attend to, and he needed time with his son when he wasn't giving orders.

They rode up past the new church and a blacksmith that had built a shop nearby. One of the overlanders. They called the area St. Louis, the church establishing the name.

He and Pierre crossed the Willamette by ferry, then rode on north past Michel LaFramboise's farm, on toward Scappoose, where he hoped Tom McKay might be working horses. Farther south, Tom had built a flourmill on Champoeg Creek, and French Canadians and now Americans, too, brought their wheat to him. At his Scappoose ranch, hundreds of fine horses grazed. Tom painted a place with prosperity.

Baptiste hoped to talk to his old friend, to catch up on how his sons were doing in the schools back East, and how he fared with his brother, a man who'd lived long on French Prairie. Baptiste had just learned the two were related. For some reason, McLoughlin didn't talk much of this other son, Joseph. Family secrets, Baptiste supposed. He guessed all families had them.

Most of all, he wanted to ask Tom what he'd heard of the rumblings from Waiilatpu. And he wondered if Tom knew of any British plans to secure the area if trouble arose, and was he looking to a British-led militia to help protect his interests? What Tom was thinking always interested Baptiste.

Josette didn't want him carrying arms, and he'd given in mostly to her wishes. Instead he'd hunted and trapped and used his adz to make an oaken canoe he sold to the Americans, who either didn't know how to form a worthy craft or who had little time to spare from breaking sod for seed. He had barter for trade, ammunition, and enough food stored to keep his family safe. That was all that mattered. That and living beside Josette without strife.

Baptiste hadn't actually spent any time with men who said they'd form a militia. The provisional government had no money to support an army. Robert Newell had been named one of three to head the area newly named Champoeg County. Josette said the Americans named it by mistake, thinking it a French word, but it was an Indian word for *root,* the *champoo.*

"Maybe it's both French and Indian," he'd told her once. "French for *field* is *champ,* and *pooich* the word for *root.*"

"Like our sons, both French and Indian," she'd said.

The district formed a militia, though the few hostilities near Oregon City involving Indians had been handled by White and his constables assigned to the city. Perhaps a full-blown militia on the prairie wasn't needed. Maybe the American flow into the region would slow so the things that brought friction between people who wanted to conquer the land and the people who wed it wouldn't increase. Maybe, as Josette said, the presence of a militia suggested trouble rather than prevented it. "A militia merely enflames dying embers."

He hoped they were dying, the fires between Indians and non. Tom would know.

But Tom wasn't there.

Louis LaBonte and Kilakotah, who looked after Tom's ranch, insisted Baptiste and Pierre spend the night, and they did, liking the idea of a dry roof to shelter them away from a late season downpour.

"This is that little boy?" Kilakotah said.

"I'm not little," Pierre told her. He had his arms over his chest, his legs wide. He wore only buckskin leggings even in the hot weather, something Baptiste allowed.

Baptiste elbowed his son. "You speak good to her. She's a grandmother."

"He should speak well to all women," Kilakotah said. "Even a young woman becomes a grandmother if she's fortunate. He looks like you," Kilakotah said. "Are you tough like your father?"

Pierre nodded. Baptiste elbowed him again. "Yes, Grandmother," he added.

"Your mother is well?" Kilakotah asked then.

Baptiste nodded. "She takes on two new little ones, my mother."

"Children flocked to her like lambs to their mothers," Louis said. "I remember how they'd come announcing the brigades and run first to your mother. Boys your son's age."

"So she'd know when Jean arrived," he said.

"That Toupin, he made a good catch with your mother," LaBonte said.

"She has help?" Kilakotah asked. "She takes on two new lives to raise. She must have a slave then finally. Good."

"No," Baptiste said. "And the woman child, Barbe, left, so it is just her new little ones. Including an infant. It tires her," Baptiste said then. "She looks older since that one came four months ago."

"I miss visiting her," Kilakotah said. "With the weather changing, maybe we'll see her more."

The men talked then of tensions between those newly coming West and those who'd been here, of the British and Americans, even of Dr. John McLoughlin and his land troubles at Oregon City.

"Always arguing over something, you men," Kilakotah said as she served Baptiste and his son bacon and beans with hard bread to soak up the juices.

"And you don't argue, you women?" LaBonte said. He winked at Baptiste.

"We tend each other," she said.

"Plenty of that needed," LaBonte said. He chewed, then said, "You know about the measles." Baptiste nodded. "Several cases here, more farther east. Among the tribes."

"I knew. I thought it passed."

"Still going. Last year was a bad one. Cayuse might be down by half."

The loss alarmed him. He'd made a good choice then, bringing his family back here, away from the disease. If they stayed to themselves, they could avoid the pox too…if it stayed very long.

As he and Pierre rode toward Fort Vancouver, he considered whether he should arrange to go to Walla Walla, find out if Josette's mother and uncle's family were safe. Had Dr. White talked to them about how to manage the disease? Maybe there wasn't any way to contain it; maybe like the Americans coming West, it just did what it did no matter how anyone tried to prevent it.

Maybe the Americans traveling in had even brought it.

Upon arriving at the fort, Baptiste noticed fewer ships docked and inside the post, the piles of corduroy pants were smaller. Not as many bales lined the shipping section prepared for transport. Supplies to serve the Walla Walla country and farther east still came through here and for the Willamette country. In fact, the Company had built a warehouse near the sandy crossing at Champoeg, and he could have merely taken his pelts there for trade. But he'd wanted to see how the fort had changed. And he'd wanted to talk with Tom. He'd wanted a good journey with his son beside him.

Things appeared to wind down at the fort. Only two hundred men served here, though thousands now lived in the valley. And thousands more were coming. The HMS *Modest,* a big British ship, had eased into and then out of the harbor. A subtle message that the Brits were giving in to the fledgling American provisional government? Who would protect the settlers if the tribes united and took back their lands? Perhaps the chief factor of Hudson's Bay, George Simpson, now groomed Fort Victoria farther north as the British center, closer to that Puget Sound port. The British might well abandon those in the south. These Kalapuya were wiped out, but hundreds of strong warriors had come to treat with White. If they chose to attack the Americans and people in this valley, there'd be little to stop them.

His son pulled at his sleeve, nodded with his chin to men talking.

"He actually nailed a sign, right on a post near their cabin," Baptiste overheard an *engagé* say.

"They get pretty brassy, those Americans. Don't seem to notice territories or boundaries," another said.

"'Meddle not with this house nor claim, for under is the master's name.' That's what the American wrote and then he signed his name. Big as life. Henry Williamson."

"At least he writes," Baptiste said.

"Aye, that he does. Yells, too. McLoughlin had the sign removed, stripped from the tree, and the fellow and his friend came in howling. They'd built their cabin a stone's throw from the fort, but nothing to say the Brits own the land. McLoughlin had the man's house torn down too. Pulled down the cat-and-clay chimney and all. Just a stain where that cabin once stood."

"This Williamson took issue with that," Baptiste said.

"He did. A man's home belongs to him. No one can take it from him, no one, without expecting a fight. McLoughlin might learn that himself with his property at the falls."

"When I was a boy coming through here with Hunt," Baptiste said, "this land wasn't McLoughlin's nor Williamson's."

"You mean McLoughlin squatted first?" the *engagé* wanted to know.

"He did," Baptiste said.

"Whose was it?"

"Multnomah's land, and a few dozen other people's who aren't even here anymore."

"That's the facts of life, eh?" the *engagé* said.

"One McLoughlin might have to learn," the second man said. "A man arrives, builds his house, and then someone tries to take it away. If it's worth having, it's worth fighting for, I say."

"The Brits might say the same. And the Americans. And the Cayuse," Baptiste said.

"Best we arm ourselves then," the *engagé* said. He lifted a painted paddle. "I've my weapon of choice."

"My papa has a rifle," Pierre said. "Better than your paddle."

"Is it now. Well, this ol' paddle of my grandfather will help me beat the buggers off if they try to take my home."

"It paddles your canoe," Pierre said with disgust.

The *engagé* laughed. "It can take me up the river to a safer place."

"Williamson might have to do that too," the other man added.

Baptiste picked up the supplies he'd come for. He added extra quinine. It might forestall the measles if it came to this region. He found a sewing kit for Denise. She was old enough now to be of more help to her mother. Pierre asked for a maple sugar cone, and he traded for it, the child still a child, though he'd overheard men's talk these past few days.

Baptiste remembered he'd been along when his father had some difficult encounters. He'd heard him shout and threaten, sometimes at the gambling tables playing *vingt et un.* He remembered huddling in the corner, torn because he so wanted to be with his father and yet fearful that something might happen, that he might not be safe. Once he'd dreamed that his father had shoved another boy at him, someone who stood beside his father. "Meet your brother," he'd said. When Baptiste told his father about the dream later, his father struck his face and told him never to mention it again, not ever. That's when he'd begun having the looping dreams.

His father had fought once over money on a gaming table. Baptiste cried, and his father had turned on him and told him to act like a man, to stop his sniveling. He'd cried for his mother then, an act that enraged his father more. Later, after his father had slept and morning came into the corner, Baptiste awoke to find his father kneeling down, pulling him to him, saying *"Pardon, pardon."* Words that soothed his soul.

He wanted his son to feel soothed by a father's presence, but without the agony that preceded those embraces. He didn't want him ever to know such unpredictable, uncertain ways.

"What do we need for Mama?" Pierre asked, pulling on the fringe of his shirt.

What did they need for a siege, to hold out against disease or invaders, the uncertainty of family and days? Josette would say they needed prayers.

Baptiste bought ammunition.

15

Revelation

"When?" Marianne asked her husband. She took the carrots David handed her, rubbed the dirt from the tubers, then stuck them into her apron. "We do almost everything together and I…oh, David, you don't suppose I've been exposed to the measles too?"

"I don't think that's what it is," David said. "She doesn't have scabs or—"

"That little Angele living with Mother and Papa. She had it. That's where we've gotten it from, right?" Marianne felt her cheeks grow warm and knew it wasn't all from the July heat because a light breeze brushed at her face.

"Angele hasn't been sick. But the Sisters have been. And people at the mission. Indians by the dozens," David said. "But none have the marks. They spasm and cramp and get clammy, and they can't keep anything in them. Father says maybe it started from the ship, *Modest.* That captain traveled to the mission, and not long after—"

"You can tell by her face? Does it work that way? If you've had it and survive, do you just go on and keep spreading it?" She could hear her voice rising in pitch.

"Mama?" Joseph said.

"Ooh," Marianne said. "Put that down. I hate those things." Joseph laughed as he let the slug ooze its way around his fingers and then over the back of his pudgy palm.

David cleared his throat. "Julie's husband wondered if you could, if you would, come and look after Julie and the baby."

"Can't Angelique?"

"She has her hands full, with my brothers at home and her youngest is only three."

"But I've got a home too, and a family to care for."

She carried the carrots to the basket at the edge of the garden, dumped them in. She liked the hard sound of them, their stiffness thumping into the basket. She stomped back, the feel of the earth against her bare feet, affirming and solid. Her mother would say to follow her *métier,* to do that work to which she was best suited. Tending the sick wasn't it.

Joseph had followed her, and she brushed the slug from his hand then picked him up and plopped him on her hip. She patted his leg as she stood over David, still bent to his work.

"Not so hard, Mama."

She rubbed her son's leg now, brushed the tight frizz of hair from his neck. She needed to cut his hair. She had things to do too. She took a deep breath. "Why don't I stay with Angelique's children and cook for all of you and she can go look after Julie."

"She's asked for you."

"It was that little Angele."

"There's no sense looking for blame," David said. "It just keeps you from deciding something."

Marianne didn't have Barbe to blame anymore. The girl had simply disappeared, along with Archange, who had once worked for her brother. No one knew truly if the infant her mother looked after was Barbe's or not, but it had to be. Barbe couldn't possibly raise a child on her own. It took a responsible adult to do that, and as limited as her mind was, Barbe must have known it.

"No one knows how the sickness moves between people, Marianne. Marie Anne," he corrected. "Dr. Barclay at the fort says maybe it's related to waste, to sewage and water. Maybe that's why people get so thirsty."

"Maybe Marguerite could do it."

"She'll have her baby soon. And don't offer up Josette, either."

"I wasn't going to. I know she's ill. They haven't even been to Mass to baptize Philomene yet." She brightened. "I hope they ask me to be godmother. What about that Marie Anne Ouvre that Julie took into her home? Can't she help? Why can't she look after Julie?"

"My sister asks for you. You're her friend. I'd think you'd be pleased to know you could help her, and that she wants that from you. It's not easy for her to ask."

"She'll get better, won't she David? I mean, she won't...die, will she? She's so young and so healthy. Even her babies didn't wear her out. She had an easy birth, not like mine with Joseph. She'll pull through, won't she?"

"Disease is no respecter of hardiness," he said. He used his folding knife to scrape dirt from the carrot, then bit into it.

"Aren't you worried that something might happen to me?"

"I don't want you sick." David swallowed. "You know that. But you're strong. And father says to use lye soap often and maybe it won't spread."

"What do our hands have to do with it if it's in the air?"

David sighed. "Taking care of Julie now is what matters, getting her back to health. You always liked spending time there."

"When we can do things together." Joseph wiggled to be let down, throwing himself back. As soon as his feet hit the ground, he was off and running.

"Would I have to...give her things, to make her throw up?"

"Your mother says that's not the treatment. Julie hasn't wanted to eat, and still she has the bloody flux."

Marianne shivered. She had a weak stomach; David knew that.

"The fluid's just a part of us," David said. "Nothing to shiver over."

"But what'll I give her then?"

"Your mother's made a syrup. Julie will need it every twelve hours. She needs you, Marianne. She'd be there for you."

Marianne bent to pull carrots herself, yanking at the leafy green. Why did this have to happen to Julie? She hated illness. She'd never told a soul, but people who were sickly always preyed on her, clutched at her as though they had talons. She was impatient and easily frustrated caring for sick ones. For Joseph, if he got ill, she could do it. A mother could always do it for a child, but for others? She could never nurse them to health the way her mother did for strangers.

Her skill lived in treating the spirit, helping people laugh and forget their troubles. That was part of healing too, as important as syrups.

Maybe Julie would just get better. She'd ask for that in her prayers. Light a candle at Sunday Mass just for her friend.

Father Desmet had been ill fifteen days with the flux last summer, though, and if anyone had access to powerful prayers, it would surely be him.

"Well?" David said.

"After the Fourth of July celebration," she said. "Tell her I'll come then. I've promised to help with the food and the music. It'll be our first celebration at the St. Louis church." David frowned. "I have obligations to keep too."

Barbe had once brought the sorrel plant to her, pulled it from the wheat field. Marie had taken the pounding stone and ground the seeds and then cooked it to a broth. "For tummy," she said and acted out cramps. Marie preferred vinegar and salt for the flux. She'd given it to her grandson once, and he'd healed. Angelique made syrups, and Marie had done that as well, of rose water and ash and rhubarb cooked slow over a fire with two slivers of maple sugar. Marie made that recipe now with plans to take it to Julie's household. She hoped it would bring comfort.

It would be better, of course, to know what caused this flux, but some things couldn't be known; a good response was the only cure.

A good response. She missed Barbe more than she expected. She'd been pleased to have time without her when she met for David Mongrain's lessons, pleased when she arrived home warmed by the fires the girl kept burning. Barbe's hands were eager and extra, something Marie hadn't appreciated when she lived there.

Archange must have found them so. She hoped he gave Barbe a gentle love. Marie clucked her tongue. She hadn't even known the girl was pregnant. Maybe Barbe didn't realize it either. And yet she had known enough to keep the infant alive and take it where it would be tended. Why hadn't she just brought the infant in to Marie? Did she think Marie would scold or lack compassion? Was that how the girl saw her after years of sharing in her household?

The thought made Marie place the stirring spoon in its holder beside the fire. She removed the syrup. "Watch Baby," she told Angele, who busily pressed lead around the letters of *Oregon Spectator,* a newly published newspaper Jean brought home. She had breadcrumbs she rubbed to erase.

Written in English, the paper wasn't one Jean could read, but the advertisements interested him, and Angele liked finding the letters she could copy and name. She was so quick to learn her letters, unlike Marie.

"Yes, Mama," Angele said.

Marie looked at the sleeping infant who had outgrown her salt-box and now slept in a baby board Marie had made. She nodded approval, then walked to the storeroom in the barn.

In the years Barbe lived with them, she and Jean had placed hides there, salt, candles, currency of the prairie, and told Barbe these were hers to trade as they were payment for her work. "You are not a slave," Marie had told her but never really knew if she understood this.

She pushed open the storeroom door. The baskets that once held Barbe's currency were gone.

"So she did understand," Marie said out loud. Knuck scooted around her to sniff the history of the room. "Come, we'll go back. Finish the syrup," Marie said.

Barbe understood so much more than Marie had imagined, even her own limitations. But why had she left, and why give her baby away? Marie would have let her continue living there with the baby. She would have helped her raise her child. If she and Archange had chosen to marry, she would have allowed Barbe to move in with him. *I would have allowed,* Marie thought, as if she'd had a say in the matter.

But perhaps Barbe knew how difficult that might be, to live her own life. Maybe the girl did understand what pain there would be in watching another raise a child you had birthed. And so she'd found the safest place for the child and then…let her go.

Marie walked slowly back toward the house. She sniffed the summer air, heard birds trill their songs. In the distance, she could see François and Baptiste working on a canoe together, the curls of adzed wood like foam at their feet while Jean pointed, offering direction. Jean looked up and waved, said something to his sons, and then started toward her.

Jean hovered close since her revelation. She was grateful. He hadn't pushed for a further explanation, but she knew one day she'd tell him. She had to. But she looked for answers to explain it to herself. Pain that once smothered like a blanket over fire had now burned through to the surface of her soul. It hurt too much to carry the wondering alone. She had done it for nearly fifty years.

"You take a walk, eh? This is good," Jean said.

"I wondered if Barbe remembered her currency, the payment we set aside for her. I don't know why I didn't think of it before," she said. "It is gone. I'm glad she understood those things were hers for the taking."

Jean looked quizzical. "I told you the baskets were empty."

"Did you? I don't remember."

"We went out to look together, a day or two after Baby came here." He stood up straighter, lightened his voice. "You've had much on your mind," he said.

"Oui."

Together they went into the house, and Marie returned the syrup to the fire. Her eyes cast toward Baby and Angele beyond.

"You'll take it to Julie tomorrow? Or will Marianne stop by for it?"

"Our Marianne has yet to come as she plans," Marie said. "I think the illness scares her. She still talks of it as though it were the pox. She touches her face each time she says Julie's name. I've told her this is something different, but she insists on being worried."

"A family trait," Jean said.

"I don't worry over such things," Marie said. Jean raised an eyebrow, smiled. "Not often," she added.

"I think of myself," Jean said. "I worry too."

Marie stirred, lifted the spoon to see if the coating stuck to the pewter, just enough to make swallowing easy, neither too thick or thin. "This is good now," she said.

"Let's take it to her ourselves, then," he said.

"The children…"

"We take them along but I stay out in the wagon, *n'est-ce pas?* I'll keep them safe while you go in or I go in. Maybe Marianne is already there and you see her, too."

Angele begged to stay and work on her letters, and François said he'd look after her as long as she brought her paper outside so he could continue forming the boat. The two argued a bit, Angele protesting that the breeze might take her Papa's paper, and François showing her how to put the paper over a hard piece of leather, lay pebbles on the edges to fool the breeze. That left only the baby, who slept still in the board laid across Marie's knees.

"We could have ridden the horses," Marie said. "Saved you the effort of the harnessing."

"But I don't get to sit so close to you then," Jean said. He patted her knee and smiled. "And my hearing goes, so I have trouble when you talk, your voice so soft. On horseback, we ride together yet alone."

"I like that," she said.

"I know," he told her. "But not all the time, eh?"

For many years she and Jean had lived separate lives, years she'd refused to go with him on the brigades that welcomed women and children too. These past four though, they'd lived as white people did, in wooden houses that didn't move.

"The baby sleeps well in her board," Jean commented. "She's found a good home." Marie nodded. "A family, too. Arguing brothers and sisters, at least until François decides he wants to live on his own."

"At least the parents don't quarrel," Marie said.

"I hate cross words more than anything," he said. He hesitated, cleared his throat, then said, "It's why I don't push to know the story of what you said. Of this John. Your…son. I don't want to lasso something wild. I only throw the rope out to gently lead, Marie."

Marie looked at her husband. At times, he could sound profound. Always, he'd been a patient man with her. She supposed there was little she could tell him that he wouldn't accept, and yet, could anyone be sure of the largeness of another's heart? He had always given unlimited love, a gift she had trouble opening. But he was a man, and there might be a bottom to his basket.

"He was my firstborn," Marie said.

"His father?"

"Pierre," she said, surprised he might think otherwise.

"Then..."

"*Oui.* You wonder why we do not have three sons we take with us across the mountains." She stayed quiet a long time. "We gave our first away."

The very words made her wince. *Gave our first away.*

Baby fussed, and the wheels rolled over a rut in the road, causing the seat to bounce hard. Marie grabbed the infant, held on, and kept Baby safe. The baby cried now, and Marie unlaced the thongs, folded back the soft leather flaps, and removed the child, held her to her shoulder, patting her back. The motion must have comforted her, for the five-month-old infant slept again within Marie's arms.

"You decide this for a good reason," Jean said. He didn't ask it as a question, and his confidence that she would do something so despicable for only the best of reasons warmed her more than he could know. Tears formed and she blinked them away.

"To let a thing happen decides, *n'est-ce pas?* I learn this later."

"Was the child sickly?"

"No! He was a beautiful child. Eyes the color of a buffalo, his skin the color of wet sand. He was a long child, with long fingers and toes and would have been—" She stopped. "Might still be, tall. He might still be." The thought that he lived on took root in her soul. "For so long I don't think of him, not ever. It's as though he never was. As Paul died to me after a time. But I still think of Paul, not every day. Maybe because he chose to go while John was... I didn't fight for him as a mother should. I let John go."

She didn't want to cry now. She'd cried for days after Baby came, and when Marianne or Marguerite stopped by, they commented on how tired she looked, never knowing how she aged and ached, not from her efforts at mothering but from a frigid memory now thawing.

Baby made smacking sounds, and Marie lowered her from her shoulder, placing the infant's head against the pillow of tree moss that lined the board. She fluffed the green threads up under the infant's knees, and the baby slept on.

"Another mother had lost her baby," Marie said. "They had tried for many years my husband told me. Three times she held an infant in her arms, and three times before the sunset, she sang the mourning song. That's what he told me. He played *vingt et un* with this woman's husband, he told me. They exchanged debts. He knew of their losses. I didn't know. I was young, so young. I held my infant, nursed him."

She whispered then, the scene running through her mind. "I didn't...feel what everyone said a mother must. The sight of him... frightened. What if I dropped him or forgot him somewhere? What if I didn't feed him enough or too much? Would I make the right choices for him? Sickness. If he got sick, I didn't know if I could keep him well. Would I be enough?"

"You had a mother-in-law," Jean said.

Marie turned to him. "We were gone from there soon after John was born. We stayed at Crawford's fort on the upper Des Moines. St. Louis, little Fort St. Louis. I was alone while Pierre traveled with the trader. Afraid. I was afraid. There were no women to ask, no grandmothers sharing wisdom."

Jean pulled the team up and stopped, wrapped the reins around the iron whip-holder. He bent forward, his forearms on his knees, his head bowed as he listened. He gripped his hands together. In disgust? In rage? She couldn't tell.

"He told me of this woman, another mother, and then he said the child should go to her."

"His own son, his first he just gives away?"

"I didn't disagree. He had been ill. John cried and cried, and I walked him and he coughed, so hard I thought his insides would spill out. I couldn't sleep for fear he'd choke and I might not hear him. I couldn't sleep. I sometimes thought to drop him, wondered what might happen if I did. The thought was like a night terror crawling inside my skin." She swallowed, and Jean sat straighter, still didn't look at her, just let her talk. "I laid him down, afraid that if I held him any longer I'd do something I'd regret. So when my husband said we should let this woman get him well, I told Pierre one night to 'Take him! Let him find a loving mother. There is none here.' And then I slept."

"When you awoke—"

"The child was gone."

Julie Gervais Laderoute died the morning of July 9, 1845. Word went out in that prairie way, and everyone gathered for the service on the eleventh under a cloudless sky, the Jesuit Father Buldoc officiating. Dozens of children were shushed into silence while the incense punctuated the priest's mournful words. Marguerite kept her arms at Xavier's shoulders as he stood to her side, her stomach too huge for him to stand before her. She shouldn't even be out in public, as large as she was.

But JB had said, "We must go. To support my friend Joseph Gervais who has only one young daughter left. The fresh air will be good for you, eh?"

"Angelique says her people don't allow pregnant women near the dead," Marguerite said.

"Superstition," JB said. "What would your mother say?"

"I don't know. I don't think her people thought that way. They're known for compassion, for their great love of children, for—"

"You see? Another *should* to hammer yourself with," JB said. "You shouldn't do this, you shouldn't do that."

"The trip over might well bring on the baby," Marguerite said. "Those rutted roads are as hard as George Gay's brick."

"I'll be with you then, Etoile, if that happens. That should make you happy."

She wrinkled her nose at him.

"We go. It is the thing to do."

His sons had ridden in the wagon box, and Xavier had begged to ride back with them, but she'd said no. She didn't trust them with her son. They were bigger and stronger, and no telling what they might do to her *enfant* while her back was turned.

The boys jumped off when they reached the parish and scattered while Xavier raced to follow them. "No, François Xavier," she shouted. "You stay with me now." He'd know she was serious when she used his full name.

St. Paul parish had grown considerably since the arrival of the Dutch Sisters and the new Jesuits. Marguerite could see construction of a building above St. Ignatius Lake, and there were now thirty boarders at a college for boys. The students often signed as witnesses to baptisms and deaths as they probably would today.

She'd nodded to her mother but hadn't yet had a chance to talk with her. If Marianne were here, she'd be close to Mother, that was certain. Marguerite scanned the gathering. Her sister had to be present. What would people think if she didn't come? David was here, his head bowed, tears wet on his cheeks. It would be hard to lose a sister, the only sister he had who shared the memories of their mother. He'd have no one now to say, "Remember when Mama used to make neat's-foot oil, how she boiled those hooves and how that oil tanned her leathers smooth? Remember? Remember how she sang to us. Remember?" Those shared memories kept a parent alive. It kept the child alive too, that little person who still lived inside a grown-up body.

Her body was certainly grown. *Blown-up* might be a better word for it. A smile formed on her face. *Stop it. It's not seemly. I should be solemn.*

Where was her sister? Marguerite would have words with her about not coming to her best friend's funeral. It would be another quarrel between her and Marianne. Marie Anne. But if it weren't for a sister, who would correct someone like Marianne who behaved like a child, though she already had a child of her own. Only one child. She should have two or more by now.

Marguerite wondered if she might be doing something to prevent that from happening. Maybe she'd ask. Julie's children had been born evenly spaced, one every three years since she was fifteen. Maybe

Marianne and Julie shared a secret. She'd ask Marianne if she knew a way to manage when a child would arrive. But if she wasn't planning it, if Marianne wanted more children but something interfered, Marguerite's asking would either hurt her feelings or Marianne would fry her with the heat of her words. She'd have to think twice before bringing up an issue pregnant with dispute.

Pregnant with dispute. Marguerite heard herself suck in a chortle. Laughing at a funeral! What kind of woman did that? She was at a burial, for heaven's sake. A young mother gone, leaving behind four young children, and here she was smiling over a poor choice of words. She was as *impropre* as her sister.

Her baby kicked, hard enough that Xavier turned to look at her. He thumped her stomach back.

"No, no," she whispered. "It's your brother."

He stared at her stomach, then at her.

Did people turn to look? What must they think? She never should have come here.

The priest spoke his prayers. Death was such a part of life that sometimes its presence just washed over her like a numbing poultice. She hadn't felt anything when JB told her of Julie's passing. Julie had been sick for at least two months, and if it hadn't been for her own pregnancy, she would have been there to help. Her mother had visited Julie. She knew that. Papa Jean, too. That's what her mother did around illness, tended to others.

She still couldn't locate her sister. Marianne must have stayed home out of guilt for never visiting Julie. She'd have to have a talk with her. She had some experience with guilt as an older sister, and Marianne rarely tapped it, acting instead like she was an only child demanding all attention, doing everything on her own.

Personally, she thought Marianne had gotten married too soon and probably just because Marguerite had. Marianne never took it seriously, the demands of marriage. Watching David grieve alone without his wife at his side told her that.

She doubted, too, that Julie ever confronted Marianne about her willful ways. The girls just laughed together, came up with antics and plans. The weathering of a conflict strengthened a friendship. If friends kept everything smooth and never noticed the nubbins, the relationship would soon just wear down out of boredom. To deepen, a kinship needed differences stitched through to understanding.

Marriages did as well. She was still troubled by her husband's sons, but she had tried to notice when they did something agreeable and speak only one negative word out of every three that came to mind. That hadn't been easy these past months with her morning sickness putting her on edge and Xavier demanding more of her time just when her body required she pay attention to this new one. The smell of lye on the ash while she made soap, the butchering of a lamb, even JB's pipe, all rolled her stomach as though on a windswept river.

Xavier pulled away from her now as the graveside service broke up. The long building that housed the college was open for the food brought for the family, and he ran off in that direction. She started after him. JB touched her arm, shook his head. The child did need to be more independent. She couldn't possibly give all that she should to this new child if Xavier continued to demand. She'd have to ask her mother about that.

No, she'd handle it her own way. She didn't need her mother raising that one eyebrow in judgment at something her oldest daughter might say.

The Ouvre girl who lived with Julie and her husband held Julie's baby in her arms. The baby was still of nursing age, barely seven months old. The girl was barely sixteen. She walked away and returned with little Isadore in tow, the child all dressed in black. His father lifted him, and the child rested his forehead on his father's chest. He didn't even know yet what it meant to be without one parent. Thank goodness the boy still had his father. Marguerite had lost her father at the same age.

Julie's oldest daughter sat kicking her feet up as she sat beside her father at the table. Her brother, already ten, held her hand. Julie had made her family a tightly tied one. She might have been a young mother, but she must have been a good one, too.

Loneliness draped Marguerite in the midst of the crowd. She spied Xavier through the legs of men. He had his head bent to something, someone, she couldn't see.

Did Julie realize she was dying? Perhaps that was why they'd taken the Ouvre girl in when they did. So she could keep the routines and the children's loss would be lessened. Even in her death, Julie touched the lives of her children, wanting to give them what they needed after she was gone. She'd asked for Marianne those days before she died. She must have hoped Marianne would be a part of that bridge. Marianne had frittered away any chance to help Julie and left herself just a loose thread, detached from someone she loved.

It was stitching on through a relationship that mattered, staying until all the threads were tied up, not backing away when things got uncomfortable. She hadn't backed away from JB, and they were stitching the pieces together.

Watching David grieve his sister pained her almost as much as watching Julie's husband. He had the children to comfort him and that Ouvre girl to keep things steady. David had only his volatile wife.

She vowed to spend more time with her sister. She'd try not to correct her when she did. Marianne would eventually face what she'd done, Marguerite imagined, and wear a guilty robe for not having done what she should have.

Marguerite made her way to Xavier just as she heard his scream. The family group scattered, leaving Marguerite's son rushing from a snake Julie's girl held in her hand.

"He brought it to frighten her, but he's the one running now," someone said.

She should have watched him more closely.

There was that word again. But there were times when what one should do wasn't a judgment. It wasn't a way to keep a body bent in guilty prayer. Sometimes what a person should do was the keeping of a commitment to something or someone that mattered.

Her mother stepped out of the gathering and reached for Xavier, pulling her to him. He looked startled but hid behind his kasa's skirts, watching as Julie's girl approached with the snake. Marie said something to the girl, and she dropped the reptile and nearly fell into the arms of Marie. Her mother pulled the child into her skirts and brushed her dark hair, talking softly. The child's slender shoulders shook as she cried. Her mother, always there, always giving just what was needed, just what she should.

Marguerite watched as her son reached around and gently patted the girl's head. He showed her kindness. He'd learned it. It was what he should do.

16

The Work of Living

1845

"I teach you, Mama," Angele said. She pressed her small hand over Marie's fingers, gripping the lead. It reminded Marie of Mr. Hall, the one who brought the printing press to the Spaldings and showed her what her name looked like. He'd pressed his hand over hers so she could scrape out letters in the sand. Now a child did it.

"It's no good now," Marie told her. "I have a baby to feed. Things to do. You work on your letters."

"But we haven't been at school. They miss us. I need to show Sister Celeste what I write."

"She doesn't teach in the summer," Marie reminded her. "We are all busy, tending our gardens, getting ready for winter. Sister Celeste, too."

"You're always getting ready for a time that isn't now," Angele complained. She threw the lead down on the newspaper. "I'm sorry, I'm sorry," she said when Marie raised an eyebrow. She picked the lead up and laid it gently.

"Bon," she said. "Sometimes we must consider the future or we will not be ready for it when it comes," she said. "I go now. Baby cries. You have eggs to collect, *n'est-ce pas?*"

Angele nodded. "They smell bad. I don't like those chickens. And the rooster chases me."

"You do it anyway," Marie said. "It is your duty."

Angele scowled and kicked the side of the stool when she slipped off it. Then she shuffled out to the chicken house. "Stinky chickens," she said under her breath. Knuck followed her out, tail wagging against the girl's slender legs. Marie smiled. The girl acted like a child at last instead of an angel all the time. A good sign. Though she apologized often, it was good to see her protest. Being difficult was part of a child's living. A child had to feel protected in order to test the waters. Marie had worried that she might always try to be good for fear of being sent away if she did something bad.

Was that a part of living too, this fear that doing bad meant separation? She'd been disobedient as a child, and the result had torn her from her mother and her sister forever. But David Mongrain suggested their deaths weren't related to what Marie had done at all. And that the greatest separation was her distance from her faith, the years of space when she had refused to receive the unending love, had refused to be baptized. Yet choosing hadn't washed away those past mistakes either. Instead, grievances she'd long sunk into the bottom of a well had been dragged up. How deep a faith was that?

Maybe she should ask him that question since the other had been too troubling for anyone to answer. Sister Celeste might have some thoughts on this, too. She had only talked of lessons with that woman, and Marie had disappointed her in that. She knew it, despite how kindly the Sister treated her, how patiently she still offered her assistance in the class.

At least she had an excuse for not being reminded of her dull mind. With the summer season, no one expected the thirty or so students ranging from six to sixty to pursue their letterings and numbers. But when she returned in the fall, that trial would begin again. She had told the Sister she would come, but perhaps it was time to tell her it would be her last term sitting in the class. Marie must tell herself the truth about her thinking. She had given this wish enough effort. Opportunity had come too late for her stubbornness. There was little hope for a mind that let her forget that she'd given up a son.

Baby scooted on her bottom toward Marie. The child at eight months or so showed no interest in crawling but instead had found a way to propel herself across the floor. Jean kept the puncheon smooth as vellum, and Marie dressed her in skins so no wayward slivers landed where they shouldn't. Baby pulled herself up against Marie's knees, wobbly but wearing a grin so large her dimples looked deep as finger swipes across a chocolate cake.

A butterfly chose the moment to enter through the open door. The wings dipped and startled and landed on Baby's pudgy hand. The child's eyes grew large in wonder. She looked up at Marie but didn't move. Such wisdom at her early age, to know not to move, to let this wispy being blink its wings back and forth like breathing. She would remember to tell Jean of this moment of pure joy watching a child's first understanding of the kiss of living things.

Marianne wiped at the playing cards, removing sticky jam that Joseph must have smudged on them. David loved his cards, and he'd be upset that she'd let the boy play with them, worse still that his hands had been dirty when he did. She spit on her apron and rubbed. A pale pink now scummed the yellowing ace.

Her father had told her. She hadn't even known the baby was born until days after the event. Why, if she'd missed Mass that month, she might not have known until Christmas.

"Maybe if you had been at Julie's funeral she would have asked you," her mother told her. "I know Marguerite looked for you there."

Her words jabbed like a bone needle to her heart. Since Julie's death, everyone poked at her almost as though she were responsible for her friend's dying. Didn't they know she cried for Julie and the family she left behind? Didn't they know she, too, wore that robe of regret her mother once described, so much regret she didn't believe she would ever be able to push it off?

How she wished she'd gone to help Julie, been with Julie, taken care of Julie's children for her. She just couldn't imagine seeing Julie's face all strained, her body all cramped as though she gave birth when she didn't. Fruitless work, that's what illness was, and Marianne just couldn't stand it.

She rubbed at the playing cards. Her efforts would have to do. Maybe David wouldn't notice. He didn't notice much of late.

She wished she'd said her good-byes while her friend still lived, she did. But what did you say to someone dying? Julie might have lived, and then if Marianne had acted as though their hours together were their last, what kind of experience would that have been for Julie? Maybe a friend's long face at death would hasten the departing song instead of bringing ease to it.

That was it! By staying away, she'd allowed Julie better time with her husband and family. It was a gift of hope she'd given Julie by saying with her absence that all would be well.

Besides, who knew how flux spread? She couldn't risk exposure to Joseph from Julie's family too, could she? Baptiste's baby boy was still ill too. She couldn't expose vulnerable children.

She put the deck of cards into a leather pouch and shook her finger at Joseph. "You leave these alone now. They belong to your papa."

The boy ran outside to his father then and crawled up onto his lap. David, her father, and her brother smoked pipes on her parents' porch. Marianne watched as her husband lifted his son and brushed his lips against the child's head, his eyes red and worn.

"I wonder if David will grieve me as much as he does his sister's death," she said out loud.

"This is a true question you have?" her mother asked. Marianne turned, startled. She'd forgotten where she was for a moment, helping her mother prepare a meal on a hot August evening.

"What other kind of question is there?"

"One that seeks attention," her mother said, "and already knows the answer."

"I don't know the answer. I don't know if David would miss me as he does his sister."

"A brother and sister are twined in a singular way. Like you and François, *n'est-ce pas?* David knew Julie as only a brother can. But I see how he looks at you. Adoration fills his eyes."

"You think so?" The confirmation lifted her spirits.

"Falling from a high branch can be painful," her mother said. Marianne wrinkled her brow. "It can take a little time to recover."

"Who fell?" Marianne asked.

Her mother shook her head, returned to her stirring.

Sometimes she talked in riddles, her mother. But at least she talked with Marianne. Marguerite of late spoke barely a word and avoided her eyes as well at the baptism. Maybe all her energy went into Baptiste's family. They were pretty close, she and Josette, all of them living under foot with each other. The only time Marianne saw her sister these days was at a funeral, a baptism, or Mass. *Am I some kind of disease?*

Marianne picked up Baby, sat her on her hip, and with the other hand carried to the table a platter of pork that her mother handed her.

"Angele, go wash your hands," her mother directed. The girl moved obediently away from Marianne's Joseph, who'd been running back and forth from where the men talked to where the food platters sprouted up like fresh mushrooms onto the table. Joseph eyed his mother, looked at Baby. "Pick me too, Mama. I'm tired. Pick me too." He lifted his arms.

"We'll eat soon. You wash your hands, now," she said. It couldn't hurt this practice her mother insisted on, though what wet hands had to do with disease was beyond her.

Joseph left to wiggle beside Angele at the washbasin and splashed her. She laughed and splashed back. "Joseph," Marianne cautioned.

"They just play," her mother said as she wiped her hands on the cloth she wore folded over her buckskin waist tie. "He needs a brother or a sister." Her mother stuck her head out the door and waved the men inside with her hand.

"You have so many grandchildren already," Marianne said, setting Baby on a highchair Jean had made for her. "You don't need another from me."

"Why not make room for more?"

"What makes you think I haven't tried?" Marianne said.

"You're right. It isn't a grandmother's affair. I meddle."

"No, it is your affair. I just... Joseph takes so much time, and a baby, the birth..."

"Marguerite had no trouble, and this time, JB was there for her. He came and got me, and the baby was born in an instant."

"She's built for having babies," Marianne said. "I'm narrow." She swallowed.

"There's room enough in you," her mother said and smiled.

The men entered then, children following. All this talk about babies troubled Marianne. Julie had been weakened by the births of her children. So when the flux came into their household, she, not the children, succumbed.

Marianne was a disloyal friend and a distant wife who couldn't comfort her husband. She was probably a terrible mother, too, so of course God hadn't granted them another child. He probably never would.

"Have you set a date?" David asked her brother.

"Maybe Epiphany," François said. "Angelique says that would bode well for a marriage."

Angelique Longtain! Of course. Marguerite had named her newest baby after François' intended. François' first baby would probably be named Marguerite in return. Tears pooled in Marianne's eyes. Here she sat surrounded by family, and yet she felt as alone as if they'd all taken their plates and left the room.

"Does an ant live in your pants?" her father asked her. She looked at him. "Your feet, daughter. They move without taking you anywhere."

She shuffled her feet under the table where they all sat now, she on a bench between her husband and son, her eyes across at her mother, her palms holding tight to her son and her husband. She made herself hold her moccasins flat on the floor, her knees together in rigid quiet. The family bowed their heads while her father spoke the blessing.

"May the hands at this table hold each other through thick and thin," he said. "May the food bring nourishment to our bones and souls. And may we bring before you all the joy of our hearts to glorify you and be strengthened by all you've provided to serve you fully. Amen."

The brush of the cross they signed against their clothing was like a whisper of comfort in Marianne's ear. In that bowed moment she felt a lifting. Nothing certain, nothing clear, but her father's words were a slender thread she could hang on to.

It had been a hot summer, and the shrunken lake had grown murky in the center and then a few weeks later dry in the center sink area. "Not a good sign," Jean told Marie. "We can only hope the rains come soon."

The air felt cool with the promise of an October rain, but the clouds scudded by, leaving only a dribble. They didn't even get wet as they rode north from the lake toward the St. Paul parish for yet another funeral.

Marie was tired of funerals. The St. Louis church might not have an eighty-pound bell as the St. Paul parish did, but their small one clanged out loud enough. Today that larger bell pounded against her ears sending another loved one away. She longed for the pleasure of music and dance. Instead, grief lined her days.

Her son thumbed his eyes. "I wish I knew where the sickness comes from," Baptiste said. "Then we could stop it."

Josette paled beside him, her skin stretched tight over sharp cheekbones. Her hands once strong clutched like claws as her husband helped her to kneel at the wooden bench. For weeks, Marie had gone daily to Josette's tipi, bringing the syrup and vinegar and salt, eventually moving into Josette's tipi then, so as not to expose Marguerite's family. Marie boiled the water they drank that had been drawn from the streams when the wells went dry, to better skim the murky scum. She woke to the slightest sounds of the infant in the night, able to reach the child even before Josette could, the mother had weakened so much. She had Angele and Baby with her, and some days even Jean spent the night, hurrying home to help François with morning milking.

Baptiste pushed his worry into the adz. His mother had watched him as he worked on the wooden craft, then tried to smooth his furrowed brow when he leaned over Philomene, his son.

"You and I are bound by the death of children, *Mère,*" he said once when he rose in the night to see her holding his ill child.

"This one doesn't die," she said.

"He will. There is nothing I can do to halt his suffering. What kind of father can't stop the suffering of his children?"

"You relieve it," she said. "You give comfort to his mother, his brothers and sisters. You're here. We do what we can do." He'd grunted in that way he had.

All their efforts had not forestalled this newest loss.

Philomene, baptized just the month before with Marie Anne Ouvre as the godmother, had died of the same thing Julie Gervais Laderoute had. A bloody flux. It emptied his body while causing a burning thirst. Baptiste said it was a miracle the infant held on for as long as he did and a miracle, too, that he held on no longer.

"Suffering a child's death is more work than anything I do," Baptiste said.

Children fell first to the disease, Indian children even before the French or Americans. Marie tried to remember if it had always been that way.

"The diseases travel strangely," Jean said when she commented about so many children newly buried. "Who can say on which back the flux rides? We have many orphans to care for, eh? So the disease spares some young, takes their mothers, too. We're not given all the answers, my Marie. It takes more courage to walk when we're not sure where we're headed. It means we must rely on other hands to carry us along."

After the funeral and with the autumn leaves calling to them, Marie and Jean and their little family made their usual trek south of the Lake to an area with a timbered mound in the distance. They stayed at the smaller cabin while Jean hunted and, mercifully, the rain came. More steadily now, but there were long hours when the sky cleared and the earth gave up the heady scent of transformation, soil nurtured by decay for the growth of next year's harvests.

They saw evidence of new settlers, chimney smoke rising in the distance. Several thousand more Americans had arrived that fall, brought their cattle, their hogs, and their lust for land. Jean encountered people he'd never met before, and he wondered if there was any place a man could go with his family where he could live alone without having to negotiate everyday differences of broken fences or wayward stock.

Marie and Angele and Baby did little work the first days there, except what was needed for daily life. No making candles. No soap making. No drying berries or gathering acorns.

"All the work is done now?" Angele asked when Marie said they'd play the moccasin game, a tradition of her Ioway people.

"Is that all we do, you think?" Marie asked her. She laid three moccasins out between the two of them.

"Papa works."

"He hunts. He calls it work, but it is what he loves to do."

Marie watched as Baby poked with a stick at an anthill. She looked back at Angele. "When he brings in a deer, we'll work too, but this is a restful place. We fill up here until then," she said. "So when we go home, we'll have a full basket."

Angele looked around. "We work to fill the basket? What basket?"

Marie touched her chest. "The basket inside," she said. "It holds laughter and kind touches and songs and good thoughts."

"Gifts," Angele said.

"Yes, gifts."

Marie placed the little stone before them and showed Angele that the game involved guessing which moccasin hid the stone.

"But that's easy," Angele said. "I watch you do it."

"Where's the stone, then?" Marie asked. Angele pointed, and Marie lifted the moccasin. "No stone," Marie said and smiled.

Angele's eyes widened. Then, "My turn."

There were tricks to the game, and Marie remembered watching her mother and sister play. How long she'd watched before she could see the subtle shifts in their fingers, the tiny adjustments as their bodies pointed to the right moccasin without their knowing. She'd become quite good at it, but she'd spent hours learning. The elders must have placed bets on their right choices, since piles of beaded bags and bones like markers exchanged hands many times during the hours of play. The songs her parents sang during those games drifted into her head, and she sang one now while she watched Angele, the child's eyes intent. She hadn't realized that song still lived inside her head.

"You can't see through my hands," Marie said.

Angele stared. The child could put all other thoughts aside to learn a thing. It was how she understood the Sisters' lessons and could write several words in English now while Marie still struggled. Some might say Angele attacked her tasks with fierceness, rarely wavering. "Prideful," Marianne described the girl. But Marie saw Angele's efforts as a sharpness that had kept the child alive.

In all these months since the girl had chosen them as family, Angele had never talked of where she'd come from or what she remembered of her past. She lived here now, as though only this time mattered. But Marie knew she set aside bad memories, had to, in order to do the work that made her way to a safe place.

"You can blink," Marie said.

Angele shook her head. "I miss what your hands do."

"I'm not that fast." Marie laughed.

For Angele, the challenge consumed. Barbe had never held an interest in the moccasin game when Marie had tried to show her.

"Yes, that's the right one. *Bon,*" Marie said when Angele made a correct choice in the moccasin game.

"Again," Angele said.

"Don't you want to try to trick me?" Marie asked.

"I'd rather see how you do it before I try on my own."

Baby dug at the anthill now, her cloth dress hiked up around her knees as she sat. It looked like sweat beaded at her brow. A fever? No, just effort, Marie decided.

Work. Was it work when Angele tried her hand with a bow and arrow and failed to notice hunger or when Baby took her first steps across the cabin's uneven floor and wanted only to repeat it instead of being held? A woman's work meant molding, kneading, shaping, not just things but people, and it was part of the human spirit to forget the pain of empty places inside work. She hoped Baptiste could learn this. He was right: To watch a child suffer was the hardest work of a parent, even a grandparent.

Maybe that was how Marie set aside such torments. She worked, stayed busy. When she paused to let a breeze blow by to cool her face, her mind went quickly to another place.

That day she last saw her son.

Pierre's blank look when she asked where John was.

His slap to her face when she spoke her son's name. She could still feel the sting when she let herself remember.

"We do not speak the name of the dead," he'd said.

"John's—"

He'd struck her again. "To us, he lives no more. Remember this, *Femme.*"

Had she ever told Baptiste he had an older brother? No, Baptiste would have asked questions, and he hadn't. Only that once when he told of a looping dream. Only she and Pierre had known this secret, and now she'd threaded Jean into the weave.

And the family who took him in, they know. What must they think of her? She should have been told who they were, where he'd gone, been allowed to sing a departing song. A mother must know, so she could protect her son from some future time when he might fall in love and not know that the woman who won his heart shared his family blood. It was a mother's work to do this, and she hadn't.

She should have gone after him, tried to find him. Pierre told her to think of him as dead, and maybe he was.

Don't say his name, Pierre told her. Put the child from the mother's mind. She'd forgotten. She was weak. So weak.

She had pushed John's presence from her, put all she had to give into her other sons and daughters. But it was not enough. She was not enough. She'd made no room for him, so it was better to forget, to erase the memory the way breadcrumbs wiped out lead words written onto paper.

She smelled tobacco. "No more peaceful time for *les femmes,*" Jean said, approaching. Marie looked at him, uncertain for a moment of where she was. She blinked. He dropped the deer carcass on the leaves. "You'll have work to do now."

Marie nodded. He'd rescued her. She found the greatest peace when her hands taught, tended, and accomplished, when her thoughts were bundled with work and held no room for remorse.

17

Prodigal

1846

They held the wedding in late January, and the couple moved into the upstairs loft of the Toupin household the day after. It caused some rearranging, but that was what families did, rearrange. Jean liked that his son would be close by. A man never stopped learning about his son as he aged. His daughters moved on to lives of their own, became foreign, almost, as they lived in a matrimonial state. He watched loyalties shift from him as the father being the one who could heal the wounds of a daughter's heart to her husband, who could do it better, he supposed, much as he hated to admit it.

But a son's standing after marriage brought a father closer. He could become a comrade rather than a combatant.

Jean approved François' choice of a bride. Angelique was a soft-spoken, lanky girl, nearly as tall as her new husband. She didn't correct him in front of others and only rarely touched her slender hand to François' arm with what looked to Jean as a warning to "hold his horses." His son had his own interpreter now. Jean's teaching days were over. His children had their own lives. Everything changed.

A town of sorts grew around St. Louis with coopers and shoemakers and even a gunsmith. Nearly three thousand emigrants had spilled into the valley, and he'd heard rumblings that their worries arrived from Waiilatpu with them. The supposed British spies had left on the *Modest* last winter with no one quite sure how they assessed this valley's loyalties, should the boundary line be tested by conflict. The Methodists and Catholics in this little valley lived side by side without much rancor, at least the old families did.

No one had need of an old negotiator on French Prairie, though. Jean was just a farmer now. A man who tilled soil for garden produce and who hunted as he must to feed his family. He milked his cows. He made butter enough to put on trade at the Company. He drove his family to Mass. He tended his wife, wary about her lapses, the wounds she hung on to that she never let heal.

Jean finished the wooden bed he'd made for the girls. The two were alone in the barn where he worked the file to smooth the sides. This little bed could slide under his and Marie's bed.

"Where's Baby's bed?" Angele asked.

"There's room enough for both of you. See how wide it is?" Jean said.

"She'll wet. I want something different."

Angele rarely complained, not even about moving down from the loft to allow François and Angelique to have it. In fact, he'd rarely heard her protest any request he or Marie gave. It worried him a little. Children always protested something. It was how they learned to negotiate, to practice knowing they were loved despite not getting their way. Angele rarely expressed a preference. When she did, he took notice.

"What do you propose?" Jean said.

"A hard floor is better than a wet bed."

"You say this from your years of experience?" Jean said, and he laughed.

Angele nodded her head, her face as solemn as a rock.

There was something more here. "Did you have a little sister or brother who wet a bed you shared?" he said.

The child had never talked of her beginnings the way most children did, at least the way his son and daughter had. He thought maybe children remembered only the stories adults told around them, and since they had no stories of her beginnings to relay time and again, she'd have nothing to talk about of her earlier years. He'd proposed that to Marie once, and she'd nodded. "Those stories become their own when they hear what adults tell them happened," Marie had said. "But I remember things I don't believe my mother could have told me or my father." Even Marguerite told stories about shoes the first time he'd met Marie's daughter. It was not a story Marie had told her; it was what Marguerite remembered.

Angele, though, never spoke of what had been, until now.

"A sister," she said. "She wet."

Jean simply nodded. A man didn't want to startle a fawn shivering alone, and that's how he saw Angele at this moment.

"So you slept on the floor."

"On the ground. I found leaves. They're soft, but she wet them."

Just let her know that I'm listening. "Soft leaves were right there where you could make a bed of them." Angele nodded. "And your sister lay beside you."

"Until she couldn't get up." Angele's voice rode on short breaths now.

"You woke up and she didn't."

Angele nodded. "I roll over on her." Her eyes were wide, and she looked far away. Her lips looked almost blue. She held her breath.

What a weight the child carries. How to help her lift it?

"Here," Jean said. "I need you to hold my hammer for me. Are you strong enough?" She looked down at the tool, looked back at Jean. "Take it now," he said. He used a firm voice, couched in encouragement. "It's cold and heavy. Can you handle it? I know you're very strong, but this is my heaviest hammer." She nodded. "*Bon.* See there, how you help me. You're good. I'll make two beds," he said. "You made a bed of leaves that must have been soft, just right for you and your sister, *n'est-ce pas?*"

"They died," she said. "They died."

"And you took your sister to find help."

She nodded, gripped the hammer.

"Heavy, eh? A rock with a good horn handle is heavier than this iron one. But this one makes it easier to hit the pegs with. We make glue now, with salmon eggs so the pegs will stay even tighter. You'll help. You have much strength to give away." Jean said.

"Because I slept in a hard place and woke up?"

Jean smiled. "Because you did what you could for one you loved. That makes you strong as a hammer. It does."

Jean patted her shoulder. Angele smiled up at him. There might still be a need for an old interpreter.

"It's been a long time, Madame Toupin," David Mongrain said. "I miss our times together. I thought your school studies might keep you away." She sat on the bench in front of the St. Louis church. He came south of St. Paul, worked with the priest at this parish, too.

"His name was John Dorion," Marie told David Mongrain. "The name you couldn't remember."

He looked surprised, his hands rubbing his chin. "That's right. You thought it might be a Paul?"

"I did."

"So is this John Dorion someone you know, then?"

"How well do you remember him?" Marie asked.

"It's been some time," David said. He ran his tongue over his bottom lip. "He was a young man. Me too, then," David said. "I was thinner than he was too. Well, he may still be. We pushed a *bateau* together in the Athabascan country and later on the Saskatchewan River. For the Company."

"Was he… How did this man look?"

He concentrated. "Dark curly hair. He had a temper, I remember. Liked to play cards and didn't like to lose." He searched for details. "Married. He was married. I remember that. He said he'd leave the service of the Company soon, to stay with his wife. I left soon after myself, 1834. To assist the priests."

"John assisted the priests?" Marie asked.

David shook his head. "No. This was my work after I stopped being a *milieu* and began my studies. I don't know his vocation. He liked horses. It stood out since so many of us *voyageurs* like our sea legs better than on a mount."

"Is there a Ladder story for a lost son?" she asked. "Different from the Joseph story?"

David looked at her, his brow furrowed. "There is. One who came back after doing something despicable and dishonoring to his father. One son remained behind, and it's a story of his journey too."

"The one who went away, how did he decide to come back?"

"He looked around one day and said, 'this is a terrible place I've put myself into.' He slopped pigs and ate what they ate after he squandered…wasted what his father had given him. His share of an inheritance he'd blown to the wind, and one day, he told himself a truth. 'Ye shall know the truth, and the truth shall make you free,' " David Mongrain said. "A favorite scripture of mine. He set himself free by admitting his mistake, by turning around and going back. He did not deserve forgiveness from his father, but he received it. We all do when we turn around."

"And the son who did not leave, who stayed?"

"Some…resentment there. His story required that he, too, tell himself the truth. His father had always loved him. He still had his inheritance, and his father had room enough to lavish gifts on the returning son while still loving the one who had stayed beside him."

"But the remaining son, he had trouble seeing this?"

"Yes. Grace is unwarranted forgiveness, a removal of a debt. Both sons could have received it, but only the returning son was willing to accept the gift. The other believed he had earned it by staying and working and doing well. We can't earn it," David Mongrain said. "If we earn it, it's not truly a gift, *n'est-ce pas?*"

She imagined her sons returning to her: one giving her the gift of grace, forgiving her for having let him go; the other offering her the opportunity to grant the same to him. And Baptiste, who had stayed behind with her, in his way, what did he harbor in his heart? Was he a receiver or a grantor? He'd certainly forgiven her for her part in his daughter's death, but what about all those years when her mind had wandered on to Paul? Had she failed to notice Baptiste's efforts to be a good son, a good husband and father? Even a good brother to his sisters and, yes, to Paul, too. Baptiste had put feet to her prayers and tried to find him.

She considered telling him of John, but if he'd encountered any Dorion on his journey back, he would have told her. Perhaps this is a family secret that should be kept.

"Your pictures have stories for everyone," Marie said.

"We could talk of this story, see the thread that runs through it from that time to this," David Mongrain said. "Would you like to do this?"

"Threads held too tightly break."

"Not this one. It can never break. You can let go of it, but it won't break. He knew the Columbia country," David said. "I remember that little bit since we talked." They heard meadowlarks flitter by, land on leggy grasses that grew beside the church. "I remember him telling us what we could expect if we went all the way to Spokane House and maybe beyond. He was right about it too. Described the round hills of Okanogan. He said he'd been there once, that it held great beauty."

"He'd been in the Columbia country." Marie held her breath.

"Didn't say where. Do you want to know the story thread then? We call it the Prodigal Returns. *Prodigal* means 'wasteful,' and both sons wasted, *n'est-ce pas?*"

Marie said, "My thread will need a knot tied in it, or it will just pull through."

"So you'll go," Marguerite said. "Leave me here again, alone."

"Joseph Gervais needs help," her husband told her.

"And I don't?"

"Ask your sister. She would come."

"She's too busy," Marguerite said.

"Then Josette."

He was so helpful at finding others to do what she wanted him to do.

"She's been ill and has her hands full with her own children." Marguerite patted Angelique's bottom. Her mother had made a board for her using rosewood and willow, but Angelique didn't like it. At least that's what she told her mother. Right now, as the child fussed, Marguerite wished she had gotten her accustomed to that board so she could lay her in a safe place and prop her up to watch while she talked with her husband, prepared food for his journey. Marguerite noticed that when Baby fussed, it took mere seconds before her mother unlaced the board, placed Baby in it, and the child, even as big as she was, found peace there. Marguerite had nothing that worked so well with her babies.

At least she had children. She should be grateful. Josette had lost Philomene, and her sister, Marianne, still showed no signs of her family expanding. She supposed she should be happy with a healthy child, two healthy children. Well, four counting JB's sons. Would she ever count them all as hers?

"Will the provisional government pay you?"

He grunted. "I take no government money."

"But Joseph Gervais goes to see if that pass along the Santiam will allow for wagons to come through there, something the government wants. Why would you assist if you don't care to be involved with the government? I don't understand this."

"To help my friend," he said. "It's a kindness."

"There must be something more," she told him.

"To aid a friend is not enough?"

"You should stay with your wife and children," she said.

"No. No shoulds, Etoile," he said.

She sighed. The word came onto her tongue as easily as spit. "I need you here," she told him. "This is the better way to say it."

"Toussaint and Doublé will do well for you. They're big boys now. They can milk the cows alone and be pleased they can. A son needs to feel confidence in accomplishment. They'll teach Xavier."

"Yes, but what will they teach him?"

"They get along well, Etoile. See, they plant melons even now together."

She looked out the window, confirmed what he said. Did she just stir up trouble that went nowhere? Her mother might ask her what her worries about such things kept her from doing.

Their daughter wailed now, and Marguerite handed Angelique to JB. He nuzzled the girl, his whiskers tickling her chubby chin. She quieted, and Marguerite bit her lip to stop herself from saying what she was thinking, *She should quiet like that for me.*

"She knows I leave, and she wants to please," JB said. "Tell your mother, eh?" He spoke to the baby. "Tell her she should do the same." He looked up at Marguerite and grinned.

"A farmer should stay on his farm," Marguerite said.

"Maybe I am not so good at farming, Etoile." His voice turned serious. "The land grows almost by itself. Oh, a good mule would help the boys. But to help my neighbors and friends, to find a wagon route that will go both east and west, to help the emigrants who come, I like this. I can pay my tax this way. It is worthy work."

Marguerite reached for a calmed infant who slept in her arms. "I miss you," she said. She didn't look at JB, but at the child instead. "I worry when you're gone, when you'll be back. If you'll come back." Her eyes watered. This was not the time.

"Ah, so this is your tangle with me when I leave." He struck his palm to his head as though he were a dense thinker who just figured something out. "I don't intend to die on that mountain looking for a wagon trail," he told her. He lifted her chin. "Is this what worries you?"

"What would I do?" she said. "How would I keep four children without you? When you're not here, it is what I think about. My father died and—"

"What is it that priest says, 'Give unto them beauty for ashes, the oil of joy for mourning, the garment of praise for the spirit of heaviness.' The priest says these words, eh? You remember? At Julie Gervais' sepulcher?"

"I didn't really know what it meant," Marguerite said.

"We must seek what brings comfort in all times. Beauty. The oil of joy. But most of all, praising the heavens for all things, especially when we are sad or worried. There is nothing else that can bring us comfort, eh? Even an old trapper like me knows that the peace here"—he touched her forehead and her chest at her heart—"does not come from what we make happen but from wrapping ourselves in thankfulness. You wrap yourself in those thoughts while I am gone, and then even when bad things happen—no, no, I do not expect anything bad will happen, Etoile—you will know you are not alone."

"What became of Joseph Gervais' petition for a canal around the falls?" Marguerite asked then. "Or for the railroad? Maybe he gets involved in things that are good ideas but nothing comes of them. Is this one of his ideas, too, this trail over the mountains? Wasted effort for you, husband?"

JB pulled Marguerite to his chest then, the baby still asleep between them. "You will not be successful in having a fight with me before I leave," he said. "There will always be trials. There will be wars. Boundaries will need changing, and people will come and change what we do, eh? Our sons will grow up and away; our daughter, too. I cannot keep all bad things from happening. I can't keep you from your worries. But you wear a good wrap, eh? You are a wise and faithful mother, and you know what to do to cover the worries."

Alone here in the St. Louis church was best, even in the cool March morning. Marie believed that Jean understood or at least he did not question her going except for that first time. After that, he said he'd look after Baby if she woke. "Take your time, my Marie. Find there what you want and then come back to me."

She didn't know what she wanted, but she felt closer to receiving it when she sat on the wooden benches, alone. She'd sit and think and pray, such as she knew how to. She knew none of the strange language the priests used that were said to be ancient prayers. Instead, she talked as though to a friend, fingering the beads she wore at her neck.

"At least I can remember the words," Marie said out loud. She'd not recognized Sister Celeste when she saw her at St. Paul at the little store. She knew she was a Sister, of course; the habit announced that. But her name escaped, and then it came to her with the blue eyes sparkling and Marie had been relieved, so relieved. But then her mind had wandered off on its own, and in the middle of her talking, her thoughts had stopped. She could not remember what she intended to say. The Sister had touched her hand and asked if she was well. Marie had shaken her head and walked away.

At this St. Louis church, she cleaned, hoping the work would be tasks she could finish and would remember having completed.

She scrubbed the whitewashed wooden floors, wiped down each

bench. The hard brush scraped across the wood. The scent of lye soap, with just a touch of rose water she had added in the making, seeped out both memory and hope. At the windows, she scraped off fly marks before washing, then wiped at her wrists as the water drained back to her elbows. The discomfort honored. Her chapped hands were gifts she could give.

While she cleaned, she listened. She reasoned with herself and with the voice inside her head that said she must forgive. Forgive her forgetfulness. This happened with the wearing of years. It should not be alarming. Forgive Pierre for having given John away, yes, but forgive herself, too, for having let him. Forgive herself for not going after him, dragging back her son, for not enlisting the priest's help, for putting her son away in her mind. She was young when she chose that act of protecting silence.

She needed to be grateful she had lived, married, had sons and daughters. She'd given them a good life. Perhaps because she had done her best, been faithful as she knew how, perhaps that was why she could now remember what had once been. She had let the silent pain surface. She did not need to pay penance for it any longer.

There would be no way to find him, even if she searched. David Mongrain said the John Dorion he knew had left the Company over fifteen years before. She'd have no way to track him, and in all these years, even with the Dorion name spread now as some said around the world, he'd not appeared, even with Baptiste out seeking Paul those years before. But should a mother begin the making of a coat only if it had a chance to be finished or even worn by the one she intended? Or did the gifts of the threads require working toward the wrap regardless of how it turned out? It was this question she had struggled with, and so far, the answer twirling in her head had said to "cease striving." It was from a proverb. She'd had to ask Jean the meaning of the word *striving.*

"It means to struggle or contend with something," he said. "Though we are French, we say it as a drive, too."

"As when we drive the cattle to the stanchion?" she'd asked.

He'd been thoughtful. "*Oui.* We are not to push ahead or propel in such a way we can only see that one way. It may not be the best way at all."

"The opposite of a *métier*," Marie had said. "One calls, the other is hit with a stick into a place."

Jean had smiled at her. "You should have been the interpreter," he said.

"But this is always the question, *n'est-ce pas?* Whether we strive or are called? Whether we hold tight or let go? How to sort this?"

"Maybe we can't," Jean had said. "Maybe it's done without us." He'd shrugged his shoulders then, his bad arm swinging on like an afterthought.

That had been weeks ago. She could remember that conversation. She lifted the wooden bucket of dirty water and carried it outside the church, splashing the wooden steps with it. She scrubbed now, her knees straddling the rough-hewn logs. The verse said to cease striving. Maybe if she could, then other things would fill the space. She came closest to allowing that within this wooden structure while working on her knees.

She didn't hear them come upon her, but she felt them beside her, saw two sets of feet.

"Papa told us you were here," Marianne said. She turned to look.

She gasped. A striving, ceased.

"What did mother say?" Baptiste asked.

The children of Marie, minus some exceptions, had gathered at Marguerite and JB's home. Josette showed signs of another birth, and Marguerite wondered at the wisdom of that. It hadn't been a year since their son's death. But maybe choosing life again was the best course. It wasn't her choice to make.

"She sat with her mouth open for a time and then she stood and wrapped her arms around them and just cried," Marianne said. "Her welcome song, she said it was."

"It was good you found her at the church. She takes strength from that place," Josette said.

"I wish I could have been there," Marguerite said. "I love reunions, even this one that brings us all together here with things of sadness to consider."

"You should have let us know," Marianne said. "We would have waited for you."

Marguerite felt her face grow hot. She'd gone to the St. Louis church where her mother cleaned and arrived in time to see the dust of a small gathering ride out. Marguerite had shouted, but the wind was in her face and her horse a slow one, and they hadn't waited up for her. Angelique rode in a board tied to the saddle, her eyes searching the world.

Marguerite's eyes pooled with tears. It was such a silly thing. They couldn't have known she watched them ride away. They hadn't left her behind intentionally, and yet it was as though she'd been purposefully excluded, as though she was someone not worthy to be inside this family. Baptiste and Paul were true brothers; François and Marianne blood brothers and sisters. She was an only child, and a lonely one at that.

She'd caught up with them at her mother's, and when she watched the woman step down from the horse, she knew instantly from that waddle and walk that it was Barbe, though she'd lost much weight. Archange's wide shoulders marked him, and he had his hand on Barbe's elbow, walking beside her. Her mother welcomed them back with open arms, hardly a question asked.

But now, only a few days later, the children gathered, minus Barbe, whom Marianne said she would not claim as a sister. Together, the children of Marie Dorion Venier Toupin would decide what to do.

"We can't have them continuing to stay at Papa and Mother's," François said.

"Because there's nearly three in the loft already?" Baptiste teased. Angelique blushed, barely let her hand flutter at her abdomen before leaning over to pick up some needlework she now placed on her lap.

"No. Because it's too hard on Mother. Papa sees it too, but he doesn't know what to say. Mother can be stubborn."

"Persistent, she calls it," Marguerite said. "And she gave it to all of us."

"To the women anyway," David Gervais said to Marianne's wrinkled nose.

"We two are closer to it now than any of you," François said. "We see it every day."

"Angele's there. What does she say?" Josette asked.

"What child of nine knows anything of help to an adult?" François said. "She stays busy playing or doing what she's told."

"It's what a little one should do, eh?" JB said.

"Angele's a good girl," François' wife said. "But she's just a child."

"In school once," Marianne added, "Sister asked us if we knew what the word *powerful* meant, and we all gave out examples of the Hudson's Bay Company or warriors who win or talked of strong horses. But Angele said it was when you wanted to quit but kept going."

JB nodded. "Wisdom knows no age."

"That's why we let you meet with us," Marianne said. "You're old enough to be Marguerite's father. We needed that wisdom of age."

"Oh, Marianne," Josette said. "This is an unkindness, to your sister and your sister's husband."

"And to you," David said.

"I was only teasing. Must everyone be so serious?" Marianne crossed her arms now and had a pouting look. "It could be a compliment. Not every old person has wisdom. Or they lose it. Isn't that why we're all here?"

"I know I'm not with Mother much, but what I see," Marguerite said, "is that she's working very hard taking care of everyone. She's at the church almost every day. She's baking bread to give away. Papa Jean's garden goes mostly to orphans and the priests and those in the schools. When she's not doing that, she travels around tending people's ills. She's been exposed to every illness. It'll weaken her. And she sometimes looks confused. That worries me the most."

"We need a French-speaking doctor," JB said. "That Bailey didn't learn much from Dr. White. Or at least he doesn't show it."

"She's constantly giving," Marguerite continued. "Tireless. It's like she…atones for something. With Barbe back it's worse, not better. She tries to let Barbe be the child's mother and she can't be, and then Mother steps in and there's conflict. Isn't that right, Angelique?" François' wife nodded agreement. "She isn't able, much as Barbe might think otherwise.

She's...well, we have to speak the truth here. Barbe can't make the choices that will keep a child safe and growing into an adult."

"But with Mother there, she can," Baptiste said.

"Mama can't help her all the time," Marianne said. "She's getting... forgetful."

"And that's the gnawing, as I see it," François said. "She wants to do what's right, but it can't happen. Barbe's...a child herself, and Mother won't say it."

"Barbe can't raise her own child," David said. "Do we agree with this?"

"Without help," Marguerite said.

"My wife does what she can," François defended.

"No one's accusing," Marguerite said.

"Mother doesn't want to take a child from her mother's hands," Baptiste said.

"Barbe gave her baby away," Marianne said. "She lost the power to say anything about it."

"How do you know that?" Baptiste said.

Josette said, "Maybe she didn't intend for another to raise her child."

"You think she was coming back for it when the Sisters found it?" Marguerite said. It had never occurred to her. How awful to seek your child and not find her! Maybe that was why she'd run away with Archange.

"But why did Barbe wait so long to return, then? Why didn't she come forward as soon as it happened and claim her instead of disappearing?" Marianne said.

"It's been over a year," François said.

"What kind of mother would do that, just let someone take your baby away without protest?" Marianne said.

"A poor one, that's certain," Marguerite agreed. "No, Baby's like a toy to Barbe. She can't be allowed to raise this child alone."

"She has Archange," David said. "Doesn't he have a say in this?"

The room fell silent.

"We could build them a house of their own," JB said.

"While Archange works, who would look after Baby? And could he do the cooking and tending and feed his wife as well?" François said. "Sometimes I think he's as witless as Barbe."

"She does need someone to cook for her," Marianne said. "Barbe has quite an appetite."

"She and Angele are the only two children Mother claimed the name of godmother for. They're very special to her. We can't keep mother from this circle," Baptiste said.

"Or Papa Jean."

"Or Barbe and Archange," Josette said.

Marguerite said, "What we want for Mother is for her not to worry over Barbe and Baby. And even if they weren't underfoot, lived in their own house, it would just be one more place she'd want to tend to each day. I know she would." Silence again. "Maybe we should include Archange and Papa Jean in our decisions, though. Maybe we all need to talk together, the whole family. I hate feeling excluded in what matters to me."

Marianne thumped her foot against the table as she swung it. "It isn't right us talking about all this without everyone included."

"There will always be a missing one," Baptiste said.

"Let's go ahead and eat," Marianne said. "We can try another day—"

"There is a missing brother, *n'est-ce pas?*" JB said. "I forget this."

"No one has seen Paul for years," Marianne said, disgusted.

"Baptiste has," Marguerite said.

"What? When? How come I don't know about it?" Marianne said. "No one tells me anything."

"I didn't know either," François said.

Josette nudged Baptiste. "Tell them."

"Paul was at Waiilatpu," Baptiste said. "Two years back. No one has seen him since. No one has heard from him. He's not a part of this journey."

"And the rest," Josette said. "Maybe it's better if all secrets are unwrapped."

Marguerite felt her heart begin to pound as though her body knew before her mind that something lurked inside this den of secrets they called family.

"There is another brother," Baptiste said. "Paul's and mine," Baptiste said.

"How do you know?"

"Mother told me."

"Why would she?" Marianne asked.

"I had a looping dream, a memory of my father pushing a boy toward me at a *vingt et un* game he played. Papa said never to speak of it and I didn't, but I remembered, not long ago when I traveled with my own son."

"And you asked her?" Marguerite said.

"I'd asked Mama before, and she didn't answer. I thought she hadn't heard me, and my heart pounded so loudly I didn't know if I wanted to hear the answer. But this time I persisted and she said yes, there had been an older brother."

"What happened to him?" François said.

Baptiste swallowed. "I think my father arranged for the child to go away to someone else. Maybe to pay off a debt."

Marguerite heard herself gasp. "Mother wouldn't have let that happen."

"Who knows what any of us will do when we're grieving," Marianne said.

Baptiste said, "But she let the child go and returns now in her aging to visit her regret."

Penance. Marianne was paying penance for not being a worthy daughter. Yes, Marianne had seen her mother looking tired and weary, but she hadn't remembered her ever looking sprightly or young. A mother's face rained wrinkles from the hot east winds of Walla Walla, and her knees creaked as she walked. As for her mother being more forgetful, Marianne had been the first to notice those occurrences, and yet none of her older brothers and sisters had taken her observations seriously at all. Until now, when they noticed it too, when they decided something should be done. And Marianne should do it.

She felt that anxious feeling, as though she needed to sit close to the front, to be ready to jump in before they told her to, and yet she hesitated. Oh how hard this was, being the youngest. She so wanted to do it right.

She listened to them talk back and forth, her sister and brothers, their families. All with opinions, all making her stomach ache with anticipation. If she were a bird, she'd take flight now, perch like a hawk on the lip of a tree overlooking the river. No, she *was* the tree, sturdy and tall, or was that her sister who best fit that picture, as unbending as oak. Maybe Marguerite formed the solid trunk of a tree growing up straight and firm. Maybe Marianne was the taproot of such an oak. The oak's roots didn't branch out the way some trees did but they nourished well. That was Marianne, strong but not too complicated. No, that was their mother, the one who drew deep as an oak tree taproot and gave them all life. What did that leave Marianne? The leaves of branches spread out wide and offering shade. Showy. Comforting. Ever-changing. That was Marianne, and what was wrong with that?

She had to offer first, before they asked, to honor Julie.

Her rosary beads felt solid in her fingers. She said a prayer before she offered. It might not be so bad. Maybe she wouldn't have to take Barbe, too. Baby and Angele she could handle. Angele might even be of help with Joseph. While the little one slept, Angele and her son could pull weeds in the garden and Marianne could patch David's pants and darn the holes in his cotton socks. A wifely thing to do. David complained about his sore toes hitting against his boot ends, and she did notice a tiny sore that hadn't healed, just at the tip of his toe. Good socks might help that.

She was a good wife, and surely not just noticing a need but tending it would make her a worthy one. Maybe even a noticeable daughter. She hoped, a forgiven friend.

Marianne was about to offer, to open her mouth to do what she must, when Marguerite, the tree trunk, had to spoil it by saying it was Marguerite's duty as the oldest daughter to do it first, and she, of course, would take all of them, Barbe and Archange included.

Archange would work again with Baptiste and help her father as much as he would let them. Marianne's father had his own way. But Archange knew Baptiste's routines.

"They should get married," Marguerite said. "That should happen first."

The thought of that girl-child being married startled. It didn't seem right, yet she was already a mother. Legitimizing the child made sense.

Why Baptiste didn't take them all to his tipi, Marianne didn't understand. Another tipi could be easily erected, and they'd have their own little place then right next to Baptiste. No family had to be disrupted. It would relieve them all of this problem they'd discussed for hours now.

Except her mother, of course. She wouldn't be relieved. Her mother felt responsible. Her mother had taken on Barbe as family, and for her mother, family was forever, and all that went with it.

She was certainly curious about that other son. What a surprise. A secret once kept, revealed.

Baptiste said he had no evidence the arrangements were made to pay a debt, and yet the story he told around it made sense. She'd heard once the Astorians reminiscing bringing up a lawsuit of Pierre's grandfather. He'd won at *vingt et un* and never been paid, and he took the issue into court. So it could be. But her mother remembered that the child had been given to another mother, a childless woman. How could she have done it? It was a side of her mother she couldn't imagine. A human side of the saint.

Marguerite's offer to invite her family into her home won her accolades.

"Why don't we commit, each of us, except for François and Angelique who are there all the time, to take them for a day or two each week," Marianne offered finally. "Between Marguerite, me, and Josette, we could give Mother a true rest. Angelique would only have evenings to help much and—"

"That only solves the Barbe problem. It doesn't address Mama's...forgetfulness," François said.

"Maybe with less to trouble her, she'll remember important things better," Marianne said.

She'd been amazed, but after some discussion, they'd agreed to give it a try.

"Did you know about this other brother?" she asked her husband on their way home.

"No," David said. "But I don't keep my ears open for such things. If news is meant to come my way, it jumps up in front of me and taps me on the shoulder. Then I pay attention."

"You miss things," Marianne told him.

"I miss worrying over absent teeth in a comb I don't much use," he said.

"It's how a person finds things out," she insisted. "By listening to what isn't said as much as to what is."

"Then how come you didn't know that your brother Paul had been so close?"

"Because Baptiste keeps a good secret," she said. "There must have been some clue about this other one. Baptiste must have guessed, and then Mother confessed. Imagine, keeping the secret all these years."

"For a reason. If there's nothing to be done about a thing or no good can come of it, it's best not to talk about it," David said.

Marianne pulled her blanket around her shoulders, listened to the jangle of harness and hames. "But how do we know if nothing good could happen from it? Maybe Mama would have gone to Paul and that empty place she must have could be filled up. I can't imagine not ever seeing or talking with Joseph. I love him so much." She turned back to see their child still asleep in the wagon box.

"I'd be furious if my son left and never made contact with me," David said. "It'd be his job to come to me if he did the disappearing."

"But he'd know you were so angry. And maybe he'd feel a terrible shame for having left, so how could he return? I don't know if I could step across that chasm."

"Then the love isn't strong enough," David said.

"Whose? Yours or your son's? You could step across the anger too. Wouldn't you want a way to be rid of it? Such a waste. Mama always said that anger filled a basket that is better filled by something else."

"Disappointment," David said.

"No," she said. "But—"

"Let's not talk of it now then," he said. "It's not real, Marianne. Our son isn't running away from us. We're not angry with him or anyone else. We waste time over nothing."

The words she wanted to say didn't come to her. Words rarely did until she'd chattered for a time, back and forth. David didn't allow for that. Marguerite didn't either. Julie had. She could have talked for hours with Julie. In the middle of a thought, a new one would form on her lips and surprise her as it passed into the air between friends. Sometimes she even said out loud, "I'm so glad that idea decided to show up." Julie always laughed with her. Julie understood.

"She didn't name this John when she and Papa said the nuptial vows and legitimized us all. I'm sure. I remember that."

"Did she name Paul?" David asked.

Marianne pulled the blankets closer around her chest. She looked back to see that Joseph slept. The wagon movement caused the fur at the hide's edges to shiver, tickling her son's nose. He sneezed without waking up.

"No. She didn't name Paul, either."

"Probably thought them both deceased," David said.

"She hesitated when Papa Jean asked her, as though she was thinking of someone. I thought she hadn't understood the priest's question or that in the excitement, her mind floated away. It was a spirited day. Maybe she was trying to decide to tell us, or—"

"Don't gossip in your mind, Marianne. It gets you in trouble."

"Why keep it a secret from your whole family your whole life and then decide to tell just one of your children? Just one!"

"It's her secret to do with as she pleases. It should stay that way. Maybe his memory was all she had of him to call her own, Bonbon," David said. "We don't easily part with the things we love. Once we do, they assume a life of their own, one we can't bring back or contain."

"Like gossipy words, you mean," she said. "Even François didn't know about John, and he still lives under her roof. And Angelique acted as surprised as the rest of us." She rode quietly for a time. "Mama might not have told me because she knows I'm not interested in gossipy things. It's such a waste of time."

David smiled and pulled her to him on the wagon seat in a one-arm pat of her shoulder. "At least now you know what everyone else knows. And you weren't the only one left in the dark."

"Just so you're not kept in the dark, husband..." Marianne paused. "We're expecting another child," she said, "and if it's a girl, I want to name her Marie."

18

Beneath the Surface

1846

Barbe did her best, but to Marie's thinking, the girl really couldn't keep a child safe day after day. She'd forget she had a child at all some days, leaving Baby near the lake while she walked up the bank to take twined water jars to Archange, who was felling an oak tree. Barbe chattered, always chattered, distracting herself and Archange, too. Marie looked out the window and saw the two, Archange, bent over his axe, and Barbe, standing with one hand on her hips pointing this way and that. Marie would look for Baby and, not seeing her, would call out. "Where's Baby? Go find her."

"Odors," Barbe would say with a wave of dismissal, but she'd look, at least. She wouldn't move to find her until Marie did, though, and then Barbe would come lumbering. "I find her, Mama. I find her."

Together, they always did. But it was a frequent wondering and a worry that someday the child might disappear inside a sink or wander into the thicker oak stands and be lost to a marauding cow or a hog let loose and gone wild. Wolves still threatened, though the bounty offered by the government had helped contain them.

Marie thought once that having told herself the truth in doing what she did to her own sons, she'd have more patience and compassion for Barbe. She and Barbe shared a memory, though she wasn't sure that Barbe could understand that; and Marie might soon forget. They were quite a pair, these two mothers. Her children failed to see the close connection, but Marie did. She knew but for the grace of God she, too, might forget to keep an eye on her child.

Marie sat up slowly on the side of the bed. Jean's steady breathing comforted. She patted her husband's blanketed back, pulled the cover over him. The dog stirred with her movement as she eased toward the fire and began mixing the flour for the bread she'd fry as the household stumbled into morning.

She poked at the embers. She could do things in these misty hours when others slept without the hovering. She reached for her porcupine quills soaking in the water and began her work.

They'd never been so attentive, her sons and daughters. Jean had postponed their annual journey south because the presence of their children blended such kindness of caring into ready, working hands.

Every day for the past month, Josette, Marianne, or Marguerite had stopped by and spent the better part of the day with them. They took over the churning and watching after Baby while Marie rode to the church to make sure the candles were ready, that the rippled windows were washed to welcome winter's meager sun. Her tasks completed, she gathered berries or rode back home to listen to her daughters and daughters-in-law, whichever were present, as they performed the work of washing, cooking, patching, and now spinning with a contraption François brought home for his bride.

When they left her alone, she often repeated what they'd done—the cleaning, beating at the rag rug that she put her feet on when she rose. Otherwise, she felt like a guest inside her own home with little required of her. A welcome guest, though. One more rested. One who slept better beside her husband at night.

Even her sons had taken on new ways. Baptiste brought dried meat and fresh tanned hides Josette had prepared. "My son's first kill," Baptiste told Marie. "His mother gifts it to you."

She would form it into a shirt and make a quill design and give it back to her grandson so he could hand it down to his own child one day. "This hide will age, and it will remind you of your first provision," she told her grandson as he watched her work. "It will also record how your family accepted your first gift and added to the story."

Working with quills took concentration and time. She had time now. She couldn't always concentrate, but this morning she could. Yesterday, she'd listened to little stories Angele wrote and even recognized the girl's name when the child wrote it as different from her own.

They'd turn this log house on the edge of Lake Labiche over to François and Angelique before long, when the winter rains came. The lake would fill in the fingers, and what was once a bountiful garden would become the sloping lake banks again where rivulets of water gouged and grated into the muddy slough. Then the water would rise to the lake edge, creating a pool of blue. The oaks would cry with their rain-soaked moss, and in the dips and hollows, when François and Angelique rode to St. Louis, the ground would swallow their horses' feet, sinking them in thick, clay mud.

But their house sat on high ground. They had no need to wonder over the height of the lake bed or even the Willamette River's rise, as did those who lived along Mission Bottom. Marie and Jean were closer to the church and family here at the lake, but once the rains began, Jean would push to go south. Jean always said it was close to Tchamoo Prairie when people asked where they wintered at, west of that mound. "Where angels watch over us and give us all we need to make it through the winter." Mount Angel. That was Jean's description.

She had never told him, but she preferred the Walla Walla country in the winter. Cold, yes, but also clear blue skies with snow that covered over dirt and mud and promised purity. She was from the tribe of gray snow people. Going to the Walla Walla country was like going home. It was a journey of several days to go there, but this year she felt rested enough to try.

She pressed several of the quills deeper into the bucket of water, making sure they soaked up as much moisture as possible. She could more easily bend them into unnatural shapes, and they complied with the requests of her hands.

This year they might go to Walla Walla. Changes here might permit it.

Her children had certainly changed, or perhaps she saw them in different ways. She wondered if Baptiste had told her other son and daughters about John. She had no reason to believe he had, but something had inspired new offerings from her daughters. Perhaps they pitied her, this old woman with memories soaked for years and now being pushed into new and different shapes.

Marianne's first new offer had caused Marie to laugh, a sound she regretted once she saw the pain flash across her daughter's eyes.

"Whatever will you do with them?" Marie asked.

"We'll…work hides together," Marianne said. "David shot a deer, and I've been soaking it. I know what to do next. You showed me years ago."

"I did," Marie said. "And you hated pressing your hands into that brain mixture. I wonder why you'd do it now." Marie had smiled at her youngest, her surprising daughter.

But Marianne crossed her arms over her chest as though to shield her heart from a hurtful blow.

"Does Barbe want to go with you?" Marie asked then.

"I didn't ask her. Don't you think I can keep Baby safe? It's just for the day. Archange can come and pick her up early if you don't trust I'll bring Baby back."

"Oh, I have no doubt you'll bring her back," Marie said, and again she noticed the flash of distress in her daughter's eyes. "Let's talk to Barbe," Marie had said.

Barbe had wanted to go, as Marie knew she would.

"Me, too," Angele said.

Marianne, surprising Marie, agreed to that child coming along. "We'll have more hands to work the hide," Marianne said. Marie suspected Angele would be looking after Baby, but that child knew what she wanted and Marie could see she longed to go. Being with an old one all day long could bind the young rather than build them up.

Marie had ridden as far as the church with Marianne, Angele, Barbe, and Baby. Apprehension and relief rode with her as she watched Marianne turn southeast and lead the way toward the Gervais house along the Willamette. Baby in her board, close to Marianne's knees, bounced at the horse's withers. Barbe's broad back leaned heavily forward as though towing Angele like a boat, the child's arms clinging to Barbe's middle on the steady mount that followed Marianne. They traveled along the oak-shaded trail at the prairie's edge and disappeared out of sight.

Another day, Marguerite had come and took her mother north to visit Kilakotah. "You never visit her," Marguerite said. "Baptiste said Kilakotah complained to him of it. They're back on Tom's farm near the Champoeg butte for a time, so we can easily make it in a day."

When Marie hesitated, Angelique said, "Baby will be fine with me. And Barbe likes to milk, so you go now with Marguerite and your grandchildren. How much time do you have with Marguerite's little ones?"

She'd had time, in truth, but had taken little of it. And through the days of allowing her children to offer their gifts of spirit and time, she awoke one morning to realize she no longer fought with herself.

Wasn't a truce what her first husband had worked for those years as an interpreter for the Company? Her son Baptiste had taken on those tasks too, carrying words and ideas between peoples who might otherwise use guns and arrows to speak. Even Jean, who could irritate in his younger days, had been called upon to help the Company's factors understand the meanings of new ways, to form peace between people. He might be called upon again if Josette's Cayuse flamed.

But for now, her husband walked beside her with comforting ways. She had a family who needed her and who gave her gifts she didn't know she longed for. Until Barbe's return, she hadn't imagined that a truce inside a soul could become a mother's *métier.*

Jean stirred. He lay for a time, and she knew he watched her work. She looked up at him, and he said, "Today, we go south. We've lounged enough, eh?"

"I don't lounge," she said. She held up the quillwork on young Pierre's shirt.

Jean folded his arms behind his head, talked through a yawn. "I'll need those hands to tan the hides I'll bring in off our angel butte this winter."

"Barbe has strong hands. She'll help," she said. "And Archange, too."

"It'll be interesting to see how the deer populations shift, eh, when people don't burn the meadows so much," Jean said.

"We should go to Walla Walla this winter instead of south," Marie said.

"Josette and Baptiste stay here now," Jean said. "She has her baby here. She doesn't even think it good to go there with the struggles between Whitman and the Cayuse. Measles, too," Jean said. "There are rumors there of that."

"The cold will kill disease off," she said. "It's a good thing about the Walla Walla country."

"You'd leave Barbe and Baby here?" he said. "You'd separate and let them live here with François and Angelique? Or alone?"

She considered. How badly did she want to go to Walla Walla?

⌖

The colors of Marie's life faded into each other, the way the vibrant tones of autumn muted into winter's pewter rains. The land healed, it did, just by one being present in it. She needed time to just sit. She'd go outside and watch the season shift.

Tiny pricks of light when she stood up too quickly from her scrubbing knees told her to wait a moment before reaching out to comfort the child. She didn't want to fall, didn't want to injure the toddler by a careless act. She had done that once already.

Despite being a young, strong, loving mother, she had allowed her firstborn son to be given away and then pushed that betrayal from any place where the pain of it might wound.

Baby's arrival in her arms those months before had given her back her own story.

The red of her outrage bled off first as she recalled how she'd failed to challenge Pierre's decision, telling herself the other mother had grieved more than she. The other mother had borne so many babies without a living form to cuddle to her breast. This other mother deserved a child to call its name. There'd be others, Pierre told her. Many others. She was young, he kept reminding her.

She was young, and she'd let others mark her boundaries.

Once in those first days while her body winced with the soreness of the child's delivery, she thought Pierre might have used the child to pay a debt. He loved *vingt et un;* he always had. Pierre's father had gambled heavily. Yet when Baptiste mentioned it, she denied the possibility, absolutely. Her husband could be reckless, yes. He and a brother threatened to scalp their father in a drunken brawl once, but the older man saved his hair and the legacy of a family murder with his words. He reminded them it was their father they threatened.

It had taken a father's strength to halt Pierre's violent ways with that story told; what chance did a wife have, a mere young woman-child wife at that? Besides, Pierre could be tender, too. Surely he wouldn't have used his own flesh and blood to remove a debt.

She'd put John away in a place inside her heart. She sewed a seam then, tight against the torture. It was how a young mother could go on despite her choice.

When Baby arrived, a stitch tore loose. When Barbe returned to claim her daughter, the seam split open.

Marie stood. What was it she was going to do next? She hated the cobwebs that thickened her thinking. She walked back inside. Yes. The bucket. Her floors needed tending.

⌖

By July, the grasses were brown and shorter than usual because the winter had seen less rain and the spring had refused to make up for it. "We can hope for a good rainy fall this year," Jean told François as they moved the cows through the timbers toward the barn. Jean liked this ritual of twice daily milking. He enjoyed the time of work with his son.

"Our Lake Labiche stays drier this year," François said. He spoke to the cows as they drove them forward, their heads shifting to brush away the ever-present flies.

"Flies don't seem to mind the heat," Jean said. "And they still like their free ride on the backs and ears of others." He swatted at his own ears now. The women had the right idea, wearing earrings they could shake and rattle at the insects.

I should try my hand at making such a pair of earrings for my Marie, Jean thought. The last pair he'd given her, before they were married, she'd traded in for seeds to save her children's lives that first winter on the Okanogan. She deserved a present. He'd like trying to make them.

They milked only a few head of cows now, leaving the milk for the calves that had sparse grazing with the dry season. They'd raise what they could for beef and hides to tan or barter. Even the Company butchered cattle these days, so beef was no longer so scarce. The influx of neat cows arriving with the ever-increasing emigrants meant milk and butter and cheese brought less in trade, though. Supply changed price, which changed demand. It was a never-ending cycle of anticipating just maintaining food for his family.

The Company had done well by its four cows brought from the Sandwich Islands to Fort George all those years before. They'd done well in other areas, too. Astoria. Talk was that the Hudson's Bay Company owned 4,430 head of cattle, had 3,000 acres under cultivation, and employed nearly 630 people.

Jean thought that the figures were an exaggeration meant to intimidate the Americans while negotiations were going on. He smiled to himself. The provisional government had erased the requirement that each resident swear loyalty to America, and McLoughlin had signed on then, a way to keep his Company protected. Any militia called upon would have to assist all signers. McLoughlin had an even greater interest as he claimed the land at Oregon City, not for the Company now, but as his. And it most likely was. The man was a good manager, and why not set aside a good income from a mill to assist him when he retired? If he ever retired. Some men didn't. Jean guessed he was one of those. He'd be pushing a cow or two, hunting, and planting his gardens for the rest of his days. He smiled. He was grateful for it.

He'd also be a landowner before long. With the boundary settled, there'd be a way to mark the property and not just describe improvements. He planned to claim three sections of 320 acres each. It was more than what was allowed, but he hoped they'd make an exception. He had improvements on two pieces of property. That way he'd have a piece for himself, one for François, and one for Baptiste. A father took care of his sons.

They pushed the cows into the stanchions, and both men bent beneath the animals to milk.

"I wonder if the factor milks his own cows," François said.

"Probably not," Jean said. "He's an old man too, like your Papa. These old knees squatting start to bend a person. He's got lots more height and age on me. I doubt he does it himself."

"He's worth a thousand dollars in cattle," François said. "His mill, they say, is worth seven thousand dollars. Probably the richest man in the region."

"How do you know such things, eh? A man's private doings."

"Meek's the collector," François said.

"Meek should keep his mouth shut," Jean said. But Meek, that old trapper, was known to drink some and show other signs of poor judgment. Why, he'd left his daughter Helen Mar with the Whitmans in '42 and had yet to go back for her. How could a man leave his children like that? He'd heard, though, that Mrs. Whitman cared for the child as if she were her own. She'd taken in Jim Bridger's half-breed children, too, and six orphans coming on a wagon train had found refuge at Waiilatpu under the Whitmans' wings.

"He has his work cut out for him from what I hear," François said.

"The factor?"

"No. Meek. People don't like him taking the collections."

"Folks rarely like to part with their funds," Jean said. "Especially if they don't think they have a say in how they'll be spent."

"They can vote. I can."

"Don't always get your way then, either."

"It's the Americans' way," François said. "Though I'd wager it wasn't what even the new arrivals expected."

The two men finished with their respective cows, turned them out, and stanchioned two more. Knuck lay in the hay not far from Jean's feet.

"That Dr. White says Cayuse have cattle. And the Coeur d'Alene.

They pack their butter west to Fort Walla Walla. Compete with the Company." François laughed. His son took delight in things that challenged the Company. He wasn't sure where that animosity came from. "Baptiste says even the priests at the Catholic Mission at St. Mary's milk thirty head now and they make their own butter, too."

"Don't tell your mother. She will want us to go there to trade, to see if we can get a neater cow to milk."

"The settlers bring some across. Thin, but they'll fatten."

The sound of the milk hitting the side of the bucket soothed. The cow swatted at a fly with her tail and hit Jean's face. He backed away. "It's good they sell the butter there now. It's a way for them to feed the people, trade to the emigrants if they have anything left to trade," Jean said. "There'll be less tension then. Maybe if the emigrants keep moving on through to here, if they don't stop and till soil and act like they want to own that land, maybe the Cayuse and the Walla Walla will simply wave at them instead of getting riled."

"Baptiste says that will never happen," François said. "He says there'll be trouble and that we're fortunate not to be there or we'd be drawn into it."

Two days before New Year's of 1847, Josette sent Baptiste on the journey around Lake Labiche to the place where his mother and Jean always wintered, east of the Methodist Institute and Mission. Baptiste reached his mother, then brought her back.

"Angelique could care for her, but Josette wanted you," he said. "Josette feels safest with you beside her." Baptiste hesitated. "I do too."

Baptiste was pleased to say it, to put the words out without rancor. He did trust his mother's tending. What had happened long ago he'd set aside.

Baptiste had been more worried his mother might insist that everyone come, that Barbe and Archange, too, would make their pallets on the floor, awaiting those first cries of life. It was Josette's way, her people's way, to witness life and death with family surrounding each as though it were a warming fire. But he wanted only to give Josette peace the way Marianne's mother-in-law had provided it for his sister the previous month by bringing his little niece, Marie, into David Gervais' arms. He'd watched his wife take more effort when she pushed up from her knees, halt midstep at times, responding to pain. She'd never been so thin so close to a birthing. He wanted his mother close and not distracted.

His newborn son, Joseph, made his appearance within three days, arriving with the silky dark hair of a Dorion to mark him as the first Dorion born of this new year. He watched to see his mother's face as she held the cord so Baptiste could cut it. Did she think of her lost sons when she did that, he wondered? She'd said nothing more about John, but Baptiste thought he understood better now why she had had him search for Paul. Two sons lost. Too much to witness or remember. Even though she hadn't let herself remember her first son, perhaps a silent part of it pushed her to pursue Paul even further.

In February, the family gathered at the St. Louis log church for Joseph's christening day. Snow spit and caught against the brittle leaning grasses. The day turned cold even for the prairie in that month. Baptiste had asked two friends to serve as godparents. His mother had enough, Baptiste thought. And she hadn't offered. Barbe and Archange had exchanged nuptial vows on that day, too.

"It's been a hard winter," David Mongrain said after the sacraments. They stood at the table where children reached for sweet pastries that Marie and her daughters had baked. "Everywhere. Father Blanchet travels east to Fort Hall, and the snow is drifted two cows deep, he said. Many Indian cattle died. He worries for the Cayuse there. So many are starving."

"They didn't need more to argue about," Baptiste said.

David nodded. He brushed crumbs from his ample chest. "It's rumored that one of Whitman's men poisoned melons last fall trying to catch wolves. But the Cayuse think it was to discourage their forays into Whitman's fields. Several became sick. There were a few deaths. Whitman tried to explain, but isn't believed."

"Do the measles continue?" Marie asked.

"That, too," David Mongrain said. "Dr. Whitman can't quell the scourge. It does seem that the natives succumb more quickly too, and with the winter hard, and cattle dying…"

"It's good we didn't go there," Jean told Marie. "I was wise to make us stay here, eh? It's been cold, but at least the snow melts after a day."

"Into mud," François noted.

His mother remained silent, as was her way. She looked well despite her tending Josette and his mother's chosen family, as Baptiste thought of Barbe and Angele. The plan his brothers and sisters made had worked out well during summer months. But this past winter, neither he nor his sisters had ventured much to the southern spot where Jean claimed squatter's rights. Baptiste had only come to fetch his mother for the birthing. His brothers and sisters had set a course for themselves and then not kept the commitments. He knew Marguerite hadn't been there much; and this past cold wet winter would be a fine excuse to keep his delicate sister, Marianne, away.

"In the spring, the provisional government might be put out of business by finalizing the boundary agreement," Jean said, taking the conversation from measles and mud. "We'll need to mark our claims and make sure no one else takes them. We'll have to start proving up, as they put it. Showing proof we're worthy citizens, we who have been here longer than the government itself."

"And you have two claims to worry over," JB told him.

"Three, if I play my cards well," Jean told him. He winked.

"They'll never allow three plots," Baptiste said.

"Does Father Blanchet travel to Walla Walla?" Marie asked David Mongrain. "To help with the sickness?"

"He goes in June to perform baptisms there."

"You'll go too?" Marie asked. David nodded.

"Measles are there," Jean said, as though anticipating what his wife would ask next. "You wouldn't want to risk Baby and Angele with that, Marie."

Baptiste's mother answered with a strong voice, one that wintered well despite the cold. "When you go there," she told David Mongrain, "you bring back any news of a Dorion, a Paul, or a John. You will do this?"

"I'll keep my ears open for news of your family."

So, she talked now of it all, even with this man who wasn't family. Maybe this was the way wounded secrets healed.

Spring. Jean and Marie returned to the claim along the Lake, planting onions and potatoes and melons and corn farther down the banks as the lake dried into its usual slough. Underground springs kept sections green all summer, though they had their faults too, luring unsuspecting cows toward the green, sucking them into the sinks. Brown grasses edged away from the sides, but the garden flourished. They had plenty to eat, plenty for trade even at the Company's prices.

Marie stood outside in the July sun. She twisted the hide hung over the pole. She'd been soaking it at the lake water for several days, having to walk quite a distance down into drying fingers to reach the stream that fed it. It was not the time of year, this hot summer time, to take a deer. The meat tasted stronger when killed in months that had no *r* in them, according to Jean.

Marie had marveled when he told her. "A tiny letter of the alphabet gives up some clue for men to know when the season of a deer would make good meat?"

"It does," Jean said.

But this doe had broken its back leg, caught in one of the beaver traps Jean set along the creek near where he'd planted fruit trees. Beavers had discovered the slender morsels, and for several days, there'd been a war of sorts between Jean and the rodents over the trees.

Then the deer had stepped into the trap. Jean had tried to free it but the doe had thrown herself against Jean's bad arm knocking him down and he'd slipped, the animal's front legs stomping, the back leg broken. He'd rolled himself away at last, come back to the cabin with blood and bruises that Marie tended. Then he went back and shot the deer. Together, they'd dragged the animal up the creek bed to the bank, then loaded it across Jean's horse.

"Worst is that I got no beaver," Jean said. "And look at the size of the beaver house. Don't know as I've seen any larger on such a small creek."

"I did once," Marie said. "A long time ago."

He sighed. "I'll have to set another trap."

"Let's wait to plant more fruit trees," Marie said. "Trap him when the pelt is prime instead of now."

She didn't know why, but she wanted Jean away from the beaver lodge. Jean grudgingly agreed. They dressed the deer, and Marie soaked the hides, setting the brains aside for the treatment that would make the hide white and soft as Knuck's ears.

She was at the task when David Mongrain found her.

"You're back," she said, wiping her hands on her skirt. "A hot drink for you?"

"On a hot day like this?" David said.

"So when the breeze blows just a little it will feel cooler still."

He'd stepped down from his horse and waved at Jean as he strode over from the oak trees. "You've cleared even more since I was here last," he said.

"Oak means good soil, and the taproot isn't so deep it takes an army to burn it out," Jean said as he patted David's horse's neck and then ducked beneath it to stand in front of the Frenchman. He shook David's hand with his palm overturned in that way Jean had of shaking hands, to adapt for his bad shoulder.

"The early farmers say on the prairie they used to be able to grow anything at all, mountains of peas and oats. Wheat so plump and sturdy McLoughlin was forced to change his gauges."

"François got into an argument once over that," Jean said. "You remember, Marie?" She nodded.

"I don't see such crops now, closer to the church. The land looks leached out. But here..." David said as he scanned the landscape.

"Here the lake looks dry in summer, but the banks of it still harbor moisture and the crops lick it up, silent and unseen," Jean said

"You knew to farm the lake bed," David said.

"Marie liked it here."

"My people farmed the oxbows of the rivers, back in Ouisconsin," Marie said. "I don't remember doing it, but the Ioways did, using the river loops to water the ground. The story stays in my head from somewhere." She shook her head. "I remember meaningless things."

"Never underestimate what runs beneath the surface," Jean said. "Come," he motioned David into the cabin. "Let's take that hot drink of my Marie's."

Marie served, aware that David lingered, talked of crops and government, told of tragedy in Waiilatpu with illnesses and emigrants wintering there too, those who made it through the mountains before such heavy snows. Something in his manner told her he harbored news, had some other reason to come here to sit on the banks of a dry lake in the summer.

After a time, David sighed and turned to Marie.

"I met a Dorion last month," he said. "Six, in fact."

"Of my family?"

David nodded. "They were there."

"Tell the story," she said. "So I can remember and know then what to do next."

19

The Threads of a Coat

"His name is Paul. His wife's a comely one. A Sioux woman from the Lower Brule."

"Near where my first husband came from," Marie said.

"'My Horse Comes Out' is her name. They had four children with them. Might have been Baptiste's family, for the similarity in names. David, Paul, Joseph, and the youngest, Mary. A mother name."

"They live at Walla Walla now?" Marie said, her mind racing to what he must look like, his family, his sons. She could see them—they were so close! They should have gone last winter!

"Not sure. Didn't say any were born there. Maybe got stuck over the winter like so many did, but they were still there in June."

"How was he?" Jean asked.

David Mongrain hesitated. "As a father should be in such circumstances."

Marie heard her heart beating loud and slow as a mourning drum.

"There was a death?" she asked.

David shook his head. "A baptism. I acted as the witness."

"We have to go," Marie said.

This time, there would be no question of it, Jean was sure of that. She'd push and prod even though it tired her out. He watched her when she stood from kneeling, groaning with the effort. This work of remembering John had more than etched her spirit, it had chiseled it, left marks that even he could see. One son left behind. Two others she held close within her heart. Another reborn to her.

He checked the growth on the apple trees as he walked, the dog trotting behind him. Baptiste had said the trees resembled those at Fort Vancouver, where the fruit grew close together almost like clusters of grapes he'd seen in drawings. They'd have fruit for cider this fall, just no new starts taking hold because of that beaver.

He walked back toward the cabin. He could see his once-orphaned family clustered to their duties, their routines a comfort to his days. Barbe and Angele and Baby and even Archange's quiet ways brought things into his days he hadn't known he'd been missing. They required more effort from Marie, the demands making her forgetful. But their presence had given her a memory, too. Like a well-crafted canoe, life leveled out in known waters.

He could try to dissuade Marie from her seeking. This woman he loved, he didn't want her to face another disappointment.

Jean rehearsed. He'd tell her, "Who'll tend the crops, milk our cows? Archange already works too hard here and for Baptiste. François can't do it all, either. Your chapel duties…your family here has need of you. Tempers rise there at Waiilatpu; should we risk being there? And there's the measles. Would you expose those you love to such as that? What makes you think he'd still be there?" He'd try these approaches, not sure if he was to let her go or make her stay. Inside the cabin, he spoke his words of concern.

The mention of measles had cautioned her, slowed her determination, but only for a moment. His suggestion that they'd be too late fell deaf on a mother's hopeful ears.

"We can go the overland route, the way the Molalla and the Cayuse go, along the Santiam River," she said, already making plans.

"Mongrain didn't say Paul lived at Walla Walla."

"But if they are."

"Baptiste said he was the same foul man."

"Did he?"

Jean dropped his eyes. "No. He didn't say much at all of him except what I heard him tell you. But Paul must be the same, or he would have tried to tell his mother he still lived. Why do you want to hit yourself with the truth of an unloving son?"

Marie stared at him. "What else can I do?" she said and held her small palms together as though in prayer.

"There are children here who need you. Josette's baby coughs, and your remedies help. Marianne still hasn't found her place. She needs you. Marguerite, too," he tried lamely, defeated now, he knew. He could hear the desperation in his own voice. He'd just gotten this woman back from the caves she could disappear into, and he didn't want to lose her to dark places again. But she made trails of her own. She always had. It was who she was.

She'd already packed her *shaptakai,* the stiff leather sides pulled open so she could load up clothes for them all. She laid out jerked venison, smoked fish, nuts and berries, her sewing kit, everything they'd need. She packed moccasins, too, a new pair with quill designs. Who had she made them for? How long ago?

"Let it rest, my Marie," he tried one last time. "David Mongrain surely told him where we are. Baptiste did too. He chose not to show himself to you."

"There are never too many chances to recover a lost son. What separates us also binds us, *n'est-ce pas?* You said this once long ago."

Jean sighed. She could use his words back on him in ways that silenced reply. He'd always thought he was the one skilled with weaving words with acts to make a difference, but it was Marie who wove those strands and Marie who tied the knots. "Don't pack so much," he said then. "You'll age the horses with the weight."

Baptiste frowned. Why did children play such games? Marriages and deaths, he thought. They should play games to make life lighter. His daughter, Denise, laughed as she rolled her younger brother up inside the robe. Baptiste would have thought the boy too old for such games. Baptiste chewed the side of his mouth. Did the death game distress those spirits or just remind the living that death was part of all they did? Josette would say it was superstition, a thing she set aside with her baptism, she'd said. But he still held to it, some. He wasn't sure why. Perhaps the mix of blood that coursed through his veins confused the answers he got when he asked questions. Josette said death should not be feared; it was a part of life. It wasn't a part of life he wanted to consider unless it ended in some honor.

He turned away from the children's game and headed from the barn toward his mother's home, where he'd seen a horse approach. The rider appeared to wait for someone. François and Angelique had made the trip to Newell's Store for supplies and would be gone for the day. Baptiste brought his oldest children along to help him with his mother's chores. As he approached the horse and the man dismounted, he saw there was a second rider. A small boy who stayed seated on the horse as the rider now stood before Baptiste.

"Josiah Parrish," the man said, introducing himself. Baptiste remembered this Methodist man, but only vaguely. The man had been in the Clatsop country for two years or more, he thought. Yet here he was and saying he was a circuit rider now, preaching on the west bank of the Willamette. "But my home is not far from your father's southern claim." Josiah wore a wry smile on his face, as though he expected life to throw balls out to him and he either had to lean to catch them or be struck. They would never come straight on.

"If your mother was here, I'd ask her," Josiah Parrish said. "She took a child in some years back."

"Several," Baptiste said.

"A woman-child, slow—"

"Barbe," Baptiste said.

"Yes. That was her name." The boy sat still as a hawk on the horse, and Josiah Parrish rested his hand on the boy's leg. Baptiste guessed that the boy might have seen ten summers. "Would you take him in too?" Only the boy's eyes moved, scanning.

"My family had enough trouble with the one we have. She has a child now too, and my mother takes in a girl not much younger than this one." He nodded to the boy. "He has a round head. Was he a slave?"

"This young lad was whisked away from a funeral pyre on an island near Dalles City. He was to be buried with a chief's son. He'd been living with that family when the chief's son died. Don't know the circumstances of how he came to be with them. Slave seems likely."

"You intervened?" Baptiste said. "You went to the burial site and removed him?"

"The Wallers did," Josiah told him. "They waited the night to be able to handle the rapids they had to cross between them and the island. Made their way to the burial grounds, where he'd been literally tied to the dead boy." Josiah held his wrists up together to show how the boy would have been kept tight to death. "They swallowed their fears of what others would say, about violating custom, if that's what you're thinking. This child's life was too precious. Every child's life is."

A child that cheated death could be dangerous to have around. No wonder this Josiah Parrish wanted the boy gone.

"Imagine a small child being bound, tied among skeletons and rotting vermin. Imagine how he suffered not able to get free, believing no one would ever come for him. He was dead in his mind, and the Wallers gave him back his life," Josiah said. "He wasn't safe at Dalles City. Too close to the happenings. They had to get him out, and they whisked him downriver to Fort George with a brigade. My wife and I received him at Clatsop, but it was the Wallers who untied those ropes." He shook his head, cleared his throat. He wore the rounded brim hat of the missionaries, and he adjusted it now, pushed it back so no shadow hit his face. "My wife, Elizabeth, is sickly."

Baptiste raised his eyebrows. Death spirits were strong ones. He could guess why she was sickly, harboring a death cheater in her house.

Josiah said, "She, we, lost a son, and she can't care for more than our own three."

"The boy can't help?"

"He tries. He...struggles. I thought your mother—"

"She goes to Walla Walla. Looking for my brother," Baptiste said.

"He's been lost?"

"A long, long time."

The child listened without speaking, and yet throughout, his eyes moved wildly back and forth. "Your mother has a good way with children held together with pretty slender threads. His name is Joseph Klickitat, pronounced for the tribe that lives beyond the falls."

"It's a village name I know," Baptiste said. "We came through it with Hunt long years ago." The boy's eyes stopped moving back and forth, and he sat still as a striking snake. His eyes stared beyond, and Baptiste looked to see what had captured the child's attention.

In the distance, Pierre had rolled Denise inside a buffalo robe and tied it. He wailed a grieving song, and then the two laughed at his poor tones. "They play the death game," Baptiste said. "Children play it here."

Josiah nodded, patted the Klickitat boy's leg. "Come down," he told him. Baptiste watched the child swallow and sigh relief when Denise pulled free of her cocoon. She and Pierre now chased the dog shouting, "He's next! Catch him!" They laughed.

"Maybe this is not so good a place for him," Baptiste said.

"It's perfect," Josiah said. "Your children put death in its proper place. It requires reverence, yes, but celebration, too."

The boy's eyes shifted then to Baptiste's. He felt his stomach make a lurch. The boy reminded him of someone, but Baptiste couldn't say whom.

Later, when Baptiste tried to explain to Josette why he took the child in, he described the death bondage. "He must have suffered," Josette agreed.

"And wondered, if he would ever be set free."

⌖

Jean led the little party, followed by Marie and Angele and Barbe with Baby, already two years old, riding in front of her mother. Archange brought up the rear.

Marie watched as Baby bounced and slid to the side, pulled herself up. Barbe's eyes wandered, but Marie said nothing. Marguerite had told Marie perhaps she should allow Barbe to do more mothering. Until then, she hadn't thought she interfered, but Marguerite was right. Barbe had to make some decisions on her own.

Still, she noted relief when Archange trotted up beside Barbe and reached for his daughter, setting the child firmly in front of his saddle. He placed the child's hands where she could hold on.

Knuck trotted along beside when not scaring up rabbits. They were the typical traveling family. Marie smiled with the thought. There was little typical about them.

The mountain crossing proved cool with snow still two feet deep in places. Knuck whined to be lifted when the snow caked at the bottom of his feet. Despite the occasional drifts, they rode a mostly straight line through the timber, rising ever higher toward a summit of massive fir trees and high mountain peaks. They'd never gone this way, always before taking the Columbia and Willamette Rivers. She liked the solid feeling of earth beneath her horse's feet, liked the rhythm of the animals as they walked. They camped one night in the high country and then descended, found only spotty snow near the mountain's base. They faced a high plain before them with grass that reached the briskets of their mounts. The air felt drier here, and they followed a trail along a rushing river Jean said he thought was Ogden's *Rivière des Chutes.*

"This is that place," Jean said, his voice excited. "The Indians, they keep the canoes here. Remember I tell you of this?"

She shook her head, no.

"I find them and they help us cross. I got in trouble, remember?"

"Which time?" she asked, feeling foolish that she couldn't recall.

On the east side of that river, they headed northeast through tall grasses and wide vistas. Marie could think while riding horses. While traveling on water, she felt an apprehension, never knowing what might lie around the bend. Her sons were little when they made the overland trip, and she worried for their safety on the rapids. Shifting bales of supplies could topple the crafts and send them all into black swirling water.

On this journey, she had time to imagine. If the past slipped from her unexpectedly, then perhaps the future could fill her thinking.

Who did her grandchildren look like? What kind of woman had Paul found? What called him back to the Walla Walla place yet stood in his way of seeking her?

He'd been baptized. It must mean something.

Three days later, they approached Fort Walla Walla from the south;

Marie noticed the carcasses of cattle, mostly bones now, the vultures having scavenged all they wanted. She pointed out evidence of smaller animals dead too: dogs or wolves, perhaps, victims of the winter's long freeze. The grasses that had danced with winds looked shrunken and brittle as the old bones scattered within them.

They went immediately to find Narcisse Raymond, Josette's uncle. Josette's mother lived with Narcisse's family now too. The wiry woman had seen a dozen years since Marie had thought she would never live to see another summer. She missed two fingers, though. Frostbite, Marie imagined. Marie noticed pockmarks on the faces of young men who lounged around the fort's entrance.

Narcisse greeted them with a welcoming pipe, which Jean and Archange smoked with pleasure sounds, bringing the smoke toward their throats, a sign of their trust and commitment to each other.

Jean hadn't complained, not once. Having made the choice to come to Walla Walla, he wouldn't then find fault. He never beat a decision with a regretful stick.

So here they were with a roll of tulle mats to put around the lodge poles. This was a familiar place beside this Walla Walla River. But something was very different here too.

Dogs scattered old bones in the dust, and the usual warm appearance of the tipis set around a circle looked instead like scattered hearth rocks meant to put a fire out, each lying separate and cold. Even Narcisse's home revealed gaping holes in the matting. Not far from the river, Marie could see burial pyres rising near the cottonwoods. A village of them.

She adjusted her spectacles and looked around for Barbe to be sure the girl was within sight. She wasn't sure where Archange had disappeared to, but she spied Angele and Barbe with Baby near the river and she walked toward them.

Angele and Barbe moved side by side, and the two talked, Baby in between them, urging them to swing her up so her fringed dress tickled her chubby legs. The size of them, their full faces, the smiles, spoke of food and health and made them stand out among these lean and hungry-looking Cayuse people. Marie breathed out gratitude for her family's abundance, felt a twinge of worry over what such a desperate people might be compelled to do to keep their families safe as invaders moved through with their neat cows and carts.

"Big ears," Barbe said and pointed.

Marie caught her breath. Was Paul here? He had unusual ears. But when she looked to where Barbe laughed, she saw instead two women, their bonnet pokes dusty as they shaded their faces against the August sun. They wore long skirts and aprons as they approached the fort's rebuilt entrance. Marie squinted.

"They're some that arrived late last winter," Narcisse told her. "They stayed on with the Whitmans. They've started building on land not far from Waiilatpu. Others are moving out soon they say. To where you are, near the falls at Oregon City. We've seen many these past years, coming, going, a few staying. This year, they won't be so welcome when we've more dead cows than live ones and many still sick with measles. These people have to be fed. Too many mouths still have to be fed," he said. His hand shook when he passed back the pipe.

Jean said. "Something isn't right here."

Narcisse nodded agreement. "Everyone feeds on suspicion," he said. "Gray Eagle says Whitman's medicine heals white babies and white skin but nothing heals the Cayuse. They don't trust the medicine anymore. Last week, Chief Tiloukaikt sent his horses into the Whitmans' cornfield and demanded again that Whitman pay what was owed for his taking the Cayuse land."

"What did Whitman say?" Jean asked.

"That they'd been invited here those years before. It is always his argument. It may have been truth then, but the misunderstanding is truth now. It is an old bone Whitman wants buried but keeps getting dug up. It may choke Whitman one day," Narcisse said.

"I thought things were better," Marie said. "Baptiste said Mrs. Whitman took in children, mixed-blood children, and raised them as her own."

Narcisse nodded. "And others. Orphans. But she tires. Her students and those converts who support them grow weary. We have priests now in the region." He coughed, then inhaled again the pungent tobacco.

"Many come here for a priest baptism. I think Whitman feels they betray him."

"My son was baptized," Marie said.

"Baptiste? Good. He was due to change," Narcisse said. "A man with his love of fast horses and, well, the other. He needed the cleansing waters."

"Oui," Marie said. "But I speak of Paul. Remember him? You adjusted a bride's price for us because of that son."

"He ran off, didn't he? He was baptized, eh? Where?"

"Here," Marie said.

"I don't remember this," Narcisse said. He frowned.

"David Mongrain was the witness," Marie said.

Narcisse shrugged. "I'm old and forget." He smiled at her.

"Father Blanchet's brother, the bishop did it, just a month ago," she said.

Could Paul have left so soon? Was there some mistake? She had prepared herself for this, the possibility that the threads she wove might never make a coat.

"Mostly infants come for baptisms then," Narcisse said. "And I don't remember any Dorion. But I didn't attend them all. My wife coughs and stays ill."

"Maybe David Mongrain got the name wrong, my Marie." Jean patted her back.

"Non."

She wished she could read the priest's sacramental book. She could see for herself the day and name of her son being baptized. No one would question it then. Words allowed for linking.

It came to her as a way to honor her mother. Marianne wasn't much for cleaning or doing those parish things her mother did, but while her mother visited Walla Walla, she could. It would be only a short time. It would be duty.

The little room in the back of the St. Louis church that housed the visiting priest needed freshening up, not that there was much to that. A bed, a table with candle lantern, and wall pegs to hold his vestments. A small alter with a crucifix and a stool filled the sparse room. But she could get down on her knees and scrub this room, the baptistery, even the wooden pews. She'd bring her son along; he could look at the Catholic Ladder hanging on the wall, and she could tell him the stories that went with it. He'd like that. She knew them all by heart. The work would be good. Make her tougher, something everyone seemed to think she should be.

She wouldn't even tell David, at least not at first. That way if she didn't keep it up, there'd be no one to chastise her, remind her that once again she'd started something she failed to finish. It was easier to break a promise to herself than to someone else, wasn't it?

The first morning after her mother left, Marianne saddled a horse and took the trail up from the river heading into the morning sun then slightly north toward the St. Louis church. Joseph rode before her. "What's that?" he asked, pointing to a flowering plant.

"I don't know its name," she said.

"What's that?" A flower caught his eye.

"Which one?" she asked him, buying for time. She didn't know any of their names. Her mother would have. Even Barbe probably knew them. Joseph pulled on the reins, wanting her to stop. "No," she said. "We'll pick them on the way home, and we can ask your father. Or maybe Kasa Angelique knows."

Julie would have known. She might have asked her. She might have used the time with her friend not just for foolish dodging of her duties, but to know her.

Joseph sighed, resigned that they wouldn't stop, but he continued to point and Marianne continued to tell him she didn't know. It was hateful to not know things, especially when your children needed information. How did her mother do it? However did Julie do it, responding to four children with her but two years older than Marianne?

Will I ever stop thinking of Julie? Will this ever stop hurting? Sometimes she tried to imagine what Julie would do if she, Marianne, had been the one to die. She would have tried to comfort David. Well,

Marianne didn't need to comfort Julie's husband; he'd already moved Marie Ouvre into his bed.

Julie would have made sure Joseph was well taken care of and remembered his birthdays and found ways to honor his mother. She had no idea if Marie Ouvre spoke of Julie or not. Some families didn't, not for a year or more, never saying the name of the departed. Kasa Angelique's tradition was like that. She had yet to say Julie's name, and she frowned when that woman attended a funeral saying pregnant women should protect their unborn babies from the clutching baby spirits of the dead. Marianne shivered. Her mother had never expressed such beliefs, and she was an Indian too. It just varied with the tribe, with how one was raised.

Her mother had raised her to be compassionate and caring, to look after those in need, and hadn't she done that this past year, taking that Barbe into her home for visits? Such charity would surely be marked down in the Lord's book of worthy duty, completed. She wished that thought gave her more comfort.

They reached the St. Louis church and dismounted. Marianne pulled the water from the shallow well, filling the wooden bucket her mother always used. "You go pick what flowers you want," Marianne told her son. "We'll take them home and see if Kasa can name them. Maybe we'll dry them and write their names down. Would you like that?"

Her son smiled and scampered off. The sun felt warm on her face. The undergrowth of vines and berries formed a kind of boundary around the churchyard, and she inhaled the fresh scent of rich foliage now. Blackbirds landed in a flock and pecked at the ground. She might come to like this time of morning giving.

She stepped inside the log church. The quietness gentled on her shoulders. She'd never been alone inside a church in all these years. So cool, so quiet. She could say her morning prayers here in this still place. Perhaps that was why her mother came.

She'd keep this to herself and ask the priest to say nothing either, if he learned who scrubbed now that her mother was gone. What good was a charitable gift if everyone knew you did it? Besides, it would count more toward her penance, she was sure, if she did it without an audience.

She licked the perspiration from her upper lip, wiped her forehead with her arm. She'd better start to work before the building heated. Scrubbing the rough wood benches brought slivers to her fingers. Next week, she'd bring an adz and smooth some of the spots. Not that she knew how to use that tool, but she'd seen David use it, so she was sure she could too. Julie would laugh at her for trying such a thing.

Marianne sat back on her heels, her hands wet and her fingers aching from the push with the brush.

"Oh, Julie," Marianne said. "I'm going to tackle an adz. How I wish that you were here to watch me learn something new. How I wish that you were just here, not for any reason at all except because I miss you so."

She couldn't stop the tears then, the recognition that long days and months and years would pass and Julie would know nothing of them. Julie would never share another silly moment with her friends, wouldn't watch her daughter marry, wouldn't hold a grandchild in her arms. It was so unfair, so unjust! A mother like Barbe lived happily on with people to tend to her children while Julie, a good, fine, faithful mother, was gone. What was the sense of it? Why did it happen? "Why?" She whispered. "Why Julie and not me?" She spoke the last out loud.

She didn't expect any answer. She hadn't suffered enough.

When Marguerite let long weeks pass without talking to her, it was harder to find anything to say to her younger, foolish sister. It was how she thought of Marianne, the foolish one, and she'd done nothing much as a wife and mother to change Marguerite's view of that.

But then who was she to judge? All her brothers and sisters had loosened their ties before their parents left. Offering proved much easier than actually doing. They'd had a good plan, though, the taking care of their mother, and maybe each had given enough that together it strengthened her mother, allowed her to make the long journey to Walla Walla. She wouldn't have been strong enough if they hadn't given her those months of special respite.

Marguerite had actually been pleased to see her mother want to travel. It was selfish, she knew. Truth was, she didn't like spending all that time with Barbe. She wanted to be helpful, she did, but Barbe was such a strain. She couldn't imagine how that girl would live when her mother died.

Whatever will we do when Mama dies?

Marguerite swallowed hard. What would Jean or any of them do?

Papa Jean had been so secretive about the reasons for all of them leaving. "Your mother needs a rest," he'd said. But they all knew about Paul being sighted and about this John, though certainly not details. Maybe Jean didn't know they knew. Marguerite sighed. Keeping family secrets took time that might be better spent.

"Her children failed her," Marguerite said when Jean told them they would head to Walla Walla. Jean had frowned. Marguerite continued, "We haven't kept our duty to her as we did early in the summer, and now she wants to leave us."

"I didn't know it was a task," he said.

"No, I didn't mean it that way. We all committed to giving you two more time, more help," Marguerite said. *Was she supposed to tell them this? Hadn't Baptiste already told Jean what they'd been doing?*

"Who? What's this?"

He sounded irritated, and Marguerite wondered why she'd said anything at all. Baptiste had been the one who shared the reason for their mother's recent strain. Baptiste should have given Jean the story of their hopes to serve them.

"Who thinks I needed help?" he said.

"We just wanted to give you all more time," she said.

"For what? We have plenty of time. Don't know why you'd worry about our time," he said. His right arm took on an agitated move, and he pushed his shoulder back, twisted his neck back and forth. "That's why all the visits last summer? Taking Barbe and Baby away while your mother worked at the church? That was a planning by our children?"

"Mother worked at the church then? Didn't she rest? We only meant to offer assistance. Mother looked so…tired."

"I took care of her. She's fine. She'll be fine."

Jean had changed the subject then, and any thought Marguerite had to relieve her mother after that came with discomfort.

She hadn't told the others of Jean's reaction. They'd probably snarl at her for having let their secret out. Worse was that she didn't feel now she could talk freely around Papa Jean, ask him about how her mother might be doing, or about either Paul or this John either.

The next thing she knew, her Mother and Jean and their brood were headed for Walla Walla. Her mother did still have a life of her own. It was just strange to think of it that way when her children had once been all that defined her.

"You do well with boys," Baptiste told her.

Marguerite lifted her skirts to show her moccasins. "You lick a boot," she said. "I don't wear my leather shoes today."

"Non," he said and smiled. "I don't use words to flatter. You are good with boys. Look how your Xavier rides his horse. As good as my Pierre who's much older." They looked to the pasture where the boys raced side by side. "I used to do that," he said. "Miss it some."

"JB trains the horses," she said. "And he works with Xavier. His other sons, too. It isn't me," she said. "I give them nothing they can take into their work."

"They're well fed," he told her. "You do that for them."

She looked at him. "Are you using words now to slick a trail?"

Baptiste had never spoken of her as someone worthy. He'd been remiss.

"No," he said. "You do for them, as a mother should."

"I feed these boys, but my husband provides even that. So..." She lifted the palms of her hands as though what she had to give her sons weighed less than a feather.

"This boy eats like he can never be filled," Baptiste said. "Parrish, the Methodist one, would help provide food if you needed it."

"Can't Josette use this boy's labor? With Archange gone, he'd be an extra hand."

"He does." Baptiste hesitated. "He wears still the healing flesh of his wrists where they bound him to the dead child. Death rode beside him. He stepped off that racing mount."

"You aren't worrying about that, are you? There are no such things as ghosts like that," she said. "You know this."

He shrugged. "This child had a strong desire to live. Those who choose death for him might travel far to find him."

"The ones who put him in the death place might, but not spirits," she clarified.

Baptiste shrugged, adjusted his tall hat. "You milk more cows," he said. "I thought you could use the child's help. Our little one hungers and doesn't grow. This Klickitat boy hungers with his stomach and his eyes." He hesitated. "He looks to me of Paul," he said then. "And a winter I remember. We, too, cheated death and have the scars to show it."

"Paul. Is he like—?"

"No. He is a good boy. He listens. He wants to please. You would be a good teacher for him. If I ever had to ask someone to look after my children because his mother couldn't, I'd want you, Marguerite. These are not empty words."

"I would have to ask JB," she said.

The child had listened to their conversation. Baptiste had not seen the boy blink, although he must have. He stared at Marguerite now, his wounded wrists showing pink beyond his shirtsleeves even after all this time. Scars. Everyone had them. Some just showed on the outside.

Xavier raced up on his horse, leaped down, letting the reins fall. He pushed through the door, followed by his older half-brothers. In seconds they were out, each with fistfuls of cheek bread. The Klickitat boy moved aside, aware who ruled. Xavier looked at him through slits of eyes.

Doublé walked over to the boy. They would be about the same age, and JB's son handed him half the chunk of bread he'd picked up. The boy hesitated, looked at Baptiste, who nodded his assent. The Klickitat boy began to chew.

"You're a kind boy," Marguerite told Doublé. The boy's face lit up, his dimples deep.

Marguerite looked pleased.

"It is one more good thing about you, Sister," Baptiste said. "Your children reflect your generosity."

His sister's blush of pleasure reminded him of how much power lived inside words.

20

Invitation

1847

Paul had been there, and Marie's heart lifted with the knowledge. Their coming to the Walla Walla country had been worth it.

Bishop Blanchet's book showed the entry of the baptism, but it wasn't Paul's. "'1847, June 26. David, aged one year, son of Paul Dorion and a savage woman: godfather, David Mongrain.' This is what it says," the bishop told her. "I baptized your grandchild then?"

Marie nodded. She ran her fingers across the inked page. This priest was a brother to the Father Blanchet who had come to St. Paul and St. Louis, too. He was a bishop, as high as a chief factor in the Hudson's Bay Company, Marie imagined. "I performed many baptisms," the bishop said. "I'm sad to say I don't recall this one."

"We travel to many places, far to the east," another priest said. His yellow hair fell precisely into place, and his lower lip puffed out the way Marianne's did when she wanted to be noticed. "I've done a number of baptisms on the Boise, the Green River. It's nearly impossible to remember each child." His French was formal and he spoke as though Marie might not understand, slowly, with a bite to his words. He hadn't given her his name, as though Marie was someone not worthy to receive it.

The bishop tapped his lip with his finger in thought. "But now that I hear that name again, Dorion, I do remember David Mongrain saying something of it. He'd met you and talked of Hunt and Astor. And, of course, I remembered then, hearing about you, Madame Dorion. I'd heard that name before, though mostly in the Missouri Territory."

"You've heard of Dorions?"

"The Americans, Lewis and Captain Clark, employed a Dorion," the other priest said. "That's probably why it's familiar." He spoke to the bishop as though Marie wasn't there.

"It would have been your husband," the bishop said. "Or father-in-law?"

"Both," Marie corrected, "though they traveled with the Corps of Discovery only for a short distance. But my husband had many brothers. My older son signed as interpreter for a Teton Treaty. In 1828."

She hesitated, swallowed, then had to ask. "Did you ever hear of a John Dorion in your travels?" She couldn't even describe her son, didn't have any way to mark him in her memory as an adult. He might have changed his name. "He would have had your years," she said and nodded to the younger priest.

That priest bristled.

"John?" The Bishop said. "No. Have you heard of him, Father Brouillet?"

The yellow-haired priest pursed his lips. "I can't imagine how you'd know my age," he said. "And certainly not. I've never heard of a John Dorion. I'm sure I would remember something so…significant."

"We should go home now," Jean said. He brushed at the horse's neck, scratched the animal between his ears. "We can pick berries in the foothills, and when we reach our timber claim, it will be a good time to hunt deer. We'll go directly south. Just settle in for the winter. By ourselves."

"Baptiste's mother-in-law wearies," Marie told him. "We should stay and help tend her."

"You grieve by digging in," he said. "Make no changes, even when they'd suit you better."

"Do I tell you this, husband?"

"I interpret it," Jean said. He looked at her. "From years of watching someone I love."

"You interpret." She nodded agreement. "This is what you do, husband. So do that here in Walla Walla. Go see that trader, McBean.

Maybe he has work for you to do with all these people coming through. Maybe you can help keep the Cayuse settled about Whitman while we wait here for my son."

"The priests will help settle them, Marie. They do more baptisms and have more catechisms at Walla Walla than at Waiilatpu now. The faith will gentle their hearts if those hearts aren't prodded with sticks."

"I think Whitman tries to keep white people here to balance the priest's presence, keep them from becoming too strong."

The two stood watching the horse slurp water from the trough. "Whitman said there's no good grass west of here. He tries to keep those with cattle from pushing over Barlow's road. He doesn't even tell them of the road along the Santiam that we took here."

"This man of faith tells tales?"

Jean turned to her. "Maybe he believes it. People do convince themselves of things they shouldn't." Marie winced. Jean sighed. "We should go back," he said softly. "It won't be good here, my Marie. We've done what you wanted, found out Paul baptized a son. Be pleased with this, eh? Let it be enough."

"He's come back twice. He'll return again, and this time I'll be here, waiting. I—"

"Why do you do this to yourself?" Jean said, his hands now in fists. She looked away from the pain in her husband's eyes. "It is like a piece of jerked meat you chew and never swallow. It will never fill you up."

"What else can I do?" she said, her palms up, her voice almost a wail.

"Let it go," he said. "Let. Paul. Go. Make room for someone else."

"I take them away from here," Archange said. The man so rarely spoke that Marie didn't recognize his voice at first. He'd come beside her so quietly she didn't know how long he'd waited to say his piece. She patted the flour, dropped it into the hot oil. It bubbled and puffed up like a late cloud on a hot summer day.

"Barbe does well here," she said. "And Baby, too."

"There is too much sickness here, Mother," he said.

Mother? Had this man always thought of her that way? Barbe called her Mama, and Jean had adjusted to it, but it never occurred to her how Archange might have thought of her, or if he did.

"No. The journey is too hard for you alone. Who would watch Baby?"

"The child is ours," Archange said. His voice had a roughness to it, and he cleared it now. "I take care of my family."

"But all these years, we—"

"Barbe stays to help you," he said. "Now she worries over our child. I take them from this tension, the illness. I take her home to French Prairie."

Marie's eyes pooled, her face warmed, and not only because she leaned over hot oil. With a stick, Marie lifted out the fry bread and laid it on another rock to cool.

"You gave us tools, Mother," he said. "Now we must learn to use them. Before snow flies. Before we have to fight the cold."

"On your own," she said.

"We long to be on our own," he said. "This is not a fight for us. We also long to please our mother."

Marie didn't look at him. She patted the fry bread dough with her fingertips. They were white again, so pale and white. "You will travel with others, for safety?"

Archange hesitated. "If it will make our going easier for you, then yes. We will go with some of the wagons headed to French Prairie, if they will let us."

"You know the way," Marie said. "You can be their guide."

Archange's family stood ready the next morning. Marie hadn't realized how difficult it would be to say good-bye. Barbe and Baby, too, had filled an emptiness in her life at a time when she hadn't known she carried a hollow place. Tears came, though she blinked, and finally, holding Baby in her arms, she sang the parting song. The child reached up and touched the new copper earrings Jean had given her. They tinkled at Marie's ear.

"You take good care of this baby," she told Barbe.

"I do it like Mama tells me," Barbe said. She hugged Marie, then gently lifted the child from Marie's arms. "I do what Mama tells me. I follow odors. I remember," Barbe said.

They spent the fall riding out together, Marie and Jean and Angele. Jean wondered why he stayed, why he didn't just tell Marie they were heading home. A man should be strong enough to insist when he knew it would save those he loved from the searing pain of a double-edged blade: Hope might be on one side, but a son's rejection rode on the other. He'd give it until spring, he decided. That would be long enough.

As they traveled the region, they'd hear of some hut built among the rye grasses and go there to see if sod had been turned by a Dorion. The red willows along little streams pressed out yellow leaves, and once they rode a whole day and never heard a beaver slap his tail in warning. "Do you think John trapped, or maybe he was good with horses?" Marie said.

Jean shook his head. He had no answers.

They met no Dorions. The settlers they encountered acted wary with the arrival of three people mounted on big, healthy horses, even though a woman and child rode two of them.

"They're frightened," Jean said as they left one leaning hut built by a man from "Missoura." His wife and four children huddled behind him, coming out only when they heard Jean speak English.

"They have the faces of those Shoshone we came upon in the winter months with Hunt, remember?" Marie said. "They had so little food, and our group was so large and looked so hungry."

"I'd forgotten," he said, surprised that his wife would remember this detail when he hadn't.

"Once a mother even ran away and left her little girl, shaking. She had no food, nothing to give even for her own child, and there we stood with our empty stomachs writing hard words on our faces."

Angele asked for more of the story, and Marie talked as they rode. "She left her baby behind?" Angele said after a time.

"As a prairie chicken does it, I believe she pretended woundedness, hoping to lure us away from her offspring. She had few choices," Marie said. "She must have hoped we would be merciful to her child."

"It is a protection to allow someone else to tend a soul you love when you cannot, eh?" Jean said. "A gift difficult to receive but one most worthy, *n'est-ce pas?*"

Marie looked across the head of Angele as they rode. She sent Jean a gift with her smile. Maybe it was worth this waiting. Maybe this Waiilatpu, this place of soothing rye grass, would bring a newness to his marriage as he learned to exchange new gifts with his wife.

She did not know what called her. Sister Celeste's *vocare* came to mind, though it made no sense. But Marie could no more roll over in her robe beside Jean and attempt to sleep again than she could stop seeking her lost son. She rose instead to bridle the horse.

Bareback in the moonlight, she headed toward the Whitman Mission. Her horse kicked up puffs of snow like white seeds in the roadbed. Icy November air cut at her face. Why was she going?

She reined her horse up at the shadow of the split-rail fence and waited, she didn't know for what. She breathed on her cold fingers, the warm air of her breath not keeping the chill away. Timber wolves howled as the sun rose and cast a blood red glow on the snow covering the main house. A wisp of smoke rose up from the chimney. The barns sat as sentinels to the horses and cattle inside. Her lips felt chapped, and she licked at them anyway, not knowing why she sat here atop a horse stomping its impatience in the shallow snow. A rooster crowed. Tipis in the distance marked the Whitman Cayuse, those who served the mission, and as she watched, a woman stepped out to find her morning path. Something in her rapid movement brought a memory of a lone woman running through the snow to warn Marie of a danger, danger that turned real and took her husband's life. Was that why she'd been called here, to warn of something? But she knew of nothing impending, only the constant tension of misunderstandings carried on differences never bridged. The Whitmans knew of this; so did the Cayuse. What could she do?

A young woman shot out of the house then, followed by two boys. Marie knew many suffered from measles at the mission, so she was pleased to see healthy boys carrying egg baskets. She heard laughter. It was a scene as calm as a summer lake. And yet Marie felt called to come here. She waited.

Pray for us now, and at the hour of our death. Amen. Sister Celeste had taught the prayer, and Marie spoke it now, repeating it, over and over and shivering as she reached for the rosary beads tucked within her wolf-skin coat. She sent an arrow prayer for the young woman, the boys, all who lived and worked at this place, and when she finished she knew it was all that she could do. She reined the horse and headed back. She'd responded to the call, though she didn't understand its purpose, only that her heart knew the weight of this place and nothing could forestall the Ioway farewell song that stirred now in her throat.

"They've taken hostages," Baptiste told Josette. He grabbed for his gear, what ammunition he had. He'd known this would come. Tom McKay had known too. The attack had happened on November 29, but word had just reached French Prairie, nearly a week later. "The Cayuse lost hope," he told her. "Men become desperate without hope." He nearly had, a few times in his life.

"Who?" Josette said, touching his arm. "Who's taken hostages?"

"Fifty volunteers joined up yesterday. Another forty leave tomorrow. They want five hundred more."

"What are you saying?"

"The Whitmans. They're dead. Many others. Gray Eagle, four others are accused. They've taken women and children as hostages to trade for their lives. Rounded up those they didn't kill at Waiilatpu and raided small farms along the way heading somewhere. Maybe into Nez Perce country. The rest are at Waiilatpu."

"So it's begun," Josette said.

He looked at her, her eyes brown stones inside the white. "Now they've done something that can't be brought back. They don't know the Americans. They've only seen weak-looking white people, like Whitman and those emigrants who come all tired and thin from travel. They don't know how they rise up with good feed, with their honors challenged and tarnished. The Cayuse miscalculated, Josette. They'll all be wiped out if they don't agree to a peace. The government raises money even now for guns and food for the Army. When they come for grain, after I'm gone, give it. Tell Archange to open the stores to them beyond anything we need for our family. Keep what you need."

"There are so few Cayuse left," Josette said. "All the disease. It will be over quickly."

"Not if they band together, the Walla Walla and the Nez Perce. Maybe Spokane, Yakima, all of them, who see nothing changing, just more people coming bringing their disease and staying. They could do this."

"Will we be safe here on this prairie?"

He hadn't heard the fear in her voice before. Maybe he should stay. "I go to protect you, Josette." He threw leggings and lead into his *par flèche.* The December snows there could be deadly. "The Whitman deaths…like my father's death…were brutal. Hatchets. Children, too. They'll have nothing to lose by killing more. We'll get the hostages back. It's the only hope we have to stave off the Americans from retaliating and keep the tribes from joining."

"My mother and sisters. You'd ride against—"

"I ride with Tom McKay," Baptiste said. "As a second sergeant in Company D. Many French Canadians go. We bring in the guilty or the Americans will kill them all."

"Joseph is still so sick. I need you here."

"I'll send mother back," he said, not knowing if he could. "Maybe your family, too, before they get caught in cross fires."

She started to cry.

He knelt beside her. "Dorions ride with armies. It's what we do."

"But if you die…"

"We will all die one day. You know this. You tell me it is nothing to fear. Maybe I go now to face that. I know Cayuse. Maybe the French Canadians with Tom will have a way to talk with the killers. We are more British than American. They may hear us."

"You chose the Americans."

"No. I chose the non-Indian way," he said. "For you. To keep you safe, just as my father chose from that white strand of his blood. It is what a man must do."

❖

Marguerite was present when baby Joseph Dorion died, complications of the measles. She helped his pregnant mother wrap him and complete the ritual shrouding. Marianne stood by Josette, shivering with her in the December drizzle. Five days later, on December 23, Marguerite attended another ritual, a joyous one, with the birth of a nephew, François and Angelique's first son, born in the Toupins' log home.

The next day, Christmas Eve, Marguerite witnessed that child's death. Marianne was nowhere in sight.

Since birth, little Joseph had been weakened by his hesitation with this life. No one knew what took François and Angelique's small one.

"Dr. Bailey said the child came early, that I was too active and put the babe at risk," Angelique said.

"He can't know such things," Marguerite said. "Someday we'll have a French-speaking doctor who'll understand what a mother needs for comfort."

Marguerite wiped Angelique's forehead with a damp cloth. She was feverish. It could be from just giving birth. But it might be early signs of measles. The disease came like smoke seeping into every house. Even the new emigrants told of the disease hiding in their wagons. One family named McKay who settled near the church at St. Paul had lost two small sons to it in August. They'd traveled nearly two thousand miles across the plains and prairie only to bury their boys not far from where Joseph Klickitat had once been bound.

Marguerite rubbed at her stomach. Her own baby was due in the spring.

"You should go home," Angelique said. Her lips were dry and cracked. "Maybe Marianne would come."

"I'm not superstitious," Marguerite said. "Being here with you won't harm my baby. Besides, where else should I be when my sister suffers? No, you let me stay. I want to be with François, too. A brother needs his sister at a time like this."

She worried about Josette, alone there without Baptiste. Pierre was a good boy who could chop wood and Denise was a fine little mother already looking after the younger ones, but a woman needed a husband in a loss. She wished her mother and Papa Jean would come back. The presence of her mother within riding distance would give her ease.

"Is JB back?" Angelique asked.

"Every day," Marguerite said. "He brings me news each day, though I'd rather not hear it. His war news makes one shiver for the future of a mother's sons. Hearing so much robs a person of their hope in a joyful future," Marguerite said. "Laughter is needed to get through times like these." She was beginning to sound like her sister.

The rumors JB picked up at Oregon City said one day all the hostages had been released and the next day that they were all dead. JB shared every tidbit of how the Army had trouble raising money or that the grain sent them had been wormy, that the recruits brewed their own "blue ruin" to drink, and that desertions were threatened daily. She didn't really want to hear it, but at least JB came home each night to tell her.

She had her own little family around her; there was comfort in that. Even the Klickitat boy had proven a good child, a good brother. Xavier had taken to the older boy instead of competing. He was kinder with this child, and the two played together almost as though they were the same age. Such a tall boy had to be older than her son. The Klickitat boy would point, and Xavier understood, or at least he made the effort, and Xavier would tell him something in French or the English language, and the boy would nod, his eyes not fluttering with fear but with recognition. She hadn't thought that a child could teach another, perhaps better than one older, wiser, like a parent. But she had witnessed it within her son, his teaching of another.

War news made her long for more gentleness, more responsiveness when she asked for something, more time when she heard laughter instead of scolding, more trust that she belonged to this whole family who crowded around the Gobin hearth.

The day she overheard Toussaint tell his younger brother that when he married, "I want a wife just like mother Marguerite," she sat and wept for joy.

She'd waited first, anticipating a retort, some reshaping of his generous words. None came.

There'd been only one troubling day with the arrival of the Klickitat boy. It was the first time Xavier took that child's hand and led him outside. She'd been apprehensive. "Where do you boys go?" she demanded. "You shouldn't be going out in this cold."

"Beavers build at the river," Xavier said. "I show him."

A tiny prickle started up her back. She didn't recognize its source. "Don't try to set a trap on your own. Wait for your Papa," she said.

"We will," Xavier said, and off they'd gone.

She couldn't see them from her window, but she waited until she thought a reasonable time had passed for them to view the beaver lodge and return. Then she grabbed her blanket coat, wrapped herself with it, pulling it across her abdomen. It was cold, and if they slipped near the lodge, they could fall in. She should check on them, keep them safe.

She met them happy, coming back. Both boys forced air into their cheeks, then sputtered laughter as the air poofed out. Even the Klickitat boy smiled. Xavier bent over, sucked in more air, stood tall, and held his breath again, then started to laugh so the air escaped and the two squeezed over their knees in delight. *Boys. Just happy boys.*

"What's so funny?" she asked.

"He said he could swim inside a beaver's lodge," Xavier said. He wiped at his eyes. "He'll show me when the ice goes, but I have to learn to hold my breath and to count to maybe sixty. I can't make five before I look at him and laugh."

"We do it together, Mother," the Klickitat boy said.

Marguerite liked the low sound of his voice and the words. She exhaled, then took in a deep breath and puffed out her cheeks. The boys howled as she felt her eyes bug out as they counted. She only made it to *vingt et un.*

They walked back to the house laughing, and Marguerite realized they didn't think less of her for the laughter. They weren't judging her mothering, these children. Probably not even JB. The only judge of perfection who lived in the Gobin house was named Marguerite.

"The fort trader, McBean, says you're from French Prairie, but you speak the language. Your son is married to a Cayuse, yes?" The yellow-haired priest stood inside the door wearing his black woolen vestment, while Jean ignored the snowflakes falling on his rubber coat. He'd pulled it over a skinned jacket Marie had made him. "I'm secretary to Bishop Blanchet," the priest said, "who is no longer here. He is traveling now. Such a critical time."

"I know this," Jean said.

"And do you know that I'm J.B.A. Brouillet. I'm in charge here now. The bishop wishes your intervention." His voice lowered. "If he were here, he would wish this."

Jean knew of this priest who had rushed to Waiilatpu the day after the deaths and done his best to bury the Whitmans, digging shallow graves in the frozen November ground. He acted as though he was the Cayuse priest, though he hadn't been at Walla Walla all that long. Jean had heard the Cayuse speak well of Blanchet but with less enthusiasm for this Brouillet. The priest twittered, acted like a peacock, and Jean wasn't sure he trusted him. He'd prefer hearing from the bishop directly about some way he wanted Jean involved.

"We would like a parley," Brouillet said. "We'll bring the chiefs in. I can do this. And if I can reassure them the Americans wish only those responsible for the massacre, then we believe the chiefs can hold their tribes, keep them from uniting. They'll encourage the killers to turn themselves in. Spalding's promised his Nez Perce won't join up against the Army, though I suspect they're protecting that…missionary from the chiefs as much as he's protecting them from the American Army"—he wrinkled his nose—"but I wish you to meet with us. Be the interpreter. I'll be keeping the written record. Can you do this?"

It was now nearly a month after the attack. Who knew what kinds of rumors rolled along the Columbia? Who knew if the chiefs would even speak with him? He didn't think the chiefs could speak for their tribes the way an Army captain could speak for his troops. It didn't work that way for the Cayuse or the Nez Perce or any other tribe he knew of. Perhaps the chiefs were among the murderers, holding the hostages. Maybe some renegades who fell under no one's control did it. Someone with a longstanding debt they wanted paid. It had been one of Hunt's failings, not understanding how the tribes worked, the factions and fighting and family bonds. It could fail these men too.

"Do the ones you meet with control the hostages?" Jean asked.

"We hope that you'll find this out. The Bishop makes his house available for the meeting. Will you assist? One of the chiefs complains that his young men went against him when they slaughtered the Whitmans," Brouillet continued without waiting for an answer. "He worries now the Army will fight them all. He feels forced to join up with other tribes in self-defense. Naturally, this would be unwise, just flame these dreadful fires. At least one chief wishes to petition for peace."

It was probably a journey of futility. Perhaps he rode even to his death.

How long ago he'd seen this coming and been powerless to halt it. He should have taken his family home. Maybe this had been the reason.

Jean had gone to the trader McBean and offered his services in the fall. He'd heard nothing until now, and these words were from a priest he didn't really trust.

"It's dangerous," Marie told him.

"But worthy work."

"I go with you, then," she said.

It was not the work he had trained for nor the work he'd signed on for, but it was the work he'd been given. He would hold tight to that.

Jean and Marie rode into a meadow in the foothills of the Blue Mountains. Snow spotted the shaded ridges, melted around the base of trees. They'd been told a house and barn were there and they'd be escorted in.

"Brouillet may not like it that you've come along," Jean said.

"A woman's presence soothes," Marie said. "Remember, on Hunt's journey?"

Jean nodded. "But Brouillet, he doesn't seem to hold much weight for a woman's place."

"I let myself be used this way if we can get the hostages released."

"Are you cold?" Jean asked. He looked at her hands covered with rabbit-skin gloves.

"No. But I share a secret with you." She didn't look directly at him, just let him ride. "I have this dream that someone I know is here."

"Paul? You think he—"

"In my dream there was no face."

No one came to greet them, but they kept riding, the wind blowing snow from the trail. As they approached the barn, Marie watched as several Cayuse women circled it, holding knives. She didn't recognize them, and she couldn't help herself: She looked to see if one of their knives might have once been carried by Sacagawea and found its way into another woman's hands. These were larger knives, and the women gripped them as though they would never be traded away.

A tall Cayuse came out then. "Gray Eagle," Jean whispered. He greeted Jean, grim-faced, glanced at Marie. He offered no tobacco.

"Don't hurt the captives," Jean said after words of strained greeting. "It will go hard on you."

One of the women began a high-pitched cry, which the others took up. Gray Eagle smiled. "They await the order to kill the hostages," he said. "Would you like to witness it?"

Marie's heart pounded. If they killed hostages in front of them, their lives would be next.

Five Crows and Tiloukaikt's son came out then. Five Crows's presence surprised. His mother was Nez Perce. Marie hadn't thought he'd be involved with this. Some lesser chiefs whom Marie didn't know joined them now, circling Jean and Marie's horses. They were armed.

"Your priest asks for a meeting. I'm only here to make the invitation," Jean said. Her husband shifted in his saddle, as though to see into the barn. Jean made the sign for *quiet down,* his palms down and flat then lifted up, and Five Crows signaled the women into silence.

"The Americans will not go well on you if you hurt their women and children. They may look soft, the Americans, but they are like a beaver whose fat feeds him through the winter, always rebuilding, always reclaiming. And like you, they have long memories threaded tightly to their women and children. You dishonor your people if you harm these captives."

Five Crows grunted. "I cook mine breakfast," he said. "She is treated as a queen." Several of the other men laughed. Marie knew one of the hostages was an orphan whom Mrs. Whitman had taken in. Five Crows had offered horses for the girl's hand and been rebuffed.

"Do they send an army?" Gray Eagle asked. "Or a peace commission?"

"Letters have gone to ask for a commission," Jean said. Marie wondered if this could be true. Jean would have to be truthful. An army rode closer too. Baptiste rode in it.

"There is a way to save the people from an army's guns. You have that way," Jean said. "You come to this meeting. The priest and the factor guarantee your safety there. No harm will come to you. But no harm must come to the hostages, either."

He used good words, the right words, Marie thought.

Marie scanned the side of the old barn. She sent prayers through the wood slats, willing hope to the hostages, urging them to do nothing foolish. Then she turned back to the men. Beyond, she saw movement. She could almost feel the eyes of someone she knew, there behind those snow-dusted walls.

Jean told them when and where to meet. "Father Blanchet will not be there, but his protective spirit will be."

She and Jean rode out slowly; hot holes burned into their backs by the Cayuse stares. It would be a good death, dying here, Marie thought. A good way to die, beside someone you loved and doing what you believed mattered, setting widows and orphans free.

"We may have helped keep these captives living," Jean told Marie. "But no good thing will come of this meeting with Brouillet. The Americans demand justice. If they raise the money for enough men and flour and ammunition, they'll come and kill them all, not just the guilty ones."

They rode around the base of a hill, into the area of willows. They heard no one following to overtake them.

"You have done what you could," Marie said after some distance. "To believe strongly in a thing and have courage to act toward it. Even if what results is not what we desire. Some never have this in a life."

"A life with you beside me, that is what I believe in strongly," Jean said.

"I know this." Marie smiled. "And I know too it takes courage to live with me."

⌖

"I made it myself," Marianne said. "I'd like you to have it." She held the small table out for Marie Ouvre, the wife who replaced Julie. The girl looked at it. She held an infant in her arms, while an older girl pushed around her.

"Aunt Marie Anne," the girl squealed rushing toward her. Julie's son Isadore pushed past her to grab Marianne around her waist.

"You're the only one who remembers to call me by my real name," Marianne laughed. She set the table down so she could give full attention to the hugs of these children. Julie's oldest remained back behind Marie Ouvre. He held a toddler, but he smiled at her, a straight cut of dark hair marking his high forehead. Julie's baby waddled and held a corner of Marie Ouvre's apron in his mouth.

"I'm sorry it's been so long," Marianne said.

"You come in." The children tugged at her. Marianne looked up to see if the invitation extended from Marie Ouvre. The girl nodded and stepped back.

Marianne had a moment's hesitation. To step inside this house, to know her friend would not be there, almost made her turn and run. The smells, the memories…but the children wouldn't let her turn aside. Isadore pushed from behind her. "Wait, wait," she said. "My gift."

She picked up the table. "You can use it for a music box, maybe. Julie never had one. Or as a little table by a bed," she said. She felt her face grow warm imagining Marie Ouvre in Julie's bed. With two new little ones, she'd certainly been there. She rushed on. "It's crude, I know. But it's the first of wood I've ever made. From the old Mission School. My mother's people always gave their first gifts away because they carry with them a promise of potential. And only a certain kind of person would receive them," she said. "Someone who wouldn't judge but just accept the giver as they are. I'm sorry. I'm just chattering on. You don't really know me. I have to be going."

Marie Ouvre reached out to touch her arm. She smiled now and took the table from Marianne's hands. She motioned her in. *Is she a mute? Does she speak French or English or nothing at all?*

"You are my first visitor, as Mrs. Laderoute," the woman said then. "The first Mrs. Laderoute—Julie—spoke often of you. She said you would make me laugh. Come in. I've been waiting for you. I give you the gift of invitation."

21

To Brush Against a Life

The chiefs came to Bishop Blanchet's on December 18, 1847. Jean listened, translated, and remembered now how long these meetings just for trading horses had once taken, all those years ago with Hunt or on the Company's brigades. This meeting, which negotiated for the lives of innocents, for justice for a tribe, and for people murdered, frightened him. No one deserved deaths such as the Whitmans had experienced. No one. Death with honor had a place, but not one like those the innocents at Waiilatpu suffered. And yet he understood it. He wondered if there might be something wrong with him that he could understand why the Cayuse had so savagely attacked.

There had to be a peaceful way to give survivors hope. Not just the hostages, but the Cayuse people. Otherwise, no matter what they worked out here, more attacks would come, more emigrants would lie buried in shallow graves for wolves to paw at, more tribes would die without a story to remember.

Jean concentrated on what was being said, what the chiefs required, what they agreed to do if the Army stayed away, who they'd surrender their captives to. He relayed it to the priest and the Hudson's Bay factor. No military representatives were there, no Americans.

After nearly four hours, a chief's son rose. He lifted from his *par flèche* a parchment roll. It was a Catholic Ladder, the kind Marie and Barbe learned on with David Mongrain. Jean translated word for word what the chief's son said. "This tells the history of the Catholic Church," he said. "It's covered with blood, you see?" Jean translated, waited for the priest to make sense of what this Ladder smeared with blood was doing in this Cayuse man's hands.

"He says Whitman gave it to him and told him that with priests here now, this country will be covered with blood. And so it is. Whitman's blood."

"This is what they said?" Brouillet asked. His eyes were moving quickly, back and forth. "You're certain?" Jean nodded. Brouillet wiped his hands on his long robe. He performed the act again. "I'm in charge here," he said though no one questioned it. "What do they want for the hostages?"

Jean spoke again, listened. "Three things. First, the Americans must understand that the Whitmans died because the Cayuse believed Whitman planned to kill them all, with his poisoned melons and refusal to cure diseases for their people—he treated only the white children. Whitman would starve them if nothing else. He butchered a cow the day he was killed, they said, while Cayuse children whined in hunger."

"So they defended by attacking. Self-defense," Brouillet said.

"Second, they want the killings forgiven, and the hostages will be handed to a peaceful emissary. Third, no more white people can come across Cayuse land because the chiefs say they can't protect them from their young men still angry."

Brouillet sat quietly, folded his hands, then wiped them again. "The bishop would say they have an anxious desire of self-preservation," he said. "I'll ask the bishop when he arrives to convey their wishes to the peace commission and add that if the Americans go to war, we will have all the tribes against us."

"They'll never agree to keep Americans from coming," Jean said. "The Army will arrive first. The best we can hope for is to achieve the captives' release before the slaughter starts."

The chiefs left, and Brouillet busied himself, writing quickly. "I'll want this taken to the British," he said. "At the fort. So they know what they're up against."

But before Jean could leave with it, the Britisher, Peter Skene Ogden, arrived. "Tell them we meet in four days," Ogden told McBean. He stared at Jean. "I know you," he said.

"You dismissed me," Jean said.

"The *Rivière des Chutes,*" Ogden said. "You do as you're told this time, eh?"

"Always, when the order makes sense," Jean said, Ogden squinted, then let his face break into a grin.

Jean rode out again, taking Ogden's meeting time to the chiefs. When the Cayuse rode in, Ogden took over. Brouillet said almost nothing, frantically taking notes. Ogden said, "Tell them they're weak leaders to have lost control over their braves. Tell them." Jean swallowed and did as he was told, though he was sure more than one chief understood Ogden's English well enough. "Tell them we're British who come to rescue the American women and children, and we want no British blood on what happens after, between them and Americans. Just tell them they have to give up the captives, and we'll provide them with guns and ammunition to be able to hunt meat for their families. Oxen and flour. A chief's ransom."

Jean told them, and he added that he knew this man, Ogden. He was wild and brash but trustworthy.

Gray Eagle cut Jean off. "We know this one ourselves," he said. "He isn't fat like the Americans. Like you, he takes an Indian wife. He shows some wisdom. We give him his captives for the ammunition and the oxen, but for one. Five Crows wants one of the women, for his wife."

It took more days of talking before Ogden finally said, "It's all of them or none, and we leave you to make your peace with the American Army. Let them take you all and not just the murderers—unless you give us the woman, too."

Finally, Five Crows relented. "Our people are hungry," Gray Eagle told Ogden. "To feed them on our own land is all we ever wanted."

1848

Gray Eagle brought fifty-seven captives through the crunchy snow into Fort Walla Walla on January 2. The Spaldings, too, arrived in the company of their Nez Perce followers who'd kept them safe.

When little Eliza ran to her mother's arms from the midst of the hostages, Marie knew then whose eyes watched her from behind those walls. Marie ached with the reunion of this mother and child, grateful to play a small joining part. They were fed at the fort and tended, and Marie's hands were welcome to soothe the wounds.

"Our Eliza spoke their language," Mrs. Spalding said. She hugged her daughter to her side, never let her loose. "She was the only one who could communicate with them. Imagine. Will she ever get over it, ever?" Mrs. Spalding said. She clutched her daughter, pressed her head to her breast.

"Time binds a heart wound," Marie said. But she didn't think Mrs. Spalding could hear words of comfort through her fear.

By late January, the captives felt ready to proceed back to Fort Vancouver. They believed that the peace commission approached and that treaty discussions planned for bringing the guilty to justice would keep the travelers safe.

On a drizzly February morning, Marie helped the women and children into Ogden's boats. Snow covered the Walla Walla hills partway down, reminding Marie of a winter of survival with her sons. She talked quietly with Mrs. Spalding as the boats were steadied. The woman's cold hands shook when she reached up to touch Marie's face in the saying of good-bye.

"You were there," she told Marie. "Little Eliza saw you through the barn wood slats. She wanted to cry out, to let you know, but she was so frightened. Seeing you gave her comfort. Great comfort."

"Maybe the commission will find a way to get those guilty to surrender. We'll have a true peace then. You can go back to your work among the Nez Perce printing books."

"Never!" Henry Spalding pushed Marie aside as he stepped into the *bateau.* "Let's move out," he said. "Before these priests incite them against us the way they fired the Cayuse up to kill Whitman. Jealous, that's what they are, those priests. We'll never go back, and if blame's to be laid anywhere for this outrage against God and man, it's at the feet of their black robes."

Mrs. Spalding jerked her head up to her husband. "There's no evidence of that," she said. "The priests—"

"The Army can have at the savages. There'll be no peace if I have any say. Not before all the Cayuse and any who claim their bloodline are rotting in the ground and those bloody priests are dead beside them."

"Venom," Marie told Jean later. "Spalding spoke with venom spit not at the Cayuse killers but at the priests. How can there be such a divide between those who share a *métier* washed with baptismal waters?"

"Another question for David Mongrain," Jean said.

"Or maybe Sister Celeste." Marie thought of Mrs. Spalding's willingness to forgive. "A woman might have a better understanding."

Baptiste tired of this Army, though his company was somewhat better off than the valley's recruits. At least he had a horse and he'd brought plenty of food from his own storage. And he knew most of the men, all French Canadians. The first days he'd renewed friendships with Tom McKay, a man who had once been a suitor of his mother. He was mixed blood, too, and Baptiste looked to him at times, almost as a father.

But after the first few weeks, the stories had all been told, and now they waited. They'd waited in spitting rain for orders to start up the Columbia. They'd waited for grain to reach them, to know if the provisional government raised the money to fund a war. They'd waited to separate rumors of the hostage release from their own impatience to rescue them. Finally, they learned that Ogden's brigade had split the waters of the Columbia, making its way toward Fort Vancouver, hostages on board. Within days, the brigade passed by Company D's camp.

Baptiste's eyes watered as he watched the women and children huddled under cloaks as the boats moved downriver. He recognized Spalding, other men, too. The Brits had done it. Maybe they could all go home now. What kind of man was he to tear up over such a thing as captives being freed without a shot being fired?

"We still have murderers to bring to justice," Tom told him when Baptiste wondered out loud about returning home. Murderers. It was how the Army saw them. Someone had killed innocents. But maybe it was just another kind of battle strategy. Maybe there were no other prospects the Cayuse could see but to take such actions. Desperate acts grew from hungry hope.

"We bring them in," Tom said. "A trial will calm in the long run. The law protects by giving confidence that something besides power and might keeps peace."

"The peace commission can negotiate it, maybe."

"Maybe. Maybe the Cayuse can retain their lands. Maybe." He pulled his blanket around his shoulders as they sat at the February fires.

"If it weren't for you, Tom, I'd seek leave and go home now."

"But you won't." Tom clasped Baptiste's shoulder. "You're a good man, Baptiste. Good men stay through to the end."

They'd camped one evening farther up the Columbia River, easing into Cayuse country, when at dusk they heard several men call out in English, then French. "Friends. We're friends!" and then the long-awaited peace commission made its way into camp.

Close behind a volunteer American army followed.

Baptiste's company traveled with the commission then, and at least they were moving steadily now, not waiting. Baptiste thought of his father's last days, of what thoughts went through his head as he battled cold and winter winds to make a living only to be struck by men taking revenge. Was he doing that too, just taking revenge? He didn't feel that in his heart. This was duty, and he hoped to be free of it, soon.

They camped at an area beyond Sand Hollow not far from the Umatilla River, where Baptiste had spent his youth, and were just mounting up when out of the morning mist Gray Eagle and Five Crows, two of the accused, rode into camp, meeting the French Canadian force first.

"You women," Gray Eagle told Tom McKay. He wore white and red face paint, and he kicked his big mount and the animal pushed against other mounts, the stallions snorting and arching their necks. "You come to take us?" He laughed. "What we do to Whitman, we do to you first. Then we take your women and children so they will know who is in control of their meager lives now." Gray Eagle said. His eyes glistened.

Baptiste felt like an arrow had pierced his stomach. He clutched at his gut, but what pained came from within. These were men like his father—tough, strong, but using power to their own advantage, not using their heads or hearts, just heat and blind rage. The man's posture, his ignorance of what drove these British, these French Canadians, and the American Army, too, would bring his death. It would bring many deaths unless someone stopped him.

Baptiste spurred his horse and rushed the Indians, pulling Gray Eagle from his mount. Five Crows's horse twisted and turned, the animal snorting at the fallen brave held intact by Baptiste, who'd leapt from his horse. "We're not the peace commission," Tom said. "We're here for justice, to avenge the murders of innocents."

"Whitman was no innocent," Gray Eagle charged.

"The women and children you slaughtered were," Baptiste said. He twisted Gray Eagle's arm up behind his back. "I tried to tell you," Baptiste said. "The Americans will do whatever is needed to make a way for themselves."

"Your white blood poisons your red," Gray Eagle said, and he spit at Baptiste. "You dishonor your mother by riding with the likes of them."

Baptiste felt a rush of outrage. He threw the man down and pressed his foot against his throat. "No," Baptiste said. "You dishonor that blood by choosing children for your enemies."

Gray Eagle twisted free, rolled, and pulled his knife. In one fluid motion he stood and lunged for Baptiste. Was this how his father had died at the hands of his own? Baptiste had killed a man once, when he was a boy traveling with Marguerite's father. Defending then and defending now. He and his father shared this, a point of honor worth dying for. He pulled out his pistol as Gray Eagle circled him, crouched low, smiling. "You woman," Gray Eagle said. "You white woman."

The shot rang out in Baptiste's ears. He looked at his own gun. Unfired.

Baptiste stared at Tom, still mounted. His pistol smoked.

Gray Eagle fell at Baptiste's feet.

Five Crows spurred his horse toward Tom, and Baptiste shot at the chief, shattering Five Crows's arm but keeping the man alive. Five Crows howled, grabbed at the blood.

"We'll take this one in for trial," Tom said. To Baptiste he said, "I already have a death on my hands, so I take Gray Eagle for you. It's nothing to live with, the death of a man, my friend. Besides, you have a wound on your conscience. And not just that chief's. My leg reminds me when the weather gets cold and rainy. It's enough guilt for one man to live with." Tom grinned then. "You think I didn't know about you and your little brother's escapade with the skunk-hole cover in your mother's hut? You left it open for me."

Baptiste remembered and smiled. "We were just protecting our mother."

"You started young, " Tom said. "You started young."

Marguerite asked for the St. Louis priest, and he arrived in time to baptize Joseph Klickitat, with Marguerite acting as the godmother. Ten days later, the boy died.

It was Josette who sent Barbe for Marguerite a week later. "Archange sick," Barbe said. "You come. Josette says you come."

Marguerite could hardly lift herself from the chair. Right now, she didn't know if she could nurse a fly, let alone another human being enough to keep them living. Doublé had nearly died of the measles, and she'd thought she'd kept the others distant and safe. JB had taken the healthy children and stayed in the barn while she handed out food for them there, separating them from the disease place. "Whatever do people do if they don't have two adults for this task?" she said once as she handed her husband the food.

"Ask for help, Etoile. We all need help."

Her daughter's fever had ceased with the slice of cucumber she'd put on her chest, something Marguerite's mother suggested once. Kilakotah and some of the older Indian women sweated and took cold baths, but her mother had always frowned on that as treatment for a fever. It wasn't part of her custom. Using herbs and plants was.

There'd been so many deaths of children that she wasn't sure the priest could even come to say the last rites. Joseph's death had stunned her. He'd hardly been sick, had been learning and lighting up their lives and then he'd died.

She looked at her other children with a tightness in her heart. They could all go, all be gone, within an instant. There were so many dangers, how could a mother ever let them from her sight? Even inside their home, disease lurked. A home was a place that should be safe.

This creating of another life weighed heavy. She shared her thought with JB when the fevers had subsided and they were under one roof again. "We do not create alone then," he said.

"I know. It takes two," she told him. "But what I meant was—"

"I know what you meant. We create with three," he said. "Maybe four. You. Me. The child. And God. That's how it works. So when we are too tired or the troubles are too great for you, me, the child, there is still one who never tires, eh?"

His words had comforted her, reminded her of an unending source of strength. She was powerless, after all, and yet responsible, for what she did and how she lived and what she gave away.

Now here stood Barbe with a new need. The woman paced the floor, her lumbering body shaking the dishes on the shelf. "You come. You fix. Archange very sick."

"How's Baby?" Marguerite asked as she grabbed her blanket coat and walked to the barn. She thanked Doublé and JB, who had already harnessed the team. At least they didn't have far to ride to Josette's and JB would take her. She wished her brothers were back, but this senseless war raged on between volunteers and Cayuse holdouts.

"Baby good. Just Archange not so good."

They arrived to see Marianne standing beside the bed. "Did you know he was ill?"

"That's why I asked for the priest," Marianne said. "For the last rites to be given."

Marguerite wasn't sure how Marianne had found out about Archange unless she'd been visiting. Unlikely. Marianne avoided the ill.

Through the night, the three women took turns changing the linens of this fevered man while Barbe patted her sleeping daughter's head and walked the floor beside Archange's bed. For seven days they stayed, and on the eighth, the women called back the priest to prepare the burial of Archange.

"What will we do with Baby and Barbe?" Marianne whispered to her sister. They slept together on a floor mat, the worries over their children, their own lives, these family threads as Marguerite thought of Baby and Barbe, weaving a cloak of anxiety around them.

"I don't know," Marguerite said. "Maybe Mama will come home."

"But it'll tire her to care for—"

"I know. But right now, don't you just want Mama?"

"Yes, but I'm glad you're here at least," Marianne said.

"To have another who stands with you is more than a gift. It is a treasure," Marguerite said.

"Many threads weave a warm cloak," Marianne said.

"Is that something you made up?"

Marianne nodded.

"You sounded just like Mother," Marguerite said.

Marianne sighed as she pulled her sister closer.

"But I have been doing something worthwhile," Marianne defended. "First of all, I have the cabin ready when Mama and Papa return. They'll be back soon. It's spring. Papa always wants his seeds planted early."

"I was just there," Marguerite said. She never sounded tentative, her sister, the words dropping like a surefooted horse on a hard-packed road. "You didn't need to do that. In your condition you might have overstrained."

"It's the delivery that's a problem for me," Marianne said patting her abdomen. "I do fine while I'm pregnant. Why were you there?"

"Sometimes I just go there. It's quiet."

"I'm glad Barbe stayed on at Josette's. She told me first she'd go to Papa's southern claim and live alone there with Baby."

"That would be dangerous."

"*Oui!* There've been more skirmishes with the Klamath getting into arguments with people right here in this valley. It wouldn't be good for them to be so far away, alone," Marianne said. She leaned closer to her sister, who washed eggs the boys had just brought in. "And she's an Indian. People know we have Indian blood in us. And we're Catholic, too, so there's all kinds of fingers being pointed our way on this prairie. It makes me feel looked at when I go to Oregon City."

"I thought you liked to be looked at," Marguerite said. "I meant, Barbe couldn't take care of her child alone, anywhere. Do you think she could?" Her sister looked up at her, as though seeing Marianne for the first time, treating her like a friend. "I just want them all back," Marguerite said. "I'm glad JB is too old to go to war. But Toussaint pushes, and so does Doublé. I'd hate to see them go. There's so much rancor toward the Cayuse that I don't think even bringing in all the Whitman suspects for trial will settle it soon."

"Well, I'm doing my part. To support the volunteers," Marianne said.

"They don't need entertainment," Marguerite told her. She handed her another egg. "If they could just find the murderers and bring them to trial this would all stop."

"That's the Army's job. But I have something that can help the Volunteers."

"JB said the Nez Perce harbor the suspects now, and so the Americans can violate their land to go in after them even though they agreed that the Nez Perce wouldn't be attacked. But I think the Americans will say anything."

"That's unpatriotic," Marianne said. "We're at war."

"Is it? But what can these poor tribes do? If they have the guilty ones and turn them over, their own people will rise up and attack them for collaborating, or other Cayuse will retaliate. And if they don't turn them over, the Americans will attack them. Maybe they will anyway. Sometimes I do wish we were one of those American states instead of in this purgatory between two nations and a mountain range to boot."

"I'm helping. With a petition," Marianne persisted. Would her sister not listen to her, ever? She shook a piece of paper in front of her sister's face. Marguerite frowned as she read. "Several of the young ladies in this valley have signed a letter hoping to spur more young men to be a Volunteer. I've helped compose the article, and it'll be in *The Spectator* next week. Imagine. You heard about Captain Maxon's pleas to support the men and sacrifice here in the valley? Well, now these young women have agreed to withhold their hand in marriage to any young man who *can* but *will not* take up arms and march at once to the seat of war, to punish the Indians who not only murdered our friends but who insulted our sex." She took a deep breath.

"But you're already married. You can't withhold—"

"I just helped write it," Marianne snapped. "Only single women are signing it. Fifteen have agreed so far. I'm one of the few Frenchies working on it. Mama always said 'do what you can.' So I did."

"Yes. And she said to trust God for the rest."

"I do."

"Maybe if they didn't get enough recruits the war would end," Marguerite said.

"And maybe if no one paid the new tax they couldn't feed the men. Would you want that? Your own brother, starving, because we refused to pay our tax? War demands sacrifice, it demands new thinking, it—"

"I just, oh, how I want there to be another way than war," Marguerite said. "There just should be."

"Well, I've found a way to make a difference with my article. And it's better than just standing here cleaning eggs."

Marie heard a child cry as she walked past a tipi. The child expressed such discomfort, the sobbing of frustration that spoke what she felt, that voiced what she imagined all the Cayuse felt, all the Army, all those who waited for this time to be over. Tension at the fort had lessened with the hostages' release, but now rumors ruled their world. Where the murderers were or weren't. If the French Prairie region had sent grain to the troops or not. Who would support the Americans and who wouldn't. She'd heard that Tom McKay and Baptiste had encountered two of the suspects and taken one back to Oregon City to a jail the government had yet to build and was taxing everyone to do just that.

When they weren't worrying over war, disease threatened. Father Brouillet baptized with his fussy ways, gave last rites, and buried Indian and emigrant children alike. Measles swept through the region so quickly Marie thought there was no need for the Americans to war against this people; the disease would conquer it for them.

She hadn't told Jean yet, but Marie was ready to go home, to be with her family. War had that push about it, reminding those left behind of what mattered. It had been good they'd come to Walla Walla when they did, as though it was intended. Not for the result she'd hoped for, seeing Paul, but because she had something to ease the discomfort of his absence. Jean had been here for the negotiations. How could they have known it would work this way? She remembered David Mongrain's story of the brothers, of the wayward son returning. Someone wrote those stories, and someone was writing hers. No certain way existed for a life to travel. Many trails, like streams, branched off and offered something new and different, sometimes rapids, sometimes calm. As long as she remembered that all fed into that one, large ever-flowing current. As long as she didn't step out and let the craft go on without her, she could find the still places and gain nurture there to travel on downstream.

She remembered hearing of little Eliza's comfort in recognizing her, a familiar face in the midst of her captive place. Just the face of someone familiar could be enough to sustain a child in a wilderness place.

If she could have seen the face of Paul, the face of John, again, it would have sustained her as a moment in that quiet place. She would like to be forgiven for her errors; she wondered if each man harbored ill will toward her for who she was, for what she'd done.

Some streams flowed unexplored.

She was ready to let the stream flow without her pushing it along. Maybe the lightheaded feeling she had when she stood up would go away now that she'd been here, seen where Paul might have walked with his wife and his children. Maybe she wouldn't have recognized him even if she met him again. Perhaps she was being protected from some unknown pain, wrapped in a robe she hadn't created.

She and Angele visited with Josette's mother daily, and she'd miss that. But Narcisse stayed close. Going home. She'd find out how Archange and Barbe were, how Baby fared through the winter. "Go home," Josette's mother told her. "Your daughters miss you."

But Jean still had work to do here. He'd been sent to various gatherings to interpret. There were other interpreters, too, but she could see it gave him comfort to be doing something worthwhile in his graying years. She'd wait until the season changed, so they might have the fall hunt near the Santiam. That would inspire him. She could see her children through the winter. They'd be at home for Christmas, the celebration of a birth.

Marie headed for the fort supply store. That child behind the tipi walls still cried as she returned. Probably another case of measles. She didn't recognize the tipi, didn't think it had been there earlier in the week. Someone should pick that child up, Marie thought. Offer it comfort.

Marie bent to make an offer. She opened the tipi flap and bumped into her son.

She put her fingers to her lips. She could feel throbbing at her temples. She'd waited so long, had interrupted her longing to see him again, to treat disease, to await the outcome of war. She wanted to say only peaceful words despite the confusion that swirled in her head. Her heart pounded, her fingers grew instantly cold. She recognized him. *"Merci, merci,"* she breathed. It was him, her son. It was *him.* She'd know him anywhere, those ears, that mouth, those eyes. He wore his hair long and loose. He was shorter than her, leaner. His legs were bowed like the brace of a baby's board. "Paul," she whispered.

The man squinted, his mouth open wide. "Do I know you, woman?"

Marie made herself exhale. "You're my son," she said.

Paul squinted only one eye now. He laughed. "So I am."

"We've been separated," she said.

"A way to put it," he said. He laughed again. "What do you want?"

The question startled her. What did she want? To touch her son. To feel his arms around her, to offer comfort to his heart. She wanted to know what his life had been like, what he ate now, what gave him pleasure. She wanted to discover what she'd done to make him leave; to know what kind of mother she was. Had she been truthful enough, compassionate enough, had she formed a safe place for him from the ashes of an abused and frightened childhood? Had she done all she could? Had she been driven as his mother, or did she answer to a call?

"What do I want? I...to see you. We came here last year, to find you. I heard you'd been baptized."

"Me? No. My son, David," he said. He laughed again, and she realized the sound fell from his mouth like a habit. His nose ran, and he wiped it on the sleeve of his dirty shirt, the fringe of it torn in places. "The woman, My Horse Comes Out, wanted that for our son."

"Your wife and children are all here?"

He stepped aside and pulled at the tipi flap. The child had ceased crying when Paul stepped out, and one started in again. "A whiner," Paul said. "Like me, eh?"

My Horse Comes Out lifted her face to Marie's.

She had gentle eyes set above cheekbones as sharp as a rock face. She wore her hair as Sacagawea did, in long braids, and this woman's were well greased and shiny. One fell over the face of a nursing child. The infant, maybe two years old, struggled, gasped and coughed, cried again, then tried to suckle. *A difficult child.* His mother stroked his hair, assisted him to nurse. She had long, graceful fingers. She was a patient mother.

As Marie's eyes adjusted to the dark, she could see the other children who looked out at her, curiosity fluttering in their obsidian eyes.

"Like your father," she said. "Your sons have the face of your father."

"They'll be interpreters, too, maybe. I do that some," Paul said.

My Horse Comes Out motioned with her hand, and the oldest child moved over, then reached for a piece of dried fish he handed to Marie. The baby cried again.

Marie nodded acceptance, bit into it, and chewed. Her heart steadied.

She had dreamed this moment, imagined the embrace of reunion. But it had never been like this, never filled with so much striving, ceased.

Paul sat beside her now, so close. But he didn't reach out. He didn't seek reunion. And she didn't know if he would let her reach for him. He said nothing. He fiddled with a knife holder at his belt. He'd asked no other questions of her than the one, of what she wanted.

A dozen unanswered questions fell into the space between them. What did the answers matter? The past was woven into the pattern of the present, but one party alone could transform it. It didn't require consent from all involved. Marie had changed the memories of her sons through the years until this was all that mattered: This one lived. Paul, her son, lived, and she had seen his face again before she died. She'd ask for nothing more.

"I get medicine from the fort," Paul told his wife then, unwinding his legs to stand. "Maybe he whines less." He laughed. His wife nodded.

Marie watched him leave. Perhaps she teased herself, but she felt a washing of relief flood over her as she thought of what he'd said and what she'd seen.

If he interpreted, then her son had a *métier* not unlike his father and brother, his grandfather. He was connected to his family whether he acknowledged that or not. He'd worked and thus had met an obligation, somewhere, kept commitments. He claimed a wife, someone who must care for him enough to bear four of his children and leave a place of familiarity to come this far with him. Neither she nor the children looked captive or cowed. She offered food, his wife. She had a compassionate heart and had had their son baptized.

She knew their names. David Mongrain had told her, and she matched them now to the children. The youngest being Mary.

She had found her son and what she wanted to remember of him most she could see reflected in the woman he chose as the mother of his children, his wife. If Marie received nothing more than this, it would be enough. *"Merci,"* she said as she crossed her heart with the sign of the cross. Surely this meeting was a gift from God.

22

A Place of Her Own

My Horse Comes Out protested once within Marie's hearing, saying they should not go back to the Lower Brule country until the spring.

"I decide, woman," Marie heard Paul say. "I have what I come to this country to see now. We go." If they were fortunate, their August departure east could take them beyond the Rocky Mountains before snow fell, but it was a swaggering thing to do, to take on a mountain landscape and risk one's children, too. "We'll winter where we will," Paul told his wife within hearing of his mother.

"You come from the Gray Snow people," Marie told him then. "They know how to winter in the hard places of life, to make it through to spring."

"What?" He swung around, snapped at her. "You think I need the old ones to help me through?"

"We all do," she said.

My Horse Comes Out left the tipi with the little ones trailing behind her. "She goes to the fort to trade," Paul told Marie, and she realized he offered information he hadn't needed to. He engaged in conversation.

"Does she have moccasins she makes, from your hides?" Marie asked.

"She does beadwork. On *par flèches,* knife cases." He patted his own. It showed fine work. "We trade at many forts."

"Trade brought you to Walla Walla?" Marie asked, holding her breath for fear she would say something to send him away.

"The baptism last year. Then we stay and raise grain until the sun dries it to empty heads. This country is too hot for my blood."

"I'm glad you did," Marie said. "Stay. So I could see you again." She wondered if she should tell him how Baptiste was or that she had more children. Did he wonder who Angele was, the small child who lingered not too close, but was almost always with Marie?

"Will you tell me why you left?" Marie asked then. How could she not ask?

He turned his head to her, quick as the flick of a serpent's tongue. His voice almost hissed. "Don't ride there, woman," he said. "That trail has been covered over, buried in hot ash."

Her heart pounded. She'd already stepped so close. Did she want to know? Could she hear the truth if he told her?

"Louis," she said. "His death…"

"You have to know this, eh woman?" Paul said.

"*Oui.* I have to know," she said. She dropped her eyes. "I am an old woman now. If you can tell me of that time, of what happened to Louis, I can put at least this old thought to rest."

"You have other thoughts you wrestle with?" he asked.

Marie nodded. "You have three brothers," she said. "Baptiste and one younger. And another, older than Baptiste by six years. His name is John."

A sly smile lifted one side of his face. "So you keep a secret too."

She felt the skin rise on the back of her neck, beneath the knot of hair wrapped into a coil. "Yes, I keep a secret. But now I tell it to my family, to trusted people. And it is a freedom then. Maybe you will seek such freedom from an old worry, an old…act."

He stared at her. She watched My Horse Comes Out move gracefully back toward the tipi. She stopped to shift the child she carried in her board, set another on her back. He would either tell her now…or not. She could live with either.

"I was a boy," Paul said. "Boys hide things." That habit laugh fell from his open mouth then. "Now, I'm a grown man with sons of my own, eh? Now I can't remember what I hid or where I hid it. What does it matter now?"

It was all he'd give her of those years. Paul kept silent, harbored both desires and disasters of his boyhood.

Marie spent a little more time with her grandchildren before they left. Like a hibernating bear, her Hidatsas language awoke to speak a bit with My Horse Comes Out. She hadn't used it since that time on the Missouri when she and Sacagawea exchanged words. She learned that one grandson's Brule Sioux name was Dog Soldier. "A soldier," his mother signed then, her fists closed and moving toward each other. "Strong."

Marie gave each grandchild a piece of beaded leatherwork, to one a knife case, and to another a flat bag with porcupine quills dyed and woven into a river design. "To remember your grandmother," she said. She finished working a hide and rolled the smoked, soft leather and handed it to Paul's wife. "Heart knowing," My Horse Comes Out signed. "I'll remember you."

"Memory. *Oui,*" Marie said, the words of Sacagawea coming again to her, the memory of a friend.

Marie kept herself from thinking of the stones of her son's past. She put aside the emptiness of their impending departure and instead stayed present, tasting pleasure with bread she shared with her grandchildren, the touch of a child's hand at the back of her head, the sounds of shared laughter as one released her hair bun from its bondage.

Then on a hot August morning, they left behind dry flat grasses on the spot where the tipi had been.

"They've gone," Marie said, running back to the tipi she shared with Jean. He held her with his one good arm as they walked back to the empty place, looked out across the River. It surprised her that she didn't cry, though a parting song rang through her head. Angele came to take her hand and squeezed it.

"What do you want, woman?" Paul had asked. What did she desire? To let Paul go now. Not all she'd wanted to know was answered. But she'd been given back a life, had reached beyond to Paul's wife, his children and to their children, too, she hoped. They'd brushed against each other and somehow she knew they were all forever changed, despite the distance, time, and space that lay between them.

❖

"Will you be her godmother?" David asked Marguerite. She nodded, handing the baby to Marianne. The delivery went smoothly. "Almost as good as having Mama here," Marianne said. Her damp hair frizzed and stuck to the sides of her cheeks. Marianne looked tired but happy.

"We named her for you," David said.

"Another mother name," Marguerite said, her voice light with pleasure.

What pleased her more was the return of her mother and Papa Jean and their charge, Angele, in September. Marguerite guessed she should refer to Angele as their child because she was a part of the family. It didn't take blood to make it so.

Her mother's family arrived first at Marianne's and David's. Marguerite tried not to take that as critique.

"You have to tell us what you did for a year away," Marianne said.

"I see what you were doing," Marie told her as she held Marianne's baby.

"Well, that isn't all I did," Marianne said.

"She helped compose a letter to raise recruits for the Army," Marguerite said. She kept judgment from her voice. She'd been doing better with that, she thought. At least her sons behaved as though she was less critical toward them, and she and JB grew closer. She was with child again. She hadn't told her family yet, just savoring for a time this new life that stirred within her.

"Where's Barbe and Archange and Baby?" Jean asked.

Marianne looked to her sister. "Baptiste is expected back soon. But Archange. He…died of the measles," she said. "Earlier this year."

"Measles," her mother said. She shook her head.

"Marguerite did everything she could for so many. Even a child she took care of died," Marianne said.

"You took another child in?"

Marguerite nodded. "Your Methodist friend brought him."

"And Barbe without Archange? Who takes care of her and Baby?"

Marguerite touched the back of her mother's hands. They were cold as they usually were. "We all do," she said. "But for the past few months, they've been with Josette."

"You should have been here for the armistice," David said.

"There were parties on the Fourth of July, bigger than ever before," Marianne said. "Twenty-six toasts at Sidney Moss's Main Street House in Oregon City."

"But no liquor," David said. "The citizens passed the prohibition, so all we had was Adam's Ale. Water. Not much spirit in that for a Frenchman."

"Our armistice will happen when Baptiste returns home," Marguerite said. "Then we'll all be together."

"All but a few of us," her mother said. "But it is enough."

Marie looked around for a chair, found one, and sat.

"Even though it's autumn and you always like to go south, would you stay closer to St. Louis this year?" Marianne asked. "I have a new baby who needs to get to know her grandmother."

"We will," Jean said. "Your father is asked to testify at the trial of the suspected Cayuse." His voice held pride. "They'll be tried in Oregon City. An old gray one like me still has vinegar in him to tell my part in the story."

"And I go to take food there," Marie said.

"Oh, I'm sure they'll feed all the jurors and witnesses," Marguerite said. "That won't be necessary, Mother."

"I take food to the Cayuse prisoners," Marie said. "Even those who make poor choices are worthy of remembering."

"What will people think, though, Mama?" Marianne asked.

Marie laughed. "They'll be surprised, maybe. If they even notice what an Indian woman does to fill her time. But it doesn't matter what others think. Nothing to be anxious over. You teach me this, daughter. Who looks after the St. Louis church while I'm away?"

"It always looked tended," Marguerite said. "I think Sister Celeste or one of the other sisters comes to clean each week."

Marianne nodded. "Someone did a good job anyway." She had that surprise twinkle in her eye. It had always troubled Marie. Now it comforted.

"Where's François? And Angelique? Why aren't they here?"

"François went to seek his fortune," David said. "Who knows how many others will follow."

"His fortune is lost?" Jean said.

"They discovered gold at Sutter's Mill in California. The brig *Henry* was too late to bring in ammunition for the war, but it brought news," JB said. "And half the prairie is already headed south."

"He wanted his own place, for Angelique and their family," Marianne said. "To make more room for you and Barbe and whoever else you wove into your life."

"This troubles you," Jean said.

"No. I didn't mean to criticize. I didn't."

Marie's thoughts raced with Marianne's observation. Had she deprived her own children of her love and time by extending it beyond the boundaries of blood? No, she'd turned those hard times into different gifts, as David Mongrain said she could. Gifts, she could keep giving away for as long as she remembered how.

⌖

"They did well at Josette's," Marianne told Marie. This granddaughter blew bubbles while Marie bounced her on her knee. "Baby chatters up a storm, and she doesn't sound slow and plodding like Barbe. She's quiet and gentle like Archange was, and sometimes I think she looks after Barbe. Could that be? A child raising a parent? Barbe doesn't even seem to grieve Archange's death. Maybe you have to be intelligent to grieve," Marianne said.

Marie frowned at her. "Grief is from the heart. We all have hearts if we're alive."

"I didn't mean it as a slap, Mama," Marianne said. "But maybe

Barbe's saved the pain of loss because, well, because she can't keep the memory of Archange in her heart for long. Maybe her poor memory protects her."

Marie looked at her daughter. Did she know of her own wisdom? "Not remembering can do this," Marie said, as she remembered a baby named John.

1849

Marie walked the bank of Lake Labiche, reacquainting herself with the soil and the seeds. Chickens pecked in what was left of the garden, and Barbe pounded a board into a space where a raccoon or wolf might be enticed to squeeze. The trees where she twisted hides bore scars she hadn't noticed.

Jean rode often to Oregon City, JB going with him, and once a week Marie went along and took fry bread and dried fish and berries to the jailer's wife, who received it with gratitude. "You supplement their contract," JB told her. "You get nothing for giving it."

"More than money, I get," Marie told him. "You get no pay for sitting and listening."

JB nodded. Her son-in-law liked to roam, and now the trial preparations captured his attention. Marie thought these men met to reminisce, talk of old friends gone now. Tom McKay had died of consumption. Michel LaFramboise limped with a cane.

Marguerite didn't appear to mind JB's departures. At least she didn't complain to Marie as she had in her early marriage years. Perhaps her daughter's children kept her too busy. A wife's pain could be covered beneath a mother's flapping wings, but Marguerite's face showed few wrinkles. And she'd even heard her daughter laughing with JB's older sons.

She had thought she'd travel each day to Oregon City along with Jean and JB, but the days blurred and ran together the way her eyes once had, before Jean's gift of the spectacles. The tiny pricks of light when she stood up too quickly came back here too, even though she harbored no secrets she could remember.

More than once when Marianne stopped by to ride with her to the St. Louis church she'd been confused about what day it was.

"You asked me to come here first, so we could ride together," Marianne told her. "You're going to tell Joseph and baby Marguerite stories while I clean the church."

"You clean?"

"Just scrub the steps and freshen up the priests' quarters. You remember. We do it each week."

"I remember," Marie said. She had, but it still troubled her, this needing reminding of the specifics.

When they'd arrived at the square-log church, Marie sat in the shade while her grandchildren brought plants to her. She could name them all. Baby, Barbe's little one, identified them even faster. The child had a good head for such things. Before long, they'd bring them to this child for identification, wouldn't need what Marie knew. On Sundays, new people joined the Mass. More women than men. Many of the emigrant women had wintered the year alone while their husbands and sons headed into California mining for gold. Jean said 1849 would be remembered forever because of that seeking. "Do you want to go look for gold?" she asked him. He'd told her no, he had a fortune right here, and he'd spread his arm out to take in the timber and cleared fields, then lifted and kissed her hand. The last year of the decade. Even Louis LaBonte had headed south, leaving Kilakotah to tend Tom McKay's farm below the Butte alone.

The chatter after Mass wore women's words. Marie listened to the blend of French and English, hearing of how many cows these women milked, how they harvested the grain with their men all gone. They shared words of children's illnesses and gains, spoke of the weather and even politics where it touched their hearths. This Oregon place still did not take kindly to the Catholics. Some still blamed Father Brouillet for inciting the Cayuse against the Whitmans, for causing white women to be dishonored as Indian captives.

They didn't understand, these Americans. The Cayuse didn't need religion to fuel the fires of disappointment; they'd had years of brushing up against a hope soon shattered by false words. Words were important to a peaceful life. The words that others said; the words spoken to a woman's own heart were even better. Maybe even words written down.

"Will you be coming back to school?" Sister Celeste asked Marie after the Mass one clear winter day. "Maybe with this long rest, you could try again to read."

Marie shook her head no. "But I have another idea," Marie said. "Stories are the sparks that light our ancestors' lives, the embers we blow on to illuminate our own. You could be like that Irving man and write words down for me. What I can remember. Before it's all gone." Marie tapped the side of her head. "We'll blow on old embers together."

Sister Celeste's blue eyes grew large. Her smile widened, the white wimple pressing tight against her cheeks. "You'd allow me to do that, you would? I would be so grateful. *Merci, merci!* I'll ask Mother Superior immediately," and she went off, walking fast enough Marie could see her stockinged ankles beneath the heavy skirts.

Here at this St. Louis Parish after Mass, after breaking of communal bread, mothers watched their children play, and words of the world's bias and strife weighed less. Life eased when held in palms warmed by family, friends, and faith nestled against a soothing landscape.

Once or twice, she and Jean even heard Josiah Parrish speak. His circuit now crossed to the east side of the Willamette. Marie's limited English challenged her understanding of what he said, but the tone was one of hope and comfort, not the strident outrage of a Whitman. Parrish had been appointed assistant Indian agent too. He had a heart for people, and Marie felt him a hopeful choice for making plans for a long-lasting peace.

In April, 1849, Marguerite gave birth to Julie and named Marianne as godmother. She told her mother the priest wrote "Marianne Toupin" in his sacramental register, and she didn't seem to mind that neither her married name nor the one she'd chosen for herself, Marie Anne, had been acknowledged. "I've named myself," Marianne told her mother. "That's really all that matters." Her daughter never failed to surprise.

A month later, Josette gave birth. She and Baptiste named the baby

Marianne. Marie was pleased for her daughter and pleased that her son resisted the call of the rush to gold, holding instead to the bounty of his land and his wife.

Marianne became her niece's godmother.

"Would you like to be her godmother?" Baptiste had asked his mother first.

"Non," she said. "Where there are other mothers of your blood, you use them. I give myself for those with no one."

"Weave more threads into the coat that way," he'd told her, approval in his voice.

Hadn't there been a time when he'd questioned her taking on so many others? Yes. There'd been a time, but now she didn't remember what had happened for him to even raise that question.

She felt a flutter in her chest, a lightness in her head. Sometimes she awoke and didn't know where she was for a moment, a bad taste rising in her mouth. Her legs would tingle as they did when she walked long distances as a child. She feared telling Jean. So far, her memory had always come back, this knowing of her place, where she was. She guessed, though, that she might ask him if he noticed, if it happened to him, too.

Questions. It was impolite anyway, to ask questions. "Questions dress up complaints. Especially those posed in prayer." Her mother taught her that. She was sure that was where she'd heard it. "Why don't you heal a child? Why did my mother die? is saying, You should heal my child, you shouldn't let my mother die, you're not listening to me!" All are really telling God what should be done. A mind can still grow, even though it's surrounded by a pool of questions without answers. Hold tight to the thread of your faith," her mother told her. "When all else fails, that thread is still there."

Jean didn't know how to tell her. He'd only had two children of his loins, and his ache for them when they struggled had caused him pain unlike any other. Marguerite was almost like his. He claimed her, and yet there was a distance not painful, but one allowed to be a witness to her father, Louis Venier, a man who'd lived and loved and left behind a daughter who was now a good woman. Little Marie, Barbe, Angele, Baby, he claimed them, too. The love he had for them surprised him at times with its intensity overcoming the occasional frustration. Love did allow for frustration, for disappointment, he knew that. He didn't think love could deepen without sloshing through those flooded times. The crafts that beached on higher ground were always stronger for the challenge of the harder passage.

But the suffering of Baptiste and Paul when they were young on Hunt's journey joined him to Marie in a binding way. He had no memory of John. He was pleased to comfort her whenever she brought John up. It was a person's choice whom they shared sorrow with, one he honored.

But he'd taken a special interest in the Dorion sons on that Astor trip, tried to keep them safe and entertained. They'd reminded him of his younger brothers and sisters. Baptiste and Paul, those boys and his wife had tied them all to the French Canadians and former Astorians. Her love for her sons, her endurance with a difficult man, had endeared her to men she never saw again but who wrote of her and told her story.

He'd had a special bond with Marie and her sons. He never imagined one day he'd be the conveyer to the mother of one's death.

"Marie?"

She sat up slowly. "Is it morning?"

"No. Late afternoon. You nap," he said.

"That's all I seem to do," she said. She sat on the side of the bed. She yawned.

He knelt down. "Baptiste…" He cleared his throat.

"He's back? Did he bring gold for Josette?"

"He's been back. He didn't go to California. He was in the war. You don't remember? He came by to see you."

She raised her eyebrows, shrugged her shoulder, and smiled meekly.

"I have sad news," he said. "Baptiste…is dead. Consumption, Dr. Poujade says. His lungs filled with water."

"He's ill?"

"No, Marie. He's dead. I'm so sorry. Your son is dead."

"He's with another mother," she told him. "You gave him to another mother?"

He held her hand. Tears welled up in his eyes. Should he try to make her understand or tell her later? Maybe he shouldn't have told her at all. He didn't know.

"Marie. It's me. Jean Toupin."

"That's right," Marie said. Her face brightened. "She lost so many children. This one was a gift. They're all gifts."

"Yes, they are." Jean stood. "Would you like tea?" he said. "It's cool for September. Might taste good."

"I never take tea in the morning," she said. "You know that."

"How could I forget," Jean said.

"You're getting old," she told him. "Just accept it," and she smiled.

"Baptiste wanted me to take David?" Marguerite asked.

Josette nodded. "My husband said you were a good mother with a protective heart."

"His mother protected him as best she could," Jean said. "I witnessed that when he was just a boy."

"She gave him much," Josette said. "A love of learning. A wish to care for others. Even a questioning faith stirred by a servant's heart. But safety, this one especially he remembered and said that of our children, David needed it more."

"I wonder why," Marguerite said. "He's a sweet child." They looked out the Gobins' newly installed French doors toward the River where the children threw rocks and played.

"The child learns differently," Josette said. "Baptiste said he reminded him of Paul a little. Up and down. Such children need what he thought you gave best."

Marguerite felt her face grow warm. She considered herself the least prepared for mothering of any woman she knew. And JB's sons had fallen victim to her fright and insecurity. But her brother had seen something she hoped she'd grown into. Perhaps she did provide a place of routine and predictability, safety, the first ingredient for a child's learning stew.

"Will it truly help you, Josette? Or make it harder for you, being separated from your son?"

"It is what he wished. David, too. You will be his other mother. I am grateful."

Marguerite turned to JB. Her husband nodded. "My mother always said that 'One boy's a boy. Two boys together is a half a boy. And three boys together are no boys at all.' I don't know what four boys will be, eh?"

"An army," Marianne said. "An army to frustrate their mother."

"I don't think...oh," Marguerite said. "You're joking."

"With four boys around, you'll be wanting to stir up your sense of humor," Marianne said.

Her little sister's wisdom still surprised.

⯐

Marie wondered if Baptiste's David was in the wrong place. He should go home with his mother. But he was here, with Marguerite. All the family visited Marguerite. Because Baptiste had died. Her oldest son...no, the son she'd spent the most time with, was dead. They'd had the funeral. Marie sang the mourning song, and Angele joined in. Josette had cut her braids for him. Marie outlived another child. It made no sense to her. It was what living looked like.

"From ashes to ashes" the priest said as he swung the incense over the casket. Ashes covered pain, brushed out memories unless she hung tight to them. Others, she must simply let go.

23

What Living Looks Like

1850

Jean wasn't sure he wanted to attend this family gathering. They often disintegrated into differences of opinion. As he got older, he found he wanted more and more time alone, with just Marie and him. Even Sister Celeste's coming to write down what Marie remembered now took time away from him, lost time he found he resented. It seemed to ease Marie, though. She laughed out loud with Sister Celeste, and even after the Sister departed, Marie would remember tales, and she and Jean would talk together over tea for hours, like the old friends they were. He wanted more times like that with his wife. But his family also wanted her presence. His, too. He knew that. They were good children, all of them. He sighed. This was what living looked like, the adjustments, the wrinkles of change.

After Baptiste's death, they'd stayed through the winter closer to St. Louis, Barbe and Baby, Angele, and Marie and him all huddled together with Angelique and François when he returned penniless from California. Jean helped Josette as he could, and her daughters, especially Denise, worked the fields. A Catholic school had opened in Oregon City, and Jean still wished all his grandchildren would go, but maybe the next generation. Maybe all of them would know the catechism well and learn both French and English, reading as well as writing. It was something he'd wanted for Marie, but she had never gained it. And now it was too late for that. Her mind spilled out familiar things but left no room for something new.

As they rode to Marguerite's for this gathering, he smelled the spring air. They'd had moisture through the winter and yet could get into the fields for early planting. The smells of a prairie spring were unlike anything he'd ever known, even back in his Canadian province. It was enough to stir the juices of a man's throat and make him want to try new recipes. He snorted to himself. He'd have to push Angelique aside for that. That woman loved her kitchen and sent any who tried to use it their own way, scurrying. At least he had those trips to Oregon City to consume some of his time. But that would be over soon too. And they'd find the Cayuse guilty, he knew that already. They'd even built the hanging scaffold, the hammering going on while inside testimony got written down.

But here they all were, gathered together for no special reason at all, or at least that was what Marianne had told them they were gathering for. "Just to have time together. Do we need a birthday or New Year's or a christening?" she said.

Barbe wandered toward the river as soon as they arrived. Marie and some of the grandchildren puttered with the dog near there too.

Angelique and François spoke of the new doctor moving closer to French Prairie. To his other daughters Jean said, "It'll be good for your mother to have a doctor near. Some of the miners brought back yellow fever with them, and cholera. She's run down, and those diseases might easily attack. I worry for her. She's been coughing lately too." He wondered if he should tell them his larger worry. He decided he would. This was family, after all. "Your mother has been, at times…disagreeable. Stubborn over simple things."

"Mother's always been stubborn," Marguerite said.

"Persistent," Jean said. "And over things that mattered. But now, well, she reminds me of Barbe sometimes."

"I noticed that too," Marianne said. She set sliced melon on the table. "When we checked the candles at the church last week, she slapped at my hand when I tried to help her put one in the holder."

"I didn't know you went with her," Marguerite said.

"She's never raised a hand to me, not ever," Marianne said. "And she looked…scared."

"I've seen that too, the fearful look," Angelique said. She wiped her hands on her apron, set a bowl of blackberries freshly washed on the table. "Sometimes when Mother scans the room she squints, and it's as though she's trying to name us each one but can't remember us all, Barbe, Angele, Baby, Papa Jean, François."

"She knows who I am," François said.

"Not always," Angelique countered. "She called you Baptiste once." Jean thought his son winced. "It's as though we were strangers instead of family."

"What did you do, Marianne?" Jean asked. "When she did that, when she struck at you?"

"I just stepped back. Then she asked who I was."

"Oh, Marianne," Marguerite said, her fingers to her face. "How awful."

"Not really. I just told her my name and she said, 'Do I know you?' and I told her she did and that I was a very likeable person who came from a very fine family."

Jean smiled.

"One time she told me that I was Marguerite and I just nodded."

"You didn't try to correct her?" Angelique said.

"Why?"

"To be truthful," Marguerite said. "We should be truthful. She'd want to be treated with the truth. It's respectful."

Marianne shook her head. "It's not a lie. For her, right then, I was you, Marguerite. And she was happy with me, so why would I make her upset trying to convince her of something that doesn't really matter. Besides, she isn't always confused. After she struck at me that day, she later asked if she'd done something strange earlier, and I said maybe a little but not to worry, that I liked surprises. She laughed and told me she didn't always know what she was doing and could surprise herself sometimes. I told her neither did I. We had a good laugh together." Marianne waved at Xavier through the French doors. "That little moment might not have happened if I'd tried to convince Mama she'd done something wrong. She fell asleep within a few minutes after she tried to slap me. I let her rest while I finished up, and she was fine on the way back."

Jean looked out the Gervais' window. Marie walked hand in hand with Marianne's Marguerite, almost two now. They stopped every few steps, and it looked like Marie took in deep breaths. Barbe had followed her out and shouted for them to wait. The three walked out of sight toward the river, and he was aware he worried.

He turned to look at his children. "We've been speaking of your mother like we once spoke of Barbe, *n'est-ce pas?* As though she's someone who needs...special caring."

Angelique would need help with this new baby. She'd need support, not just for her own baby when it arrived but for Barbe and for Baby. Angele had assumed more adult duties, and that might not be well either. Jean wanted her in school.

He could see something he needed to do now, gleaned out of this family conversation. They'd have to do something for Marie.

It was Marguerite's idea. "Let's ask Mother what she'd like."

"We can tell her we want her advice while we can do it all together," Marianne said. "I like that."

"She'll get upset," Angelique said.

"Not if we tell her we just want to know what she'd like, how we could best take care of her. She knows sometimes she doesn't remember or isn't herself. That's what scares her. So when she is herself, that's when we'll talk."

"She won't remember," François said, "and she'll still get mad at you."

"Then we'll deal with the adventure of that," Marianne said. "We may as well do it now," she added.

"Now?" her Papa said.

"We're all here. Why not?"

When Marie and Barbe and Marianne's daughter came back from their walk, Marianne brought up the subject.

"We're worried about you, Mama. Just a little."

"Me." Her mother stood taller, towering an inch or so over Marianne. *Formidable* was a word Marianne thought described her. "What about?"

"Loving you well," Marianne said. It was a phrase she'd practiced saying.

"Oh, you all do that with no trouble," she said.

"On the days you're feeling not so well, when you wake up but can't remember when you last went to sleep, we're worried about those days and how we can love you best then, too."

Marie looked around the room. Marianne didn't think she had fear in her eyes, but she couldn't name what she saw there.

"Angelique will have a new baby soon. And we know you don't want to be a trouble to them."

Her mother's shoulders dropped. She coughed. "No. I don't want that," she said.

"What would make you comfortable, Mother?" Marguerite asked. "You should do something about that cough. Or we should."

"To love my children," her mother said. "That's what I want."

"You do that, Mama," Marguerite told her. "You've always done that well."

"That's enough then."

"Papa Jean worries," Marguerite said.

"Do you?" Her mother looked at Jean.

Her Papa said, "What do you want, my Marie?"

"Well," her mother said. "That's a surprising question, 'What do I want?' What do you want?"

"I'd like you and Papa to come live with David and me," Marianne said then. "We have the most room. Papa can still get to Oregon City as he needs to. You, too, when you want to. And then there's the garden to occupy our time. You'll be closer to Sister Celeste and to the St. Louis church, too."

"And Barbe and Baby and Angele?" Marie said.

Marianne hesitated. "They come, too, if David approves."

"My sister would be proud of you, Bonbon," her husband said.

"It's settled then. Mama, you haven't shown me yet how to quill with those porcupines. Would you like that? You can live with us and teach me all sorts of things."

Her mother tugged at the tulle shawl laid loosely around her shoulders. The Thompson clock on its stand ticked into the quiet.

"I'll go," she said. Then whispered, "But I don't know how I'll be." Her voice cracked. "I just don't know how I'll be."

Marianne sprang up to put her arms around her. She held her mother's bony shoulders as though they were a child's most precious gift. "Oh, Mama, it doesn't matter how you'll be. It doesn't. We'll love you no matter how you are, the way you always loved each of us."

"I dreamed last night," Marie told Jean.

"It was a good one, eh?" he said. "You laughed in your sleep."

Marie nodded. "I dreamed of John."

"Did you? What was it then?"

She turned to Jean, her hand on the white hair of his chest. Marianne's sheets smelled of August sunshine, and Marie pulled the patched linen of the sheet up over her shoulder. "I don't remember my dreams very often," she said. "This one felt real. I touched him. He had a gift he gave me. Pulled it out of the air. Plucked it like a feather and laid it in my hand. I could feel the cold of it, the smoothness of the blade." She held her palm up, almost expected to see it lying there.

"A knife." Jean said.

"Not just any knife," Marie said. "It was one I lost once, a stiletto one my mother gave me. At least I thought I'd lost it. Sacagawea gave me one of hers to replace it, and the last time I saw her I went to give it back but only asked her questions instead. About the trip ahead and whether I would be enough."

"And you gave it away to your Louis."

She nodded. "In the dream, the stiletto knife turned into that Sacagawea gift. And then into the copper earrings you gave me."

"My earrings were in your dream?"

"That was why I laughed. They felt so light." She quieted, remembering. "He was a good man, my son. Horses grazed behind him at a river. Many children crowded around him, calling him Papa. His voice was deep, and he spoke only French in my dream."

"Do you remember what he said?"

"No," she said. "Only that he came to me carrying gifts."

"Sometimes I wish I could have given all to him," Marie told Sister Celeste, "not stayed in my cave in those troubling times. I regret being so selfish. Jean only wanted to comfort me. I could have given him that gift of closeness."

Sister Celeste sat on the edge of the bed. She laid her writing lead down before she spoke. "I think a strong woman must stay a little separate from her husband or her father or her brothers or sons so she isn't swept away by her wish to love so fully, to give so much. It isn't selfish, I don't think, to hold back a little of herself. She's asked to give all of herself only to the One who said 'bring it all to me.' No man, however much he loves a woman, can truly understand this need for separateness inside a woman's heart. It is a distinction of being bound and yet set free that only a woman knows."

"Can you write this down?" Marie asked Sister Celeste. "It's not a story I remember but a dream instead. Will you write it and maybe, afterward, you share it with Jean."

"Whatever would bring you comfort, Madame Dorion," the Sister said. She stepped over the dog lying on the floor beside Marie's bed. A September breeze carried the sound of a music box in through the open window. "They play *Frère Jacque,*" Sister Celeste said. "*Dormez-vous?*"

Marie opened her eyes. "*Non.* I am awake. You have your lead? Good. In this dream, I am with Jean and I am not fearful for him or anyone else. I've waved good-bye to my children and grandchildren, all behind me. Jean and I watch stars filter to the night. I recognize it as a time and place familiar and that we are held in hands that have carried me along without my knowing. In the morning, I walk on a path with Jean and words spill out of me and I toss them across the sky. Like falling stars, they drop down and land as flowers beside the river for others to water and pluck. Seeds burst from the brush of Knuck running by." The dog's tail struck the floor at the sound of his name.

"The words take on new shapes," Marie said. "And I write faster as I have so little time and yet I stop and smell them, tiny stars of beauty. A horse runs out and nuzzles me and flicks a word flower to the wind. It lands in other soil. I am a part of it, but I know it isn't mine. None of them belong only to me. Then Jean leaves. Before he does, I plant a dozen flower words around him, and he tells me it is a comfort he has never felt before. 'You'll share this garden with our children,' I tell him, and Jean agrees." Marie paused.

"That's...lovely," Sister Celeste said.

"Then we part, Jean and me. He plucks some flowers and gives them to me, and I know he will carry words of memory and comfort with him too after I am gone. Flowers bloom behind me, and I am shown a door, a lovely door, opened up. A man stands there, and I thank him for the flower words. He says that I may keep them, not to dry them, but to pass them on to others so they will not die."

Sister Celeste sat crying. "My tears, like raindrops, blur the scratches on my paper."

⌖

"I wouldn't get too close," Dr. Poujade said. "It's highly contagious."

"We'll be careful," Marguerite said. "But the cool bath should help her breathe better."

"It will do that," he said.

The two girls rinsed their mother's limbs with rose water and talked quietly as they did. Marie's breath came between long pauses, but her eyes followed them, a faint smile fixed upon her face. They were good girls, her daughters. Angele sang a song Marie recognized as a good-bye song of her Ioway people. The song would go on even after she was gone.

"We should summon Father Delorme," Angele said. "And David Mongrain. They're friends."

Marianne started to cry, and Marguerite held her. Marguerite told Angele. "Tell Papa Jean."

Men's voices rose and fell in the second room while her breathing brushed the air. Marianne crawled up beside her then, and lifted her head. It felt so heavy. Marguerite wiped the cool rag beneath her neck. The threads of her hair wrapped around Marianne's fingers, and Marie liked feeling the tingle of the tug between them. She could still feel. She still knew where she was.

She listened to the girls' soft chatter, Marianne's word. "I brought the cross over. I couldn't carve a crucifix, but I made the cross," she said. "And I carved your name in it, Mama."

"Did you? What name did you use?"

Marguerite raised her eyebrows. "Marie Toupin? Don't you want that name?"

"I thought *Mother* would be nice," she said.

"It would," Marianne said. "I can do another."

"Here," Marie said then. "Help me take this cross off of my neck. It was a gift from my friend Sarah." The girls eased it over her head. "For you, Marguerite," she said. "You're the oldest." She could almost hear Marianne's cry at her throat.

"Thank you, Mother. I'll treasure it forever."

"Now, Marianne, you go to my *shaptakai.* There's something there for you, too."

"For me?" She moved to the leather suitcase, folded down the flaps.

"A rosary and crucifix. You lost yours to the Methodists." Marie smiled, and her lips cracked. "Give the *shaptakai* to François when he comes in. I painted the scenes myself. He can use it when he packs his animals to mining camps. A better way to make money from the gold than panning for it."

The narrow bed required that the women work together and roll their mother's frail body toward the wall, so her back could be washed too. They ran their fingers down her spine, touching each sharp bone.

"They stick out like the rocks overlooking the Umatilla River," Marianne said.

"They're strong," Marguerite said. "You've always been strong."

With the gentleness of the starlight that fell on this warm September night, they eased her back. She saw Marguerite's tears and wished she could remove them. It hurt to breathe, but she wasn't troubled. She'd never felt so rested.

Jean pulled a stool up, and he sat beside her, holding her hand. "There's a gift," she said.

"You give me too much," Jean said.

Marie smiled. "You're the gift giver."

"Of things," he said. "You gave yourself."

"Not all of me," she said. "But Sister Celeste says not to hold regrets. This time I give you a thing," she said. "In the trunk." She nodded with her chin, and Jean lifted the cover of the box. "Inside the corduroy," she said. He unwrapped the pale green cloth. He brushed at his eyes with his thumbs. "A pair of gloves," he said. "With a porcupine quill design."

"Better than any other pair I ever made. The first with this design. I give the first away," she said. "To one who will see my promise."

Jean gripped the gloves inside his good hand, told her he'd be back, then left the room. She heard his gulp of grief, felt sad for him that she had to go so soon. But she'd left words behind. Many words planted now as flowers in her children's hearts.

The priest came then and conducted the sacrament of the last words, words to send her on her journey. He sprinkled water over her. "I was once named Her to Be Baptized," she told him.

She dozed. She opened her eyes. "Ah, you're awake," David Mongrain said.

"You have another Ladder story for me?" she asked. François lit lanterns, and Jean sat back beside her.

"Your voice is certainly strong," David Mongrain told her.

"My *vocare?*" she asked.

"Your calling." He chuckled. "And your words today."

"Did you bring me an answer?" she asked. He looked puzzled. "To my question. The one of what was wrong with me that the baptismal water hadn't washed away my worries?"

"Ah, that one. I think I have an answer now, better than what I said before."

"You didn't," Marie said.

"It isn't the water," he told her. "It's the love that washes."

"And my worries? Is this a sign my faith is frail, weak as old bones ready to be ash?"

"Not your faith in God, Madame Toupin. But perhaps the confidence in your own worthiness, that you deserve a life of hope. Life is not made up of smooth waters alone. But of troubles and celebrations, of living through lost loves, noticing wrong turns, letting others help you turn around. Finding the lessons wherever they're offered, not just when you thought you were ready. Living looks like what you did: You took in gifts then gave them away."

She thought of her sister and mother, then. Of Baptiste and grandchildren already gone before her. Of Paul and John and the children who lived and would carry on.

She couldn't see Marianne, who held Marie's head in her lap. Marguerite sat at her side, pulling up the single sheet beneath Marie's chin. Barbe waddled in through the door, and she stood at the foot of the bed, helped Baby crawl up to sit close to Marie's knees, her own short legs swinging over the bedside. Angele sat on the floor, her head pressed against the bed, and Marie raised her hand to stroke Angele's cheek.

Sister Celeste sang. Marie hadn't known a voice so sweet. She felt swaddled inside a loving, protective robe, bound forever. She'd been given gifts, received them, then let them go. It was what living looked like.

"My daughters," she said then, letting go. Baby laid her head on Marie's stomach, causing everyone to shift, a slight adjustment. "I didn't leave much room for you girls, did I?" Marie said.

"You left enough," Marguerite said.

Marie smiled. There was that psalm, an old one of her mother's friars. "I am poured out like water, and all my bones are out of joint: my heart is like wax; it is melted." More words came to her. "Ye shall know the truth, and the truth shall make you free." She felt free and light. The words blended with the faces of those in this room transformed into her mother's face. Her mother reached out to give a flower, then took her hand. It was enough. She held tight and followed.

Epilogue

"We should do something special," Louis LaBonte said. "There won't ever be another like her." They stood outside the St. Louis church. It was the sixth of September, 1850. A cloudless sky marked the day when hundreds filled the log church to share in the celebration of the sepulchral Mass for Marie Ioway Dorion Venier Toupin. People came for miles, people who had recovered from an illness through her herbs, families given extra food because of her, the Sisters from surrounding towns who knew a certain student came because of encouragement Marie had given. Josiah Parrish brought his wife with him. Natives rode north from the Klamath country, some south from Walla Walla. Jean wondered if word might reach the Lower Brule or farther to that unknown son. But neither appeared.

Cayuse stood off to the side, drumming and singing traveling songs. The families of those who'd been convicted and hanged just a few months before knew her name and risked the wrath of settlers to stand outside the church, bringing music to Marie's journey.

"Even the priests know she was unique among women. To be buried in the church, not in the cemetery," Michel LaFramboise said. "These is amazing for a woman."

"Especially an Indian woman," Joseph Gervais said. "She was extraordinary."

Her wooden casket had been lowered into a hole dug into the floor of the church itself, along the southern wall. Father Delorme's decision surprised even Jean. "It is almost like the cathedrals in Europe," Sister Celeste told him, "where dignitaries and people of royalty are buried inside the church. Your wife is so deserving of such an honor."

"We should carve a stone or something," LaBonte said. "To remind everyone that she made that crossing, the only woman with Hunt. That she kept her children living then and later."

"And the rest of us," George Gay said. The old Astorians present nodded their heads in agreement. They were tied to Marie's death. It reminded them of their own mortality, their own troubled history, and took them closer to their end, too.

"It should say 'Madame' on it. Give her the distinction she deserves," Jean said. He knew his eyes must look like two embers burned into snow, but what did it matter? He was among friends who knew how to grieve a loved wife. He had never done this before, lived through the loss of such love.

"Madame Toupin?" LaBonte said. "Should it read that way?"

That didn't sound right, not even to Jean. "No," Jean said. "Let it read Madame Dorion. It links her to Hunt's journey west for Astor, ties us all together. She would like this, each of us here to help the other."

"That's what we'll do then," LaBonte said. "Madame Dorion it is."

Jean wiped his eyes. "Her children will remember her as mother. And I…I will remember her as my Marie. The name she claimed as her own."

TITRE D'ASCENDANCE

Jacob D'Orion	Jeanne de Caupenne
1681	1637 1707
Salies-de-Bearn	Bearn, France

FIRST GENERATION

Pierre	D'Orion	Jeanne-Andrée	Hédouin
1658	1724	1670	1747
2nd Marriage			
18 January	1688	Notre-Dame-of-Québec, Canada	

SECOND GENERATION

Jean-Marie	Dorion	Thérèse	Le Normand
1704	1761	1712	
19 Febuary	1730	Notre-Dame-of-Québec, Canada	

THIRD GENERATION

Pierre	Dorion	Holy	Rainbow
1740	1810	1760	
	1779	Yankton, South Dakota, United States	

FOURTH GENERATION

Pierre	Dorion	Marie	Iowa
1780	1814	1789	1850
	1804	South Dakota, United States	

FIFTH GENERATION

John	Jean-Baptiste	Paul	Infant
1800-	1805-1849	1809-1889	1811-1812

SIXTH GENERATION

His descendants are in Manitoba and Saskatchewan, Canada.	His descendants are in Oregon and Washington, USA.	His descendants are in Kansas, Missouri, and South Dakota, USA.	First white child to be born and die on the Oregon Trail, Orégon, USA.

(prepared by Léonard Dorion)

Author's Notes and Acknowledgments

Many readers tell me they scan my author's notes before reading the story to sort out fact from fiction. For those who don't like surprises spoiled, you may want to delay that practice this time as some of the surprise of the story will be revealed here. Or, you may read this now and forget it or, better yet, decide if my version makes sense. You might have a better one. Such is the nature of speculative fiction.

If fame is a name with a promise in it, then Madame Dorion has kept the promise. I hope I've been faithful to the telling. I had much help in this third and last book in the Tender Ties Historical Series. The errors and omissions are all mine.

The early 1840s in Oregon country offered tension and conflict. Several factions wove the fabric of that prairie, all tugging at the seams: the Hudson's Bay Company and the British interests they represented; the former Astorians, mostly French Canadian with their Indian wives who spoke French, followed the Catholic faith, and farmed in their retirement south of the Columbia River; the missionaries, both Protestant and Catholic; various native tribes, whose numbers had already been decimated by disease in the Willamette Valley by the time Marie and Jean moved there; retired fur traders and trappers settling in a mild climate as the fur trade declined; and American merchants and entrepreneurs, arriving first from the East by ship and later by emigrant wagon trains. Place this in the context of joint occupation of land claimed by two nations, Great Britain and America. The presence of the Hudson's Bay Company and its domination of commerce posed real conflict for how territorial decisions would play out. Consider the strength of many Western tribes (Cayuse, Shoshone, Klamath, Nez Perce) not decimated yet by disease or disappointment who held the knowledge of the terrors affecting eastern tribes in the wake of American settlement. Add the influx of thousands within a few years to the uncertainty of government and war, and the inevitability of conflict comes well founded.

Into this world stepped a woman, a wife, a mother, Marie.

The legacy of Marie is based on fact. The births, baptisms, deaths, and affiliations were kept as closely as possible to what is revealed by keepers of the Dorion story. The Catholic Church records as translated by Harriet Munnick, all seven volumes, found their way into my life, and in them the birth of David Dorion, son of Paul, and his baptism in Walla Walla was noted, giving us speculation of his presence in the West. All other information about Paul and his wife, My Horse Comes Out, is part of genealogist and descendant Pat Smith's research, including information from the Cut-Beef Records kept for Indians living on reservations such as those along the Lower Brule. Paul had several children there and is believed to have died there in 1889.

Some minor characters were also real. David Mongrain is listed as a servant to Father Blanchet and as the witness to David Dorion's baptism in 1847, and for a time after David Gervais' death, Marianne (or Marie Anne) Toupin lived with him and his wife until her later marriage. In addition, David Mongrain served for a time in the Hudson's Bay employ at a place in Canada that had significance to later parts of the story. Because of these connections, I did make Mr. Mongrain someone of importance, a lay catechist or teacher in Marie's life and someone who might have allowed her to safely discover secrets kept to prevent the pain of her "heart knowing," as the word for memory is signed in Indian languages. Sister Celeste is a composite of those Sisters of Namur who arrived from Europe, French speakers willing to risk the wilderness of distance to establish St. Mary's on the Willamette (pronounced Wi-LAM-it). The first days of the school began under trees in the St. Paul community with tuition paid by eggs and cheese. Students ages six to sixty were recorded. Both English and French were taught. Student names are somewhere in the archives of the Order in the Netherlands; I chose to speculate that Marie might have been one of those students.

Oregonian Sandra K. Woodruff in an act of love created two volumes called *Family Relationships on the Old French Prairie.* These volumes were loaned to me by Roger and Brenda Howard of French Prairie, the true keepers of Marie's story. Ms. Woodruff's work confirmed the presence of Angele Indian and Marie Indian (named Baby in this book).

They were the only two children for whom Marie Dorion served as godmother. Their ages at the time of baptism are recorded as provided. In Ms. Woodruff's work as well as the Munnick works, the alliances of who was godmother, who didn't attend a baptism (Jean Baptiste Gobin, for example, missed his son's with Marguerite Venier but arrived for his son's from a first marriage a few weeks later), when people married, and when they died, provided grist for speculation about early French Prairie lives, losses, and loves.

Marie Ouvre was a real person in the household of Julie Gervais and later married François Laderoute. Archange did work for Baptiste Dorion, was baptized and died as portrayed. Barbe is a fictional character, and her relationship with Archange is as well.

Josiah Parrish, ancestor of Portlander Audrey Slater who graces my life as friend, was selected as one of the Methodists serving at the Champoeg governmental meetings but who also lived close to where Jean and Marie are believed to have had at least one of their claims. He spent time in Clatsop not far from where Marie and Pierre had been while at Astoria, and he had a passion for Indian children and their survival and education. He was later made subagent for the Indians under Joel Palmer. I'm indebted to Audrey for copies of family documents that lent authenticity to this story.

The boy Joseph Klickitat existed, and his story of bondage and rescue is retold in documents of the Methodist missionaries. He was sent to the Clatsop Mission for rescue, and one such boy's death at French Prairie is recorded at the home of Marguerite and JB Gobin. I speculated how he arrived from Clatsop to there.

David Gervais was the husband of Marie Dorion's youngest, Marianne (sometimes written Marie Anne). Marianne married four times in her life following the deaths of her husbands. She did marry at age fifteen, shortly after her older sister's marriage. That her mother and father lived with them in later years is speculation, but Marie was not present at the census of 1850, January, though Jean was and with her later illness, it seemed reasonable that Marie might have been in the Gervais home while her husband still worked their claim during the days.

Marguerite Venier Gobin raised two of her husband's children, and together they had six of their own. She also took in David Dorion, son of Baptiste, following her half-brother's death in 1849 in the Willamette Valley, causes unknown.

François Toupin married Angelique Longtain, and they had three children together. The first surviving child was born after the death of Marie.

Baptiste Dorion did serve as an interpreter with Dr. E. White, Indian subagent, whose story does twist and wind around ambition, service, and women. Marie did give Dr. White a pair of moccasins beautiful enough that White recalled them in his memoir. Jean Baptiste served with Tom McKay during the Cayuse war. He is said to have confronted Five Crows and been present at the death by Tom McKay's hand of Gray Eagle. Whether he struggled with his ties to a violent father is speculation, but founded. The story of his father nearly killing his grandfather is legend. The sacramental records do note that Jean Baptiste fathered a child with someone other than Josette while living on French Prairie. Genevieve lived to be twelve years of age. His marriage to Josette is also recorded as noted along with his baptism. He may well have kept up a friendship with Tom McKay who did have a mill on Champoeg Creek near present day Butteville and ran a horse ranch near Scappoose, Oregon, across from present day Vancouver, Washington.

While some records about Jean Baptiste Dorion call him "farmer," there are no official land claims in his name. I proposed that he lived in his wife's tipi on the land later claimed by Jean and Marie Toupin. Cayuse women claimed the lodges.

The examination by historians of the Oregon-Idaho United Methodist Church archival records proved very helpful. Special thanks go to John Hook (posthumously). Shirley Knepp, Charlotte and Charles Holmes, Karin Lightner, and Ina Simms reviewed and made recommendations on an early manuscript. They provided me with a copy of "The Stick From Heaven" used by both Protestants and Catholics and known also as the Catholic Ladder found in the archives of the Annual Conference of the United Methodist Church. They understood when we couldn't include a picture in this book. Their questions and answers and tender care of history have made this a truer story. I'm grateful. Kuri

Gill of the Methodist Mission Mill Museum helped me locate contemporary Methodist historians there, and I thank her.

We know a bit about Jean and Marie's lives during this time because of the activities of their children, property documents, and early census records. JB Gobin did refuse to give information in 1842; Jean Toupin cooperated and thus we know how many acres he and his son tilled, how many horses he had, the number of cattle. There is also reason to believe he was the interpreter sent to gather the Cayuse chiefs for a meeting with Father Brouillet. The Toupins had affiliation with the Cayuse tribe through Jean Baptiste Dorion and Josette. In the records at the trial, Jean Toupin testified, and there is some evidence that he and Father Brouillet did not see eye to eye. Others document an equal frustration with the priest who buried the Whitmans and other victims at Waiilatpu.

In an archeological dig (see the Suggested Reading List for annotations) completed at the Mission Bottom area, a single crucifix was found along with buttons described in this text. French Prairie residents had few luxuries, though they lived well. A music box and stand were considered fine gifts. People danced and played cards such as *vingt et un* (twenty-one) and Pierre Dorion's father did at one time sue to recover a gambling debt. One might speculate: Like father, like son.

Somewhere near the completion of the writing of *Every Fixed Star,* word reached the Iowa Tribe of Oklahoma, Marie Dorion's tribe, that evidence had recently been uncovered confirming the existence of a third son named John who married a Thérèse Constant at Cumberland House, Canada, around 1825. John signed an affidavit reporting that he was the son of Pierre Dorion and Marie Ioway born in 1800. Rarihokwats, founder and editor of *Akwesasne Notes,* a plains and Iroquois history and genealogy researcher, recorded this *métis* relationship, identified this son with the oral story that he was the oldest son left behind when the family headed west. John's descendants Cynthia Turner of Manitoba and Léonard Dorion of Quebec assisted in the verification of John's existence and lineage.

At the time of Marie and Jean's marriage and legitimization of their children (1841), a hesitation is recorded when Marie is asked to give the names of children from previous marriages. No explanation is given in the Catholic files. But some have speculated that she recalled Paul (whom she did not name) as a son she hadn't thought of for a time. With the uncovering of information about John, it seemed possible that he was the reason for the hesitation. Marie may well have believed that Paul was dead. John may have meant a different kind of ache. Some historians recording the Dorion journey with Hunt related "three children" while most recorded "two." This discrepancy may well have been due to awareness that the Dorions had three sons but that only two journeyed west with Hunt.

The book *Vital Lies, Simple Truths* (see Suggested Reading List) offered a plausible way to weave into this final book in the series an awareness of a son never spoken of in books one and two. Whatever one's view about past memory, it is true that the human spirit is often able to keep inner peace only by denying the pain of an incomprehensible experience. Marie's extraordinary persistence to keep her sons alive, to become a woman of great generosity and faith, to endure when others might have stopped, to take children in and serve her community wherever she lived, may well have been fueled by her struggle to accept forgiveness for what must have been a painful decisive journey of a mothering soul.

Finally, the cause of Marie's death is not known, but as local historian and writer Annabell Prantl noted, tuberculosis ran rampant in 1850. Where she died specifically is also not known. Jean filed on two separate claims even though he could not have received both since Marie was an Indian and not entitled to land. Along with local historians Bob and Nancy Noble, Roger and Brenda Howard, and Annabell Prantl, possible home sites were explored. I chose two, the Lake Labiche area and east of Salem, for story locations.

Marie's burial "in" the church is noted in Harriet Munnick's translation of the Catholic Church records and is a highly unusual acknowledgment for anyone, let alone an Indian woman. She was affiliated with the Astor Expedition and the French Canadians all her life. It explains the choice to commemorate her as Madame Dorion rather than "Toupin." Her life was deemed worthy of remembrance, her name worthy of engraving.

A working title of this book was called *Her Name Engraved* because of the variety of places throughout the West that bear Marie Dorion's name and memory. A plaque at the south corner of the plot where the St. Louis church stands in Gervais, Oregon, was placed in 1935 by the Daughters of the American Revolution in memory of Marie. A women's dormitory at Eastern Oregon State College in La Grande is named for her, Dorian Hall. (Various spellings may confuse, but the Canadian lineage does spell it Dorion.) A plaque at Vista House overlooking the Columbia River reads:

Dedicated to the memory of Marie Dorian
Red Heroine of the West
Wife of Pierre Dorian
Interpreter with the Astoria Overland Expedition
from St Louis to the mouth of the Columbia
under the leadership of
Wilson Price Hunt
That party passed this point
early in February 1812
Erected by the Oregon Society,
Daughters of the American Revolution
March 1, 1941

Marie is remembered in a bronze statue at the Fort Boise Museum in Parma, Idaho. At Milton-Freewater, Oregon, a park bears her name along with steps leading to a monument marking the place believed to designate where she came out of the Blue Mountains after surviving fifty-six days in the winter snows with her two young sons. The Frasier Farmstead Museum collection in Milton-Freewater also includes extensive information on descendants of Marie Dorion. Along the Walla Walla River where it enters the Columbia, another wood sign records her story and that she was there. Plaques near Boise marking the site of her husband's death also record her presence there during the winter of

1813–14. An Idahoan, Oliver Gregerson, maintains a private museum in her name near Boise. A plaque dedicated to Marie lies outside of North Powder, Oregon, marking the most likely site of the birth of her child during the Hunt expedition. Marie Dorion is the subject of two paintings by award-winning artist John Clymer. A third Clymer painting, *Hunt Crossing the Wind River*, shows a single woman at the end of the horse brigade who must have been Marie.

As with Sacagawea, some mystery does linger over Marie's burial site. She is commemorated in documents of South Dakota indicating she returned there and died there and was known as Holy Rainbow. Because of other records naming Holy Rainbow as her mother-in-law and with several documents relaying her death in Oregon, I have written her last years as tied to the Oregon story.

Finally, let me acknowledge a variety of people without whom this book wouldn't have been written. To the many descendants of John, Jean Baptiste, Paul, Marguerite, Marianne, and François who have been in contact with me through the writing of this series: Thank you for allowing me, someone who lacked the privilege of family stories of this woman, to make the tender tie between stories of the past and present. Léonard Dorion of Quebec, who did not live to see this final book, and Pat Smith of Salt Lake hold special places in my life for their encouragement and kindnesses. I am grateful to the members of the Iowa Tribe of Oklahoma, especially historian Victor Robidoux and Lawrence Murray and historian Marianne Long; and to the Museum at Warm Springs of the Confederated Tribes of Warm Springs for the use of the replica bag on each cover. Roger and Brenda Howard's early and sustained enthusiasm for this story not only opened doors for me on French Prairie, but also brought into our lives two fine people who, as with Sacagawea and Marie, have touched our lives forever.

My colleagues at WaterBrook Press, a division of Random House, continue to nurture me in amazing ways. Special recognition goes to Don Pape, publisher and friend; Steve Cobb, president; editors Dudley Delffs and Erin Healy, for finding the essence of Marie's life and helping me weave it into the fabric of history; John Hamilton, for perusing those forty thousand Edwin Curtis photographs to find the distinctive ones to enhance this story; Laura Wright, for catching my wrongs; Rod Schumacher, special markets; and all the other sales and production people whose names I may not even know. I send the deepest appreciation for this team effort.

Finally, for support closer to home: Madeleine Ladd once again provided insights for my French language. Blair Fredstrom restrained herself from calling during final revisions. Nieces Arlene Hurtley (publicity) and Michelle Hurtley, keeper of the Web site, formed a valued team. Thanks also to Susan Holton, publicist; Joyce Hart, literary agent; Terry Porter of Agape Productions, media agent; and Carol Tedder, a prayer partner extraordinaire. Friends too numerous to mention gave moral support I treasure. To Jerry and Mariah, thank you for understanding my need to live in the nineteenth century so much of my year. Finally, to my readers, I thank you for telling me of your stories, how the study guides have extended discussions, and most of all, for making room in your hearts for Marie.

As with Marie, I do believe that stories are both sparks and embers that illuminate our lives. It is my fervent hope that others will tell their stories to their children, however ordinary they might think those stories are, remembering that each of us is worthy to be remembered and to have a name of our own.

Sincerely,
Jane Kirkpatrick
www.jkbooks.com

An Author Discussion and Questions for Reflection

In this last book of the Tender Ties Historical Series, I wished to portray a strong woman in her declining years who I believed saw herself as unremarkable, still struggling despite a growing faith while those around her found reason to admire her and even memorialize her.

With the receipt of previously unknown information about a possible older son, I needed to explore the ideas of stories we forget, stories made up of such pain or shame that we are unable to carry them into our conscious experience. In Indian sign language, even the word *memory* is signed as "heart-knowing," suggesting we don't always remember the details of an event but rather the emotions of that experience. A man once told me that he and his twin brother both had a memory of a family story in which each brother remembered that their parents (with many children) had considered allowing another relative to adopt the "other" brother. The memory is vivid to each, but each protected himself from the potential pain by "remembering" that it was the *other* brother who was chosen to leave the family. Neither did, but the memory itself provided an interesting way of exploring the existence, and forgetting, of John.

I had also recently learned of a neurological disorder called prosopagnosia, the inability to recognize faces, often even familiar ones. This disorder can develop later in life, be very disconcerting, and cause uncertainty in everyday interactions. I used its existence to help frame Marie's struggle with a distant memory against her discomfort with memory loss in present time. You, the readers, will ultimately decide if this struggle rings true inside the story.

Marie Dorion was a strong and compassionate woman. She demonstrated complexity and willfulness as well as a deepening faith and fallibility. As the poet William Stafford wrote, "Tragedies happen. People get hurt and die.... You don't ever let go of the thread." I wanted to portray the threads that held Marie Dorion together despite her life tragedies and, in so doing, to explore the threads that tenderly tie each of us together across centuries and generations. It is my hope I did.

1. What threads did Marie hang on to in her life? Which of the threads served to keep her from getting lost, and which led her astray?

2. What scenes portray the threads of landscape, family, and faith? How do these three threads remain consistent amid the inevitable changes of her life? Do you find them in your own?

3. Which qualities of Marie's character are reflected in those of her children? As you think about your own life, which of your mother's and father's qualities are alive and well in you? Are these characteristics you particularly admire? Have others recognized them? What did your parents do to transfer those qualities to you? What family story do you remember about one of those qualities?

4. Are the threads that sustained Marie different for her as a mother and wife and friend than as an individual woman? Can a woman separate herself from those relationships that seek to define her?

5. Why do you think the former Astorians and others from the French Prairie community chose to bury this Indian woman inside the church rather than in the cemetery where ordinary people and even the priests were buried?

6. Have you experienced a false memory, something that you know did not happen to you and yet you have a memory of it

or an event that was later brought to your consciousness by a sibling or parent, which then triggered the memory of the event for you? What were your stages toward trusting that memory or denying it?

7. Did Marie's "reading," the unveiling of her mystery of John, ring true? Why or why not?

8. Did Paul kill Louis Venier? What makes you think that? How does Marie's lack of certainty affect her feelings toward Paul? Toward herself as his mother?

9. Was the French-speaking community of French Prairie safer than the larger outside community, or were they as isolated as they thought from political dissension? What threads bring safety from family conflicts, neighborhood disagreements, changing demographics, or the rumors of war?

10. In fiction, characters are drawn forward by their desires. The quality of their character is revealed by how they overcome the barriers keeping them from those desires. What are the desires of Marguerite? of Marianne? of Baptiste? of Paul? of François? of Jean Toupin? Can you identify some of the barriers in their lives?

11. Some say that human desire is the longing for past pleasures. Such desires suggest they are never attainable as they belong to memory and the past. But the proverb reads, "Desire realized is sweet to the soul." How would you define desire? What gets in the way of your achieving the desire of your heart?

12. Did Marie achieve the desire of her heart? Why or why not?

While meeting with schoolchildren around the country about this woman and her story, I often ask them to define a powerful person, which to me means the ability to set a goal and gather resources to accomplish that goal. The children often answer with words like *strong, wealthy,* and *forceful.* One second-grader took my breath away with this definition: "It's when you want to stop but keep going anyway." For me, Marie Dorion was that kind of powerful woman, wife, and mother.

I hope you see reflections of your own power in Marie's story and that you hold tight to the thread that sustains you.

Sincerely,
Jane Kirkpatrick
www.jkbooks.com

Suggested Additional Reading

Bagley, C. B. *Early Catholic Missions in Oregon.* Seattle: Lowman and Hanford, 1832.

Bailey, Margaret J. "French Prairie Farm, 1839–1850." *Oregon Historical Quarterly* vol. 5, Portland: Oregon Historical Society.

Bancroft, Hubert Howard. *Bancroft's Works,* vol. XXVII, *History of Northwest Coast, 1800–1871.* San Francisco: A. L. Bancroft and Co., 1884.

Barry, Neilson. "Madame Dorion of the Astorians." *Oregon Historical Quarterly.* Portland: Oregon Historical Society, September 1929. Numerous additional articles from the *Oregon Historical Quarterly.*

Betts, Robert B. *In Search of York: The Slave Who Went to the Pacific with Lewis and Clark.* Boulder: University Press of Colorado and the Lewis and Clark Trail Heritage Foundation, 2000.

Blaine, Martha Royce. *The Ioway Indians.* Norman: University of Oklahoma Press, 1995.

Boyd, Robert, ed. *Indians, Fire and the Land in the Pacific Northwest.* Corvallis: Oregon State University, 1999.

Brown, George Thomas. *The Hand of Catherine.* Fairfield, Wash.: Ye Galleon Press, 1998.

Carlson, Laurie Winn. *Cattle: An Informal Social History.* Chicago: Ivan R. Dee, 2001.

———. *Sidesaddles to Heaven.* Caldwell, Idaho: Caxton Press, 1998.

Dee, Henry Drumond. Introduction to *Journal of John Work,* January to October, 1835. Victoria B.C.: Charles F. Banfield, 1945.

Dobbs, Caroline C. *Men of Champoeg.* Portland: Metropolitan Press, 1993.

Goleman, Daniel. *Vital Lies, Simple Truths: The Psychology of Self-Deception.* New York: Lippincott, 1964.

Hafen, LeRoy R. *Mountain Men and the Fur Trade of the Far West.* vols. I, II, VI, VII, VIII, and IX. Glendale, Calif.: Arthur H. Clark, 1971.

Haines, Francis. *The Nez Perces, Tribesmen of the Columbia Plateau.* Norman: University of Oklahoma Press, 1955.

Haines Jr., Francis D. "The Snake Country Expedition of 1830–1831," *John Work's Field Journal,* vol. 59, *The American Exploration and Travel Series.* Norman: University of Oklahoma Press, 1971.

Hook, John & Litner, Karin, eds. *The Diary of Cyrus Shepard, Willamette Mission Teacher.* Salem, Oreg.: The Commission on Archives and History Oregon-Idaho Conference, United Methodist Church, Janice Barclay, Chair. 2002

Hook, John and Charlotte. *Daniel Lee Reminisces* vol. 1, II, typescript. Salem, Oreg.: The Commission on Archives and History Oregon-Idaho Conference, United Methodist Church, Janice Barclay, Chair, 2002.

Horace, Robert. *History of the Silverton Country.* Portland: Berncliff Press, 1926.

Howard, Harold P. *Sacagawea.* Norman: University of Oklahoma Press, 1971.

Hunsaker, Joyce Badgley. *Sacagawea Speaks: Beyond the Shining Mountains with Lewis and Clark.* Guilford, Conn.: Twodot Press, 2001.

Irving, Washington. *Astoria.* Clatsop edition, 1836. Portland: Binford and Mort, 1967.

Jackson, John C. *Children of the Fur Trade: Forgotten Métis of the Pacific Northwest.* Missoula, Mont.: Mountain Press, 1995.

Jones, Robert F., ed. *Annals of Astoria, 1811–1813.* New York: Fordham University Press, 1999.

———. *Astoria Adventure: The Journal of Alfred Seton, 1811–1815.* New York: Fordham University Press, 1993.

Josephy, Alvin M. Jr. *The Nez Perce Indians and the Opening of the Northwest.* New York: Houghton Mifflin, 1965.

Klein, Laura, and Ackerman, Lillian, eds. *Women and Power in Native North America.* Norman: University of Oklahoma Press, 1995.

Lewis, William S. and Paul C. Phillips. *Journal of John Work.* Cleveland: Arthur H. Clark, 1923.

Maloney, Alice Bay. "California Rendezvous," *The Beaver,* Outfit 275, December, 1944 (a quarterly publication of the Hudson's Bay Company, Oregon State Library collection, Salem).

McKay, Harvey J. *St. Paul, Oregon 1830–1890.* Portland: Binford and Mort, 1980.

Morin, Gail. *Northwest Half-Breed Script.* Pawtucket, R.I.: Quintin Publications. 1997.

Morrison, Dorothy Nafus. *Outpost: John McLoughlin and the Far Northwest.* Portland: Oregon Historical Society Press, 1999.

Moulton, Gary, ed. *The Journals of the Lewis and Clark Expedition.* Lincoln: University of Nebraska Press, 1986–2001.

Munnick, Harriet D. "The Transition Decades on French Prairie—1830–1850," *Marion County History* vol. IV. Salem, Oreg.: Statesman Publishing, June 1958.

———, comp. *Catholic Church Records of the Pacific Northwest,* St. Louis, 1982, vol. I (1845–1868), and *Catholic Church Records of the Pacific Northwest,* St. Paul, 1979, vols. I, II, and III (1839–1898). Portland: Binford and Mort.

Nichols, M. Leona. *The Mantle of Elias. The Story of Fathers Blanchet and Demers in Early Oregon.* Portland: Binford and Mort, 1941.

Nisbet, Jack. *Sources of the Rivers: Tracking David Thompson Across Western North America.* Seattle: Sasquatch Books, 1994.

O'Donnel, Terrence. *Arrow in the Earth.* Portland: Oregon Historical Society Press, 1992.

O'Meara, Walter. *Daughters of the Country: The Women of the Fur Traders and Mountain Men.* New York: Harcourt Brace, 1968.

Peltier, James. *Madame Dorion.* Fairfield, Wash.: Ye Galleon Press, 1980.

Pipher, Mary. *Another Country: Navigating the Emotional Terrain of Our Elders.* New York: Riverhead, 1999.

Prantl, Annabell. *The Gold on the Pudding.* Gervais, Oreg.: Carlana, 1994.

Robertson, R. G. *Competitive Struggle: America's Western Fur Trading Posts 1764–1865.* Boise, Idaho: Tamarack Books, 1999.

Ronda, James P. *Astoria and Empire.* Lincoln: University of Nebraska Press, 1990.

Ross, Alexander. *Adventures of the First Settlers on the Oregon or Columbia River, 1810–1813.* Corvallis: Northwest Reprints, Oregon State University Press, 2000.

Russell, Carl P. *Firearms, Traps, and Tools of the Mountain Men.* Albuquerque: University of New Mexico Press, 1998.

Sanders, Judith, et al. *Willamette Mission Archeological Project. Phase III Assessment.* Corvallis: Oregon State University, 1983.

Schaefer, Arlington "Buckskin Slim." *The Indian Art of Tanning Buckskin.* Roseburg, Oreg.: Schaefer-Knudtson, 1977.

Schmerber, Ruth. *Only the Earth: The Story of Marie Dorion* (fiction). Woodburn, Oreg.: Pacific Printers, 1990.

Shirley, Gayle C. *More Than Petticoats: Remarkable Oregon Women.* Boise, Idaho: Twodot Press, 1998.

Thwaites, Reuben G., and Brackenridge, H. M., ed. *Journal of a Voyage up River Missouri, Performed in 1811.* Cleveland: Arthur C. Clark, 1904.

Tilford, Gregory L. *Edible and Medicinal Plants of the West.* Missoula, Mont.: Mountain Press, 1997.

Van Kirk, Sylvia. *Many Tender Ties: Women in Fur-Trade Society, 1670–1870.* Norman: University of Oklahoma Press, 1980.

Vaughan, Thomas; Winch, Martin. "Joseph Gervais, A Familiar Mystery Man," *Oregon Historical Quarterly,* Portland: Oregon Historical Society, December 1965.

White, Elijah. *Ten Years in Oregon.* Ithaca, N.Y.: Andrus Gauntlett, 1850. Provided by the United Methodist Archives Oregon-Idaho Conference, Salem, Oregon.